New Fire

by

Philip Dickinson

Grosvenor House

This book is published by
Grosvenor House Publishing Ltd
28-30 High Street, Guildford, Surrey, GU1 3EL.
www.grosvenorhousepublishing.co.uk

A CIP record for this book
is available from the British Library

ISBN 978-1-78148-789-1

To my mother, for all the time
she spent helping me learn to read.
A gift beyond mere words!

And to my father,
for doing the Piglet voice so well.

Acknowledgements

I am indebted to a number of people who helped me turn this book into a reality. Jean Norton's editorial advice and encouragement has been invaluable over the last year in helping me over the finishing line. My thanks to my sister, Melanie, who has always believed in me and still managed to give objective advice. Owen Benwell has given generously of his time to do the jacket design. Many thanks to Rob Cooper for checking the latest draft for inconsistencies and providing the last minute feedback that I so desperately needed. Nelson Solorio has been a star, checking my use of Nahuatl names. I am relieved that my old friend Ben Heywood kept a diplomatic veneer to his comments after seeing an early draft. I am grateful too to my wife Diana and to my children for their forbearance.

I need to give special thanks to Byron Pearson, who is probably the only person to have read the first draft in its entirety and whose lack of censure gave me hope.

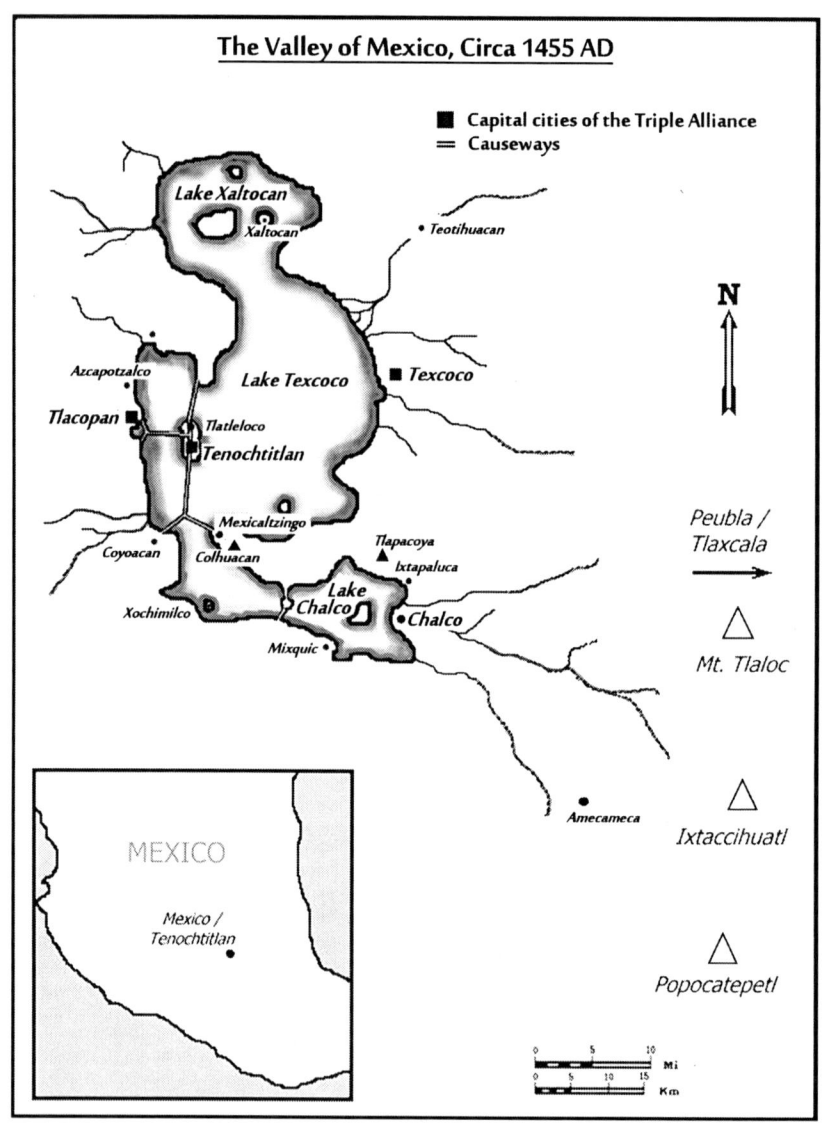

The Valley of Mexico, Circa 1455 AD

■ Capital cities of the Triple Alliance
= Causeways

N

Lake Xaltocan
Xaltocan
• Teotihuacan

Azcapotzalco
Lake Texcoco
■ Texcoco

Tlacopan ■
Tlatleloco
■ Tenochtitlan

Mexicaltzingo
Tlapacoya
Coyoacan
Colhuacan
Ixtapaluca

Lake Chalco
Xochimilco
• Chalco
Mixquic •

Peubla / Tlaxcala
→

△ Mt. Tlaloc

• Amecameca
△ Ixtaccihuatl

MEXICO

Mexico / Tenochtitlan •

△ Popocatepetl

0   5   10   Mi
0   5   10   15   Km

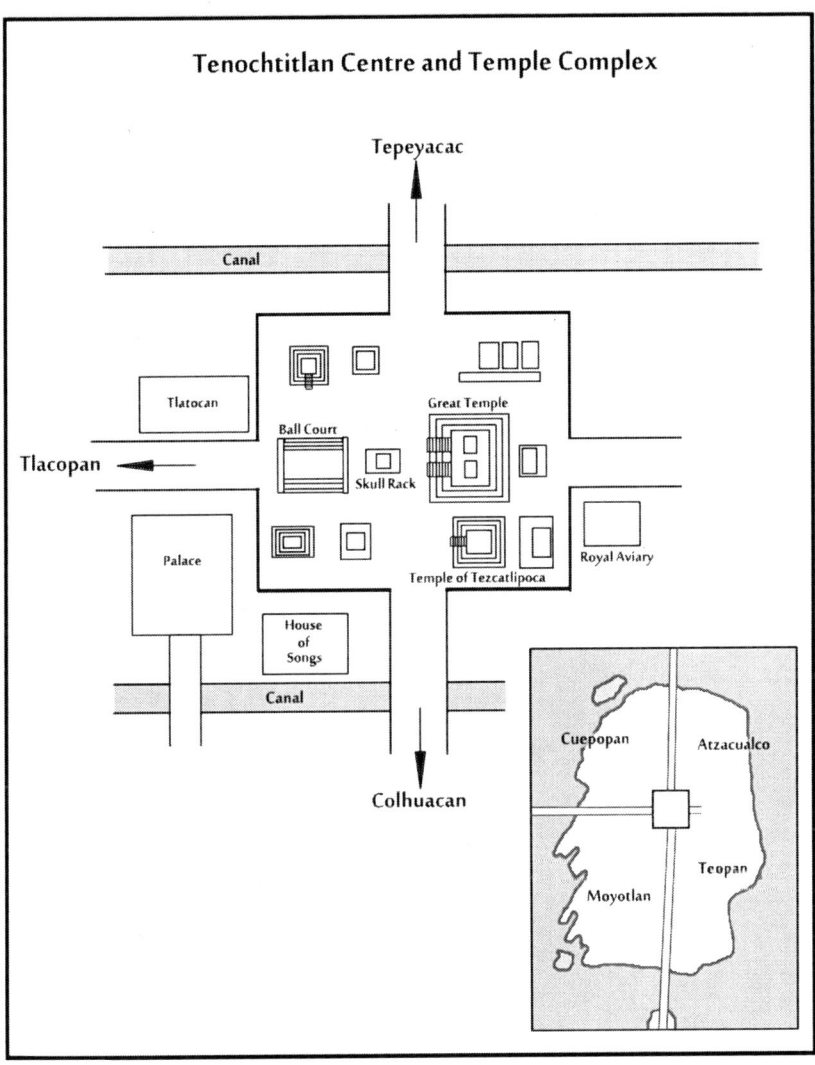

Tenochtitlan Centre and Temple Complex

Tepeyacac

Canal

Tlatocan

Great Temple

Ball Court

Skull Rack

Tlacopan

Palace

Temple of Tezcatlipoca

Royal Aviary

House
of
Songs

Canal

Colhuacan

Cuepopan

Atzacualco

Teopan

Moyotlan

Prologue

In the 11th century AD, a nomadic tribe of warriors, who called themselves the Mexica, settled in a verdant valley at the apex of two massive mountain ranges in Central America.

For a long time, the Mexica acted as servants to the powerful rulers in the area, lending their expertise in the art of war. But the Mexica were not trusted by the local people, so that when they asked for land to set up their own community, they were offered a small, rocky, snake infested island in Lake Texcoco in the hope that it would break them. Undaunted, the Mexica cleared the island and founded the city of Tenochtitlan in 1325 AD.

Through a series of clever deals with rival rulers, the Mexica then rose up and defeated their overlords. Within a few years, the Mexica city-state, together with neighbouring Tlacopan and Texcoco, was at the head of the most powerful alliance in the area, which began to spread its tendrils of conquest in all directions.

These people were to become known as the Aztecs.

Chapter I - Cipactli

Late afternoon shadows crept across the city's dusty streets as the busy sounds of traders, priests and messengers gave way to the gentler sounds of evening traffic. Children shrieked and babbled as they played between the whitewashed, mud-walled houses. An argument was taking place in one of the nearby buildings, accompanied by the intermittent wailing of a child. Every time the shouting stopped, the child paused too, only to resume as the dispute flared up again. A subtle, slightly sweet smell was detectable in patches, as pockets of air wafted over the city from the lake's rotting reed beds, ever more exposed to the warming spring air.

Clawfoot and Little Maize moved cautiously through the gradually emptying streets with Little Maize's brother, Indigo, and another boy called Shield of Gold in tow. They used the doorways and dingy alleys to pause and watch the dwindling crowds. The clamour of the Cuepopan district was beginning to settle down as market stall holders made their way back to the mainland via the north and west causeways. Weary porters trudged by with enormous reed baskets on their backs. Although empty now, the baskets would have contained maize cobs, fruit, string-beans, tomatoes, chillies and tortillas on the inward journey earlier in the day. The Tlatleloco market was a much subdued affair nowadays when compared with the pre-famine bustle, but people still did business there, with those who could afford to pay the inflated prices. The prolonged drought and repeated crop failures of the last four years were taking their toll. Labourers were struggling to pay for the basic foodstuffs and those without regular work were beginning to starve. Things were bad enough in the valley around

Tenochtitlan, but Clawfoot had heard that, rather than starve, the people on the Totonicapán plateau had been selling themselves into slavery in such numbers that the place was deserted. He had no intention of following suit, but it would be a grim summer unless the rains returned.

Clawfoot paused and looked back at Little Maize, the only girl in the gang. Like the boys, she was thin to the point of emaciation. She had a small, button nose and a chaos of tangled hair that Clawfoot found attractive in a way he didn't understand. She had a rough weave sack slung over her back that contained their meagre pickings from the day: a maize cake, dented on one side; three tomatoes, one of which had partially burst open; and a small wooden doll that Little Maize had convinced them she could sell to buy more provisions. At ten years old, she was a year younger than Clawfoot but already fiercely independent.

'Do you want me to take the bag for a while?' Clawfoot offered again.

Little Maize just scowled back at him.

The other two caught up with them. Indigo had been the leader of their gang when Clawfoot had come across them. Little Maize's brother had large ears and an untidy collection of teeth, but he was tall for his age and with a long reach, so Clawfoot had had to use all his speed and cunning to beat him in a fight to take control of the group.

'I'm hungry!' whined Shield of Gold for the hundredth time that day. His eyes had a sunken, hollow look and he had the same kind of listless look about him that had caught hold of Flying Star before they had lost him to the hunger. The youngest member of the gang had become increasingly lethargic and then caught a cough that he couldn't shake. Then one day, Flying Star had been too weak even to cough and the others knew that he would not make it through the night. There wasn't a day that went by when Clawfoot didn't recall that night in the hovel they all shared, listening to the boy's breathing grow quieter until with a small, trembling sigh it had stopped entirely. He had listened as Little Maize sobbed gently when she too realised that Flying Star had died and there had been more tears the next day from the others when they'd helped

Clawfoot carry the featherweight corpse from their dilapidated shack for the city undertakers to dispose of. Clawfoot had not cried. He had no more tears to give up for the famine.

Ordinarily, one of the gang would have snapped at Shield of Gold and told him to be quiet, but they had all gone for nearly two days now with nothing more than a tamale each and they were all hungry. Clawfoot's stomach ached and two of his teeth hurt like hell. He could only hope that they would drop out soon and take the pain with them.

For a while, the gang wandered along Coyote Street. From the high ground here, they could just see a few canoes in the distance, making their way back across the sparkling lake surface to Texcoco. Eventually, they turned north, onto Turquoise Street, where the wealthy merchants lived. The pickings would be richer here, but they would have to be more careful, the city watch was more active in this area. The passers-by went about their business, scarcely noticing the children. Soon the gang arrived at the entrance to a courtyard, the other side of which fronted the North Canal. Here they stopped and moved just inside, where they could keep the street in view.

A large man wearing the peasant hat and brown fibre cloak of a mayeque briefly held their attention. He was heading towards the northern causeway, with a rolling gait, which made the sack on his shoulder swing from one side of his back to the other. As he passed the gateway that hid the lurking children, they saw that the sack was empty, so they settled down to wait.

From their vantage-point, Clawfoot could just make out the top of the Great Temple of the Sun and Rain. The twin crenellated shrines perched on top of the lofty, stepped stone pyramid basked in the full gaze of the sinking sun and radiated a fiery orange colour against the darkening, purple sky. For a while the street was empty. The evening rush was at an end. Shield of Gold began kicking impatiently at the remains of a woodpile, disturbing a nest of beetles in the process. The others stopped him as they caught sight of a tall figure heading in their direction.

The man was barefoot, which would have marked him out as a commoner except that he was clothed in a black, ankle-length, cotton mantle that spoke of important connections. He strolled along the deserted thoroughfare with a measured, unhurried gait and paused once, briefly, to run a hand through the long hair that hung below his shoulders. His long, black apparel flowed easily about him as he approached the waiting children. Hanging from the man's left hand was a large, dead turkey, which he held by the legs.

The children shrank into the shadows as the tall man passed the spot where they were hiding.

'Look at the size of that bird!' Indigo whispered to Clawfoot. 'With the money that will make us in the market, we can live like royalty for a week.'

'Why sell it? My father can cook it for us,' said Shield of Gold. He was the only one who wasn't orphaned, although he'd lost his mother to a fever the year before and his father was infirm and incapable of any paid work.

'We're not sharing with your father,' insisted Indigo.

'He won't want a share of his own. He and I can halve my share.'

Clawfoot waved them both to silence. 'I don't like it. Why's he heading towards the centre if he's on his way home?'

'Oh, who cares!' groaned Shield of Gold. 'I have to eat.'

'Yeah, come on. When will we get another chance like this?' added Indigo.

Clawfoot nodded slowly. 'Alright, take a log from that pile and hand me one too.'

The children burst forth from the courtyard at a run, their bare feet soundless on the dusty earth. Clawfoot and Indigo were in the lead. As they ran, they each wielded one of the logs as a weapon. When they caught up with the man in black, they swung at the backs of his legs with all their might. His knees buckled and he let out a cry, releasing the turkey to break his fall with both hands. Man and bird impacted the street with a thud, one sending up a cloud of dust and the other an explosion of feathers.

'Quick!' squeaked Little Maize, pointing at the turkey. 'Get it!'

Shield of Gold gathered the load and the four of them turned tail and fled, whooping with relief and delight, but their joy was short-lived. Three young, shaven-headed priests with fierce expressions blocked the street ahead.

'Stop where you are!' commanded one of them.

'Shit! It's a trap!' shouted Clawfoot. 'This way,' he cried and headed back towards their victim, his heart pounding a fearful quick-time in his throat, thinking they could make it past him as he lay stretched out on the ground. To his horror, the pile of black robes was unfolding eerily and getting to its feet. He glared at the children with triumph in his eyes. Clawfoot had dismissed the stories of Catchers as nothing more than exaggerated tales told by frightened street urchins who had escaped the clutches of the clan sheriffs. Catchers weren't supposed to exist. The priests had no mandate to keep the streets free of muggers, but still the rumours persisted that they were short of offerings for the gods. These four were definitely not clan sheriffs and Clawfoot had no intention of finding out what they wanted.

Somehow, all four children instantly knew the peril. Some innate understanding between them communicated the danger they were in. Young children weren't allowed to watch the more brutal ceremonies, but they all knew about them. Sometimes they awoke in the dead of night to the sound of drums, and often, cutting through the momentary gaps in the beat, the terrible, tearing, high-pitched shrieks.

Clawfoot and Little Maize ducked around the figure in black and ran until they were beyond his reach then stopped to check on Indigo and Shield of Gold. The shock had jolted Shield of Gold from his torpor. Deciding that the turkey would slow him down, he lobbed it at the sinister man and used the distraction to get around him to safety. Indigo had been less lucky. He was gangly and slower to react to the threat, so when he finally tried to follow his friends, he found his path blocked and the priests behind him were advancing to close the gap.

'Run!' screeched Little Maize, but it was no use. The man in black caught her brother by the arm and twisted it brutally around until he was forced to the ground. When the other three priests saw that Indigo was firmly held, they gave chase.

Clawfoot grabbed Little Maize's arm. 'Come on!'

Together the children fled up Turquoise Street, squeezed through a narrow passage and leaped over a ditch with the sound of pursuit loud in their ears. They ran north, towards Cuepopan before doubling back into the filthy warrens of Moyotlan, where they hoped the priests would not follow. They ran until their starved bodies gave up for lack of energy and hid in a disused warehouse gasping for breath. Little Maize was wracked with sobs and tears rolled down her grimy cheeks. Shield of Gold looked too shocked for tears. He leant up against the wall of the warehouse, his jaw opening and closing as he fought to get his breath back.

'Who were they?' he said after a while.

'Chachalmeca,' said Clawfoot, using the name for the priests who presided over sacrificial rites. Nobody knew if the Catchers were the same priests who presided over the bloody temple ceremonies, but the more terrifying the notion, the firmer it seemed to take root.

Clawfoot held Little Maize's arm gently to comfort her and she looked up at him with a plaintive expression that was unmistakable.

'I'll go back and see if I can get him,' he volunteered.

Moments later, Clawfoot was cursing himself as he took a circuitous route back to where they had been ambushed, loping along through the lengthening shadows and wondering why he had offered to go on such a foolish mission. There could be no prospect of recovering Indigo from the priests if they were still there, but it had seemed the right thing to say and, as leader of the gang, he felt some responsibility for what had happened. He changed course slightly, deciding to try to intercept the priests at the East Gate as they would surely be making for the temple complex. Sure enough, when he arrived at the corner of a building that afforded him a view of the gate in the Serpent Wall, he saw the priest with dark clothes and the mane of black hair gripping Indigo by his wrist with one hand while in the other, he held the turkey. He appeared to be waiting for the other three priests to return from their hunt.

Clawfoot could see that Indigo was terrified. Even though he was nearly as tall as the priest, the boy was too skinny and malnourished to put up a fight. He was visibly shaking and a dark puddle was spreading over the flagstones at the boy's feet.

'Stop snivelling,' said the priest in a disgusted tone.

Indigo must have said something, but it was too quiet for Clawfoot to hear. Whatever it was, the priest didn't like it.

'Shut your mouth!' he replied and caught Indigo with a backhand. 'You shouldn't have been trying to rob people then, should you?'

Clawfoot wondered whether he could force the priest to let go of Little Maize's brother. Barrelling into him might just cause him to let go of Indigo long enough for the pair of them to escape. It wasn't a simple question of bravery though. There was a moral dilemma to work through as well. They could forage for food just as effectively as a team of three so Clawfoot reasoned that one less mouth to feed wasn't such a bad outcome. Clawfoot didn't waste tears on anyone since the death of his siblings and his parents, but the thought of Little Maize's face if he came back without her brother was too much for him to bear. He had just worked up enough courage to launch himself at the priest when the other Catchers returned to report their failure to apprehend the rest of the gang. There was no way to free Indigo now. Even if they escaped the clutches of the priests, they were in plain sight of the palace and its guards. Relief and guilt flooded through him in equal measures.

There was a gruff exchange between Indigo's captor and the returning search party. It was clear that the priest in black robes was very unhappy.

'Well, go out and look for them again! Post a watch on the main routes into and out of the slums. They're hungry. They'll need to go out searching again.'

One of the priests asked a question.

'I don't care how long it takes,' shouted the priest at the others, who were obviously his juniors. 'Stay out until daybreak if you have to.' With that, he led Indigo into the temple complex without a backward glance over his shoulder.

Clawfoot watched in dismay. Three wasn't much of a gang, he reflected. It also occurred to him that Indigo had been the better thief amongst them. He took careful note of which direction the three priests were heading before setting off on another rat run that would lead him back to their tumbledown shack without crossing any of the major thoroughfares.

Jaguar hurled himself at the ball and missed, sprawling face-first in the dust. Ignoring the hoots of laughter from the other players, he levered himself into a sitting position and spat to clear the dust from his mouth. He was drenched in sweat and exhausted. What had begun as a friendly knockabout, supposedly just a practice session, had turned seriously competitive.

'Twelve points to eleven!' called the referee.

Jaguar allowed himself a tight smile. 'Still in the lead,' he muttered to himself. He got to his feet and returned to his position near the centreline, breathing deeply through his nostrils. Jaguar was lean and fit, but an hour's continuous play had begun to sap his strength. The ball was out of play so he took the opportunity to refasten the tie that held his black, shoulder-length hair out of his eyes. Reaching up behind his neck, he tugged hard at the knot, determined to prevent it from coming loose and interfering with his vision again.

At seventeen, Jaguar was the youngest official player of the ball game. One of the talent scouts from Moctezuma's training academy had spotted him playing in a street game three years ago. Passing through Teopan one day, the tutor had chanced upon a group of children engaging in a rough knockabout between the houses. There he had watched as the children played out their lawless version of the sacred ullamalitzli with a homemade ball that didn't even bounce well. Jaguar was fast and agile, turning and chasing tirelessly. All of the children had been keen but none had been as committed as Jaguar. He missed fewer shots and those he hit were more accurate than his fellow players.

After the game, the tutor had invited him to one of the regular try-outs at the training academy. The others in the academy needed no persuasion after seeing the young prodigy in action.

The game was so popular with the nobility and sufficiently taxing on the players that promising recruits were highly sought after. Now Jaguar was one of the most promising stars of the game and was looking forward to the day he was allowed to participate on the main circuit against the men. In the meantime, he had to be content with practice sessions and the junior competitions.

One of his team mates had retrieved the ball and was ready to restart the game. Jaguar eyed up the players in the other half of the court. This practice court was off the main temple precinct and was run by the training academy. It was one hundred and eighty feet in length and seventy-five wide. An eight foot high wall ran the length of the court on both sides and set into each wall at the halfway point, just above head height, was a large stone hoop. The opposing team of four jockeyed for position, waiting for the ball to be put back into play.

The server bounced the ball on the ground once and then brought his knee up to connect with it, sending it looping over towards the opposition. None of the players looked very spritely. In spite of the late start, the court was still warm. The walls and dusty floor that had been baking in sunlight all day long were now pumping the heat back into the still evening air.

One of the opposition intercepted the ball on its second bounce. He turned his body neatly and nudged the ball back towards Jaguar's team with his thigh. It was a good shot, too deep into Jaguar's end for him to reach. Magic River was in position to receive it though and played a return to the right-hand side just past the halfway mark. The ball caromed off the side wall gaining spin as it did so. Too tired to notice, or too tired to make sufficient course correction as the ball skewed back towards the wall after the next bounce, the player opposite Jaguar missed the ball completely. Fortunately for him, one of his team had taken up position behind him. The rubber ball was rapidly losing impetus, so the tall player had to lunge to reach it. He just managed to get his knee under the ball and knock it back at Jaguar but there was no power left in it.

It was a gift of a shot. Any other time, Jaguar would have felt sorry for the man, but his mouth was dry, his lungs were heaving and his body was simultaneously burning from the exercise and numb from the repeated impact of the heavy rubber ball. Jaguar sidestepped once and brought his knee in behind the ball aiming it up at the nearest hoop. It was a makeable shot at this range. A ragged cheer went up as the ball clipped the inside edge of the hoop and dropped through.

Jaguar turned to the spectators' area and raised his fist to the sky. Two figures waved back at him, one of them jumping up and down in excitement.

'Game over!' called the referee.

One of Jaguar's team mates patted him on the back. 'Nice!' he said as they all made their way to the end of the court.

Magic River put his hand on Jaguar's shoulder on the way past and gave him a friendly shake. 'You did it again!' he grinned. 'I don't know how you do it.'

As the players filed through a gap in the wall, Jaguar was met by Obsidian Crocodile and Precious Flower. Crocodile got a well aimed punch to Jaguar's arm before Precious Flower threw her arms around him, oblivious to the sweat and dust that covered him head to foot.

'You won!' she exclaimed.

Precious Flower was sixteen years old and a slave in the keeping of Jaguar's family. Her dark brown hair was pinned once at the back of her head in a simple, leather grip with a wooden pin through it and from there it cascaded luxuriantly to the small of her back. She wore a plain, cream coloured dress tied simply around her waist. Jaguar suddenly became aware of how much she had changed since his family had bought her at the market. When had the frightened, fragile waif developed such a perfect oval face, dark, limpid eyes and such long eyelashes? Jaguar extricated himself quickly from her embrace to avoid this troubling train of thought.

'Pfff!' Crocodile made a sour expression. 'Did you see how neatly the ball was dropped at Jaguar's feet?' he scoffed. 'A blind monkey could have scored that!'

'Ooh Itzcipactli! You're rotten,' said Precious Flower, feigning outrage. He dodged her sideswipe easily.

'Hey!' exclaimed Crocodile. 'You shouldn't let her out Jaguar. Ever since your family announced the end of her term of slavery, she's been getting ideas above her station.'

Precious Flower shot Crocodile a venomous look from which he pretended to cower.

Jaguar couldn't resist a smile. 'What brings you two here?' asked Jaguar. He was delighted that his friends had turned up but doubted it was just to witness a practice session.

'Precious Flower wants to see Huitzilopochtli,' said Crocodile.

'Yes please,' replied the girl, her eyes sparkling, their feud instantly forgotten. 'This is the last day he's on display and the last chance I'll have to see him before Nemontomi. Crocodile came by the house to find you and when I told him where you were, he said he'd escort me here and that we could all go together.'

'You know it's just the statue on display, don't you?' said Jaguar. 'Sacred Stone has done his last procession before the New Fire.'

'Oh yes, that's fine. It's just that I haven't seen Huitzilopochtli's likeness for a while. I've seen Tezcatlipoca, Mictlan and we watched the priests anoint Quetzalcoatl in the marketplace just two months ago, didn't we?'

Jaguar laughed. 'All right, I can see how excited you are. Look at me though,' he said, looking down at his dust and sweat streaked body. 'I'm filthy. I can't go like this.'

Crocodile looked him up and down, then wrinkled his nose. 'You'll be fine. There'll be plenty of mayeques there, some of them even more disgusting. We'll just stand upwind of you. Try to avoid talking to us though,' he added. 'People might think we're friends.'

'Ha-ha.' Jaguar made a face. He and Crocodile had met at the age of ten at school. Crocodile was now a warrior in training and looked the part. He was a hand shorter than Jaguar, but he had the well-developed musculature so typical of the elite warriors of Tenochtitlan. Crocodile had a broad face with a small scar on one cheek that he had received in his first real engagement with enemy forces. Like Jaguar, he had not yet earned the right to cut his queue short. His head was shaved except for a patch on the back of his scalp that grew long and was tied neatly at its base.

Training had honed Crocodile for battle and he had proven himself a courageous fighter in several skirmishes. He had already taken three captives. One more would make him the youngest warrior ever to qualify to join the knights.

In contrast with Jaguar's very plain, dun-coloured, dust-streaked loin cloth, Crocodile's was immaculately clean, cream coloured and had short tassels. It was also embroidered with a small red eagle motif on the loose ends that hung at his knees.

'What's that?' asked Jaguar, pointing at an unsightly smudge on his friend's arm.

Crocodile looked offended. 'I'm surprised you have to ask,' he said. 'Meet my namesake and god of the river, Cipactli.' He made a flourish as though revealing the tattoo for the first time.

'Oh, I see,' said Jaguar innocently. 'I thought a bird shat on your arm.'

'You just don't appreciate high art,' complained Crocodile.

'High art? That looks like it was done by Rat Face or his boy down at the market.'

Crocodile was indignant. 'It was done by Rat Face and I got a good price for it too.'

'Well, that's a relief,' said Jaguar, 'because I could have slapped some bird shit on your arm for the price of a few cocoa beans.'

'Argh!' roared Crocodile and punched Jaguar again, this time a great deal harder. Jaguar rode the blow, grinning all the while and led his friends out onto the street where a few of the players were still discussing the game or exchanging a few parting words.

Magic River beckoned to them. Magic River was a captain in the battalion of the warriors of Island Home North, Jaguar's own clan. As such, he held an honorary rank, equivalent to that of a warrior in the Eagle Knights. He was short and stocky and his scar made Crocodile's look like the scratch it was. Magic River's lower lip was split where the blade from an enemy's sword had caught it, knocked out the two central teeth and raked down over his chin. Magic River's scalp stubble was patchy, supposedly as a result of shock from the same battle, making his round head look like the lobe of a mescal cactus. He was not often asked to look after children of a nervous disposition. 'I just wanted to remind you two,' he said, indicating the boys, 'that we're assembling at the gate to the northern causeway tomorrow.'

A cold, heavy stone of worry in the pit of Jaguar's stomach immediately replaced the last vestiges of the thrill of victory in the ball game. He fought to get control of himself. It was a scouting party round the north-eastern end of the lake. They probably wouldn't even encounter the enemy so far from Chalco.

Crocodile winked cheerily. 'We'll be there!'

Jaguar scowled. How did Crocodile make light of it so easily?

'Good! Make sure you are,' called the old veteran over his shoulder as he turned to go. 'You don't want to lose out on the chance to make your tally!'

Precious Flower looked concerned. 'You two will be careful, won't you?'

'Of course we will,' replied Crocodile. 'Anyway, Jaguar will be at the back like he always is!' Crocodile gave a deep chuckle and then yelped as Jaguar kicked his backside. 'Hey! You see!' he added with a hurt look. 'He'll probably even attack his own side.'

'Only if they're being idiots,' Jaguar retorted. 'Come on then! Are we going to see Huitzilopochtli or not?'

Precious Flower made an excited noise and Crocodile made a long-suffering face at Jaguar over her head. Daylight was fading fast when they arrived at the Black House near the southern exit from the temple complex. A few people had gathered to see the statue, which had been placed on display near the palace for one final time before it was returned to the temple in preparation for the ceremony of the New Fire. Eight stern warrior priests from the order of Huitzilopochtli stood in formation around the statue in dark grey robes and watched everyone with suspicion.

The God of the Sun and of War was about the size of a stout child of ten, seated on a blue wooden litter. From each corner emerged a serpent-headed pole, long enough for a man to bear on his shoulder. Huitzilopochtli was festooned with gold jewellery; necklaces, bracelets and anklets that hung around his sandals. The god's forehead was blue and on his head was a rich headdress in the shape of a bird's beak wrought of shining gold. The idol wore a green mantle and over this, hanging from the neck, an apron made of iridescent green feathers, stitched thickly together. In his left hand he held a white shield with a border of yellow feathers and upon which was mounted a cross made of white feathers. A golden banner protruded from the top of the shield as well as four golden arrows that had been sent down from heaven. In his right hand, the god held an undulating serpent staff of aquamarine from the top of which sprouted a forked tongue in vivid red.

'Oh,' breathed Precious Flower. 'He's so beautiful! I wish I'd brought some flowers!'

Jaguar and Crocodile noticed the tribute that had been laid down reverently all around the plinth on which Huitzilopochtli's litter rested. Bright yellow marigolds, dahlias, poinsettias and even some white cactus blossom carpeted the flagstones, fresh ones overlaying the desiccated older ones from previous days. As they were watching, a wealthy family stepped forward with armfuls of silvery grass fronds and marigolds, the colour of the setting sun. The head of the family was an urbane looking man with a pronounced paunch, jowls and a shock of grey hair.

'Who's that?' whispered Precious Flower. 'That offering is worth a small fortune!'

'That's Moctezuma's uncle, Acamapichtli,' offered Crocodile. 'He's a successful merchant. They say he has trading partners all the way to the Yucatan jungles and he's one of the members of the High Council.'

The three of them watched as the warrior priests allowed Acamapichtli to approach the statue where he and an extended family, including two women and eleven children of varying ages, placed their voluminous offering.

'Come on, let's go,' said Precious Flower. She had a sour look on her face. 'It's easy for the nobility to be pious, isn't it?'

'Good. Can we go home because I'm famished?' said Jaguar. He looked at Crocodile. 'Want to join us?'

'No, I won't, but thank you,' he said, serious for a change.

Jaguar knew the reason his friend was reticent. Crocodile knew that Jaguar's family business was struggling. The proximity of the New Fire meant that commissions had dropped away entirely and the only revenue was coming from small good luck charms that were still selling in the markets.

'Oh, come on! I'm sure there will be enough to go around.'

Precious Flower chimed in. 'Yes, please do Crocodile. Musical Reed was saying only this morning that she's hardly seen anything of you recently.'

Crocodile gave in under pressure and the three of them locked arms and headed for Harbour Street, Crocodile whistling the tune to a ribald song about the 'Hill of the Prickly Bush' that Jaguar had to pretend not to know so that he didn't have to explain it to Precious Flower.

———

'Where in the name of the Creator Pair have you been?' demanded Cloud Face.

At the entrance to the Room of Souls, Feathered Darkness bowed and placed the turkey on the low table in front of the high priest. 'I'm sorry, My Lord,' he said. 'This plan to clear the streets of beggars and thieves is taking up a great deal of time. We set a trap for some of the scum but several others gave us the slip and we spent a long time trying to find them again.' He set the turkey down on a stone table that jutted out from the left-hand wall.

'Did you succeed?'

'No, My Lord Mixayacatl. I'm afraid we didn't manage to recapture the others.'

Cloud Face was displeased as Feathered Darkness had known he would be. The birthmark on Cloud Face's forehead above his left eye flushed livid red, a sure sign of his mounting anger.

'Will he fetch a good price?'

'I don't believe he'd survive the trip to Zempoala, My Lord. What would you like me to do with him?'

'Put him in the cells for now. I have a feeling we will need a supply of prisoners to practice on.' Feathered Darkness was about to run his hands through his long, black hair when he remembered how much it irritated his master. Cloud Face was utterly bald and

Feathered Darkness knew that his own luxuriant hair was a perpetual source of irritation to the old priest.

'Mictlan take these filthy urchins! What is the city coming to?' asked Cloud Face. 'And what of the Calpullicalli? They are the ones who are supposed to be dealing with law and order in the streets.'

'I saw no watchmen this evening, My Lord.'

Cloud Face rose from his seat. He was tall and slender. Like Feathered Darkness, he wore the long black robes of high office in the service of Huitzilopochtli. Feathered Darkness watched the high priest reposition the only ornament that the old man ever wore, a necklace made from a leather thong on which was strung a small bundle of black and turquoise feathers, the barely recognisable mummified remains of a Quetzal. Aside from Moctezuma himself, the high priest was the only man in Tenochtitlan who was permitted to wear the feathers of the sacred bird and the punishment for anyone found breaking this law was death.

'We cannot allow things to continue as they are,' warned the high priest. 'Fifty-two years ago, when the sacred fire was last relit, there was respect and discipline; there was rain and no one went hungry.'

Feathered Darkness had heard the lament before and had resigned himself to hearing it several more times before the year was done. The high priest was growing increasingly irascible as the date for the New Fire approached, but then the portents were not good.

'Have you summoned the others?'

'I have, My Lord. They should be here very soon.' Light from the room's single, rectangular window was fading fast. 'Shall I fetch some candles?'

'And something to drink too,' came the terse reply. 'And the turkey is mine?' added Cloud Face.

'It is yours.'

Feathered Darkness bowed and left the room to organise the supplies. He found an acolyte in the main hall and dispatched him in search of something to drink while he located the store of candles and a taper. He returned to the room a short while later and set about lighting the half-dozen candles, which threw the features of the room into stark relief. It was large and had a high ceiling, supported by a wall of ornately carved stone. The floor was made from interlocking slabs of grey stone, but inset at each adjoining corner was a highly polished, diamond-shaped piece of jade. Two hundred silver-plated skulls lined the room at head height, grinning gold teeth smiling at their brethren on the opposite side of the room. Two wooden mannequins stood smartly to attention either side of the entrance to the room, each draped with ceremonial outfits of beads, shells and a coruscating forest of black and red feathers. Above the door he had just come through hung a tapestry of the finest cotton, richly embroidered with the city's founding motif, an eagle perched upon a cactus, but the centrepiece of the room, set on the wall opposite the doorway, was a pictogram of the God of War and of the Sun that took up three panels of stone, each the height of a grown man. Cloud Face marvelled, as he always did, at the craftsmanship. Flickering yellow torchlight accentuated the shadows in the depths of the carving, which depicted the story of Huitzilopochtli's defeat of his sister, Coyolxauhqui, and made the entire scene stand out from the wall and come alive. In the middle ground of the centre panel of the triptych stood the God of War, upon a hill. The god stood with one arm thrown protectively around his mother, portrayed still pregnant, as a device to illustrate that she had only just given birth to him.

The left-hand panel showed Huitzilopochtli's vengeful sister. Coyolxauhqui was storming the hill with four hundred of her siblings, outraged at what she believed to be a preposterous story of their mother's pregnancy. On hearing that a floating ball of feathers was the cause of her brother's conception, Coyolxauhqui had vowed to cleanse her mother by violent means. The triptych was a breathtaking work of art.

'It's a fine piece, is it not?' Cloud Face had seen Feathered Darkness staring at the image as he always did whenever he visited the room.

Feathered Darkness simply nodded his head. He had always known, with absolute certainty, that he had joined the right order of priests, but the first time he had been inside the Room of Souls and had seen the huge stone tablets that told of Huitzilopochtli's victory over his sister, he had been overcome and had very nearly wept. Coyolxauhqui could have had no idea of the unimaginable power that her brother would possess as he emerged from his mother's womb, not only fully grown, but armed and ready to do battle. In his right hand, Huitzilopochtli held aloft the *Fire Serpent*, a devastating weapon that belched liquid fire. Coyolxauhqui had led her army into the very teeth of death and the right-hand panel showed her downfall. Her dismembered body and limbs rolled to the base of the hill, cut down by the righteous wrath of her newly born brother. Her army lay about her, the corpses of a thousand brave warriors, slashed and torn apart.

'...and then Huitzilopochtli did turn upon his sister and summoned the power of the heavens to tear her and her army into pieces,' spoke a new voice. Devine Cactus slouched into the room with an affable smile. Devine Cactus was the high priest of Tlaloc, a portly, middle-aged man with a ruddy complexion and a thinning straggle of jet black hair. Cactus was clearly used to the good living that the priesthood could offer, even in times of famine.

'I see Tlaloc is taking good care of you,' Cloud Face greeted him.

Devine Cactus put on a sad face. 'Mixayacatl, you know I would give up anything to see an end to the drought. Unfortunately, Tlaloc does not share all his mysteries, even with me.'

Feathered Darkness saw his master suppressing his distaste to embrace the priest of Tlaloc around his generous girth. 'He needs all the allies he can get,' thought Feathered Darkness.

'My assistant managed to procure a turkey and you sprang to mind,' said Cloud Face, stepping back and pointing at the bird.

'Oh, how kind,' replied Cactus eagerly. If he noticed the insult, he covered it well. 'What a fine fowl! And so hard to come by these days. Surely you need feeding up more than I?' Cactus patted his stomach affectionately. 'I was worried about you before the famine began, but now...' Cactus' voice trailed off.

'I want for nothing... of that you can be sure,' said Cloud Face waving the concern away with a bony arm.

Cactus' gaze wandered lazily about the room, as though taking in the surroundings for the first time. The man liked to play the fool and Feathered Darkness had to remind himself that Cactus had risen from the mire, through the cut-throat, political echelons of the order of Tlaloc without any obvious effort. He was not someone to underestimate.

The acolyte Feathered Darkness had sent for drinks put his head through the door and announced the arrival of Snake Eyes, the high priest of Xipe Totec. The acolyte deposited a jug of fruit juice, keeping a watchful eye on the minister of the God of Flayed Flesh before scurrying out. Snake Eyes was an ancient, malodorous piece of scum, who made little effort to conceal his use of poisons as the means by which he had effected his own inexorable rise through the priesthood. Feathered Darkness acknowledged that direct methods were sometimes necessary, but Snake Eyes was especially barbarous and was the kind of man who gave the priesthood a bad name. As Cloud Face often said though, it pays to keep the scum on your side.

'What's this about?' demanded Snake Eyes, his tone hostile. His gaze darted warily between Cloud Face and Cactus, then, without waiting for an answer, he darted into the room with a bird-like step and sniffed at the juice suspiciously. He was the eldest of the three with a deeply lined face, most of which seemed to be sliding downwards to collect around his jaw, giving him a lugubrious look. His thinning, ragged, grey hair rested forlornly upon his wrinkled brow. For once, the priest of Xipe Totec was not caked in blood or festooned with the decomposing flesh of his victims, but the stench of the man was still so overpowering that it was all Feathered Darkness could do to avoid gagging.

'Come now, Snake Eyes. You are among friends here,' assured Cloud Face.

The wizened priest glared back at him. 'You want our help to get rid of Tlacaelel.'

'We have spoken of Tlacaelel before,' agreed Cloud Face. 'He's a scheming little shit who will have to be dealt with, but I fear we have bigger problems.'

Cactus pursed his lips thoughtfully. 'How much bigger? Are you sure you're not over-reacting?' He sounded concerned. 'After all, we all know what a strain you must be under. Are preparations for the ceremony in hand?'

'Of course they are in hand,' snapped Cloud Face. 'You need have no fear on that account!' He gestured crossly at some wooden chairs. 'Sit down. We have a lot to discuss. My assistant will serve drinks.'

They pulled the chairs in around a low wooden table, while Feathered Darkness fetched three earthenware cups from an alcove and made a deliberate show of pouring the juice into them where the others could see him. It wasn't enough for Snake Eyes who peered carefully at all three cups.

Feathered Darkness pretended not to notice and retired to stand by the door.

Cloud Face pulled his chair closer to the other two. 'Tlacaelel is a dreamer and a heretic who hides behind his brother. Ever since Itzcoatl granted him the role of Woman Snake and made him the tlatoani's chief advisor he has been meddling in the affairs of state. Until then the tlatoani always consulted with the priests.'

'Well, you actually,' Cactus pointed out.

'And my predecessors,' corrected Cloud Face. 'The point being that Huitzilopochtli is the God of War and it has always been his priests who have been the tlatoani's advisors in matters of strategy and battle plans.'

Devine Cactus sighed theatrically. 'Mixayacatl, we know the hierarchy of the gods, please continue with your explanation.'

'Oh dear, Mixayacatl's star is on the wane,' Snake Eyes observed drily. He chose the cup furthest from him but waited for the others to drink before he put it to his own lips. It was now dark outside and the only light in the room came from the flickering yellow flames of the handful of tallow candles that reflected from the polished skulls on the walls and cast the corners of the wall into pitch-blackness. The shadows of the three priests lurched and wobbled on the walls around the room.

Feathered Darkness wondered if Snake Eyes had gone too far. Cloud Face was notoriously short tempered and the long pause suggested he was struggling to contain his anger.

'You may believe this has nothing to do with you,' said the high priest of Huitzilopochtli in icy tones, 'but I can assure you that it does, and what's more, this is only the start!' He paused to check that he still held their attention and took a small sip from his own cup. 'Tlacaelel means to prevent us from carrying out sacrifices.'

'What?!' Snake Eyes jumped to his feet and even the placid Cactus started, knocking his own drink over.

'He can't do that,' frowned Cactus. 'We must make offerings to the gods!'

'He has no power over us!' cried Snake Eyes. 'How would he achieve such a thing?'

'That's true. Tlacaelel has no direct power over us or our ceremonies, yet he does command the armies of the Triple Alliance and I have a spy in the Woman Snake's staff who tells me that he is trying to persuade Moctezuma to call for a reduction in the number of captives we take.' He raised his hands, appealing for the chance to continue. 'Even now, he is redrawing the plans for our first fight with the Chalca with the express intention of reducing the number of captives taken.'

Cactus raised one eyebrow. 'I have always thought Tlacaelel a reasonable man, but now I am not so sure! Does he want the Fifth World to come to an end?'

Snake Eyes banged his fist on the table. 'Leave it to me!' he croaked hoarsely. 'I can arrange for him to get sick, the kind of sickness no one recovers from.'

'Hold on a moment,' Cloud Face eased them back to their seats with a wave of his hand. 'We mustn't act too hastily. As I already explained, it's not just Tlacaelel who is the problem. Tlacaelel's position is secure as long as these pestilential, godless clans continue to exert influence through the Council of Twelve.'

'The Calpullicalli?' Cactus said. 'What can we do about the House of Clans?'

Feathered Darkness listened to Cloud Face's explanation as he set it out for the other two priests. Since the founding of the city, the ruler of Tenochtitlan had come to the priests for advice, from advice on sacred events and the most auspicious dates for war with neighbouring states, from marriage guidance to the city layout least likely to cause offence to the gods. As the city had grown though, so too had the need for administrators. Tax collectors, engineers, drainage experts, builders, wardens, legal advisors and a profusion of other ancillary posts had ballooned, a situation that had been resolved only by devolving more power to the clans who organised and ran their own districts.

'If we priests allow our power to be eroded anymore,' said Cloud Face, 'we'll be reduced to ceremonial roles; for aesthetic or entertainment purposes only.'

'You're a member of the High Council though,' Devine Cactus pointed out, referring to Moctezuma's inner circle of advisors that consisted of Cloud Face, Tlacaelel and two of Moctezuma's cousins. 'Can't you have the existing members of the Council of Twelve replaced?'

Cloud Face shook his head. 'Assuming we could find grounds to have them dismissed, the appointments are decided within the Calpullicalli so we'd be no better off. Anyway, I know that we'd struggle to persuade Acamapichtli and Zipactonal to support any attempts to undermine the Council of Twelve, they're too giddy with the power their own positions in the Tlatocan gives them. You have given me an idea though. If we could make the Council of Twelve look weak, Moctezuma would look to the High Council on the key decisions. Then all we need to do is oust Tlacaelel and maybe even one of Moctezuma's cousins and have them replaced with priests...'

Cloud Face sat back, his hands steepled in front of him and his eyes closed. Devine Cactus slurped at his juice. Snake Eyes watched them both.

When Cloud Face spoke again, his eyes were like the darkest obsidian, glinting in the guttering light of the candles. He moved closer to the two other men and in a quiet voice that was cold and measured, he made his pitch. 'I believe I have a plan that might just work. I'll need your help, but understand that absolutely nothing must be traced back to us!'

Devine Cactus made a concerned noise and Snake Eyes grunted in agreement.

'If we can turn Tlacaelel's plans to our advantage, with a few supporting initiatives of our own, we may be able to get rid of him, greatly weaken the Council of Twelve and exert greater influence over whatever remains.'

Chapter 2 - Ehêcatl

Two Sign climbed the last flight of decaying stairs that led to Tlacaelel's apartments, his stomach grumbling at the lack of food. The commander of the Eagle Knights was used to pre-dawn starts but hadn't had time to find something to eat. He wondered if Tlacaelel's staff would provide some breakfast but did not hold out much hope. The general didn't eat much. Two Sign looked at the once beautiful frescos that lined the stairwell, depicting a menagerie of animals in various poses. Fish leaped, snakes reared and deer pranced. All were cracked and faded, and the ancient limestone plaster they were painted on was dropping off in chunks. The stone steps themselves were kept clean, but they were worn and in desperate need of repair.

The big warrior shook his head. Tlacaelel could have the most fabulous living quarters in Tenochtitlan. Instead, Moctezuma's brother and right-hand man had chosen an old disused section of the royal palace to make his home, steadfastly refusing any offers to have the place refurbished.

The guard at the entrance recognised Two Sign and stood smartly to attention. Not many people in Tenochtitlan did not know or recognise the famous warrior Two Sign. He was dark and tall with a muscular torso and broad shoulders. He wore his hair long and tied back but with shorn sides in the traditional manner of the warriors. His nose had a squashed and tortured appearance as the result of being broken two or three times in battle. Two Sign raised a half-hand in friendly recognition of the guard. The two smallest fingers on his right hand were missing, cloven from his fist by a blow from a battle-mace years ago in combat deep inside Oaxaca.

Two Sign gave the guard a brief nod in acknowledgement and stepped into Tlacaelel's private apartments. Two Sign knew the layout well. He was standing in the largest of eight rooms that had once been home to one of Chimalpopoca's concubines. Tlacaelel used this room as a reception area and meeting room. His servants and four personal bodyguards used the five rooms leading off it to the right, while the first room on the left was used by Tlacaelel as an office; beyond that was his bedchamber. By Tenochtitlan's standards, the arrangement was extremely frugal and the stark, utilitarian nature of the furnishings served to illustrate Tlacaelel's contempt for frippery. The only items in the room were a map of the lake and its surroundings pinned to the far wall and four low stools arranged neatly in the centre of the tiled floor. The map was the only one of its kind that Two Sign had ever seen. It was the height of two men and almost as wide. Made of grey cotton – by design or as a result of ageing, Two Sign could not tell – the contours of the lake were painted on in a brown dye. A swathe of forest was stippled in green, stretching in a crescent from the north of the lake, through Teotihuacan to the east and on until it encircled Chalco to the south and beyond the forest, in the south-east corner smoked the mighty, brooding volcano Popocatepetl.

'Two Sign,' called Tlacaelel from the doorway on the left. 'Through here, I need your advice.'

Two Sign had to duck to walk through the opening. Tlacaelel's office was well lit. It was on a corner of the building and had two windows that Tlacaelel had had enlarged so that the soft, early morning light streamed in. One looked out across the northern edge of the Moyotlan quarter and a portion of the temple precinct could just be seen through the other. Tlacaelel was sitting cross-legged on the floor examining a sheaf of parchments that lay spread out before him. Tlacaelel could read and write better than anyone Two Sign knew and the general kept enormous quantities of notes. He kept details on every military campaign that he was involved in, claiming that the official records from The House of Ordered Progression were too sparse and consisted of nothing more than naked triumphalism. Apparently, he also spent many hours each night recording things that he had seen or had heard during the day. The papers arranged on the floor meant little to Two Sign, but Tlacaelel was studying them with a fierce intensity. Above his bushy eyebrows his forehead was furrowed with lines of concentration and he stroked the bridge of his nose. The downturn of his mouth was more pronounced than usual giving his gaunt features a sombre expression. Tlacaelel's head was shaven in the same style as Two Sign's but unlike other experienced warriors, his queue reached halfway down his back. Two Sign noticed that the general, normally deeply tanned because of the time he spent with his troops, looked pale and tired. 'Spare me from planning and politics,' thought Two Sign.

'General. How may I help?' he asked.

Tlacaelel bade him sit down. 'The scouting parties have left?'

Two Sign nodded.

'Excellent,' exclaimed Tlacaelel with a twinkle in his eye. 'I want to change the plans we've made for the battle after the New Fire and I need you to check I haven't made any mistakes.'

'Didn't we already agree these plans with the Tlatocan,' said Two Sign.

'We did,' agreed Tlacaelel, looking up from his notes. 'I wasn't particularly happy then but I've been over them several times and now I'm sure they're wrong.'

'What about Last Medicine, My Lord? Shouldn't he be part of this discussion?' Two Sign wondered why the commander of the Jaguar Knights wasn't present.

'Ideally, yes, but he's too busy organising security for the Binding of the Years. I'll find time to advise him of any changes. I'm sure he'll trust your judgement.'

Tlacaelel was a brilliant strategist. Two Sign had learned much as his second-in-command and had no wish to disappoint his mentor, so tried to recall the details. Tlacaelel found a parchment amongst the others at his feet. It was another map, made from the bark of the fig tree. Tenochtitlan and Lake Texcoco occupied the top left-hand corner and Chalco the bottom right-hand corner.

'This is the area we're talking about.' Tlacaelel indicated an area the other side of Colhuacan roughly halfway between the two cities. 'We all know this area well.'

Two Sign looked at the map. It was another work of art. Tlacaelel certainly liked his maps. 'It's a lightly wooded area with lots of cover. On one side we'd have the marshes on the northern edge of Lake Chalco.' Two Sign's attention drifted from the map and he turned his eyes to the ceiling as he recalled the area he knew so well. 'We'd have an advantage as the land runs slightly downhill, away from Colhuacan. As I recall, that and the cover afforded were the reasons why the council approved.'

'Indeed,' Tlacaelel acknowledged. He pulled gently at his lower lip. 'And you agree with this?'

'I would do,' laughed Two Sign, 'except that your gloomy expression and the tone of your voice suggest I do otherwise!' He watched the general carefully for a moment before considering the map again. After a few minutes, Two Sign shrugged. 'I give up. I see nothing unusual or worrying about this choice of site for the battle. We have fought the Chalca here before.'

'That's exactly what's wrong with it,' sighed Tlacaelel. 'Tradition is going to be the death of us. More importantly, our line of retreat consists of just one causeway,' he added. 'If the Chalca ever gain the upper hand, they might be able to turn a minor defeat into a catastrophic rout.'

'That's never happened though.'

'Not yet,' said Tlacaelel. He moved to the window where he stood for a while in stark silhouette against the morning light. The disc of the sun was incandescent above Mount Tlaloc.

'Do you believe the gods protect us, Two Sign?'

'Yes, My Lord.'

'Do you believe the gods enjoy looking after those who make stupid mistakes?'

'Ah, no, My Lord.' Two Sign could see the logic in that.

'We need to be more careful, Two Sign, and less arrogant. As the empire grows, we will be fighting further from home on territory that is less familiar to us. We must take care to examine all the factors. Even small mistakes or flaws in our plans could have disastrous consequences. Huitzilopochtli has no interest in details like this.'

'I understand, Tlacaelel, My Lord.'

'How many of the warriors who trained alongside you are still alive, Two Sign?'

'I'm sorry, what was that?'

'You heard me,' insisted Tlacaelel. 'How many of your friends from – what is it? – ten, twelve years ago are left alive?'

Two Sign knew the answer but he'd locked it away. These were memories that usually only surfaced in the small hours of the morning when his defences were down; memories of fights and battles, some triumphant and some less so. So many of the memories carried losses with them; another face that would never smile again, another friend who would never tell another joke.

'Three,' whispered Two Sign. 'There were six of us I would have called good friends and five more who we knew well. Only three of us remain.'

Tlacaelel said nothing, simply staring out of the window for a long time.

'What a waste!' Tlacaelel said at last. The words caught in his throat. 'We can't keep throwing our good men away.'

'But we have made extraordinary gains, My Lord!' Two Sign countered.

Tlacaelel gritted his teeth. 'But not when we fight the Chalca! We must put a stop to this futile war.'

'Huitzilopochtli demands more sacrifice,' pointed out Two Sign. 'The priests are adamant that we must increase our offering in order to end the famine.'

Tlacaelel turned on him, angry now. 'Do you believe that? This time last year, they sacrificed eight hundred warriors from Chalco, and to what effect?' Tlacaelel paced round the room and waved in frustration at nothing in particular. 'Meanwhile, in Chalco, three hundred of our own men were put to death, along with one hundred and fifty from Texcoco, and still the drought continues, if anything worse than ever.'

Tlacaelel suddenly swept the map from the floor and spread it out on a stone table and beckoned to Two Sign. 'Look here!' He jabbed at an area of the map roughly eight miles directly north of Chalco. 'I went to look at this plain yesterday. It's flat and mostly covered with grasses. No scrub or wooded areas; no surprises.'

Tlacaelel turned to Two Sign. 'With our superior numbers and training, how well do you think we will fare against Chalco in these conditions?'

The big warrior nodded, beginning to see what Tlacaelel was after.

'The Chalca will have nowhere to hide if we fight in this location,' continued Tlacaelel, 'but it will be harder to take captives.'

Two Sign's stomach loudly protested its emptiness again. He rushed into his reasoning, hoping to cover the noise. 'I agree. This open ground will suit us better but the entire army will have to somehow coordinate the moment when the fighting is done and it's time to take prisoners. Are you certain we don't need captives?'

'Of course we need to pay our respects to the gods, but how will we honour Huitzilopochtli if we become so weakened by the loss of our warriors that our empire crumbles?' Tlacaelel picked the rest of his papers off the floor. 'Anyway, I'm not suggesting we stop taking captives. I'm just determined that we crush Chalco first, that way we'll have less trouble from them later.'

'Will the tlatoani approve the change of plans?' asked the big warrior.

Clutching his precious papers to his chest, the general approached Two Sign and poked him in the chest with one finger. 'Moctezuma will love it!' he exclaimed. 'It's a chance for him to put one over Amihuatzin, and if it all goes to plan, we should still be able to take plenty of captives, which should keep that scheming madman, Cloud Face, and his cronies quiet!'

Two Sign didn't share Tlacaelel's dislike of the priests. His parents had instilled in him a deep respect for the gods and their servants. As with most people, Two Sign's parents had consulted the priests regularly for guidance, especially when their son had been born exactly between the days Serpent and Death's Head, neither of which was deemed sufficiently auspicious. Their family priest, Fire of the Earth, had proscribed the name Two Sign and bound the child to both days, thus avoiding any firm association with either.

'What scheming do you suspect the high priest of?' inquired Two Sign.

Tlacaelel gave the Eagle Knight a sorrowful look. 'Come over here, my friend.' He drew the big man over to the window where their voices would not echo and lowered his voice. 'The priests detest me. They believe I hold this post because my brother is the tlatoani. You know this much.'

Two Sign opened his mouth to speak but the general cut him short.

'You know, of course, that we have a number of informants. You're responsible for one or two of them yourself.'

'Of course. "Information is everything",' said Two Sign, repeating one of Tlacaelel's favourite sayings. '"The rest is preparation."'

Tlacaelel lowered his voice again. 'Most of them are useless, a drain on our time and my brother's purse, but there is one in particular who is close to Mixayacatl.'

'Do you have any details?' Two Sign frowned.

'No. Just vague ideas at the moment, but I'm hoping to speak to him again soon.'

'Have you discussed this with the tlatoani?'

Tlacaelel snorted. 'I wouldn't trouble him with this even if I had more information. No, this is a personal matter and running to my brother for help would only fuel the priests' dislike of me.'

'How is your son getting on anyway?' asked Tlacaelel, suddenly changing the subject. I hear he looks set to make you very proud.'

'Crocodile is doing very well, My Lord, it's very kind of you to ask. As you well know he is adopted so it has very little to do with me!'

Tlacaelel laughed warmly and reached up to pat Two Sign on the shoulder. 'Typically modest, my friend. We both know you work very hard to make up for the loss of his parents.' With an entirely innocent look he added, 'Have you eaten this morning?'

Two Sign said that he had not.

'Very well, then,' Tlacaelel proposed, 'let's go and see if Moctezuma's palace kitchens have opened for breakfast.' The general deposited his documents on a table and headed for the door.

'By the Skin of Xipe, slow down!' called Crocodile, ducking to avoid an overhanging branch as he followed in Jaguar's footsteps.

Jaguar could hear his friend's breathing coming in ragged gasps. With his light and easy gait, Jaguar was having no trouble keeping pace with the pack ahead. Jaguar was lean and well toned because of the constant practice at the ball game. He reflected that this might be the only part of war in which he would ever excel over Crocodile. Jaguar decided that his friend was just one of those people with a solid build, no matter what they ate or what exercise they did. His frame was too solid and muscular to fall into the graceful rhythm of the chase, especially over the rough terrain and thick vegetation they found themselves in now. Crocodile was a fighter, not a runner. Last summer, when Jaguar had captured his first enemy in a battle against the Tlaxcala, he had turned, triumphant, only to discover that Crocodile had increased his own tally by two.

Jaguar and Crocodile were at the rear of a twelve man scouting party sent to secure captives for the ceremony of the New Fire and to stir up trouble with the Chalca. All of this was traditional in the run-up to a major battle, but this year the tensions were running especially high as the great cycle of the years was at an end.

The sun was already high in the sky as the scouting party made its way quickly up a valley to the east of Teotihuacan. In the distance rose the ghostly outline of Mount Tlaloc, a few wispy clouds clung to its peak, like fledgling birds uneasy at the prospect of their first flight. Jaguar was glad he hadn't brought his cloak. The loin cloth and light battle tunic he was wearing were already drenched with sweat from the exertion of the run. The spring weather was hot for the fourth year in a row. For months on end there seemed to have been only sporadic, light showers that barely seemed to touch the ground before they stopped again.

Jaguar listened to the noise of the pursuit. Behind him, Crocodile was puffing and blowing; ahead, the rest of the pack were quieter so that Jaguar could hear the crackling of dry twigs and rustling of the long grasses as the warriors wove their way through the desiccated landscape.

The shallow valley narrowed and began to slope upwards to a saddle between two low peaks, leading Jaguar to conclude that their objective must be close. A short while ago, Magic River had spotted what looked like a platoon of Chalca in an adjacent valley and was now leading his own men on an intercept course.

Up ahead, a mother quail and her mottled brown chicks scattered, squeaking through the clumps of bunchgrass. Their black and white faces made the chicks look crestfallen as they fell over each other in their haste to escape the line of running warriors. The bunchgrass was thick here in the light shade of the valley, but the large tufts looked dry and brown, as though it was still mid-summer.

The valley floor climbed more steeply now. The oak that thrived in the valley basin gradually gave way to a mixture of pine and gnarled juniper trees. Large gaps in the canopy appeared, revealing a brilliant azure sky, set high above with stretched-thin clouds that crept quietly in the direction of Huexotzingo.

Magic River stopped his warriors before they reached the top of the rise and sent Archer Eagle ahead to reconnoitre. The others gathered round for some last minute instructions. Magic River's stocky frame was not ideally suited to running long distances. His face was puce and the sweat poured from his scarred face and body. In spite of his discomfort, he stood bolt upright with his arms folded, his chest rising and falling quickly.

'You wanted a fight,' he growled, 'and now you've got one! Any of you changed your minds and want to go home?' He scanned the faces in front of him. The men stood, frozen into immobility for fear that any movement, no matter how small, would be interpreted as a sign of weakness.

'Good!' said Magic River. 'We are Mexica!' He made a fist and thumped his chest, sneering as he did. 'Mexica do not turn from battle!' He wiped the perspiration that beaded on his forehead.

'Storm Light,' Magic River called to the youngest warrior. 'What is the most important weapon you have?'

Storm Light's wiry frame, sallow complexion and the wispy hair reminded Jaguar of a wind damaged maize cob and he had to suppress the urge to laugh. He did not look like the warrior type, Jaguar decided.

'You find this funny, Jaguar?'

'No, My Lord!'

'Just because your father is one of the Council of Twelve doesn't mean that you're above all this,' said Magic River with a stern expression.

Jaguar hung his head. 'No, My Lord.'

'Well then, perhaps you can answer for our friend, Storm Light...'

'My hands,' Jaguar muttered.

'I didn't hear that! Again, please.'

'My hands, My Lord!'

'And why is that?' asked Magic River in a voice that echoed his severe looking scar.

'Hands make gifts for gods,' Jaguar replied, somewhat louder.

'Good.' Magic River nodded thoughtfully and addressed the rest of the party. 'We must take as many captives as we can. Tlacaelel has put out a general call asking for more intelligence on what the Chalca are up to and, as you all know, the New Fire approaches and the gods must have their tribute.' He turned his face towards the sun, signalling a prayer.

'Sturdy souls, once more we raise our arms in battle,' he began in a solemn tone. 'Huitzilopochtli, we call on you for courage, O Lord! Send us the power of your rage and fire our souls with vengeance so that we may purge the world of our enemies!' Magic River turned back to the warriors and addressed the younger members of the party. 'Remember this as you pursue our enemies: though we Mexica are the chosen people, protected by our gods, so must we honour them and return to them their portion. Therefore, secure your enemies and bring them forth, so that we may appease the guardians of Motion.'

A brief silence was interrupted by a clatter of stones as Archer Eagle returned.

'Magic River,' he puffed, drawing level with the group. 'The men we saw are Chalca.' Beads of sweat traced lines over the man's dusty pectoral muscles as he described what he had seen. 'Perhaps twenty warriors escorting two dignitaries, approaching from the West. They will pass beneath our position in a few minutes.'

'No doubt seeking military assistance from Tlaxcala,' Magic River spat through his cleft lip.

Several of the warriors shook their heads sadly at this cowardly behaviour.

'Is there a route down the other side?' Magic River asked, nodding at the crest.

'The path is steep,' Archer Eagle replied, 'but there is a ravine, which will provide us cover on the descent.'

'Very well, we must be quick!' Magic River motioned the troops forward and then held his right hand in the shape of the closed beak of a bird, requesting silence.

Jaguar crested the hill. The forest fell away sharply on this side, but was gouged by a sharp, V-shape that cut precipitously down the slope. The trees on the edges leant in towards the middle of the ravine where their fanning branches met giving the appearance of a tunnel below.

The war party descended cautiously to avoid dislodging any scree. The few trees that grew in the shade of the fissure were thin and contorted. Their exposed roots writhed and twisted against the rocks that held them captive. Rivulets of clear water emerged from many places, pushed up from aquifers deep in the volcanic rock. Jaguar couldn't resist the temptation to brush one of the soft, furry clumps of bright green moss that thrived in the damp conditions but it did little to sooth his churning stomach. Clusters of drooping ferns trembled as the warriors pushed on downwards.

They all reached the bottom of the ravine with Crocodile and Jaguar still bringing up the rear as they had been ordered to. Magic River was listening for sounds of the approaching enemy. When he was sure they weren't close, he stepped out to survey the situation in more detail. The ravine ended on the floor of a narrow defile that was one of the less well known routes east towards the mountains. Aside from the route they had just come down, the only way in and out was along the sandy path. Elsewhere, the walls were far too steep.

Magic River completed his assessment and picked out two warriors.

'You two come with me,' his voice was a harsh whisper. 'The rest of you stay here with Archer Eagle and try and stay out of sight.' He patted Archer Eagle on the shoulder. 'Wait until they draw level with you. We will block their escape route.' With that the stocky warrior strode off towards the approaching foe to look for a suitable hiding place.

Jaguar watched him go.

'By the sacred skin!' said a voice at his side. Storm Light was watching the three warriors depart. 'He's mad!' the boy whispered, glancing at Jaguar. He stared, wide-eyed, looking paler than usual. 'Three of them... against twenty Chalca!'

'Nine of us attacking from this end,' Jaguar pointed out.

'What if they try to break out that way?' Storm Light pointed at the three warriors as they disappeared from view round a jagged, rocky outcrop.

'You haven't seen Magic River in action yet, have you?'

Storm Light shook his head.

Crocodile overheard the conversation and cut in. 'He was a knight for ten years, you know!' Crocodile grinned, knowing the trouble that was in store for the Chalca.

'What happened?' asked the younger warrior.

'He took that injury to his face,' said Crocodile in a whisper. 'When he recovered, he quit the knights and went back to his family.'

'So now he only fights with his clan?'

'That's right,' replied Crocodile. 'He says he's done his bit for the tlatoani.'

Archer Eagle hissed at them to be quiet and waved everyone back into the shadows to wait. Several of the warriors used the opportunity to empty their bladders.

Jaguar felt nervous again. He always did. His hands were cold and they looked pale. He looked at Crocodile and was annoyed to see him looking relaxed. The threat of imminent violence didn't seem to bother him. He gave off an air of indestructibility, as though his powerful frame was too big to suffer any serious damage. There was some strange magic at work for Two Sign to have adopted Crocodile; they were so alike in looks and build.

When he was ten years old, Crocodile's village had been wiped out by a retaliation strike by the people of Oaxaca. A dozen outlying Mexica villages were torched by the raiders and their people put to death or hauled away as slaves or sacrificial offerings in the great city of Oaxaca. When the news got back to Tenochtitlan, every unit of Eagle Knights and Jaguar Knights was dispatched to re-secure the area and search for survivors. Two Sign had been with the platoon that found the last village and came upon the butchered and charred remains of the oldest and the youngest in the village, piled up on the communal fire. Two Sign had found the boy huddled in the burnt out remains of a hut, gently rocking, his knees pulled up under his chin. He had been out collecting firewood and returned to find his grandparents dead and parents missing. Two Sign took him back to Tenochtitlan and the frightened boy had refused to leave the big warrior's side. Seven years later, and now a man himself, Crocodile had the same square jaw, thin lips and the same flat nose as Two Sign. It was in his eyes that Crocodile differed from the man who had taken him under his wing. Crocodile's large, friendly eyes rolled cheerfully beneath sparse eyebrows. The overall effect was to give Crocodile a benign look that had fooled many an adversary.

Jaguar watched his friend examine his sword, checking each of the blades in turn to make sure they were tight. He felt queasy and decided to check his own weapon in the hope that it would calm his nerves. He slung a bag from his shoulder and took out the shield and his own sword. Jaguar's was the traditional style, with none of the garish embellishments that most warriors favoured. Some carved the wooden hafts and tied colourful feathers to the head, but Jaguar's father had shown him that clean lines and unfussy design allowed a warrior to check the weapon for faults more easily. He turned it over in his hands a few times, feeling the balance. It was a beautiful piece of work by Achcauhtli, the clan's armourer. Six razor-sharp shards of polished obsidian gleamed even in the gloom of the ravine. The cutting stones were mounted in two rows of three, set on opposite sides to give a clean slicing action and to allow the weapon to be carried safely.

Jaguar cursed himself, irritated because of the fear that crawled over his skin.

Suddenly, Archer Eagle pulled back from the rift opening. He made a flattening motion with his hand and the warriors shrank back further into their hiding places. The enemy were close.

Jaguar unslung his wooden shield from his back and retreated behind a mossy branch. His stomach improvised new contortions and his throat felt dry.

All the warriors readied themselves, each offering up a silent prayer to Huitzilopochtli. The passing seconds slowed down until they dripped like the amber sap from a wounded pine tree. Now the sound of approaching feet could clearly be heard.

All of a sudden, the enemy came through the narrow gap and into the defile where the warriors lay in wait. Two abreast, the Chalca knights strode along the dusty track, their feathered headgear waving as they came. Jaguar held his breath as the first twelve emerged, the last of whom were noblemen, dressed in long cloaks of richly woven fabric. One of the noblemen held a long spear, upon which a human skull was mounted. The snow-white cranial dome was decorated with gold studs and framed with Quetzal feathers.

Just as the noblemen cleared the gap in the defile, Archer Eagle leaped at the two men in front, a blood-curdling scream in his throat. He crashed into them and three people fell in a thrash of legs and arms and those behind them were forced to stop abruptly. As the Chalca came to a halt, Jaguar, Crocodile, Storm Light and the other Mexica warriors rose slowly to their feet.

The tableaux held for a fraction of a second and then the Chalca reached for their weapons. Action finally dispelled Jaguar's attack of nerves. Now that the trap was sprung and he faced the enemy, it seemed as though raw fire coursed through his veins. He saw Crocodile throw himself over the struggling form of Archer Eagle at the next two Chalca and in the shatter-stop time of battle, Jaguar found himself beside his friend, sword raised high and yelling like the demons of the dead.

A yell from beyond the gap signalled that Magic River and his two warriors were engaging the enemy. From the corner of his eye, Jaguar saw Crocodile swing his sword and the nearest warrior raised his shield to parry the shot, suffering a jarring shock to his wrist in the process. Immediately, Crocodile began a reverse rotation of his right arm that should have disembowelled his foe.

Jaguar didn't see the outcome because he was forced to block a sweeping blow from his own opponent. The world slowed down and fragmented into a handful of scenes, frozen as though they were carved in stone like some legendary deed of old. Rather than stop the shot directly, Jaguar instinctively ducked and stepped in under the man's sword arm and hacked his own weapon across the man's bare stomach, peeling it to ribbons of flesh. The warrior sank to his knees with a groan as his entrails spilled out. Jaguar stepped over him to draw level with Crocodile, to prevent his friend's left flank from becoming exposed.

The next man confronting Jaguar was twice his age, muscular and had the look of a seasoned warrior. They exchanged a quick succession of blows, sword on shield, sword to sword, then shield against body, each successfully defending against the other's attack. Jaguar's arm began to tire so he stepped back to buy himself more time and slow the pace a little. As he stepped back, Jaguar tripped over the body of the first man he had dispatched. Unwilling to let go of his shield or sword, Jaguar fell heavily on his backside. He cried out in pain and, sensing victory, the Chalca warrior rushed forward with his club raised high.

Jaguar could only look up at his opponent, silhouetted against the brilliant green canopy of overhanging trees, sword poised to deliver the final blow. Scintillating motes of dust swirled above, caught in the shafts of sunlight that pierced the foliage. Through the sounds of battle, Jaguar thought he heard Crocodile shouting as though in the far distance. Jaguar tried to raise his shield to defend himself but a searing bolt of pain in his left shoulder prevented him from moving. Suddenly, a huge weight fell across him. As he struggled out from underneath it, he saw it was the body of his opponent. Blood poured in shockingly crimson gouts from the warrior's skull, mixed with slivers of white bone. In his haste to kill Jaguar, the man had forgotten the other six Mexica who stood waiting behind the battle line to get into the action.

Jaguar stood up, expecting to rejoin the fray, but another warrior had taken his position and there was no room in the confines of the rift for Jaguar to get to the front. He took advantage of the enforced rest, breathing deeply as the world slewed back into normal focus.

'Are you all right?' asked Storm Light.

'Yes.' Jaguar rubbed his shoulder. 'Who took that big man down?' He noticed Storm Light was trembling. 'Was it you?'

Storm Light nodded and managed a rueful smile.

'Wow! Thanks,' said Jaguar, eyeing the lad with new respect.

'What's it like in there?' Storm Light agitated. His eyes kept flicking from Jaguar to the fight, perhaps worried that the enemy might break through.

'Tight,' was all Jaguar managed.

'Did you see Magic River?'

Jaguar replied that he hadn't.

Suddenly, a high-pitched scream rose above the general clangour. Jaguar tried to identify the source of the noise, but the scene was too chaotic. It looked as though another Mexica warrior had advanced to fill a gap up front. The fighting had retreated a small way down the gully, but it was impossible to tell whether it was due to Magic River retreating or whether it was caused by a contraction of the Chalca ranks. Jaguar thought he could just make out Crocodile's sword, rising and falling amidst the flailing arms and weapons.

Storm Light and Jaguar moved closer to the rear of the action, ready in case the enemy should try and break through.

Just then a sharp command cut through the noise. The fighting stopped abruptly. Warily, the Mexica warriors lowered their weapons. Five Mexica stood alongside Crocodile. It wasn't easy for Jaguar to get a clear view from the back, but it looked as though Archer Eagle was lying sprawled, face up amongst the ferns to the right of the path. Another Mexica lay close by, slumped over a large boulder with a vicious looking war club embedded in his skull by its glistening blades. It was the boat builder's son.

Trapped in the narrow pass, seven Chalca warriors stood in a protective huddle around the two dignitaries. They were all liberally splashed with blood and they clutched their weapons and shields with fierce desperation.

Magic River stood beyond the huddle of Chalca, blocking the defile with his solid frame. His face and arms were splashed with gore and the front of his once-white tunic was now almost entirely red. In spite of this, he appeared to be unhurt. One of the warriors he had chosen to fight alongside him was still alive, his eyes blazing with savage intensity. A dozen corpses lay about them on the ground.

'What's happening?' Storm Light whispered to Jaguar.

Jaguar ignored him, annoyed at the interruption and intent upon the detail of the stand-off. The walls of the narrow pass made it impossible for the Chalca to escape, so unless they surrendered they would have to fight their way out, but Magic River had taken a huge gamble by calling a halt to the fighting so soon. With only two warriors standing between them and the way they had come, they might yet decide to try and break free.

Moctezuma's instructions were to take captives, so Island Home North's experienced captain intended to deliver. Jaguar checked the numbers. Ten of the Chalca lay dead, for a loss of three Mexica, leaving the two sides more evenly matched. If Magic River's timing was good and the enemy capitulated, the rewards would be extraordinary.

The pause continued as the Chalca weighed the situation up. Jaguar could see them trying to work out which route would offer the least resistance.

'Come on,' Jaguar urged Storm Light forward so the two of them could take up position between the others to block up the gaps. The other way out certainly looked easier at first glance, but there was something about Magic River's solid, implacable presence and his calm demeanour that whispered death. Looking at him and the tangle of bodies that lay about the captain, even Jaguar had to suppress a shudder.

A ghastly moan broke the silence. Everyone turned and stared at Archer Eagle who was still alive. He had dragged himself out of the ferns and was trying to haul himself into a sitting position against a rocky outcrop. Dark, treacle-like blood lay in a sheen over his mangled shoulder, while black dirt and leaf litter mingled with the pink froth that bubbled from a wound in his chest. The warrior's once-tanned skin looked a deathly shade of grey and he struggled to draw breath. The standoff was momentarily forgotten as every warrior watched, transfixed by the dying man.

The broken warrior slowly raised one finger and pointed at the Chalca. 'Do... not... choose... this,' he breathed, barely audible. The smallest of smiles tugged briefly at the corners of his mouth. He dragged another shallow breath. 'Choose surrender...' Here Archer Eagle coughed weakly, drooling blood. His outstretched arm dropped to his lap and his eyes glazed over before refocusing again briefly.

'Choose... immortality.' Archer Eagle slowly looked to one and then the other, as though looking for something. Finally his head dropped to his chest and his bubbling wound fell still.

A shocked silence ensued but Magic River knew the moment had come to appeal to the enemy. 'Worthy sons of Chalco,' he said. 'You heard our noble friend, Archer Eagle. There is no escape for you. Fight on and die here in agony or...' he paused for effect. 'Give yourselves up and live another day, fêted as the gods' chosen ones.'

The two dignitaries stirred as though from a trance and they bent their feathered heads in conference. They whispered in short staccato, as the one with the spear started jabbing at the other's chest. His shorter colleague nodded frequently at first and then began shaking his head. Gradually, his voice got louder and then raised an octave. The one with the spear gesticulated at his colleague a couple of times and then slapped his face hard to shut him up. He waited a moment to see if he had made his point. When there was no response, he turned gracefully to face Magic River and bowed low.

'Brave children of the Sun,' began the dignitary, opening with a traditional compliment. 'We have fought valiantly. We have hurled ourselves upon the might of our enemy with terrible ferocity and yet we have been repelled.'

Magic River nodded once, looking sternly through the blackening flecks of blood across his face.

'You have fought valiantly,' he replied, according them the respect they sought. 'In truth, we were in fear of our lives, but now you are outnumbered.' Magic River twisted the truth, allowing the Chalca to save face.

The Chalca representative gratefully acknowledged Magic River's comments and formally surrendered.

'We honourably lay down our weapons and place ourselves in the care of our fathers.' So saying, the dignitary instructed his warriors to place their weapons on the ground. When they had done so, he addressed them again.

'You have acquitted yourselves well in the name of your fathers and in the true spirit of your ancestors.' He bowed to his warriors, who now stood at ease, and passed between them. He presented himself before Magic River and knelt in front of him, submitting himself in the traditional manner. The proud nobleman prostrated himself upon the ground and placed three fingers to the ground at Magic River's feet. He wiped his fingers in the dust and touched them to his lips.

'Honourable father, I am your son. Guide me until the will of the gods is known.'

His colleague followed suit, eating dirt at Crocodile's feet. With Archer Eagle dead and Crocodile occupying a central position, the emissary from Chalco naturally assumed he was next in command. The Chalca each picked an opponent from amongst the Mexica and submitted one-by-one. The last two stepped up to Jaguar and Storm Light and knelt in the leaf litter.

'Father, I am yours to guide,' they intoned.

'Son of mine, henceforth you are also son of the Sun,' recited their captors in time.

'What is your name?' Jaguar asked the man at his feet.

'Sunshine of the Seven Hills,' the man replied, his gaze fixed firmly on the dirt. Jaguar bade him stand and looked him up and down. He was a wiry individual, old enough to be Jaguar's father. His face was nearly flat and he had high cheekbones that suggested Tarascan lineage, but he had the narrow slit eyes and dark skin of the lake dwellers. 'You should call me Sunshine,' he added. He scratched nervously at his thinning black hair and gave a watery smile.

'Very well, Sunshine,' agreed Jaguar. 'Are you injured?' Jaguar looked at his captive's leg, which was bleeding from a wound in his thigh.

'It's not as bad as it looks,' replied Sunshine, dabbing at the cut with the free end of his loin cloth. Although it didn't look life threatening, the cut was deep enough to have sliced through muscle and the wound steadfastly refused to be staunched.

Just then, Crocodile came over. 'You need to close that.' He pulled a small fabric pouch from his waist and handed it to Jaguar. 'Needle and thread.'

'Right,' said Jaguar as he extracted the contents delicately. He'd seen a wound sutured closed on the battlefield once before but his only real experience of stitching was the time his mother had been unwell and he'd helped out by repairing one of his father's tunics that had been torn in battle, that and one lesson in the military school.

'Sit down,' he instructed Sunshine of the Seven Hills, pointing at the fallen tree trunk behind him. The Chalca did as he was told and Jaguar set to work as quickly as he could, talking all the while to allay his nerves. He took a bone needle and some thread made from the fibres of the agave plant out of the small pouch. He spat on the needle, wiped it clean on the fabric of the pouch and ran a thread through the eye. Jaguar tried to look confident as he pushed the needle through Sunshine's skin, as though he'd done it many times.

'You are my second captive,' said Jaguar. 'Two veterans helped me take my first captive.' He tugged the thread and made a knot before beginning again. 'That day we fought the Tlaxcalan army. They fought hard but in the end they turned in rout.' Jaguar frowned as he concentrated on pulling a knot tight. 'I managed to grab one of the warriors, but he was sweaty. He nearly wriggled out of my grasp but then one of the clan elders grabbed the man's other arm.'

Sunshine listened politely, wincing as the rough needle pierced his skin.

Jaguar remembered the thrill of taking his first captive. Another veteran had caught hold of the Tlaxcalan's queue and wrenched him to the ground, whereupon the Tlaxcalan had submitted.

Jaguar finished the last stitch in silence and for the first time, he noticed the quiet after the battle, a ghostly silence that hung over the forest. He stood up and surveyed his handiwork. Half a dozen coarse knots crossed the gouge in the captive's thigh. It looked ugly, but the blood seemed to have stopped. With luck it would hold during the long walk back to Tenochtitlan.

'Mictlan's bones,' grinned Crocodile, who had been watching. 'I thought you were trying to save him, not finish him off!'

Jaguar gave a sour look. He was still trembling from the nerves and the effort of concentration and was in no mood for jocularity.

The solemn ritual of surrender was over, so while Jaguar had been tending to his captive, Magic River had directed one of his men to collect the Chalca's weapons into a pile against the wall of the defile and line the fallen warriors up neatly along the edge of the path, ready for carrying away. With this job completed, Magic River addressed those present.

'I know this path. There's a cave to the west, not far away. We will take the dead there and give them a proper burial.' Magic River made it clear that the Chalca would have to help. Even the captured dignitaries were pressed into service. 'It's going to take two trips to get everyone down there, so we'd better get going.'

'Come on,' Jaguar indicated the nearest body to Sunshine, who stood up gingerly, testing his damaged leg. It oozed slightly but seemed to hold. They bent down to collect up the limbs of their chosen corpse and gathered it up awkwardly. Sunshine gripped under the dead man's armpits and Jaguar hooked his elbows under the limp knee joints. Sunshine nodded his head in the direction they were supposed to be going. Jaguar was puzzled until Sunshine managed to free a hand and made circular motions with his index finger. Suddenly Jaguar caught on. Sheepishly, he manhandled his end of the load until he was facing the other way, realising that his captive had spared him from ridicule.

Jaguar and his captive fell in with the others, who were already making off down the defile with their loads. The procession moved in an ungainly fashion along the path in the direction that the Chalca had been going, leaving two bodies behind to be collected later.

The volcanic landscape in the area was pockmarked with numerous caves, especially in the high country. Over time, lava outpourings from ancient eruptions had become eroded into complex and sometimes grotesque shapes or fractured by earthquakes. In some places, ash and pumice deposits, sandwiched between layers of solidified rock, had become exposed to the elements and washed away, revealing flat-roofed caves. Extensive systems of caverns formed where underground water courses cut through the softer volcanic residue. Through such caves the dead attained the afterlife. The spirits left their earthly flesh behind and wandered down the dripping sink holes, where they would eventually reunite with Mictlantecuhtli, the God of the Underworld.

Sunshine's composure was commendable. The little man had a strong hold on the body and was as committed to the task as any of the Mexica. Jaguar hoped that he would bring honour to his people if he was ever taken captive. In a recurring dream of his, he was taken by the Chalca or the Tlaxcalans – he couldn't be sure which – who prepared him for sacrifice. Priests dressed Jaguar in the ceremonial costume, presenting him as the living image of Tezcatlipoca, the God of Drought, Famine and Plagues. His memories of the dream were mostly hazy, but many details remained etched in Jaguar's mind. First the priests painted his body black and placed a crown of quail feathers upon his head. Next came the red mantle, decorated with a skull and crossed bones. In his left hand they placed a white shield and four pure-white arrows. In his right hand they placed the atlatl, the throwing spear. Jaguar could recall no sound from the dream, but the wide-open mouths of the priests and the crowd rang in his head like a condemnation. He knew he must be brave and turn to face the altar, but each time he had tried, the dream ended and Jaguar awoke to find himself awash with sweat.

Jaguar shuddered and tried to concentrate on the task in hand, shifting the weight of the dead man to relieve his aching shoulders. Up ahead, others were having trouble with their loads too. The pair in front stopped to adjust their grip allowing Jaguar and Sunshine to slip past and catch up with Crocodile. Crocodile had been in the thick of the fray for the whole battle. He must have been exhausted, but Jaguar could only detect the faintest signs that he was struggling. He was bringing up the rear of his team so Jaguar got close enough to land a kick on his backside.

'Hey, worm! You're too slow!' cried Jaguar. 'Hurry up or we'll be forced to tread on you!'

Crocodile turned his head and caught sight of the mischievous grin on his friend's face.

'At least I didn't shirk the fight by playing dead!' he retorted.

'Pah! Mictlan take you!' laughed Jaguar. He kicked Crocodile again for good measure, glad that his friend chose to fight alongside Island Home North. Technically, because Crocodile had been adopted by Two Sign, his clan was *They Who Hold Back the Water*, but since Two Sign wasn't married, he'd spent very little time with the warrior's family so he'd been given leave to fight with Jaguar's clan instead.

The two had met at telpochcalli, when Jaguar became old enough to attend the military school. Not long after Jaguar joined, he was accosted by Crocodile who, in the short time he had been there, had developed a reputation as something of a bully. An argument had broken out over the ownership of an unfortunate toad, which had been waddling dejectedly around the recreational area. Jaguar had taken pity on the creature and was about to release it in the street outside the compound, from where it would be able to make its way to the canal. At that moment, Crocodile made an accusation of theft and within a matter of seconds was pushing Jaguar repeatedly on the chest. Crocodile's regular victims winced, recognising Jaguar's mounting frustration, but were secretly pleased that Crocodile had found someone new to pick on. Everyone who witnessed the event was convinced that Jaguar would flee or cower in humiliation, probably bawling his eyes out. At fourteen, Crocodile was already larger than his contemporaries and he certainly had a weight advantage over Jaguar.

Jaguar staggered back from another shove. He looked up from the toad in a detached way. Crocodile narrowly missed treading on the creature several times. Jaguar imagined the split skin and squashed entrails that would result. Crocodile's sneering face swam into view and his fatuous expression angered Jaguar. Suddenly, he snapped. Spinning with lightning speed, Jaguar smashed the heel of his open palm directly into Crocodile's nose. The astonished antagonist fell backwards and sat down heavily. Black drops formed curious sooty pellets in the dust and Jaguar tried to work out where they had come from, until he saw Crocodile's broken nose, gushing blood into his cupped hands.

From that day on, Jaguar had Crocodile's respect and it wasn't long before the two became firm friends. They could often be seen together out in search of trouble. With a co-conspirator in the high jinks of adolescence, Crocodile's exploitation of his fellow schoolmates stopped, as Jaguar found more creative means of entertainment. On one occasion they stole a fisherman's canoe, intent on paddling it clear across to Texcoco, until they accidentally overturned it in the middle of the lake, forcing them to swim for almost half an hour to regain the shore.

'There it is,' called a voice from ahead, bringing Jaguar's attention back to the present. The convoy had at last reached the cave. Jaguar and Sunshine lowered the dead warrior to the ground and arched their backs, trying to ease the cramp. At this point in the defile, the path began to slope back downhill quite steeply and the dirt path disappeared among haphazard steps of broken rock. A massive slab of tezontle jutted out from the right-hand cliff-face, similar to the black basalt used for the sacrificial altar of the Great Temple. The slab lay at an angle, its far end lay on a level with the path, but the nearer end was propped up on a large boulder, forming a gaping horizontal crack. Yellow-green creepers festooned the sides of the dark slab and a gnarled juniper tree grew out from above it. The tree's branches pointed up the rift, combed by the channelled winter winds into a rough and threadbare alignment.

The gap beneath the slab was wide enough for two people to lie across it, but it was very low.

'The entrance isn't big enough!' exclaimed Crocodile.

'Perhaps not for a fat pig like you,' scoffed Jaguar. 'I could easily get in there.'

Just then Magic River made his way to the head of the convoy and overheard the exchange.

'You two,' he said, beckoning to Jaguar and Crocodile. He wiped at the sweat and blood that caked his forehead with a corner of his tunic. 'You seem keen to try out the cave. Get in there and check it out.'

'What, get inside?' asked Crocodile.

'Crocodile, I've got no time for your idiocies,' said Magic River, a note of exasperation creeping into his voice. 'There are two more bodies to bring down here and we're a long way from home, so get in there and make sure it's a worthy burial place for these men.'

'What are we looking for?' Jaguar asked sincerely.

'Just...' Magic River waved them away. 'You'll know when you get in there!' With that he began arranging for collection of the remaining corpses.

Jaguar and Crocodile bent down beneath the overhanging slab to inspect the entrance to the cave. Beyond the mouth itself, the darkness was profound. Jaguar could just make out a drop down to the floor.

'Move aside, blubber boy.' Jaguar prodded Crocodile's muscled torso and backed towards the ledge. He lowered himself into the opening, gingerly extending his right leg until he felt it touch solid ground. Very little light penetrated the wedge-shaped aperture. While Jaguar waited for his eyes to adjust, Crocodile wriggled through the gap and eased himself down to the floor of the cave. The basalt roof of the cave continued unbroken into the depths for two or three paces until it vanished into the inky blackness.

'How deep does it go?' asked Crocodile.

Jaguar shrugged.

'Let's find out,' he suggested and crept further into the cave. He strained his eyes into the darkness, trying to see the ground, the walls, ceiling or any discernible feature. People disappeared in caves like this and Jaguar didn't want to add his name to the list.

Jaguar became nervous. There was a fracture in the stone roof that seemed to run across the width of the cave, but Jaguar could see nothing of the floor. It had a curious velvety quality of black that he didn't like at all and the air had a pungent, earthy smell. As Crocodile drew level with him, Jaguar put out a hand to stop his friend going any further.

'Wait, Crocodile, I think there's a hole.'

Jaguar stooped and reached down to touch the floor. He stretched out a little further and the floor disappeared. Jaguar groped about until he found a stone and lobbed it into the inky darkness so that it would land a few paces in front of where they stood.

Silence.

For a second, Jaguar doubted that he'd thrown the stone at all. The almost total sensory deprivation in the cave made it hard to trust the little information coming in from his surroundings. A moment later there was a distant, muffled clank of stone bouncing off stone, a brief clatter and then silence.

'By the shredded Skin of Xipe! It is a hole,' exclaimed Crocodile. 'I wonder how close we are to the edge? It must go down all the way to the Land of the Dead.'

'No,' said Jaguar, unsure. 'I heard it hit the bottom.'

'That wasn't the bottom. It just bounced off a wall and then carried on down. We'd better get out of here in case it lands on Mictlantecuhtli's head. He won't be very pleased.'

Jaguar knew Crocodile was joking, but he still didn't like it. The Lord of the Underworld presided over a grim realm, where the mayeque, the peasants, went when they died. Also, those unfortunate enough not to die in combat or upon the sacrificial altar made the arduous journey through nine levels of infernal torture until they reached the Land of the Dead. The thought of Mictlantecuhtli's skeletal features rising from the depths to see who had disturbed him made Jaguar apprehensive.

A sudden draught of damp air blew up from the abyss, like the foetid exhalation of a dying man. Jaguar's skin went cold and the hairs on the back of his neck stood up. His flesh crawled and he stood rooted to the spot.

'Let's get out of here!' cried Crocodile and turned on his heel.

Jaguar whirled, stumbled to the entrance, and leaped through the narrow opening, out into the dazzling sunlight. Crocodile was just behind him.

'What's wrong with you two?' asked Storm Light. He looked down at the boys, who lay gasping on the warm earthen path. 'You're both as white as axolotl.'

'Did you see a snake in there?' Sunshine asked politely.

'More likely they just met the spirits of their ancestors,' laughed a Mexica.

In the warmth of the defile, Jaguar quickly regained his composure.

'No! But we did nearly fall down a huge hole,' he replied. 'It's the perfect place to put these warriors, but we'll have to stay away from the back of the cave. It's too dangerous.'

While they waited for Magic River to return with the last of the bodies, Jaguar and Crocodile described the cave to the others. When all of the bodies had been ferried to the mouth of the cave, Magic River instructed Jaguar and Crocodile to get back inside so there would be someone to pass the corpses to.

'Any of you Chalca know the burial rights?' asked Magic River, unwilling to send more of his own men into the cave.

Sunshine volunteered.

'I spent two years studying to become a priest,' he explained as he followed Jaguar under the stone slab.

Those still outside placed the bodies on the lip of the drop into the cave. From there, Jaguar, Crocodile and Sunshine could drag them in and set them against the left-hand wall. Jaguar recognised Archer Eagle's body as it was handed down, but just as he and Crocodile caught hold of the warrior's legs, his damaged shoulder tore free. Magic River lowered their comrade down by his other arm, then passed the other limb to Jaguar. Somehow the severed arm was more gruesome than its lifeless owner. Ragged strips of flesh hung about the remains of the joint and although the weight of the thing surprised Jaguar, the realisation that it was still warm was even more unsettling. He was glad to dispose of it alongside Archer Eagle's body.

Soon they were finished and thirteen warriors lay in a row, barely visible in the gloom. Sunshine said a short prayer to Huitzilopochtli, commending the souls of the dead to him and earnestly requesting that they be spared from an eternity in Mictlan's realms.

Jaguar and Crocodile helped Sunshine out of the cave. The sun had passed its zenith, casting the floor of the rift into shadow. A solemn silence descended over the scouting party and its captives as they set out for Tenochtitlan.

Chapter 3 - Calli

Two dozen priests were hard at work cleaning the platform at the top of the great pyramid of Tenochtitlan. Although the sun would soon be dipping below the western cordilleras, the stone of the sacrificial altar and twin shrines of Huitzilopochtli and Tlaloc were baking hot. The stone radiated an intense heat that had been captured during the day.

From his place by one of the huge buttresses that flanked the top of the steps, Feathered Darkness looked up briefly and drank in the surroundings that gave such meaning to his life. He cast a critical eye over the three men who had been tasked with scrubbing bloodstains from the chacmool. More priests were working their way down the two vertiginous stairways, scraping and sluicing as they went, rivulets of black water cascading down to the base of the stepped pyramid ahead of them.

The chacmool was a statue of a recumbent figure wearing a breechcloth, headpiece and splendid halter that were painted alternate colours of red, cobalt blue and brilliant white. Placed on the figure's stomach and cradled gently in his hands was the ceremonial bowl. The exterior of the receptacle was painted red, while the interior was lined with beaten gold and shone like the sun itself.

Behind the sacrificial altar sat the two shrines. The buildings tapered as they rose, ending in flat roofs fully twenty feet above the level of the sacrificial platform. Each had a single square entrance at the front. On the left was the shrine of Tlaloc, the God of Rain. The upper fascia of Tlaloc's shrine above the doorway was inset with four rectangular panels inset with gold. By contrast, the upper fascia of Huitzilopochtli's shrine had a single large recessed panel, from which square bricks protruded in a rectilinear pattern and around which danced myriad miniature warriors in relief.

The power of the gods was manifest to Feathered Darkness in this glorious structure. Its height, rising majestically as it did, above Lake Texcoco and its surroundings, imbued Feathered Darkness with wonder. To him, it was the most remarkable creation of the human race and at the same time, a reminder of the fragility of people, when it was compared with the vastness of the cosmos created by the gods.

A commotion behind Feathered Darkness alerted him to the arrival of Cloud Face. Feathered Darkness glanced down the steps. Cloud Face was shouting at the priests, who were now halfway down. Two of the priests climbed back up a few steps and bent to tackle some unseen stain while the remainder resumed their scrubbing with renewed vigour.

Feathered Darkness checked the altar and chacmool again and was relieved to see that it was spotless. As Cloud Face reached the platform, Feathered Darkness dispatched the acolytes to help clean the steps. As always, Feathered Darkness felt a mix of trepidation and awe in the presence of the high priest.

The many hours spent cleaning the chacmool seemed to have paid off. For once, Cloud Face had no criticism to offer. 'Are you done here?' he said.

'Yes, My Lord.'

'Good. I need your help.'

Feathered Darkness nodded, hiding his surprise. Cloud Face never honoured him by asking for his advice. Cloud Face walked towards the western edge of the temple that looked out over the oldest part of the city and on the far bank, beyond it, the burgeoning district of Tlatocan.

'People are forgetting the old ways,' Cloud Face said bitterly.

Feathered Darkness was well aware of the high priest's dismay over the waning power of the priests but was wise enough to let Cloud Face work his own way round to the point. Feathered Darkness' veneration of the old man had not blinded him to Cloud Face's dangerous nature. The irascible high priest was, he decided long ago, the perfect mouthpiece on earth for the God of War and Fire.

'When I was a young man,' continued Cloud Face, 'our ruler sought guidance from the gods.' He turned to check that his second-in-command was paying attention and then set off along the edge of the platform at a leisurely pace.

'The tlatoani at that time, Chimalpopoca, was a simple man, but true to the spirits of our ancestors. He understood that his power derived from the supreme authority bestowed on him by Huitzilopochtli and so his council, in all matters, was the high priest.'

Cloud Face fell silent for a moment as the two of them turned onto the northern edge of the platform. He had a pensive look, staring at his feet as they padded along the precipitous edge of the temple and then at last he spoke again. 'Feathered Darkness,' he began.

'Yes, My Lord?'

'I'm sure you consider yourself as a candidate to replace me when the time comes?' Cloud Face's tone was one of idle musing.

'It hadn't occurred to me, My Lord,' Feathered Darkness lied smoothly. 'That time must still be a long way off.'

'We must both pray that it is,' snapped Cloud Face. 'I have yet to see you realise the potential I thought you had.'

Feathered Darkness tried to quell a growing anxiety at the direction this conversation was heading and of his proximity to the steep edge of the pyramid that plunged a hundred feet to the ground below. Cloud Face's last assistant was disembowelled five years ago as punishment for fainting at a sacrificial ceremony and the high priest had not mellowed much since.

'How have I failed you?' asked Feathered Darkness, trying to keep his voice from catching.

Cloud Face stopped and turned, poised confidently at the platform's edge and fixed the younger man with eyes as black and fathomless as the night. 'You,' he said, 'are supposed to be my eyes and my ears! Your spies have provided no useful information to me.'

'My Lord!' exclaimed Feathered Darkness. 'That information about Tlacaelel...'

'What of it? Where is the detail... where is the follow up?'

The wide expanse of Lake Texcoco, spread out behind the high priest, was such a beautiful sight from way up on top of the temple, its surface sparkling and dancing. Feathered Darkness loved that view. Born on the day Four-Water, his horoscope preordained a life of priesthood, but from the moment he had stood between the twin shrines on the temple-top and looked out across that vista, Feathered Darkness had known with utter certainty that he was a servant of the gods. Remembering this, Feathered Darkness found his centre and grew calm.

'My Lord,' he began again. 'I have gleaned many fragments of information, but you would not wish me to waste your time with idle gossip and half truths.'

'You will just have to try harder. There are a number of priests who would gladly take your place. Don't give me a reason to try them out. That would put you in a precarious position, wouldn't it?' Cloud Face glanced at the ground below before continuing. 'This plan depends upon digging up some dirt we can pin on one or more clan elders! Snake Eyes and Devine Cactus have rallied to the cause, but we must show them we can make progress.'

'I understand, My Lord.' Feathered Darkness' tone was placatory. 'It's just a matter of time...'

'We don't have time!' exploded Cloud Face. 'That Snake Woman, Tlacaelel, is practically in charge already! Moctezuma seems to just grin and nod his head to everything his brother says.'

'All right,' said Feathered Darkness seriously. 'We'll redouble our efforts. I may have to make an example of one of my informers to inspire the others.'

'See that you do!' sneered Cloud Face. 'Your future depends upon it.' With that, Cloud Face stalked off back to the steps, his black robes fluttering to keep up.

Without the high priest to keep him there, Feathered Darkness moved away from the edge but continued the route around the four sides of the temple-top, thinking as he walked. He was not afraid. It was an irritating fix though. His heart was true and Huitzilopochtli would be his guide and judge, whatever happened. Feathered Darkness ran a hand through his long, well-groomed hair. Based in their tight-knit local communities, the clans were hard to infiltrate. It was nigh-on impossible for an outsider to gain their confidence, so the trick was to turn one of them on a minor misdemeanour and use them to uncover something to control another, more important member of the clan. The trouble was that after nearly three months of trying, they still had nothing to go on. As for the threat of replacement, Feathered Darkness wasn't convinced there was a long list of applicants for the post of Cloud Face's right-hand man. Still, it couldn't be ruled out entirely.

Dusk was falling by the time the scouting party secured passage to Ecatepec by canoe. The sky was clear and cold air from the mountains was seeping down to the valley floor. On the way back, Magic River's band of men had been joined by two more groups. They journeyed on together and recounted the events of the day. In all, the newcomers had taken five captives in contrast to the twelve that Magic River's group had taken. They listened in awe to the tale of the skirmish in the narrow pass.

Several hundred people turned out onto the streets of Tepeyacac to see the warriors. Magic River commandeered water and fruit from the town's elders and there were a great many questions from the townsfolk about the captives and how they had been taken. After a brief rest, the tired warriors set out onto the raised road that cut south over Lake Texcoco to Tenochtitlan. In spite of the gathering darkness, the Chalca looked keenly at everything around them. None of them had ever been this close to Tenochtitlan before.

'So this is one of the famous causeways,' exclaimed Jaguar's captive. 'How long ago were they built?'

'There have always been paths through the marsh,' replied Jaguar. 'Since our ancestors moved to the island though, each tlatoani in turn has carried out building work to improve access to the city.' In spite of his exhaustion, Jaguar felt a surge of pride. Tenochtitlan was the centre of the world and the envy of all who set eyes on her and the magnificent engineering works of the

Mexica. The causeway they were travelling was wide enough for twenty warriors to walk abreast, purposely rebuilt to move an army on and off the island quickly.

Sunshine piped up again as they approached a bridge. 'Is this one of those defences that can be dismantled or dropped into the lake at a moment's notice?'

Magic River overheard and cut in. 'We will give no answer to that question. You should not believe everything that you have heard from merchants and travellers.'

The captives dismissed Magic River's words and there was a general murmur of appreciative noises as they crossed the bridge and marvelled at the stout wooden trusses and a central section that looked as though it was built to hinge down on one side.

A bright moon shone above Texcoco to the east, providing light for the last part of their journey. Over the black expanse of Lake Texcoco, a stripe of blue-white light made a shimmering pathway to the far shore while either side, motes of brilliant silver winked in and out of existence as moonlight danced upon the ripples of the lake.

It seemed impossible to Jaguar that all this might end in five days time. The end of the fifty-two year calendar was imminent and was preying on everyone's minds. When it was discussed, it was in hushed voices. Some dismissed it as a minor obstacle, something the priests would easily put right with a well conducted ceremony. Yet if the Binding of the Years failed and the priests could not light the New Fire, then some great cataclysm would surely follow. This was where the priests and the elders were unable to shed any light. Would the end come quickly in a sudden blaze or would it come slowly? Perhaps this prolonged drought would worsen until the world was full of desiccated corpses.

Jaguar sighed and tried to put it out of his head. Ahead he could see Tenochtitlan, standing proud of the lagoon that surrounded it. The moonlight caught the edges of the darkened buildings, giving them an ethereal glow, and towering above the dwellings in the centre of the island was the Great Temple itself. Seeing it, Jaguar made a silent prayer to Huitzilopochtli.

The evening air was still and quiet. The barefoot warriors made very little noise as they walked along the causeway. The only sound was the low chattering of a disgruntled duck among the chinampa.

'No frogs,' said Sunshine of the Seven Hills suddenly.

'What?' chorused a few of the warriors.

'It's the mating season,' said Jaguar's captive, shrugging his shoulders.

'Oh, yes,' Crocodile acknowledged, looking over his shoulder. 'This time of year, they should be croaking loud enough to wake the dead!'

Bringing up the rear, Magic River overheard the comment. 'Are there any at your end of the lake?'

'None!' This time, one of the dignitaries from Chalco spoke up.

Despite the low water level of the lake, the frogs should have been in full song. 'No,' continued Magic River. 'The famine is so bad you can't even get them at the market anymore. Since the famine started everyone's been out catching what they can to feed their families; now even the frogs are gone!'

Finally, the warriors reached the outskirts of the city. Here the ditches, cultivated banks and the occasional farmer's house gave way to firmer ground, where the causeway joined the island in the quarter of Cuepopan. Torches burned on all the major street intersections.

At the sound of the approaching footfall, people crowded out of their houses to cheer the brave soldiers home. Men lit more reed torches to help light the way. Women craned their necks to see if their husbands were among the returning heroes and children bounced excitedly up and down, trying to catch a glimpse of the captured enemy. One young girl shrieked as she caught sight of the Chalca and ran to her mother's side, wailing in abject terror.

The Chalca walked in single file, flanked by their captors. They held their heads up high and tried to make a good impression. They were fierce, proud warriors. By displaying their strength, they brought glory upon their captors and therefore upon themselves as well.

Soon the Serpent Wall was visible and, rising behind it, the towering apex of the Great Temple, silent and forbidding.

Once the warriors were inside the temple complex they could see the whole magnificent stone edifice. Jaguar gazed up in wonder at the temple. It always left him feeling breathless.

'Welcome to you, brother,' boomed Moctezuma.

Tlacaelel raised an arm in salute at his brother who reclined on the far side of the great hall with several courtiers and a dozen women. Queen Chichimecacihuatzin wasn't present, presumably already retired to her bedchamber. A dozen torches added their smoky, orange light to the white moonlight that lanced in from the three large windows on the left-hand side of the hall.

'Have you been working late again?' called the tlatoani.

'Yes, My Lord,' replied Tlacaelel. As he approached his brother, Tlacaelel was careful to keep his eyes on the floor.

'Come now, Tlacaelel!' Moctezuma chided. 'How many times must I remind you that we are brothers?'

Tlacaelel loved his brother. He was not in thrall to the man, but the notion that they were equals was absurd. Moctezuma was a tall, charismatic leader of men and the people adored him as much as they worshipped the god he represented. Tlacaelel felt that if the people had not chosen his brother to rule Tenochtitlan, Huitzilopochtli himself would have blazed a fiery trail down from the heavens to correct their error.

Moctezuma put an arm around his brother's shoulder and led him out of the hall and into the wide expanse of the Emerald Garden. The moon was bright enough to make out the paths that criss-crossed through the tlatoani's garden. This recent project of Moctezuma's was beginning to take shape. What had begun as a large and dusty courtyard now had a number of large saplings and cactus. Tlacaelel admired a particularly healthy blood-spine cactus, whose five thigh-thick, ribbed trunks were covered in the most vicious looking needles that Tlacaelel had ever seen.

'My gardeners brought that all the way from Otumba,' said Moctezuma noticing his brother's gaze. 'I've decided not to plant too many water-loving trees from the lowland forests or my gardeners will spend their entire time running backwards and forwards with buckets of water. Perhaps if the rains return...' Moctezuma's voice trailed off.

'A wise decision, My Lord,' nodded Tlacaelel. 'There are so many beautiful plants from the highlands that will thrive here whatever the weather.'

The two men walked a broad avenue of ahuehuete saplings that Tlacaelel felt sure would require a monumental effort to keep alive in this drought.

'You wanted to speak to me, brother?' asked Moctezuma. Here, he turned towards a carved stone bench and sat down, gesturing for his brother to follow suit. 'Is it about the New Fire?'

'No, tlatoani, it is not.' The stone bench was cold and the night time dew had made it slightly damp. 'Of course, I am as concerned as everyone else that the ceremony proceeds without a hitch.'

Moctezuma laughed softly. 'And there was I thinking you had come to complain again about the number of sacrifices!'

'Well, there is some relevance with what I wish to discuss.'

Here Moctezuma turned sharply to his brother. Although it was too dark to make out any features on his face, it was clear that he was not happy.

'I've warned you before,' said Moctezuma. 'The priests will not countenance your plans. The gods must be honoured in the proper way!'

Not far off in the city, two dogs barked in a demented conversation of their own. Above the tallest trees in the garden, bats swooped and jinked, briefly silhouetted against the almost-full moon. Moctezuma showed no sign of continuing, so Tlacaelel began again, certain now that his brother would hear him out.

'Our people have done extraordinary things,' Tlacaelel pointed out. 'Our exodus from Aztlan, the creation of this city, the forging of the Triple Alliance...' The stone bench still felt cold.

'Brother, we still have a long way to go. Our people could make their mark. History will tell of the Mexica who conquered the world from east coast to west. First Chalco, then Tlaxcala and beyond, just imagine it! With the name of Moctezuma on their lips, the Jaguar Knights and Eagle Knights can take enlightenment back to the barbaric northern lands from whence our ancestors emerged. You could be remembered for spreading our civilisation far to the south where it is said that mountains rise ten times higher than Popocatepetl from a never ending forest.'

'Brother, you forget yourself.' There was a cautionary edge to Moctezuma's voice, but it was clear that he was interested.

'You know as well as I do that we cannot feed our people now. We rely upon the lowlands for our food and they demand such prices that we can barely pay! We can take them for ourselves but we need more men, better trained and more experienced,' continued Tlacaelel. 'I have no problem with fighting the Chalca, but if we must do it, let us crush them and put an end to it.'

'But we will not succeed without Huitzilopochtli. Balance is what we need. Sacrifices must be made.'

'Mixayacatl is a menace. Are you just repeating what he says?'

'Yes, and with good reason. You know that I am Huitzilopochtli's chosen one and that means I have certain responsibilities.' Moctezuma's voice had a hard edge to it so Tlacaelel knew that he would have to choose his next words carefully.

'Balance was your word, brother, and I agree with that.' Tlacaelel watched the silhouette for a change but there was none. 'What I am suggesting is not that we stop taking captives, in fact it is to the contrary. If you gave our warriors free reign against our enemies, I believe we would take more captives, not fewer, but more importantly, we would lose fewer of our own people!'

'What has that to do with balance?' asked Moctezuma.

'Right now, the balance is wrong.' Tlacaelel shrugged. 'Our army is constrained by the choice of enemy and battlefield.'

'How so?'

'If we field all of our forces and choose a different location, we could end this ceremonial war against Chalco that costs us so many men.' There, it was said. Tlacaelel breathed a little easier now that he had aired the main argument. He watched as the ruler of Tenochtitlan gazed at the moon.

'I'm just beginning to understand the sweep of your ambition, dear brother,' said Moctezuma after a while. 'And you believe that enemies further afield will provide for our gods?'

'I do.'

Here Moctezuma stood up and Tlacaelel was pleased to follow suit as his backside had almost gone completely numb sitting on the frigid granite bench.

'It seems I have underestimated you again, Tlacaelel. Do you have a plan?'

'Two Sign and I have redrawn the plans for the coming battle with Chalco,' explained Tlacaelel as the two headed back for the warmth of the palace.

'And you want me to help you get these approved at tomorrow's Great Council?'

Tlacaelel nodded and here his brother laughed aloud, surprising him with the warmth of his voice and by putting an arm round his shoulder.

'You know what's funny?' asked Moctezuma and continued without waiting for an answer. 'There you are thinking big, serious thoughts about world domination, all of which I heartily approve of, but what appeals to me most is putting one over that pompous idiot Amihuatzin! Yes, let's teach the ruler of Chalco a lesson he won't forget in a long time,' added Moctezuma with a twinkle in his eye. 'After that, we'll see about the rest of our troublesome neighbours!'

Tlacaelel gave a wan smile, still too cold to enjoy his brother's mirth.

'What?' exclaimed Moctezuma, misunderstanding. He burst out laughing again. 'You think I enjoy that overstuffed upstart sitting in his foetid palace a few leagues from here and sending his ill-mannered envoys to me with their demands and their petty threats?'

The two men reached the outer hall where two Grey Privy Knights stood guard.

'Go make your plans, brother. I'll support you at the council meeting but you must bring me victory.'

Moctezuma winked as Tlacaelel took his leave.

News of the returning warriors preceded them so that Feathered Darkness had time to assemble an appropriate reception party of priests. Two dozen raiding parties had already returned before nightfall and a rumour had begun to circulate that the remainder had been captured, so there was widespread relief when they were seen crossing the causeway to Tlatleloco. The temple precinct was mostly unlit so Feathered Darkness dispatched four priests to set up torches around the central courtyard to light the proceedings. The yellow flames guttered unenthusiastically and lent a sickly colour to the priests' pale skin. Their cinnamon-coloured garments looked black in the feeble light.

In the centre of the courtyard and directly opposite the Great Temple stood Tizoc's stone and behind that stood the skull-rack. As the flickering torches added to the flat, grey light of the moon, the skull-rack seemed to come alive. The skull-rack was a rectangular stone plinth, about thirty feet long that stood about four feet high. It was finely carved and decorated, the main motif of the carvings being that of a skeletal face. Row-upon-row of tall wooden poles, set six feet apart, pointed up at the night sky from the top of the plinth like a palisade. Hundreds of tiny holes were drilled at regular intervals up the poles, through which thin rods were threaded horizontally, and suspended from the rods in their thousands were human skulls, the heads of sacrificial victims. Ten layers deep, suspended from the wooden rods by a pair of matching holes in each temple, the grinning skulls shone coldly in the moonlight, their empty eye-sockets the colour of the night sky. Feathered Darkness was delighted with the effect that the recent cleaning of the temple had had on this structure.

There wasn't a lot to do but wait for the warriors to arrive and for a while, Feathered Darkness caught himself listening to a couple of the priests, one of whom was new to the priesthood and clearly obsessed with the minutia and the proper running of things.

'The overriding problem,' said the acolyte at one point, 'seems to be due to poor calculation and implementation of proportional tribute to the gods, which, quite naturally, has resulted in the unfavourable weather and poor crop yields.'

'You've explained this to me already,' said the second man. He made a sour face as he attended to one of the torches that was reluctant to stay alight. He was clearly unimpressed with his new charge.

'Yes, but unless we start acting on the natural balance, we won't be able to bring back the rains. Tlaloc is under-represented.'

'Give it a rest,' said the other. 'You've been on about theological balance all day.'

'It's very important,' retorted the acolyte, clearly hurt. 'Anyway, it's Proportional Pantheistic Attribution not theological balance!'

'Hmph!' said his mentor, prodding at the end of the torch with a doubtful expression.

'As I was saying,' said the acolyte, his enthusiasm undiminished. 'The multitude of deities who protect and control every aspect of our lives must see a fair and even handed apportioning of the dues that we have to offer, based on seniority, time of year and other relevant circumstances.'

Feathered Darkness could see the older man nodding casually, evidently hoping the gloom would mask his indifference. The eager acolyte showed no signs of drawing his monologue to any immediate conclusion. The younger members of the priesthood could always be counted on to latch onto new ideas.

'It should be clear that a problem of this complexity can only be handled with any degree of competence by persons fully trained in such matters...'

Feathered Darkness stopped listening when he noticed an armed guard of warrior-priests entering the courtyard. They began to form two lines leading out to the holding cells where the captives would be kept until the ceremony. They had just sorted themselves out when the warriors entered from the opposite side.

Of the returning warriors, Feathered Darkness recognised very few. In truth, it wasn't very easy to distinguish one from the other, so blackened were they with blood and dust. A thick-set, ugly looking man separated from the group and walked over to the priest. There was no mistaking Magic River. The leader of each of the other two scouting parties followed the big man to begin the formal handover. Feathered Darkness greeted the warriors and asked each of them how many captives their respective groups had taken.

Then it was Magic River's turn. 'Twelve,' he answered.

'No,' said Feathered Darkness as though to a child. 'Just for your group.'

'Twelve, My Lord,' Magic River repeated.

Feathered Darkness shook his head. 'Extraordinary!' He looked at the ring of warriors who stood encircling the Chalca. 'Nine of you took twelve captive?'

'That's right, My Lord. It was an unusual encounter.'

Feathered Darkness congratulated Magic River and began the formal proceedings to accept the captives.

'Brave warriors, we greet your safe return with joy.'

'Your humble servants bring these gifts, O Lord!' responded Magic River gesturing behind him.

Here Feathered Darkness summoned three of the attendant priests, one each from the major deities of Tlaloc, Xipe Totec and Mictlantecuhtli. He noticed that one of them was the one who had been arguing with the young acolyte. At least with the ceremony underway he had been able to escape the tyrannical theorising of his young charge.

'In the name of the Lord of War and of Fire and of the God of Water and of Rain and in the name of "He of the Flayed Flesh" and of the Lord of the Underworld, we accept your gifts and name them "Sacrifice".'

'We place our charges into your care,' replied Magic River in a serious tone.

Feathered Darkness and the other three priests now pushed back the long sleeves of their robes to expose their upper arms.

Each of them then produced in their other hand, as if by magic, a long bone needle.

'Accept this offering of ours as a promise upon the lives of these captives,' intoned all four priests. As the final words were uttered, each priest plunged the needle smoothly through the crook of his own elbow under the tendon. Staring fixedly at Magic River, who had by default become the undisputed leader of all three raiding parties, the priests worked the needles back and forth until the blood ran freely from the wound. Each then withdrew the needle, cleaned it with the hem of their robes and hid them away.

Now Feathered Darkness summoned for the captives to be brought forward. One after another, the warriors presented their captives. Each was named and blessed in turn.

'Now is the parting of the ways,' chanted the priests, as each was introduced.

One after another, their captors recited The Severance.

'Treasured Son, now you are one with our gods!'

Here the captive could respond if he spoke nahuatl and knew the words. All these captives were from Chalco and knew the ceremony.

'Honoured Father, may the Gods watch over you.'

Two of the warrior-priests then escorted the captives to the armed guard that led from the courtyard.

Feathered Darkness breathed a sigh of contentment and rubbed his arm where he had pushed the bone needle through. It hurt more than usual but that was no bad thing. The act of auto-sacrifice gave Feathered Darkness a strong sense of being in control of himself and it always left him feeling calm.

No more warriors were expected that evening, so the priests' duties were over. These late additions to the number of captives being prepared for the ceremony of the Binding of the Years brought the total to six hundred and fifteen, a figure that Feathered Darkness was very pleased with. Cloud Face had set him the target of five hundred and twenty, exactly two for each day in the calendar year, so they were well past that. Perhaps, if the ceremony was successful they would set some free as a gesture of goodwill.

Feathered Darkness watched as the warriors filed out of the courtyard. It was only then that he recognised one of them by his gait. The street outside was too dark to be able to make out their features, but this young man's movement was powerful, yet distinctively fluid. Feathered Darkness was not a great lover of the ball game, it seemed a frivolous distraction from the more important things in life, but there were few people in Tenochtitlan who had not heard of Ocelotyolotl, Heart of the Jaguar. Feathered Darkness had even seen him play once and remembered a drunken nobleman amongst the spectators telling him that Jaguar was the youngest and best exponent of the ball game in Tenochtitlan.

The priests who had assisted with the reception were collecting the torches and preparing to leave. The warriors had made it out of the courtyard where, freed from the constraints imposed by religious decorum in the temple complex, they were chattering excitedly amongst themselves, congratulating each other. There were even one or two whoops of joy.

Feathered Darkness smiled. He turned and was about to leave when he remembered something else the nobleman had said in slurred words, something about the young man being the son of a commoner and a clan leader. Without any real volition of his own, he found himself drifting over to the gates through which the warriors had left, from where he could hear what they were saying.

'Two more!' said a solid looking young warrior, slapping Heart of the Jaguar on the back. 'You only need to take two more captives and you will be eligible to join the knights.'

Magic River said something, but Feathered Darkness couldn't make it out. Whatever he said it had to have been funny as the warriors all laughed.

'Never mind me,' replied Jaguar. 'What about Crocodile? After today's haul, he's already eligible to sign up with the knights!'

One of the young men piped up, 'How old are you, Crocodile?' There was some more conversation that was too faint to hear and then the same man exclaimed in astonishment. 'No, no one that young!'

Feathered Darkness pretended to check the torches and got a bit closer just as the warriors were beginning to disband and head for home. No one noticed the priest with black hair and dark robes in an unlit passageway.

Jaguar and the one he called Crocodile were slower than the others to move off. Feathered Darkness heard something about a girl called Precious Flower and Jaguar mentioned the name Two Sign. The priest wondered why the commander of the Eagle Knights had been mentioned. At last the two young men finally moved off and all Feathered Darkness heard as they departed was something to do with Island Home.

The one called Crocodile looked very young to have taken his fifth captive but there was no reason to doubt the story, especially as he had handed over two captives just this evening. If it was true, it would be all over the city tomorrow. There was enough in the tale of a small raiding party of a dozen warriors returning with an equal number of captives to report back to Cloud Face but Feathered Darkness decided he would do some investigation. A tight feeling at the base of his stomach told him that there was more to know about these two warriors.

Chapter 4 - Cuetzpalin

The first day of Nemontomi dawned with a white, frosty mist that clung to the lake and seeped into parts of the city nearest to the water. The sky above was clear though and, after a while, the warmth of the sun began to penetrate all but the shadiest of nooks.

Jaguar awoke to find the room he shared with his parents empty. White light lanced through a handful of gaps in the woven rushes of the roof and gave sparkling life to the dust that spiralled gracefully about the room. Jaguar sat upright on the low palliasse and rubbed his face. Worn out from the exertions of the previous day, he had slept through the noise of the others getting up. As he sat stretching, the smell of honey and hot tamales wafted through to him from the adjacent room.

There were no windows in the room that served as their sleeping quarters, but a mellow light crept in through the gap between the top of the walls and the reed-thatched roof. The air coming in through the opening felt cold.

Jaguar stood up gingerly. His lower back and left buttock were sore from the fall he had taken during the fight. He still had his hair tied back from the day before and the roots ached from being pulled flat back for so long. He loosened the string, holding it and rubbed at his scalp to ease the pain. Negotiating the other two beds, Jaguar gave himself a wash using cold water from the earthenware bowl by the door. Then he towelled himself dry with a cotton cloth that hung above the door-post, and collected a grey maguey-cloth mantle before ducking out of the room.

The family was in the main room of the house, having breakfast. The workshop benches and bric-a-brac had been moved aside to make space for the eating area. Jaguar's father, Blade of the South, was seated on the floor at one end of the low table.

Jaguar's sister, Beetle, and her husband, Arrow One, sat on one side of the table. Together, Beetle and Arrow One shared the only other room in the house with the slave-girl, Precious Flower. Jaguar's mother was prodding at the fire on the open hearth against the end wall.

'Musical Reed,' Jaguar's father called to his wife. 'Put some more tamales on the fire. Our hero is awake!'

'Good morning!' Jaguar said as he joined them. He placed his mantle on the ground opposite his father and sat on it, folding his legs under the table. He reached for a wooden plate from the middle of the table and scooped the last tamales onto it before his mother whisked the tray back to the fire. Jaguar spooned some beans from a bowl onto the side of his plate, as well as some honey and the few berries that were left.

'So?' asked his father. 'How did it go?' He always wanted a full account of Jaguar's sorties into battle. Blade of the South was a wiry man with a slight paunch. He had a thick crop of unruly black hair that sat on top of a slightly lopsided face. It looked as though he was squinting at a particularly small carving. In fact his eyesight was deteriorating because of his work, but in spite of this, he insisted on coming into battle whenever there was a general callout.

'How did it go?' he asked.

'Yes,' answered Jaguar. He carefully rolled some beans into his tamale and drizzled honey over it. 'I took another captive.'

Blade of the South smiled and nodded. Beetle clapped her hands. Arrow One said nothing.

'And what about Crocodile?' urged Blade eagerly.

Jaguar nodded, but in the cold light of day, the loss of Archer Eagle overshadowed the evening's accomplishments. He swallowed his food and then, between mouthfuls, set about relating the events, right up to the point Crocodile handed over his two captives.

'Two!' exclaimed Blade in disbelief.

Jaguar's mother brought the tray back to the table. 'Isn't that good?' she said. On the plate were two more piping hot tamales, fresh from the earthenware skillet. 'I mean, last time, the whole company went out and only brought back three captives.'

'Yes,' replied Blade. 'That is good. Crocodile always wanted to join the Eagle Knights, didn't he, Jaguar?'

'Uh-huh,' acknowledged Jaguar round another mouthful of breakfast.

Here Arrow One cut in angrily. 'You mean they just laid down their weapons, just like that? That doesn't sound very honourable.' Beetle's husband was an unimpressive man with a pinched face, jet-black hair and beady black eyes. His skin was a pasty colour. Jaguar could not remember a time the man had ever looked healthy and he wondered why his sister had agreed to marry the man. It was not that he disliked Arrow One; it was just that they had nothing in common. Arrow One was a junior administrator for the clan of Island Home North, whose chief responsibility was the upkeep of the paths and chinampa in Teopan. It was generally acknowledged that he did a good job but more importantly, he looked after Little Beetle well, so Jaguar had no complaints.

'They had no choice.' Jaguar explained, feeling an irrational need to defend the Chalca. 'If they had tried to fight their way out they would have died.' Jaguar spooned some more honey onto his plate.

'Magic River is good, isn't he?' asked Blade.

Jaguar nodded and took another bite from his tamale. His father and Magic River were both representatives for their clan to the House of Clans.

Blade could sense his son's uneasiness and tried to find some encouraging words. 'Well, now you only have to take two more captives to earn full warrior status.'

Jaguar managed a smile as he swallowed the last mouthful. He was still hungry, but didn't ask for more. He knew that his family, like so many others, was struggling to make ends meet, what with the soaring food prices. Even the patronage their jade carving business enjoyed from the nobility had dwindled in the last few months. Jaguar complimented his mother on the tamales and made satisfied noises.

'Peppers and mesquite seasoning,' explained Musical Reed with a smile as she gathered up the plates.

'Where is Precious Flower?' asked Jaguar, suddenly realising she was nowhere to be seen.

'She's gone out,' his mother replied.

'You shouldn't have let her go,' accused Arrow One. 'It's Nemontomi. She should stay inside.'

'Precious Flower will be fine,' said Blade of the South, rising to his wife's defence. 'Children can't be cooped up for five whole days. Everyone knows that and it's why the curfew is only enforced in the last day of the year. It's just as well too, times are hard enough for businesses as it is.'

Arrow One fell silent and busied himself clearing the breakfast away.

Beetle reached across to Jaguar and touched his arm. 'Jaguar, can you go and have a word with her?' she asked.

Jaguar smiled fondly at his sister. Beetle was tall and her long, dark hair fell to her slender shoulders and waist. Jaguar felt she was too thin and suspected she was denying herself food for the sake of the family.

'She's worried,' continued Beetle. 'This is a confusing time for her.'

'What about my work?'

'Don't worry about that,' said Blade. 'No one's placed any new orders because of the New Fire and nothing we're working on needs finishing until after the ceremony.'

His mother added her weight to the general opinion. 'You find Precious Flower and talk to her. She likes you.'

There was something about his mother's tone that caught Jaguar's attention. He looked across at Musical Reed as much as to ask 'What do you mean by that?' but her expression was inscrutable.

'Alright, does anyone know where she is?' Jaguar looked at each of his family in turn before casting a quizzical glance at his mother.

'No,' replied his mother, 'but you know how she likes the harbour.'

Jaguar picked his cloak up and left the house. The azure sky had that crystal clarity that only comes with the cold and the bright sunlight hurt Jaguar's eyes. He had to squint until they became accustomed to the glare. Dewdrop bejewelled spiders' webs hung from every thatched roof in the street. The air was still, which meant that the sulphurous smell of the lake's decaying vegetation was even stronger than usual. Jaguar pulled his cloak around his shoulders and set out on a roundabout route for the harbour, his naturally buoyant mood resurgent.

Jaguar had never seen the streets so empty. People must be taking the priests of Huitzilopochtli seriously. Even the beggars, who usually thronged about the gates of the Serpent Wall, were scarce. He was tempted to make a detour through the Tlatleloco marketplace to see how many stall-holders were still doing business.

A knot formed in Jaguar's stomach at the prospect of seeing Precious Flower again. He pictured her long, dark hair and the way it swept down to her generously curved hips. He remembered the way her hips swayed as she walked and the way she had thrown her arms around him after the ball practice the day before yesterday. Precious Flower had been in the family for so long now it seemed that they had grown up together. He had always thought of her as a sister, but something had changed and Jaguar wondered whether it was just something inside him.

Deep in reverie, Jaguar negotiated the network of canals and city streets without even noticing them. He turned into Coyote Street before he realised he was heading for the practice court. The Serpent Wall loomed ahead, so Jaguar re-orientated himself and circumnavigated the temple precinct, then headed back towards the southern end of the harbour in Teopan. He picked up the pace a little, hoping the detour would not cause him to miss Precious Flower.

A shimmering-blue dragonfly rattled past Jaguar's ear and dipped towards the water of the canal that ran alongside the path. Shoulder-to-shoulder, empty canoes lined the waterway, moored diagonally from the banks. The slender craft wore a profusion of colours; some painted red and some yellow, but the majority had green flanks above the waterline and whitewashed decking inside.

A single canoe passed Jaguar, sculled by a youth in a brown cloak. The resulting wake set the tethered canoes bobbing gently at their stations until they knocked hollowly against each other.

Jaguar followed the canal and eventually emerged at the southern end of the harbour where it faced out over the lake towards Texcoco. The eastern rim of the valley formed the far horizon that ran south until it met Popocatepetl and the White Lady. Five wooden jetties of varying length extended out over the shallow water of the bay with more boats tied up alongside. The harbour was nearly deserted. One old man sat on the quayside repairing a net. On the northernmost jetty, one man stood gesticulating at another who knelt in a boat, hammering at something Jaguar couldn't see. A young couple silently washed their craft that they had pulled up the slipway and sitting at the end of the southernmost jetty was the forlorn looking figure of Precious Flower.

Jaguar's mother had guessed correctly. Precious Flower was sitting with her legs crossed, staring out across the mirror surface of the lake. Jaguar clattered along the planking and sat down beside her. He allowed his legs to hang over the edge of the dock.

'Hello,' said Precious Flower, smiling briefly.

Jaguar had sat here many times and dangled his feet in the water. Now, the level of the lake was so low, Jaguar could only just touch the surface of the water by extending his toes straight down.

'Look at that!' exclaimed Jaguar. 'I've walked three times around the city trying to find you and now I don't even get to cool my feet.' He smiled back at Precious Flower but realised that she had been crying. Her eyes were puffy and her skin was blotchy. Looking at her, Jaguar understood that she was a grown woman. The realisation was brought home by the fact that her term of slavery was nearly done. Jaguar leant over and gave her a hug. She was thin, not painfully so, but the ravages of malnutrition had left their mark upon her.

When she had first come to live with Jaguar's family, she had been almost too weak to walk.

'Why have you bought this poor thing?' Musical Reed had asked her husband, while Beetle had taken her for a wash and a change of clothes. At the time, Blade had very few convincing arguments to defend his choice, but in a short space of time he was proved right. Somehow he had sensed the girl's artistic talent. Within weeks, Precious Flower was carving pieces of jade as though she had been at it all her life. Lately, Blade had even entrusted her with some of the most important commissions.

In spite of the famine, Jaguar's family had fed Precious Flower as though she was one of them and, although she was still on the thin side, she had regained her strength and a healthy glow. Her long hair was tied up so that it didn't get in the way of her work.

Eventually, Jaguar broke into the companionable silence before it became too intense.

'This is my favourite place.'

'I remember when you and Beetle first brought me here,' said Precious Flower in a small voice. 'I was so weak. The walk here nearly finished me off!'

'Sorry about that,' replied Jaguar ruefully. 'I guess we just didn't know how bad it was for you back then.'

'That's alright,' said Precious Flower with another small smile.

Jaguar liked that smile. He suddenly noticed the tiny dimples that formed on the tops of her cheeks and the way her eyes crinkled up at the edges as they closed almost completely. It made Precious Flower's face light up and Jaguar wondered why he'd never noticed it before. He felt he should say more, find out why she was crying, but wasn't sure what to say.

'Are you, uh... alright?'

'Yes,' she sighed. 'I'll be fine.'

Jaguar admitted to himself that he was no expert with girls. That said, an idiot could see that she was lying. 'Only, it looks like you've been crying,' he tried.

Precious Flower pursed her lips together and looked sad again briefly before trying another small smile that was decidedly unconvincing.

'Is it the New Fire?' Jaguar asked.

Precious Flower shrugged.

'It will all work out, you know.' This time it was Jaguar's turn to be unconvincing.

Finally, Precious Flower found her voice. 'Do you think the New Fire will light?'

Jaguar scoffed, trying to inject more confidence into his tone. 'Of course it will. I heard that the high priests have been practising for over a year now!'

'I'm sure you're right,' agreed Precious Flower after a pause. She nodded once, opened her mouth as if to say something more and then closed it again.

Jaguar raised an eyebrow inquiringly.

'Oh Jaguar! Even if we get through that, I don't know what's going to happen to me.' Precious Flower finally blurted out.

'You mean because you'll be free?'

Precious Flower sighed again and looked across the lake to the distant mountains. A small tear formed on her lower lash and clung there for a moment before dripping onto her lap. Jaguar felt embarrassed watching her cry and followed her gaze while he tried to work out what to say. He felt a momentary surge of irritation directed at his sister. Curse Beetle for suggesting he do this. Why hadn't she come to speak to Precious Flower? She would have been much better at this kind of thing.

Wavelets lapped at the thick wooden piles that supported the jetty. Sunshine shone through the shallow water revealing the lakebed in detail. Strands of algae waved gently to-and-fro under the surface, all in time, as though dancing to some unheard mystical music. Thin wisps of silt disturbed by the waves above danced variations to the same tune, twisting in eddies and minuscule currents around the rocks. Tiny, pale freshwater shrimp clung stubbornly to the rocks, unwilling to join in the rhythmic sway. There was little vegetation on this side of the island, but on the opposite shore, a mass of reeds swathed the exposed coastline. Flocks of geese and ducks bobbed and ducked out near the centre of the lake, where they were safe from hungry humans. Three canoes passed close to the birds and sent a cloud of them crashing into the air, honking their alarm. Most landed a short distance away, but a few birds circled higher and higher above the lake, and then flew south towards Popocatepetl. The volcano's vast, rounded cone was white almost down to its base due to the winter snowfall. At that distance the perennial wisps of cloud that clung to the crater rim looked like plumes of smoke, as though from an eruption.

'Would you like to find your family again?' asked Jaguar. This was seemingly not the right thing to say because the trickle of tears suddenly turned into a stream and Precious Flower made a small sobbing noise. Jaguar cursed himself silently.

'If we did find my family,' breathed Precious Flower eventually. 'Would I have to leave yours?'

Jaguar blinked, suddenly realising how stupid he had been. They were her family now. 'I, er... no. That is, we'd all be very sorry to lose you. You know,' continued Jaguar, trying to make amends, 'you're the best carver in the family. The business really took off when you started work for father.' Jaguar took hold of Precious Flower's hand and gave it a squeeze.

Precious Flower uncrossed her legs, leaned over and gave Jaguar a hug. 'That's a lovely thing to say!' She let go of him and wiped at her eyes. Smiling again, she said, 'It's lovely, but completely untrue. Things have been getting worse and worse.'

Jaguar scowled. 'That's only because of the worries about the New Fire. You'll see, once the priests have safely re-started the fire, everything will go back to normal and trade will pick up.'

Precious Flower bit her lower lip. 'You think so?'

'Of course! Hey, did you know that the wife of Tlatleloco's Chief of Justice asked for you by name when she gave us that commission last year?'

Precious Flower beamed proudly. She looked a lot more cheerful now and she gave Jaguar another hug.

'Come on,' said Jaguar, beginning to feel awkward. 'The others will wonder what's happened to us.'

Precious Flower put a hand on Jaguar's leg to stop him. Jaguar was intensely aware of the heat of her hand on his thigh.

'I made something for you,' she said. She took her hand off Jaguar's leg and pulled something from the waistband of her skirt. It was the figurine of an ocelot fashioned entirely from dried grass stalks. Ochre coloured stems of Bunch Grass had been gathered together to form the limbs and torso of the creature, bent to shape and bound at the joints with several loops of cotton thread to keep them from springing straight. Jaguar was amazed. The tough fibrous nature of the grass must have made complex shaping very difficult, but somehow Precious Flower had managed to capture the likeness of the jungle cat. Even its face, down to the teeth and small rounded ears were perfectly formed.

Jaguar stared at Precious Flower.

'It's fantastic!' he breathed. He lifted the cat gently from her hand, turning it over, wondering how many hours she had spent on it. Its front paw was raised off the ground, half curled inwards towards its body in an unmistakably feline poise and its tail had the characteristic, graceful, drooping curve.

'How did you do that?' Jaguar pointed.

'Oh, that's easy,' replied Precious Flower. 'You've just got to make sure that none of the kinks in the stalks line up when you tie them together.' She smiled at Jaguar's evident delight.

Jaguar hugged her, holding the effigy away so that it didn't get crushed.

'Thank you,' he said warmly. Suddenly he had a thought. 'Has anyone else seen this?'

Precious Flower shook her head. Somehow, she had managed to conceal her work so that no one in the cramped house had noticed.

'Come on. Let's go and show the others,' said Jaguar and hauled Precious Flower upright. 'If we can make more of these we might be able to sell them as lucky charms!'

'*Curse the shitty arsehole of Xipe Totec!*' roared Cloud Face and delivered a blood-soaked backhand to Snake Eyes that sent him crashing to the floor where he dropped a smouldering pile of wood shavings.

There was a sour atmosphere in the tiny, high-walled courtyard and the stench of piss and blood hung in an acrid cloud. Seven of the most senior priests were gathered in this hidden place of worship to practice the New Fire. Devine Cactus was present, as were the priests of Quetzalcoatl, Tezcatlipoca, Mictlantecuhtli and the high priest of Itzli, all dressed in sombre brown robes. Feathered Darkness knew that the same group had already met a dozen times in the last year in order to prepare for the most demanding ceremony of all. The year One Rabbit was set to end in four days' time as the interlocking wheels of the calendar came full circle as it did every fifty-two years. To usher in the new year successfully required the most skilfully executed ceremony of all, a carefully choreographed event also known as the Binding of the Years. On the sacred hill of Colhuacan, a specially appointed sacrifice would be held over the black altar and have his heart cut out. Then, with the correct incantations and a fire kindled in the dark of night, the burning embers had to be thrust into the vacant chest cavity of the dying man to ensure the successful transition to the next day, Two Reed and the year that bore its name. The ceremony could not be allowed to fail as the alternative was too awful to contemplate. The soothsayers and the astrologers, who pored over the ancient lore, talked of children mutating into creatures, cracks opening in the earth and swallowing towns and temples, and cataclysms tearing rents in the fabric of the world.

Feathered Darkness had seen Cloud Face in a bad mood before but this was on an altogether new level. Even the usually laconic and imperturbable Devine Cactus was wide eyed and the other priests looked genuinely terrified. A pale twitching drew Feathered Darkness' attention to the subject on the altar. The dying boy was still pinned down by five priests, the one at his head clamping down a large wooden yoke over his neck. Feathered Darkness recognised the snaggle-toothed youngster he had apprehended two nights earlier. A cloth had been thrust into his mouth to stifle the screams. His lips were blue and his eyes had rolled up into his head until only the whites were visible. Below the boy's chest, his torso was all slick wreckage where it had been torn in two down the middle and Cloud Face had reached in under the heaving chest to slice out the heart. Only the legs gave any sign that the victim was not entirely dead. They trembled slightly, flexing at the knee as though still nursing their own faint hope of flight.

Feathered Darkness hurried over and helped Snake Eyes to his feet, wondering why he always had to smooth over the ruffled feathers that Cloud Face left in his wake. He dabbed helpfully at a puddle of blood that was pooling on the priest's upper lip and Snake Eyes swept his straggly hair from his face and shot a murderous look back at Cloud Face, but the high priest wasn't finished with him yet.

'That was your cue to gently cradle the kindling *next* to the embers, you witless turd!' Spittle sprayed as Cloud Face ranted on. 'If you dump that stuff all over the fire-drill at Colhuacan we are all going to die! *Do you understand?*'

Snake Eyes nodded but it wasn't enough. The high priest of Huitzilopochtli spat contemptuously and glanced down at the gangly youth on the altar, or what was left of him. Something deep inside the shattered human remains was trying to stay alive. The jaw worked and the eyes rolled down and looked up at the skeletal frame of Cloud Face looming above him. The high priest transferred the dark knife to his right hand and bent over his victim, then slowly, almost tenderly pushed the knife down through the boy's eye socket until the hilt jammed against his face. The body spasmed weakly and then lay still. Cloud Face retracted the blade and examined it as though trying to understand why it was covered in blood and then he advanced on Snake Eyes.

Feathered Darkness stepped between them, heart hammering in his chest. 'This is a difficult procedure. Why don't we have a rest and try again later?'

Cloud Face locked eyes with Feathered Darkness as he pointed the dripping end of his knife over his shoulder at Snake Eyes. 'Fine, but you tell that feral shit-for-brains that if he does it wrong again, he'll be the one on the altar for the next practice run!' With that, Cloud Face turned and swept from the courtyard.

Feathered Darkness marched over to Devine Cactus and grabbed a cloth from him. 'I'll calm Mixayacatl down,' he hissed. 'You get this place cleaned up and ready for another go.'

Devine Cactus nodded and began flapping at the four other priests in the room, urging them into action while Feathered Darkness followed the high priest.

'*Five times*!' shouted Cloud face, still on the verge of apoplexy when Feathered Darkness caught up with him. 'I don't need to use those idiots. These two would do a better job.' He pointed at two acolytes, who stood ready with a bowl of water and another cloth.

Feathered Darkness let the old man carry out his ablutions. Cloud Face dipped the cloth in the bowl of water and wiped his arms down with one half of the cloth before splashing his face with water and using the clean end of the cloth to towel his face dry.

'Would you like me to assist?' offered Feathered Darkness.

'No. I have to work with these half-wits,' spat Cloud Face. He was beginning to calm down. 'You know what a special event this is. All of the orders of priests must be represented.'

Feathered Darkness decided that his master was ready to hear his news. 'I have some information, My Lord.' There was no answer from the high priest so he continued. 'One of the raiding parties that returned last night took two high-ranking figures from Chalco.'

'What of it?' said Cloud Face dismissively. 'Just inform the council so they can be interrogated as usual.' The old man threw the towel at one of the acolytes.

Feathered Darkness recounted the previous night's exchange. 'The warriors said these two men had been on their way to Tlaxcala to seek military assistance.'

Cloud Face's demeanour changed in an instant. His frown faded. He tilted his face up at the ceiling and then reached up to run a hand over his bald pate.

'Now that is interesting,' said the old man eventually. He discarded his spattered cloak for one of the acolytes to collect. The old man looked as though he was wearing a borrowed skin that hung from him in small folds. 'Forget what I said about informing the council,' he added. 'Come and find me first thing tomorrow. We'll go and question them ourselves.'

Feathered Darkness nodded.

'Is that all?'

'No, My Lord,' said the priest. 'After the captives had been taken into our care, I overheard two of the young warriors talking. I recognised one of them as an ullamalitzli player; I saw him in one of the junior games. After asking around, I discovered that his name is Ocelotyolotl and his father is Blade of the South, Teopan's representative in the House of Clans.'

'Get to the point!' growled Cloud Face. 'I have to go to the Tlatocan now.'

'From what you've said, we need some leverage against the clans. What better way than through the family members?'

'What about the other one?'

'Itzcipactli,' said Feathered Darkness. 'He is Two Sign's adopted son.'

'Do you have anything we can use?'

'Not yet, My Lord,' replied Feathered Darkness, 'but I'm going to have them both followed to see what we can learn.'

Cloud Face sighed and pulled a clean, black cloak around his shoulders. 'Is that the best you can do? It sounds like a waste of time to me.' He took a long drink from a pitcher of water and swept from the room.

Feathered Darkness stared at the rows of parchments that lined one wall of the high priest's room and wondered, not for the first time, whether the old man was still up to the job. His belief was strong, of that there could be no doubt. He still had an excellent grasp of the politics and knew all the rites and observances in meticulous detail; all qualities that had been sufficient twenty years ago and had helped to elevate Cloud Face to his current position. The trouble was that the world had moved on; Tenochtitlan had tripled its population in the last two decades. A single man couldn't hope to handle the flow of information single-handedly. It was, Feathered Darkness reflected, a bit like a fisherman trying to land a crocodile with the same tackle he'd used all his life to catch perch. Cloud Face just didn't seem to see the value of the groundwork and so, partly with the high priest's blessing, he had quietly built a network of informants and odd-job men who could feed the order of Huitzilopochtli with information and, just as importantly, distribute lies and misinformation back into that dark, ephemeral web. The time had come to extract some real value from his endeavours and show Cloud Face why he was indispensible.

Cloud Face drew savage delight from the fact that everyone in the Tlatocan had been waiting for him. There wasn't a spare seat. Apparently no one wanted to miss out on the last Great Council meeting before the New Fire and everyone had arrived early at the drab building that lay just outside the north-west corner of the temple complex. Moctezuma cast him a reproachful look. The tlatoani had donned one of his most ostentatious outfits as he always did when Nezahualcoyotl visited. Moctezuma occupied a chair in the central well and appeared to be dressed in the likeness of Quetzalcoatl. His feather mantle was a rippling carpet of red, white and black butterflies and was so long it dragged on the ground behind him. His ankles were heavy with gold ornaments that tinkled when he moved. He wore a black, knee-length breechcloth with a raptor's head picked out in shimmering gold, a design that was echoed by a magnificent headdress of the same bird with its cruel, red beak curving down over his forehead. Cloud Face thought it was tasteless.

The Tlatocan was unusual in that it was the only communal room in which Moctezuma sat at the lowest level. It was about the only thing Cloud Face liked about the meeting place for the Great Council. Here, he was on equal terms with Moctezuma and the other four members of the council; Tlacaelel, Moctezuma's uncle, Acamapichtli and Zipactonal, the Lord Administrator of Tenochtitlan, and yet another of Moctezuma's relatives. The two men were already engaged in a heated debate over something. Cloud Face reflected on the happy circumstances that meant Moctezuma's family were at each others' throats most of the time. He knew that if they ever succeeded in setting their own family squabbles aside he'd have a lot more trouble manoeuvring one or other of them to his own point of view.

The clan leaders who made up the Council of Twelve sat on a stone bench that described a graceful ellipse around the lowered central well. Waist high above them again was a third and final gallery that seated roughly thirty more people including scribes, astrologer-priests and there was even a dais for visiting dignitaries or outside observers. This was where the ruler of Texcoco was seated. Above them, twenty windows looked out over the city and higher still sat the large, flat roof spanned with the trunks of gigantic trees hauled from the forests of Yucatan.

In addition to four knights of his imperial guard, Nezahualcoyotl had brought one of his sons with him – Cloud Face couldn't tell which one, he had so many – who shared his proud, aquiline features. Both had long hair tied back in impeccable, shoulder-length queues, the only difference being that Nezahualcoyotl's was predominantly a striking grey. The ruler of Texcoco held a long staff of polished bocote wood, whose rich, dark grain swirled so animatedly that it looked alive. Beside Moctezuma's absurd outfit, Nezahualcoyotl's grey, feather cloak looked sombre and stately. He wore the mantle of power easily after nearly three decades in charge of Texcoco.

'Silence!' Moctezuma's voice cut across the chatter. 'Everyone is here now. Let us begin. Zipactonal, the floor of the council is yours.'

Zipactonal mushroomed from his chair, expanding as though he meant to cover the discussion floor. The Tlatocan was his empire and he milked it hard. Unlike his second cousin, Acamapichtli, he hadn't a mercantile bone in his body and he was too small and scrawny to have ever gained any notoriety in battle. Cloud Face had never been able to rid himself of Devine Cactus' description of the man; 'too tiny and too stuffed full of pompous to allow room for anything else,' he had said. The stipend Zipactonal received from Moctezuma must have been fairly generous though. He was dressed in a shimmering white cotton cloak embroidered on both shoulders with the emblem of the city's founding, the eagle alighting on a cactus.

'Yes, My Lord and My Lords,' Zipactonal began in obsequious tones. 'As you all know, the main subject of today's meeting is to ensure that the preparations are complete for the Binding of the Years and the subsequent celebrations.' There were some muttered approvals but Zipactonal held up his hand. 'The tlatoani has asked me to reopen the debate on the plans for the coming battle with Chalco.'

Cloud Face had been expecting this, thanks to a source inside the palace, but the pronouncement was greeted with disappointment from the Council of Twelve. The representative for Teopan stood.

'Yes?' enquired Zipactonal.

'We have already approved the tactics for that battle. What is there left to discuss?' said Blade of the South. The members on either side of him nodded sagely. It was a fair question, observed Cloud Face. Of all the clan heads, the high priest despised Blade of the South the least.

Zipactonal refused to be drawn, insisting that the matter would not be discussed until after the main business had been dealt with. Blade of the South took his seat and allowed the Lord Administrator to call on Cloud Face and reassure everyone that preparations for the ceremony were in-hand and that everything would run smoothly.

Cloud Face suppressed his own boiling emotions about the scene he had just left behind him in the temple and gave the broadest smile he could.

'Everything is progressing exceptionally well, My Lords,' he beamed. He described aspects of the preparation that were genuinely in order such as the clean up and renovation of the temple at Colhuacan, selection of the priests and other key figures who would be allowed to witness the main event and followed this up with a recap on the number of priests who would be involved in the ceremony in Tenochtitlan, the one that the general public would be able to see. Cloud Face avoided any mention of the difficulties he was experiencing in the training of the other priests he would be utterly reliant on during the ceremony. No ceremony in the religious calendar was more demanding or more daunting.

Split-second timing held the key and in today's practice attempts, only one of eight had succeeded. Cloud Face finished his summary and asked if there were any questions. There were none, but then he hadn't expected anyone in the clans to understand the difficulties involved, less still have any insightful questions.

Zipactonal thanked Cloud Face and addressed Tlacaelel with glacial formality.

'My Lord Tlacaelel, you appointed Last Medicine to oversee security. Why is he not present?'

'Lord Administrator,' answered the general smoothly, 'it's the information you need, not the man. I have the information.'

'I repeat my question. Why is Last Medicine not here?'

Tlacaelel showed no irritation at Zipactonal's peevishness. Cloud Face had to admire the general's urbane demeanour.

'My Lords, I apologise on behalf of our commander of the Jaguar Knights. As I'm sure you'll appreciate, he still has a great deal of work to complete the arrangements. He humbly begs you accept a situation update from me.'

Zipactonal glowered. 'Proceed,' he replied brusquely. 'Have all the watch duties been handed out to the Jaguar and Eagle Knights? These celebrations must not be an excuse to let our defences down.'

'They have, Lord Administrator. Last Medicine has assigned a division of seventy-six knights to guard the entrance to the city from the southern causeway, fifty to guard the northern approach and a further forty-two to guard the bridge from Tlacopan. The commander has agreed with Our Lord, Moctezuma, a rota of no fewer than eighteen Grey Privy Knights on duty at each entrance to the palace throughout the ceremony and through to the next evening. That's three times the usual roster. We have a further ninety knights consigned to barracks to be called on in the event of a crisis. I have personally approved the appointment of each of the commanders in charge. I commend these preparations to the Tlatocan.'

Zipactonal grudgingly put the matter to the Council of Twelve who approved, but before the Lord Administrator could introduce the next topic, Cloud Face interrupted.

'Lord Tlacaelel! What of patrols for the streets? Just two days ago one of my priests was mugged... by children.'

This question provoked a commotion as everyone tried to make themselves heard. The clansman representing Tlatleloco began listing recent crimes committed in his neighbourhood. The council member from Xochimilco, a heavy-set man with hands like shovels, was on his feet demanding to know why this matter had not been discussed more in the Tlatocan and the man representing Atzacualco was shaking his fist across the room, but Cloud Face couldn't make out the nature of the complaint above the clamour.

The Lord Administrator bleated ineffectually for a while. Cloud Face glanced up at Nezahualcoyotl. The ruler of Texcoco was whispering something humorous to his son. It was plain that the chaotic display in the Tlatocan was not making the best impression on them. Moctezuma watched with a look of growing despair, until he could stand it no more. He stood up, his eyes dark like thunder beneath the raptor headdress and doused the room in opprobrium. The silence was complete.

'I recall that we have discussed the issue of patrols before,' complained Moctezuma at last. 'Didn't we conclude that the clans would provide additional watchmen to patrol the streets during the ceremony and the celebrations?'

The Lord Administrator mopped his brow. 'Yes, My Lord. That is what was agreed.'

Having manoeuvred the conversation round to where he wanted it, Cloud Face seized the opportunity. 'With the greatest respect to the Calpullicalli, perhaps we are asking too much of them. After all, the watchmen struggle to maintain law and order day-to-day and I fear these celebrations will be rather rowdy.' To the high priest's immense satisfaction, the room erupted once more. This time the only member of the Council of Twelve not on his feet was Blade of the South. He was looking directly at Cloud Face. Their gazes locked and held before the clansman from Teopan looked away to catch the Lord Administrator's eye. Order was restored and Blade was invited to take the floor.

'Lord Moctezuma, my Lord Administrator and members of the Tlatocan,' Blade began his address. 'We have discussed the issue of crime on Tenochtitlan's streets before and doubtless, we will be discussing it many times over the coming years. I thank our Lord, High Priest Mixayacatl for raising the subject again.' Blade of the South inclined himself fractionally in the high priest's direction. 'I cannot deny his claim that things are not as they should be, however, I must point out that the watchmen are funded from a fixed budget that is set aside by the Tlatocan; a budget that has many other drains on it.'

Muted cries of approval echoed around the chamber.

'To increase the number of men on the watch and provide more frequent patrols,' continued Blade, 'we would be forced to reduce spending on the sanitation works and irrigation, or cease improvements on the docks or several other minor projects.'

'No one disputes the need for these works, My Lord,' the honorary title used for clansmen in the Tlatocan tasted sour in Cloud Face's mouth. 'Perhaps it would be right for the council to report on just what the existing funding of the city watch buys? I've heard some people complain they can go for days without seeing a single patrol.'

'I'd be happy to report back to the council with this information,' said Blade of the South. 'The area the city watch has to cover is large. I doubt that there would be any serious dispute over the need to invest more in this area.'

The Lord Administrator seized on the ensuing pause to regain control of the meeting and presented a brief statement from the palace kitchens in which the Procurator General made it clear that the banquet, planned for the eve of the ceremony, to which nobility, the clan elders and high-ranking knights of the realm would be invited, was provisioned and planned for, down to the last detail. No one was inclined to challenge the head of Moctezuma's household servants, an especially futile move since the man wasn't even present, so without further ado, Zipactonal addressed the Tlatocan.

'Are preparations complete for the festivities after the ceremony?' he asked.

Mahuizoh, the member of council for Cuepopan, who had been put in charge of this area, was circumspect. He licked his lips and fought the wispy strands of hair that invaded his beady brow with an embroidered sleeve and explained that, although progress had been good, there was too little food to go around.

Moctezuma called across the room in a voice like grated ice, 'What do you mean "too little food"? I agreed that whatever funds the Calpullicalli decided to contribute to food for the poor and the sick, the treasury would double it. What's happened to all the money?'

Cloud Face watched the man struggle. Mahuizoh's task ought to have been simple enough. He was supposed to distribute produce to all those groups who had agreed to hand out food to the needy on the dawn of the New Fire. Several orders of priesthood were involved including Tezcatlipoca and Cloud Face's own order. As usual, the Sisters of Penitence would be dispensing charity across the city without making the least attempt to check the eligibility of the supplicants. All Mahuizoh had to do was take monies he had been provided and make the necessary arrangements, but this was evidently beyond him. He was another spineless administrator with no real power and no god-given authority, appointed to a position he was hopelessly ill-equipped for.

'Ah, My Lord, I, er...' Mahuizoh licked his lips again and rubbed his hands. He bowed nervously in Moctezuma's direction avoiding direct eye contact. 'It's all gone,' he said at last in a small voice.

'Gone?' exclaimed Moctezuma. 'That cannot be so. I authorised payments to the Calpullicalli for this exact purpose. What has happened to these funds?'

Blade of the South stood again. 'May I be allowed to explain, My Lord?' Mahuizoh looked relieved when Moctezuma and Zipactonal both gave their consent. 'I'm afraid that the purchase of the foodstuffs required has proven much more costly than was expected. It's very hard to plan anything with the prices rising at the rate they are. Also, My Lord, the very act of trying to buy large quantities of provisions has artificially inflated the prices further.'

'What's the shortfall?' demanded the tlatoani.

Mahuizoh was made to read out from a list of supplies and state how far short of the target they were. Stocks of amaranth, maize flour, fruits and peppers were half as plentiful as the Tlatocan had envisaged. The story for meat was even worse with pledged supplies to be delivered on the eve of the ceremony itself running at a quarter of what had been planned. The thunderous look on Moctezuma's face darkened as the disastrous situation was aired in front of Nezahualcoyotl.

'Enough!' said Moctezuma at last. 'There are still reserves of food in the palace warehouses. Zipactonal, you and Mahuizoh are to see to it that this is distributed to those groups dispensing charity at the celebrations.'

'All of it, My Lord?'

'Yes, all of it!' raged Moctezuma, carefully avoiding Nezahualcoyotl's gaze. 'I will not have my people starving on the first day of the new world.'

With that, the matter was settled and the Tlatocan ground out the rest of the afternoon haggling over every last detail of the run up to the ceremony and the aftermath of the celebrations, which were expected to last throughout the following day. The clean-up effort alone was expected to take five hundred people as much as eight hours. Special barges had been commissioned to ferry the waste to Xaltocan where the townspeople had already dug a monstrous hole to bury it in.

Finally, the Lord Administrator was able to steer the conversation on to the subject of the battle with Chalco, whereupon Tlacaelel was invited to step forward and explain the proposed changes to the plan. Cloud Face already knew that the appointed place of battle was to change but his informant, a member of Tlacaelel's staff, understood nothing of warfare. Tlacaelel began with an appeal to the council that Chalco needed to be crushed. Having such a powerful enemy so close at hand was a terrible drain on the armies of the Triple Alliance.

'We have no need of this artificially arranged conflict to provide captives,' said Tlacaelel. 'Enemies can be hauled back from real wars at the frontier. The War of the Flowers must be stopped.'

Cloud Face listened as the general described the revised tactics that he wanted to use on the day of the battle, how the strongest units would be placed on the wings in the hope of drawing the opposition into a trap in the centre. The description was thorough but dry. Cloud Face yawned. One thing was certain; the man lacked the oratory skills of his brother.

Cloud Face had prepared a lengthy list of objections to the new plans and had intended to finish up with some fairly direct threats of the consequences for the people of the valley if the decline in the number of captives continued, but as he listened to Tlacaelel describe the placement of the battalions of knights and realised that the clans would be used as bait in the middle of the field of battle, a different idea began to take shape in the high priest's mind. If Cloud Face had struggled to concentrate on Tlacaelel's turgid style of delivery at the outset, by the end, he was hanging on to every word the general spoke. The possibility that Chalco might be able to summon help from the Tlaxcala was also a new and intriguing development. At last, when Zipactonal threw the floor open to questions, instead of rising to his feet to complain, Cloud Face said nothing. He watched the council and realised with grim humour that if anyone opposed Tlacaelel's revised strategy, he would have to come to the support of his enemy. That was something he had not expected. He was still marvelling at this extraordinary turn of events and trying to think of ways to ensure the battle turned out in his favour when Nezahualcoyotl addressed the Lord Administrator and asked for permission to speak. He stood when Zipactonal introduced him.

'I don't like this plan.' His voice was deep and melodious, in keeping with his size, but the message was curt. Nezahualcoyotl was always polite and especially careful in his dealings with the Tlatocan so his abrupt announcement caught everyone by surprise. Before anyone could recover, he added, 'This plan puts the battleground on a direct line to Texcoco. If our armies fail, there will be nothing between Amihuatzin and my people.'

'My Lord, if the people of Texcoco stand with Tenochtitlan and Tlacopan and our allies, Amihuatzin's army will find no way to get past the Triple Alliance.'

'With respect, Tlacaelel, it's not your people at risk.' The ruler of Texcoco inclined his head sagely. 'If the worst were to happen and the Chalca did get past us, they'd have a clear run to a city defended only by old men and women.'

It dawned on Cloud Face that Nezahualcoyotl was seriously considering withholding his forces in order to protect Texcoco. He estimated the size of the armies of the Triple Alliance without one of the partners and then tried to recall the fighting strength of the Chalca. Elation swept through him as he began to understand the likely change in the dynamics of the battle if Texcoco did not join the fight. He held his breath to see what Nezahualcoyotl would say.

'Again, My Lord, I cannot see how the Chalca would get past our combined armies. If your men fight with us, we will defeat the Chalca on their own doorstep. If you do not join us and the enemy somehow get past us, you invite them to fight in Texcoco itself.'

'My good friend Tlacaelel, I must insist on disagreeing with you.' Nezahualcoyotl smiled down at Tlacaelel. 'Please don't take it personally, but I simply cannot take any risks in this matter. It is different for you, Tenochtitlan is easily defensible with a small force of men, but Texcoco is not an island. Lord Moctezuma?'

'Yes cousin, what is it?'

'I deeply regret any offence, but if you insist on fighting the Chalca such a short distance from my door, I can only offer you a token force. One battalion of my Jaguar Knights and anyone from Texcoco disposed to volunteer; I'll have the city criers sent out this evening. The majority of the army will stand in defence of the city.'

'The council has not made a decision yet,' Moctezuma pointed out. 'Your concerns are noted, cousin. Shall we hear what the Tlatocan has to say?'

Nezahualcoyotl nodded graciously and sat down, then, one by one, the members of the Council of Twelve took their turn on the floor. As usual there was no consensus. Mahuizoh and Ueman, the clan representative of Atzacualco agreed to the change but spoke at length of their concern that Texcoco would not be taking part. Here, Tlacaelel was called upon to give an estimate of the fighting strength of the Chalca. The council member for Moyotlan, a bilious old man, agreed on condition that the role call, previously set at twelve hundred for his quarter, was reduced to eight hundred souls, there being a sickness sweeping the residents at present. Blade of the South approved the change as did the youth appointed to speak on behalf of Tlatleloco, but only after Tlacaelel had been returned to the floor to describe in great detail the distribution of the various divisions across the line of battle. Xaltocan and Xochimilco objected vociferously, the first insisting that it was a breach of tradition and the second on the grounds that the location was a great deal further for their warriors to travel. Cloud Face watched them all, carefully keeping his contempt for this absurdly inefficient process from his face and when he was called upon to give his own verdict, he conjured an apologetic smile and waved in Tlacaelel's direction.

'I'm afraid I haven't the Woman Snake's expertise in warfare. If this is the general's best plan, I feel we should follow his advice.'

A short while later, the Tlatocan approved the changes and Cloud Face picked his way to the exit through the still-bickering parties with a feeling that his plans had just been handed a much needed fillip.

That evening, everyone was full of admiration for the lifelike effigy of the ocelot. Blade of the South was evidently impressed and agreed that there might be a good market for them as talismans to ward off evil spirits. Moments later, Jaguar knocked the figurine into the fire. The family had just finished their evening meal and Jaguar was helping his mother tidy the cooking area. He was brushing with one hand and collecting the crumbs with his other when he accidentally caught the handle of a jar that fell over and rolled towards the edge of the table. As he lunged for the jar, Jaguar knocked the figurine from the table. Somehow he managed to get a hand to the jar but had to watch aghast as the little cat sailed towards the fire. Everyone had turned to see what the noise was so there was a general sigh of relief as it caught on a bundle of twigs standing just to the left of the hearth. The sighs turned to a communal gasp of horror as the bundle of twigs, unbalanced by the collision, toppled slowly into the fire, taking the little figurine with it.

Musical Reed panicked as she saw flames licking at the delicate straw effigy.

'Oh, quick, do something!' she flapped her hands at Jaguar, but he was already moving. Deftly he snatched up one of the twigs from the bundle that lay half in and half out of the fire. The other end was already alight, but there was no time to spare trying to extinguish it. The heat of the fire scorched Jaguar's outstretched hand as he tried to hook the twig under the ocelot. Twice, the intense heat drove Jaguar away, but on the third attempt he succeeded.

'Watch out!' he cried as he flicked the figurine out of the fire and across the room. Arrow One ducked and Precious Flower shrieked as it sailed past her like a meteorite, leaving a trail of smoke. The straw ocelot landed at the feet of Blade of the South, who calmly emptied a jug of water over it.

Everyone gathered to look at the smouldering remains, but it was Blade of the South who was closest and who reacted first. He gave a sharp intake of breath as he looked at the floor.

Jaguar was already apologising to Precious Flower and Musical Reed wrung her hands apologising to both of them, convinced that the disaster was her own fault. They all stopped talking when they saw the expression on Blade's face. His mouth was open and he was still staring at the floor, utterly speechless. Everyone peered at the puddle that lay at his feet.

Arrow One shouted in disbelief. 'Look at that!' The figurine lay on its side, wet and a little blackened, but seemingly unharmed.

Blade bent down and delicately picked up the figurine between forefinger and thumb. He turned it over several times to check, but there was no sign of damage other than a few charred spots that made the animal look even more lifelike than before. In a voice of solemn respect, Blade recited from an ancient history.

'...and into the conflagration that was the creation of the Fifth Sun and Moon, plunged the eagle and the jaguar...' He solemnly handed the effigy back to Jaguar as he continued, '...yet both emerged alive, and that is why the majestic eagle's wings are black and how the regal jaguar got his spots.'

The bundle of twigs blazed in the hearth, but everyone in the room felt a chill and no one spoke for a while.

Blade of the South handed the figurine to his son. 'It's an omen!'

They all knew something unusual had happened. It seemed impossible that the grass could have survived that inferno. It should have flashed, briefly incandescent, before floating up the chimney in a million feathery, grey particles of ash. Instead, it survived, the legend of Creation brought to life.

'What does it mean?' asked Precious Flower tremulously.

Musical Reed took hold of Precious Flower's hand. 'We need an astrologer to tell us more, my dear. We can't work this out.'

'Perhaps the city is going to burn down,' suggested Beetle, with a worried frown. 'Maybe we should all leave Tenochtitlan.'

An intense debate on the interpretation of the omen followed. Even Musical Reed had plenty to say in spite of her earlier insistence to the contrary. She was a taciturn woman, who usually only spoke when she wanted someone to do something. The loudest noise anyone had ever heard her make was the sharp intake of breath when she pricked herself with a bone needle when sewing.

Arrow One was still sceptical. He tried to steer the conversation towards an examination of the facts. How long had the straw jaguar been in the flames? Had it caught at all? Had the bundle of twigs protected it from the flames? Perhaps the straw had been damp, he suggested, but his wife would have none it.

'You saw that thing,' exclaimed Beetle. 'It was as dry as a creosote bush!'

Jaguar and his father argued over whether the omen referred to the first battle planned for the year Two Reed.

Eventually, Arrow One grew bored and tried to draw Jaguar's attention to the game of patolli he had begun to set up before the accident.

'Do you want to play a few rounds with us?' he said, including Jaguar's father in the group.

'All right,' said Jaguar reluctantly. Patolli infuriated him. He considered himself a good player and yet, whenever he played with his father, Blade always beat him. Jaguar always started each game knowing that he could win and always enjoyed it up until the moment it became clear that his position was hopeless. His record against Arrow One was only marginally better.

Jaguar's mother stoked the fire again. She poked the remains of the bundle into the blaze and bade the others goodnight. A short while later Beetle and Precious Flower also turned in.

Jaguar sat down in front of the game and pulled his mantle closer around his shoulders. The fire was having a limited impact on the unseasonably cold night air. Jaguar took the four wooden counters allocated to him and placed them in the safe-zone nearest to him, from where all his pieces would start. The safe-zone was one of four, which lay at the ends of the cross-shaped playing area painted onto the patolli mat in liquid-rubber.

Arrow One and Blade each threw the four beans that served as dice onto the table to see who would start. Arrow One rolled a six and Blade scored nine. Jaguar threw the beans and only managed a five.

Blade got the game underway. He scooped up the beans and muttered into the palm of his hand briefly before tossing them across the mat. He moved one of his counters out of his safe-zone and along the arm of the cross.

'You know,' said Blade as he pushed the beans towards Arrow One. 'The more I consider it, the more I'm convinced Precious Flower's little ocelot is a good omen for the coming battle.'

Jaguar nodded as he watched Arrow One throw the beans. Arrow One took his turn. Beetle's husband wasn't a warrior and avoided conversations on the subject of war.

Jaguar reached out and took the beans from Arrow One. Throwing an eight, he advanced one of his pieces until it was almost at the intersection of the cross.

'Will Magic River be fighting with us?'

'Yes,' said Blade, taking the beans from his son. 'Fire Mountain too. Have you seen him in action?'

'No, but I hear he's good.'

Arrow One shifted uncomfortably. 'Will you be fighting too, Blade?'

Blade cast the beans and moved one of his counters, catching one of Jaguar's pieces and taking it out of the game.

'Yes.'

'I don't think that's a good idea,' said Arrow One, shaking his head. 'All three of our clan leaders putting themselves in danger?'

'You know that we macehualtin must fight and be seen to fight,' observed Blade. 'We must earn our respect with the pipiltin.'

'Pipiltin!' scoffed Arrow One. 'What do the nobility know about respect?'

'We need their support,' Blade insisted. 'Here, it's your turn.' He passed the beans to Arrow One. 'Whatever you think of the ruling classes, their patronage is vital to us and therefore to the city.'

'Why is that?' asked Jaguar, watching as Arrow One advanced a piece and took out the piece Blade had just used in the attack against Jaguar.

'Since the founding of this city, the tlatoani has ruled with only the priests at his side, but a big change is underway. The priests aren't in control anymore, at least not the everyday administration of the city. That power is gradually passing over to the Council of Twelve and to the clans from whom the council is drawn.' Blade's voice was strong but very quiet and it occurred to Jaguar that he didn't want to be overheard.

Jaguar took his turn in silence. He was in danger of having another of his trailing pieces captured. He needed a good score to move it out of reach of Arrow One's piece, but the best he could manage was a three. Jaguar weighed up the options and decided to abandon it, using the score to advance his lead counter.

Blade of the South smiled as he accepted the beans which only served to convince Jaguar that his father was on the verge of sweeping him and Arrow One from the board. It wasn't hard to see why Blade could never find adversaries to play for money.

'Arrow One is right to be concerned,' said Blade.

Jaguar noticed that his father was keeping his pieces in a loose formation, so as to avoid being drawn into the battle between his two opponents. The beans passed to Arrow One as Blade continued.

'The fact remains that the power of the clans is still weak. Administrative duties do not carry much weight on their own, however important we know they are to the smooth running of the empire. This is why we must underpin our commitment to the tlatoani in war.'

Arrow One intervened angrily. 'I don't understand,' he said. 'Collecting of taxes, maintenance of roads and ditches, tribunals, regional city guards, to name but a few! Why do the nobles consider these tasks unimportant?' Arrow One hurled the beans in disgust and then had to work to hide his delight when he realised that the numbers meant he could capture Jaguar's exposed piece.

'Moctezuma and Tlacaelel know that these activities are vital to the efficient running of the city and our conquered lands,' Blade said. His voice was soothing. 'Most of the nobility know it too. True, a few of them are out of touch with reality, just like the priests, but one of the missions of the Calpullicalli is to win the ruling classes over.'

'What about the priests?' asked Jaguar.

'The priests will eventually see that we are a part of the solution and come to accept us, but for some, like Mixayacatl, that may take a long time. In truth, I'm surprised he didn't raise any objections to Tlacaelel's new plans.' Blade was still keeping his voice down though it seemed unlikely that anyone was close enough to overhear.

'New plans?' asked Jaguar, somewhat distracted as his position in the game had suddenly begun to look frighteningly vulnerable.

'I was getting round to that part,' said Blade and summarised what had transpired in the Tlatocan, paying particular attention to the general's revised battle plans and Nezahualcoyotl's retraction of his army.

'I don't understand,' Jaguar said. 'If we still outnumber the Chalca, why would Mixayacatl object?' Jaguar managed to manoeuvre one of his pieces into a safe-zone.

Blade of the South pounced on one of his son's laggard pieces. 'Mixayacatl loathes Tlacaelel with a vengeance and he usually takes every opportunity to obstruct him.'

Arrow One looked up from the game. 'Maybe he's preoccupied at the moment.'

Blade of the South nodded slowly.

Jaguar listened to his father list the arguments that took place in the council meetings as he tried to wrest back some control over the game. A lot of it sounded very petty and eventually he gave up listening in order to concentrate on avoiding the predations of the other two players. On his next go, Jaguar whispered to the beans as he shook them, invoking the power of the Ehêcatl, the God of Wind, to blow the beans until they showed a good score. The prayer seemed to work, enabling Jaguar to take one of Blade's pieces, but the respite was short lived. From that moment on, Jaguar's position became increasingly hopeless. Eventually his last piece was captured, so he stood up and said goodnight, leaving the other two to battle it out.

Chapter 5 - Côâtl

Tlacaelel and Two Sign marched purposefully across the Bridge of Tlanextic in the heat of the midday sun, flanked by ten members of the Grey Privy Knights. Tlacaelel was the only man allowed to command members of Moctezuma's own honour guard. They were hand-picked members of the Eagle and Jaguar Knights sworn to the tlatoani's service until death. They were the toughest, most experienced warriors in Tenochtitlan and they made an imposing sight in full battle-dress of padded cuirass, coyote skins and ornate headdresses of black, brown and orange feathers. To a man, they were tall, well-muscled men, chosen for their ability to wield a two-handed macuahuitl, a six foot long, double-edged sword that could take a man's head off in a single blow. Each man carried his weapon slung over his back where the exquisite designs were on display, set with opals, topaz and ornate shell fragments. The obsidian blades inset along each edge were held in place with cured pine resin and leather bindings. When the Grey Privy Knights passed by, everyone got out of the way and watched the spectacle with bated breath.

'So your son told you these men were on their way to Tlaxcala?'

'Yes,' replied Two Sign, struggling to keep up with the smaller man. 'But then I went and questioned Magic River, who led the scouting party, and he confirmed it.'

'Cloud Face knows that important captives must be submitted to the Tlatocan for questioning!' Tlacaelel gestured impatiently. 'Why must he defy the council like this?'

Two Sign rubbed at the scars where he had lost the two middle fingers on his right hand. 'Maybe he questioned them himself and decided they have nothing useful to say,' he ventured.

'It is not his decision to make,' replied Tlacaelel. 'This is something that only the council or I can rule on. Besides, we're only a few days from war. These two must have been carrying crucial information or a request to someone. Where were they intercepted?'

'Magic River said they were on a little-known route that runs through the hills to the north of Ixtaccuihuatl, so it seems unlikely that they were heading this way to sue for peace.'

'You're right there. No one wants peace now,' Tlacaelel said at last and then added in a sombre voice, 'My brother has made sure of that.'

'I heard that Amihuatzin insulted the tlatoani,' said Two Sign, still hurrying after the man. 'Yet you say your own brother arranged this?'

'With a little help from me,' replied the general, glancing back. His frown had eased a little.

'How did you do that?'

'We made a request we knew they'd enjoy turning down.'

Two Sign smiled, beginning to understand, but was pleased when Tlacaelel continued.

'Two weeks ago, the tlatoani sent word to Chalco, begging Amihuatzin for food, explaining that our people were at death's door and insisting they convey an answer back to Moctezuma before two days had passed.'

'Doesn't the tlatoani have reserves?'

'He does have some in spite of recent handouts, but that's hardly relevant,' said the general over his shoulder.

Two Sign nodded in acknowledgement as Tlacaelel went on to explain how the ruler of Chalco had sent two of his personal aides back to Moctezuma, just before the expiry of the deadline, carrying with them a single scrawny duck from Lake Chalco. The two emissaries politely pointed out that, whilst they had every sympathy for the people of Tenochtitlan, Chalco was also suffering from the same terrible famine and regrettably, this single bird was all the people of Chalco could spare.

Two Sign burst out laughing at the effrontery. 'I hope they said a fond farewell to their loved ones before they left home!' said the warrior.

100

The crowds grew thicker as the party approached the Serpent Wall. It was the last market day before the ceremony of the New Fire and everyone was trying to stock up on essentials before the curfew began. Men and women argued furiously over the little produce that was on display. Shoppers jostled each other, muttering darkly as they waited their turn and then hotly contested the extortionate prices with the apologetic stallholders. A fight had broken out over a single tomato and clan-appointed militia, identified by their red sashes, waded in with cudgels to restore order.

Two Sign had to raise his voice to be heard over the clamour. 'What happened to them?'

Tlacaelel chuckled as he recalled the ruse and explained how the two men had been separated while they watched a ball game that had been hastily arranged in their honour.

'We brought the other one back to the palace for a banquet,' said Tlacaelel. 'We told him that his colleague had been taken unwell and had asked to lie down somewhere for a while and that he had given explicit instructions that we should proceed without him. A banquet was brought in and the emissary remarked on how tasty it was and then he asked Moctezuma how, with so much food in evidence, he had thought to request more from the people of Chalco.'

'Don't tell me,' said Two Sign ruefully. 'The meat was delicious.'

Tlacaelel threw his head back and roared with laughter. The people around them were caught unawares and jumped back, startled.

'You guessed it!' managed the general, overcome with mirth. 'It was only when he commented on the quality of the meat that he began to have a sneaking suspicion of what had happened.' The general paused to wipe tears of joy from his eye. 'He asked after his friend once again, this time with one eye on the roasted joint in front of him.'

The effect of watching Tlacaelel trying to control his laughter set Two Sign off and suddenly the two men were nearly doubled up, unable even to walk. The dour knights on either side of them slowed down and waited, expressionless.

'You should have seen his face!' wheezed Tlacaelel when he had recovered.

'So you let him go back and tell Amihuatzin what had happened.'

'Of course,' agreed Tlacaelel. 'The tlatoani had just handed him the excuse he was looking for. The next day we received a note from Chalco with a formal invitation to restart the War of Flowers.'

By the time the troops reached the entrance to the temple complex, Two Sign and Tlacaelel had recovered their composure.

'We are here to see Mixayacatl,' Tlacaelel announced to the wizened man at the door. The stooped figure muttered something unintelligible from under a monstrous set of greying eyebrows. Tlacaelel stared at him for a long moment before his patience ran out.

'Don't worry. I'll tell him myself,' said Tlacaelel and stalked through the entrance without waiting for permission.

Two Sign and the knights followed as Tlacaelel made his way to the priest's accommodation on the east side of the temple complex. A youthful looking warrior priest stood guard and looked as though he was about to make a stand until he saw the Grey Privy Knights advancing on him like a small avalanche.

'We're here to see Mixayacatl,' barked the general. 'Go and tell him we're here.' Tlacaelel didn't wait at the door but followed the man as he hurried inside.

The air inside the building was pleasantly cool but Two Sign was several paces in before his eyes adjusted to the gloom. They followed the youth around a couple of twists and turns before he ducked through a doorway. Two Sign slowed down, worried that they were intruding on sacred ground. Tlacaelel showed no such inhibitions and plunged straight in. Stopping to make sure the Grey Privy Knights were behind them, Two Sign stepped through the entrance.

The interior was better lit than the corridor and carried the faint aroma of beeswax that Two Sign assumed was from the candles placed on a stone ledge running around the room at head height. The meagre light from the candles was supplemented by a small rectangle of light high on the facing wall. Tlacaelel was standing next to a small table, carved from the lustrous white substance that seemed to glow with a light of its own. The length of the left-hand wall was set with alcoves packed with parchments in their thousands so that Two Sign wondered if there were more scrolls here than in Tlacaelel's rooms. Cloud Face stood opposite the general. He had dark puddles under his eyes and looked as though he'd just been woken up. Two Sign moved to stand at Tlacaelel's side. The Grey Privy Knights trooped in, unheeding of the crackling tension in the air.

'Tlacaelel!' Cloud Face rolled the name around his mouth as though it was tainted. A smile oozed uncomfortably across his face. 'What an honour to receive the Woman Snake here!' His tone was smooth and perfectly poised, but Two Sign saw the mockery in every angle of the high priest's stance.

'Lord Mixayacatl!' Tlacaelel inclined his body forward by the width of a hummingbird's feather.

'You must excuse this interruption, but I have learned that two of the captives taken in the most recent raids were taking a message to Tlaxcala. I must question these two men.'

Cloud Face ignored Tlacaelel and gazed at Two Sign. It was as though a cold draught had washed over him. Eventually the high priest allowed his eyes to drift disdainfully across Tlacaelel's corps of knights, as though he'd uncovered a nest of maggots in his chipotle stew. By slow degrees he rotated his head back to regard Moctezuma's brother with a stony stare. 'I have no idea what you're talking about.'

'I'm sure I don't need to remind you of the proper protocol regarding the questioning of captured noblemen and elite warriors?'

Cloud Face glided forward until he was inches from the general and glared down at him. Two Sign felt the temperature in the room drop.

'Nor then shall I need to remind you,' Cloud Face hissed into Tlacaelel's unblinking face, 'that the proper protocol for gaining an audience with the high priest is to submit a request through the master of the House of Souls! The temple and the grounds within the Serpent Wall are sacred,' he added. His voice was calm but contained a germ of menace that grew as he went on. 'No one is allowed upon this hallowed ground except by invitation. You,' he pointed at Moctezuma's brother, 'were not invited! The fact that you are the tlatoani's brother does not make you exempt!'

The confrontation made Two Sign feel deeply uncomfortable. Tlacaelel might have been at home dealing with the politics, the factions and power struggles of the court and the Tlatocan, but his own place was the battlefield where the only protocol was survival. It was clean and simple and there was honour and a strange, brutal beauty to it. In his haste to take on the high priest, Tlacaelel had transgressed and put himself at a disadvantage and the old man knew exactly how to get under the general's skin. Two Sign could only watch as Tlacaelel, incandescent with rage and determined not to back down, fixed Cloud Face with a venomous look.

'You have one of your boys find those two emissaries and bring them to me now!' he spat.

'Or what?'

As if on cue there was a commotion behind Two Sign. Feathered Darkness shouldered his way into the room accompanied by a dozen, heavily armoured warrior priests. Four of the Grey Privy Knights closed ranks to shield Tlacaelel and Two Sign while the warrior priests threaded their way through to stand behind Cloud Face. Two Sign noticed the short, stabbing spears that the priests were carrying and decided that these would be more effective in the confined space than the knights' great swords. Tlacaelel said nothing and Two Sign began to think the standoff might get ugly. Used to assessing the combative situations, he found himself trying to predict who would begin the fight and what the possible outcomes might be. The Grey Privy Knights were well-trained, battle-hardened veterans who would die rather than allow Tlacaelel to come to any harm. If Two Sign was lucky, one or two of the knights would rally to him. The warrior priests had fanaticism and more appropriate weapons on their side. Two Sign looked at their tattoos and scars and decided that these priests were not just for show and hoped that Cloud Face would not start anything in such confined quarters. There would be many casualties and no certain outcome.

Cloud Face broke the silence. 'As you seem to be unaware of the seriousness of this transgression, Tlacaelel,' he said, 'I'll remind you that trespassing on hallowed soil carries a maximum penalty of death. Your family connections won't buy you leniency!'

'I look forward to hearing your submission to the council,' Tlacaelel replied angrily. 'They will hear that the reason for my visit is your failure to hand over important enemy combatants for questioning. I wonder what the punishment is for withholding information vital to the wellbeing of our people?'

Neither the high priest nor the general looked like they were prepared to stand down and then, quite suddenly, with a casual shrug, Cloud Face questioned his assistant.

'Feathered Darkness?'

'Yes, My Lord.'

'The Woman Snake claims we have two senior figures from Chalco in captivity. Is this true?'

Feathered Darkness' eyes remained locked on Tlacaelel as he replied. 'Yes, My Lord. That is correct.'

'Extraordinary! Tlacaelel, it seems you were right after all,' said Cloud Face in astonished tones. 'Feathered Darkness, kindly arrange for them to be brought here immediately.'

Feathered Darkness stalked past Tlacaelel and the knights and left, but he was back within two minutes, during which time a frosty silence had reigned. Feathered Darkness had a large magucy sack in one hand that looked heavy. He handed it to Cloud Face who opened the neck and peered in with an expression of mild surprise.

'What is this?!' growled the general, sensing something was up.

Cloud Face handed the sack over.

Tlacaelel examined the contents. 'Is this them?' he said, clearly outraged.

Two Sign was convinced from the apparent weight of the bag and its shape that it contained the heads of the two men they were after and he was also certain that the high priest had known this.

Cloud Face looked at his assistant with a raised eyebrow.

'I'm sorry, My Lord,' said Feathered Darkness. 'These men were injured when they were captured and in their weakened state, they did not survive questioning.'

Tlacaelel started shouting then. Two Sign had never seen the general so angry before. He trembled with suppressed rage and stood on tiptoe to blast Cloud Face, shaking the sack at him and accusing him of reckless behaviour.

'And how were they supposed to answer your questions with their heads severed from their bodies? What were you and your bloodthirsty goons doing questioning these men anyway? That is not your business!'

Cloud Face wiped spittle from his face and ran a hand over his hairless head.

'You know as well as I do that the priests have always had the authority to question captives. You seem to forget that we are the appointed ministers of the gods and that we've always been close advisors to the tlatoani.'

'And you seem to forget that those days have gone!' Tlacaelel lobbed the bag containing the heads at Two Sign, who caught it deftly.

'Come on,' said the general. 'We're going. The tlatoani needs to hear about this.'

Two Sign signalled to the Grey Privy Knights to form up and while he stood by the door, they followed the general from the room. When the last of the knights had ducked out, Two Sign stood for a moment, eyes flicking between the high priest, his assistant and the phalanx of warrior priests. This kind of bad tempered feud between two people, supposedly on the same side, was why Two Sign was grateful he had no noble blood in him. He would never be promoted to Tlacaelel's position where petty politics seemed to consume so much of everybody's time. Like it or not though, he was a part of this fight and although he had a deep respect for the priesthood and prayed to Quetzalcoatl every morning when he awoke, he was sworn to the general's cause.

Two Sign bowed briefly, then left.

Jaguar awoke from a troubled night's sleep. In his dreams he had been back to the cave in the gorge up above Chalco. Instead of the cave being cool as Jaguar remembered it, the air was hot and humid, flowing back and forth like the foetid breath of Mictlantecuhtli himself. As he stood on the edge of the inky abyss with Crocodile, a priest came up behind them wearing Quetzalcoatl's shimmering green cloak over his black robes. Perched on the priest's shoulder was an enormous eagle that glowered at Jaguar. In the murky depths of the cave, the whole scene was inexplicably lit so that Jaguar saw everything in great detail. Apparently oblivious to the eagle's presence, the priest opened his hand revealing the straw figurine of the ocelot, which he showed the two warriors.

'Fetch me the Crocodile,' intoned the priest and promptly pushed the two warriors over the edge so that they fell, tumbling end over end through the cloying darkness. Jaguar remembered thinking as he fell what an odd thing the priest had said, because there was no figurine of a crocodile.

The detail of the dream then became somewhat imprecise, but they must have survived the fall, because the vision crystallised once more to reveal a variation on Jaguar's recurring nightmare. Now he and Crocodile were being held down on two immense slabs of tezontle and poised over them with a sacrificial knife was Arrow One, already bloody from sacrifice and dressed in the flayed skin of Xipe Totec. Arrow One's beady black eyes stared out through the eyeholes in the scalp that was pulled taught over his narrow features. Behind him stretched a long queue of citizens from all the towns and cities of the lake; Tenochtitlan, Texcoco, Tlatleloco, Chapultepec and even Chalco, all waiting their turn to offer themselves up to Tlaloc and praying for the rain.

Jaguar got out of bed and rubbed his shoulders that ached as though he had spent the night rowing back and forth across the lake.

Blade had declared that as they were in Nemontomi, the unlucky last five days of the year, no more carving was to be done until after the New Fire. So after breakfast, Jaguar spent some time examining the work in hand, but there was very little to see.

The end of the fifty-two year cycle meant the order book was even more sparse than usual.

Musical Reed prepared the last of the maize kernels by soaking them in water and lime. The family had been unable to purchase food for two days because of the soaring prices. Everyone who could still afford it was hoarding food against the potential horrors of the next few days.

'We have enough to last for a day or two after the New Fire,' said Musical Reed in one of her very rare references to the ceremony. She tried hard to avoid sounding worried. No one was deceived for a moment. In the small house, apprehension about the transition from the year One Rabbit to Two Reed was so tangible it could almost be cut with a knife. Any subject that was discussed very soon became examined in the light of its relevance to the New Fire.

Finally, Jaguar was forced to leave the house to escape the air of gloom and despondency. For variety, he chose a long route through Moyotlan, which he did not know well. The western edge of the quarter was built over marshland that looked out towards Chapultepec, a grubby, stilt-city in its own right and nothing like the more affluent edge of the district that bordered on the city-proper. The houses were rickety wooden affairs, standing on slender stilts, and interconnected by a devilish maze of walkways and frail bridges. This was home to the mayeque, the poorest people in Tenochtitlan. They worked as farm labourers or porters, or if they were unable to perform heavy manual work, they made necklaces, ear plugs and other trinkets from beans, coloured stones and dyed seed pods, selling them wherever they could. These people were Tenochtitlan's dispossessed. With little or no income, they scavenged from the surrounding countryside or netted shrimp and insect larvae from the lake to keep themselves alive. Some had been lucky and had found work on the Great Temple, but the new building had been completed some weeks ago in readiness for the big ceremony so these people were even worse off than before.

Tiny spherical clouds dotted the blue sky with surprising regularity. A few muted sounds floated over the stilt houses and, although it was the third day of Nemontomi, a few men and women going about their business, clattering along the lengths of loose planking between the jumble of houses. Large red-painted stones sat outside a number of deserted houses, which was the sign of quarantine, a warning to others not to enter for fear of catching some illness. Jaguar gave these houses a wide berth as he made his way around the more remote parts of the slum at the lake's edge. Making his way along a creaking bridge of planks, he saw a pair of emaciated legs protruding from the open doorway of a dilapidated house. At first, it looked as though the person was asleep, perhaps having toppled over from his position, propped up against the door frame where he had been watching the world go by. It was only as he drew level with the entrance that Jaguar realised his mistake. Three vultures with dark, two-toned wings and small red heads were crouched inside the open doorway; one was perched on the man's chest.

The vultures looked up nervously at Jaguar, blinking their red rimmed eyes at him. Dark blood stained their flaccid wattles. With mounting horror, Jaguar saw the hideous plunder they had wreaked upon the dead man. His eyes and lips were gone and remnants of his tongue protruded from between his teeth. Jaguar's senses were assailed by the stench of putrefaction, which he quickly decided emanated from the birds rather than from the deceased, who could not have been dead for long. The victim's skin was strangely discoloured, covered with sores and was stretched over what was little more than a skeletal frame.

Jaguar retched.

More vultures circled high above. It was a sight that had been common since last summer and one that until today had meant nothing to Jaguar. For the first time, he understood the magnitude of the disaster that had befallen the people of the valley and while his own family had been forced to eke out supplies in between the dwindling commissions, many thousands of mayeques had been far less fortunate. 'The New Fire will set things right again,' thought Jaguar. It must surely kill them all or bring the rains again.

Jaguar tried to edge closer to see if there was anyone else in the house, but he could see nothing in the dim light of the interior. The vultures backed away into the gloom, their claws scrabbling and scraping across the floorboards, then Jaguar heard a voice.

'Is there anyone in here?' he called out, but his voice alarmed the vultures and set them scuttling and flapping so any answer would have been drowned out. In an instant, Jaguar's irritation flashed over, provoked by some innate loathing of the ugly, malodorous birds. Consumed with a sudden desire to kill them, he reached for a wooden pole that was propped against the other side of the railing behind him. The pole was of the sort used to spear frogs. It was long, so Jaguar pulled it over the railing carefully to avoid making any noise. Its point was covered in mud from the marsh below, but Jaguar could see that it was sharp enough.

Jaguar hefted the makeshift spear and struck at the nearest vulture. Trapped in the doorway the bird was unable to move quickly enough and only succeeded in spreading its massive wings. The spear caught it full in the plumage on its chest. The other two vultures escaped into the house flapping furiously and screeching as they crashed around looking for a way out. The skewered bird lurched about at the end of the pole until the thin wooden shaft broke. It flapped feebly a few times and then lay still.

Throwing down the remains of the pole, Jaguar dashed through the open door and immediately collided with another of the vultures, breaking its neck as he fell on it. The sweet smell of decay filled Jaguar's nostrils so that he retched again as he tried to get to his feet. While he peered through the spiralling feathers waiting for his stomach to settle the third vulture seized its chance and flew at the doorway making its escape. Again Jaguar listened for the source of the noise, but all he could hear was the loud hammering of his heartbeat.

The ramshackle dwelling consisted of a single dingy room. Apart from a few cooking utensils and a few pots, the place was pitifully bare. The shutters were closed on the two windows, so the only light inside came from the entrance and through the loosely joined floorboards, through which Jaguar could see the mud below. As Jaguar's eyes adjusted, he noticed that the room was divided in two by a flimsy panel made of rushes. The sleeping quarters would be on the other side. Jaguar poked his head round the partition. Stretched out under a few torn and dirty blankets was a child, a boy, no more than ten years old. His condition was so poor that Jaguar could hardly bear to look as the child's pus filled eyes opened slowly. That brief effort was all he could manage, for he soon closed them again.

Jaguar knelt at the boy's side. The child might have been dying of hunger, Jaguar couldn't tell, but he was clearly very ill as well. Perspiration beaded the youngster's brow under a mop of filthy, dark brown hair and his skin was grey and clammy.

The scenario played itself out in Jaguar's imagination. The dead man was the boy's father and the remainder of the family had long since departed for the coastal plains where food was supposed to be plentiful. Staying behind to nurse the boy back to health, the father had starved himself in order to provide enough food. But the boy's sickness lingered, in spite of a visit by a medicine woman. Unable to leave his son's bedside to find work, the man had grown weaker and weaker until one day he threw himself down in the doorway to rest. Too exhausted to move and too proud to call for help, he drifted into unconsciousness from which he never awoke.

Jaguar took the child's small hand in his own.

'Don't worry,' whispered Jaguar. Tears welled in his eyes as he wondered what to do. 'I'm here. You'll be fine.'

By now, the noise of Jaguar's scuffle with the vultures had attracted some attention. Jaguar heard footfall on the planking outside the house. Knowing only that he must get the child out of the disease-ridden house, Jaguar quickly gathered the child up, still wrapped in blankets. As he staggered to his feet, a new pungent odour filled the room. The soiled bedding oozed and dripped. Jaguar gagged again and then he wept. Huge tears rolled down his cheeks as he lurched towards the door. His vision swam so much that he could hardly see his way out.

Suddenly he was out in the sunlight with the boy wrapped in his arms. People from the neighbouring houses crowded round, jabbering and asking questions, but Jaguar couldn't answer. He wanted to shout at them to be quiet. He wanted to berate them for not looking after the boy and not seeing the plight of his father earlier. He wanted to scream out loud at the gods for abandoning their people, but he found he couldn't speak. He took a step across the creaky bridge towards the crowd of onlookers with the boy held tightly in his arms. No one moved. No one wanted to brave the sickness. Jaguar took another step and then another, shaming the crowd into helping with the child. With his tears still wet upon his cheeks, he swept them all with a flinty expression, daring them to turn and run until at last someone came forward, arms extended to take the child. It was a woman, Jaguar barely noticed as he crumpled, suddenly drained and nauseous.

Someone helped Jaguar to his feet and guided him across rattling planks. Someone else gave him a wet cloth to clean his face and hands and then another put a cup in his hands and bade him drink. Others talked around him, discussing something in a string of words that Jaguar could not bring himself to care about. The first thing that Jaguar really noticed was the rough edge of the clay cup as his teeth scraped its surface. The next thing Jaguar noticed was a hand on his shoulder and he recognised the face that swam into view.

'Jaguar?' Precious Flower said anxiously.

'Precious Flower!' blurted Jaguar. 'What are you doing here?'

'I followed you.'

'You shouldn't have come out!' exclaimed Jaguar. 'It's not safe.'

Precious Flower wrinkled her nose and made a dismissive gesture. 'Why? Because of Nemontomi? Don't worry about that! I've seen hundreds of girls and children out and about. The curfew doesn't really start until tonight anyway.'

Jaguar was silent for a while, as though digesting this last statement and then remembered Precious Flower's previous reply. 'So why did you follow me?'

Precious Flower suddenly looked shifty and glanced over her shoulder. 'I'm sorry, Jaguar, I didn't mean to, but when you left the house, I came out to wave goodbye.' Precious Flower looked

round the room again and Jaguar noticed for the first time that
he was sitting in someone else's house. Precious Flower leaned
closer to Jaguar and whispered. 'You were almost at the corner of
Axolotl Street and I was just about to shout when I saw someone
watching you.'

Jaguar looked puzzled. 'Really? What did he look like?'

'I didn't say it was a man,' reproached Precious Flower.
Although she was worried for Jaguar, her tone was more spirited
because Jaguar appeared to be recovering. 'You're right though, it
was. I didn't get a look at his face because he was turned towards
you. He had long hair and was wearing simple peasant clothes.
It wasn't anyone from our clan.'

'Are you sure he didn't just glance in my direction?'

'No,' insisted Precious Flower with a frown. 'He waited
until you turned the corner and then followed. Are you in any
trouble?'

'No,' insisted Jaguar. Now it was Jaguar's turn to whisper
conspiratorially. 'Is he here now?'

Precious Flower made a face at Jaguar, which he took to mean
no. 'I followed him all the way here but he disappeared into the
crowd.'

He gazed down into his cup and noticed it was empty so he
set it aside and looked around the room again. It was a pitifully
bare and simple room in a wooden shack with an old and
decaying roof of rushes. The only ornamentation in evidence was
what looked like a good-luck charm hanging on the opposite wall.
One tiny window on the wall behind Jaguar provided the only
light in the room. It seemed likely that he had been seated next to
it for the fresh air. Four people stood close by, engaged in an
earnest discussion of their own.

'What crowd?'

'Oh,' exclaimed Precious Flower. 'Well, I caught up with
you just as you came out of that house carrying the boy in your
arms! There were a lot of people outside by then and they were
making a lot of noise.' Precious Flower became quite animated
as she told her version of events. Half of the people gathered
were arguing over what to do with the dead man. Some of them

advocated tipping him off the edge of the walkway and into the lake. Others protested that the water was too shallow and without any current to carry the body away, it would simply rot in situ bringing pestilence to the neighbourhood. Half of the throng had arrived late and were demanding to know what was going on.

Precious Flower went on to explain that when Jaguar had staggered out, looking as green as Xipe Totec with a month-old skin and holding the unfortunate child in his arms, the crowd had fallen silent. Then Jaguar had collapsed and the general din had become an uproar as everyone then wondered who the newcomer was and what was to be done with the orphaned boy. Apparently, after a lot of shoving and angry gesticulation, one woman had taken charge.

'Melody says that the boy is called Shield of Gold. Apparently he's been running with a gang of urchins, coming home with food for his father who had been unwell. Melody said she'll adopt the boy. Isn't that wonderful? Oh, here she is...'

A woman came over carrying a pitcher of water and introduced herself as Melody. There was a lot of grey in her hair and deep creases around her eyes. She had a wide face with prominent cheekbones and a ready smile that lit up when she saw that Jaguar had recovered. She refilled his cup, thanking him all the while for rescuing the boy and grumbling about the complaisance of the local people.

'Will, er... Shield of Gold be alright then?' asked Jaguar.

Melody was optimistic. 'He is very ill,' she said, 'but I think he is over the worst of it. If I keep him warm and give him lots of water he will be well again. I will try to find some fresh fruit, perhaps after Nemontomi...' her voice trailed off. The doubt in her mind as to the outcome of the ceremony was evident.

'What will happen to him then?' asked Precious Flower.

Jaguar heard the concern in her voice and realised that the loss of her own family made the boy's situation more personal to her.

'Oh, my husband and I have no children, we will look after him.' She noticed Precious Flower scanning the room. 'He's not here at the moment. He's been lucky enough to get work on clean-up duty, clearing the streets in preparation for tomorrow.'

Jaguar looked at the meagre provisions in the dwelling and wondered how well the elderly couple would be able to care for the boy. At least he might not need to roam the streets, scavenging through garbage for scraps. Jaguar held his tongue. He felt he had already interfered enough. Melody insisted on introducing Jaguar to the others in the room and several more still congregated outside, all of whom praised Jaguar for his timely intervention. Eventually, Jaguar and Precious Flower made polite excuses and managed to extricate themselves, promising, whilst avoiding any reference to the New Fire, that they would return in a few days to check on the boy's progress.

Later, in a field of tall weeds and wild flowers at the start of the southern causeway, when they had left Moyotlan far behind them, Jaguar and Precious Flower rested. The whole area was divided into roughly rectangular plots of land, often crossed by ditches that came off at right angles from the main feeder canals. Many of the plots had a simple shack that housed the family or families who worked it. For the most part, the chinampa were evenly spaced in parallel lines. Sometimes they ran for hundreds of paces, sometimes they twisted and crossed over, and sometimes they stopped after only a few paces, but everywhere there were bridges. There were bridges made of simple rough-hewn planks and decked wooden structures, all the way up to the stone bridges used along the causeways.

They sat down on the trunk of a fallen willow and breathed in the scent of the meadow. Situated next to a well-dredged chinampa, marigolds peppered the long grass and a few early dahlias dared to show their golden petals.

Jaguar looked at Precious Flower, who had her eyes closed and had turned her face up to catch the warming rays of the sun. She was kind and recalling their conversation by the lake and the effigy, Jaguar realised that she really cared for him. His spirit lifted for the first time since the incident with the vultures. Precious Flower was a beautiful girl, perhaps not the classical beauty of some of the nobility, but she possessed a simple elegance. She was radiant, outgoing and spirited, and Jaguar knew now that he had been aware of her flowering since last summer but had kept his feelings hidden, even from himself. Jaguar allowed himself to drift off into a daydream that featured Precious Flower quite heavily.

Bees contributed a continuous hum to background noise in the field, utterly unconcerned, or so it seemed, with the severity of the drought and famine that affected the rest of the valley. One bee even inspected Jaguar's tunic before making for one of the mounds of dredged up mud where the sediment from the canal bottom had been piled up, ready for use as fertiliser for the field. On the opposite bank, there were maize plants growing but they were barely knee-high and their shoots looked tender. Unbidden, the memory of the sick child returned once more.

'One more day,' thought Jaguar grimly. 'One more day until the New Fire and then we'll know!' Suddenly it occurred to Jaguar that with the future of the world hanging in the balance, nothing mattered very much except that moment when the flower stalks and grasses swayed gently in the wind and the sun touched Precious Flower's upturned face and the gentle curve of her neck.

Jaguar reached over to Precious Flower and took hold of her arm. 'If we get through the next few days safely, will you stay with us?' As soon as he said it, Jaguar wished that he hadn't. The words were innocuous but his voice sounded heavy with his unspoken feelings. Precious Flower's relaxed pose evaporated and the beatific expression on her face was replaced by a frown. Still, her eyes were closed and she said nothing for a long time.

Jaguar waited.

Eventually, Precious Flower's hand fought its way into Jaguar's and she gripped it tightly. She opened her eyes and looked at him and he realised that she had been fighting back tears again. She finally broke the silence.

'Of course I will.'

Precious Flower eased over to Jaguar and hugged him tightly and then frightened Jaguar when she recoiled immediately.

'Urgh, you stink! Get away!' she exclaimed.

Jaguar was shocked, but then remembered his collision with the vulture.

'Wait,' Jaguar smiled broadly at Precious Flower. He turned and headed for the embankment. Reaching the edge, he began to pick his way carefully down the steep, slippery slope. Precious Flower watched with amusement as Jaguar stood with one foot in the canal and undid the knot holding his mantle on. He pulled the garment from around his shoulders and stooped down to wash it. After swirling it round a few times in the still, cold water, he lifted the dripping mantle up and wrung it out. He repeated the process several times, wiping his face, torso and legs down too. Finally, he struggled back up the bank, clutching the wet mantle in one hand and as he looked up, he noticed that Precious Flower was drinking in the view. He was suddenly acutely aware of his body, fit but wiry, honed by hours of practice in the ball court. His skin was dark, even for a warrior, and the wash had left his body glistening with a thousand water droplets. A slight breeze roughened his upper arms with goose bumps. Jaguar rubbed his biceps self-consciously and smiled awkwardly back at Precious Flower. He felt a tingle of excitement as he understood the hunger in her stare and wondered briefly how many times she'd looked at him this way without him noticing. Even if Jaguar had nurtured any hopes beyond their familial relationship, he would have been forced to dismiss it as an impossible dream. Tenochtitlan had strict codes of conduct for slaves and for their owners, but now Precious Flower was no more than two days away from being a free woman.

More than anything, Jaguar hoped that Precious Flower would choose to stay with the family and then he remembered that none of his hopes would matter if they did not get past the New Fire. Tomorrow night the sun would set on the last day of the year One Rabbit. Precious Flower must have guessed what Jaguar was thinking.

'Do you think everything will be alright?' she asked in a small voice. 'You know... at Colhuacan?'

'I don't know,' he answered softly. He reached out a hand and watched, transfixed as she reached out to place her hand in his. Jaguar knew then that he wanted Precious Flower and wondered why he had never seen it before. He dropped his cloak and pulled her to him.

For a long time they simply held each other. Jaguar felt the warmth of her slender body against his wet skin and breathed the scent of her hair. He stroked Precious Flower's hair and felt the gentle curve of her waist beneath his hand. She responded, pressing her face into Jaguar's neck and running her hands over his chest. Gradually their movements became more urgent until at last, Precious Flower pulled Jaguar to the ground.

Chapter 6 - Miquitzli

With the morning prayers over, Feathered Darkness emerged from the gloom of Huitzilopochtli's shrine onto the plateau of the Great Temple. The orange orb of the sun had just cleared the mountains to the east and seemed to glare across the valley like some monstrous baleful eye. Feathered Darkness peered back at it through hooded eyes. Surely now, on the last day, there ought to be some sign; some portent of change. Somewhere in that fiery disc the future of the Fifth World should be written. He closed his eyes and span away from the searing light, covering his eyes.

Hiding his disappointment, Feathered Darkness ambled across the huge stone platform, his hands clasped behind his back, careful to avoid Tlaloc's shrine where the morning abeyances were still in progress. He could hear Devine Cactus' disembodied voice floating out of the shrine's ornate doorway. Reaching the edge, he looked out across the rooftops of Tenochtitlan, gazing at his favourite view. The morning mist spread out below him, like a veil over the city, covering all but the tallest buildings. Moctezuma's palace lay beneath the undulating silver shroud, but to the left, the temple of Tezcatlipoca rose out of the sea of white like a mountain-top above the clouds, while the roof of the shrine was all that could be seen of Xipe Totec's temple. At his feet, the steps of the Great Temple itself descended, seemingly forever, until they disappeared into the coiling tendrils of mist, and from the steep sides of the temple, the sea of white lay unbroken until it beached upon the hills of Chapultepec. It was an ethereal scene and its magic would never be lost on Feathered Darkness.

Just south of the city, the domed ridge of Colhuacan crested from the featureless mists like a vast crocodilian. Feathered

Darkness squinted, trying to make out the temple on its hallowed summit where the ceremony would take place tonight, but it was too far away. Just thinking of the ceremony made his guts turn to water and yet somehow, Cloud Face managed to go about the daily ritual as though this was just another day. From midnight, every last fire in the city had been extinguished and at the prayers just completed, the Great Temple's eternal flame had been quenched in blood, setting in motion the final sequence of events that would lead up to tonight's spectacle at Colhuacan. Now that they had entered the final hours, Feathered Darkness could not wait. He hoped Cloud Face was ready.

There was the noise of someone clearing their throat. Feathered Darkness gazed out of the corner of his eye to see Cloud Face standing beside him, black robes hanging from him like congealing pitch.

'The Chosen One is not well,' said Cloud Face. 'I've just come from his quarters.'

As the embodiment of Huitzilopochtli, Sacred Stone was not held in the common holding cells like enemy warriors. An entire suite of rooms had been made available to him and his every whim was indulged. The rooms were secure though and two warrior priests stood guard duty at the entrance at all times. More often than not the Chosen One developed misgivings about the honour bestowed on him and eventually tried to escape. Some, like Sacred Stone, became ill from the worry and lost their appetite.

'We should give him more octli,' suggested Feathered Darkness.

'Fine!' answered the high priest brusquely. 'See that he gets his octli, but make sure that he is alert tonight.'

'My Lord! He does not need to...' began Feathered Darkness.

Cloud Face spun around. *'By the bones! I want him alert!'* His arm snaked out and he grabbed Feathered Darkness by the throat. 'Why can I rely on no one? Doesn't anyone understand how important this is?'

Feathered Darkness was choking. Cloud Face's fingers were digging into the base of his neck while his thumb speared into the younger priest's windpipe. Familiar as he was with the high priest's rages, Feathered Darkness was afraid. Cloud Face's eyes were dark, as though backed by an infinite abyss and a vein pulsed urgently under the birthmark on the smooth dome of his head. Already, Feathered Darkness' vision was growing hazy. He struggled to speak but it was impossible to do anything but gurgle through his constricted larynx.

'What's that?'

Feathered Darkness made a gasping, rasping sound and then the old man shoved him so that he stumbled and fell, mercifully away from the vertiginous edge of the temple.

'You, of all people, should know better,' Cloud Face cursed. 'This is no simple game where all we need is another minor triumph like the charade we used to fool Tlacaelel!' The high priest's face was a mask of murderous rage. He shook his fist at Feathered Darkness. 'By the bones! Once we get through this night, I'll make that godless maggot pay for daring to walk upon our holy ground without my approval!'

Feathered Darkness sat on the cool stone of the temple platform and nursed his bruised neck. It was easy to see why the younger priests and acolytes were so afraid of the high priest. The sheer vitriol of his displeasure was terrifying but it was the unpredictability of his mood that they all feared. Feathered Darkness forgave the old man as he always did. Who could hold such a position, under such terrible strains and remain immune to the weight of responsibility?

'The young warrior,' croaked Feathered Darkness. 'The ball game player...'

'What of him?' spat Cloud Face. 'None of that matters now!'

'Of course not,' croaked Feathered Darkness, struggling to draw breath through his damaged windpipe. 'You know,' he continued, 'you do me an injustice. No one is more loyal to you than I. I have waited on your every word these fifteen years and done everything that you have asked of me and never once complained.'

'So I should be grateful? You've forgotten how many hours I have spent teaching you; how patient I have been.'

'No, My Lord, I am not asking for gratitude.' Feathered Darkness wondered if he had lifted a stone that should have been left well alone.

'What then?' Cloud Face was contemptuous.

'Perhaps you should trust in me a little more.'

'Ha!' the old priest snorted. He put both hands to his pate as if in disbelief. 'Has it not occurred to you that jar was emptied long ago?'

The temple-top grew busier as Tlaloc's shrine emptied out, their morning duties seen to. Feathered Darkness spoke again, this time softly.

'You cannot do this alone, My Lord,' he said. 'If you want to take on the general and the spreading tendrils of the Calpullicalli, you'll need help and people you can delegate to.'

Cloud Face sucked in a huge lungful of air. 'Very well, Feathered Darkness. What help can you offer me?'

'The information I have is of no use to you today, My Lord, but in a few days' time, when all the excitement is over, this may be just what we need.'

'Go on then!' said Cloud Face.

'The one called Heart of the Jaguar is having an affair with a slave girl.'

The old priest's look changed immediately. He narrowed his eyes and looked intently at Feathered Darkness. 'Now that is interesting! Did you say this is Blade of the South's son?'

Feathered Darkness nodded.

'Have you told anyone else yet?'

'No, My Lord, I have not.' Feathered Darkness was satisfied that Cloud Face had calmed down sufficiently to let him get to his feet so he picked himself up.

'Good!' said Cloud Face. 'And no one else knows of this?'

'That's more difficult to say,' replied the younger priest. 'I think not. My spotter saw the young man and the slave girl in a very secluded spot. It looks like they are used to concealing their relationship.'

Cloud Face checked their surroundings cautiously. 'Let's continue this elsewhere,' he said. 'Come on!'

With that the old man swept off and bounded down the temple steps with the energy of a man half his age. Feathered Darkness followed as quickly as he could, but his knee hurt from the recent fall and complained at each of the steep temple steps. He nearly tripped several times trying to keep up. The mist was clearing and when he reached the base of the temple, he saw Cloud Face was waiting for him in the shadow of the east side of the temple, scraps of the chill vapour still curled about his robes. The skull rack loomed eerily above them, four thousand sightless grins all stacked upon each other with the tall, bare poles extending patiently above, like spindly arms reaching to the skies for more.

'What's wrong with you, Feathered Darkness?' Cloud Face hissed at him. 'You're hobbling like an old man!'

'I have twisted my knee somehow,' replied Feathered Darkness carefully avoiding any mention of the high priest's responsibility.

'Come on. The main ball-court is just around the corner. It should be deserted today. We can talk there.'

A short walk later, the two priests stood at the centre of Tenochtitlan's ceremonial ball-court now basking in the early morning light. A hundred thousand silken threads draped the walls and empty seating area with a million tiny, fiery beads of dew. The court lay silent and there was no noise from the numerous rooms in which the teams and priests prepared for the games. The city beyond the walls was also quiet due to the general curfew that was now in force.

Feathered Darkness wondered why they needed to speak in such secrecy, away from Cloud Face's own quarters.

'We've got this little prick right where we want him,' said the high priest. 'You need to bring him to me tomorrow. Can you arrange that?'

Feathered Darkness nodded. 'Yes, of course.'

'No, wait!' said Cloud Face. 'I'll find someone else to do that. I need you to do something else.'

'I will do whatever you require, My Lord.'

'So you said. Here's the thing. Those two dignitaries we questioned were on their way to Tlaxcala to ask Xicotencatl for his help in battle. There's no doubt about that, is there?'

'There's no doubt, My Lord. I was there with you, at the end, when you...' Feathered Darkness didn't need to say more. 'That's what the young one said.'

'We need that message to be delivered.'

'What? But they're dead now! We killed them to stop Tlacaelel getting his hands on them.'

'That's why I need you to go to Tlaxcala and deliver the message to Xicotencatl.'

Feathered Darkness thought he'd misheard. 'You want me to go to Tlaxcala?'

'You said you wanted to help! Take a couple of our fighting men and go now. There's no time for delay. There are only a few days until the battle!'

Feathered Darkness couldn't believe his ears. 'B-b-but the New Fire...' he stuttered. It was inconceivable that he should have to miss the ceremony. This was his only chance to see this ceremony. The next time it came around he would be long dead. It would be a bitter disappointment for any priest to miss the Binding of the Years, but for Feathered Darkness, who had hoped to be at the altar at Colhuacan, it was a devastating blow.

The older priest misinterpreted Feathered Darkness' dismay.

'Don't worry about it!' soothed Cloud Face. 'We've been practising for months. In spite of the recent problems, it will go well.' He laid a hand solicitously on Feathered Darkness' shoulder and smiled. It was the smile of a mighty masacoatl wrapping its fat coils around a fat deer. Feathered Darkness preferred the old man when he didn't smile.

'Besides, if it isn't and the world comes to an end, it makes no difference whether you're in Tenochtitlan or half way to Tlaxcala, does it?' added Cloud Face.

'You want me to ask Xicotencatl to join forces with Chalco?'

Cloud Face's eyes swept the ball-court. 'Exactly. Tell him that Chalco will need his assistance in battle after the New Fire.

Xicotencatl despises us. He won't miss an opportunity to give Moctezuma a bloody nose.'

Feathered Darkness thought it highly likely that the ruler of the Tlaxcalan confederation would kill him on sight but when he shared his concern with Cloud Face, the high priest dismissed the suggestion out-of-hand explaining that he had been in touch with Xicotencatl on several occasions.

'Here, take this necklace to him.' Cloud Face untied the necklace that hung around his neck and lowered the mummified remains of the little hummingbird into Feathered Darkness' upturned hand. 'He knows this is my badge of office. It should offer you some protection and will show that your mission is genuine. Also tell him that I, Mixayacatl, have reason to seek a favourable outcome for his own people and for Chalco and that I shall lend assistance on the day.' Cloud Face looked pleased with himself. 'I have made other arrangements for the forthcoming battle but this and your ball player are the final pieces of the plan.'

Feathered Darkness was appalled. This sounded a lot like treason.

'I don't understand, My Lord!' he said faintly, reeling with the enormity of what he'd just heard. 'You seek the downfall of the Mexica?'

'Of course not,' scoffed Cloud Face. 'Our army is too strong to be entirely overrun, even if Texcoco does not come to our assistance, but we need Tlacaelel to fail badly and if we're outnumbered, things will go much less well for the weaker units.'

'Doesn't Tlacaelel see the danger?'

'He might, if he knew that he had to contend with the Tlaxcala as well,' said Cloud Face inspecting his nails nonchalantly. 'He might suspect something is up, but he won't get much from the two captives we handed over, will he?'

Feathered Darkness could see it all now. He ran both hands through his hair, momentarily covering his shock. Cloud Face had a strategy that just might work. Not only would the general's reputation take a hammering, but the clans, who were less battle hardened than the Jaguar or Eagle Knights, would suffer terribly.

'Many of our warriors will lose their lives.'

The high priest narrowed his eyes. 'Tlacaelel will only come under pressure if they do.'

Feathered Darkness nodded his head slowly. It was a savage and risky idea and what was more, it was simple, but it depended on the Tlaxcalan army being persuaded to side with Chalco.

Cloud Face shrugged and excavated his ear with his little finger and examined the results nonchalantly. 'Come on, Feathered Darkness. A few more people will perish, so what? We're waging war in the name of Huitzilopochtli and the gods are on our side. Have you not seen the plight of our people? Do you know how many people are dying every day already? Every day the famine grows worse. We must appease the gods and yet Tlacaelel and the clans weaken our power with every passing year. Perhaps this drought is but a foretaste of things to come if we continue down this route.'

Feathered Darkness wasn't entirely sure what to think but he felt certain that Cloud Face wasn't deranged. Desperate measures were necessary. The priesthood had nurtured Feathered Darkness, trained him, fed him, clothed him and Cloud Face had taught him everything he knew about the stars and their god-given procession across the sky. The high priest was dangerous and irascible, but Feathered Darkness owed his position and his good living to the priesthood, so Tlacaelel was the threat.

It was a simple decision in the end. Huitzilopochtli was fire and life and Cloud Face was the high priest. He would miss the ceremony of the Binding of the Years and that left a sour taste in his mouth, and yet, Feathered Darkness could not imagine the high priest entrusting this mission to anyone else. He had asked Cloud Face to have faith in him and that was exactly what the old man had done.

'Alright,' said Feathered Darkness at last. 'I'll arrange for one of the other priests to fetch the warrior to you tomorrow and then I'll make preparations to leave for Tlaxcala immediately!' The young priest warmed to his task as he spoke the words. Somehow, stating his intent aloud suffused him with a new strength of purpose. The righteousness of it caught his soul and, like the spark that must blossom on the breast of the captive at Colhuacan, that spark brought light and warmth.

'Excellent!' beamed Cloud Face. 'I will wish you good luck and leave you now. I must prepare for the banquet tonight. I shall pray for your safe return.' With that, Cloud Face stalked off, heading for the far corner of the ball-court and the palace beyond.

In the heat of the afternoon sun, a huge crowd of noblemen and warriors processed at a snail's pace through the entrance to the palace. There was a palpable frisson of anxiety and excitement in equal measure. It was as if, on this final day, the real fear that had been building across the land, from the seas and forests to the high mountains, could be set aside as there was absolutely nothing more that could be done. The priests had made their preparations and every individual and every family had whispered their fervent prayers to one shrine or another. Offerings had been made and the women and children were all confined to their houses until the morning. Now they could only wait and hope.

Crocodile shuffled forwards with his father, surrounded by a battalion of Eagle Knights, many of whom, like Crocodile, had never visited the palace before. Jaguar Knights were all around them too, pressing forwards and trying to muscle past everyone but nobility. The Eagle Knights and Jaguar Knights wore their battle tunics and best skirts, but the fearsome headgear of beaked eagle and toothed jaguar were not in evidence. Two Sign had explained earlier that they had been ordered not to bring headgear as this would spoil the view of the tlatoani.

The river of people narrowed to fit ten-abreast through the massive entranceway to the reception hall, the largest of the rooms encircling the tlatoani's throne-room. Everyone was talking excitedly while at the same time trying unsuccessfully to keep their voices down and as the multitude crammed through the high-ceilinged room, the growling susurration reverberated off the great walls. Crocodile had never seen his adoptive father looking so contented. He had a beatific smile stretched across his wide jaw and his eyes were half shut. It occurred to Crocodile that, in the midst of his troops, with the threat of death only hours away, Two Sign was in his element.

The palace was every bit as impressive inside as Crocodile had heard tell. The stone walls had been built by master craftsmen to a level of smooth, symmetrical perfection he had never seen before. Here and there, the wall was set with enormous blocks, six feet square, as though the builders had grown impatient with the lethargic pace imposed by working with the smaller stones. Set into the walls on both sides, at regular intervals, were rows of intricately carved wooden hooks from which hung magnificent gowns and cloaks, presented to Moctezuma by visiting dignitaries. Most were decorated with feathers from the blue mockingbird, or the characteristic red and blue of the macaw, but above the entrance to the main palace hall, folded carefully around a woven willow structure, hung the most sacred item: Quetzalcoatl's shimmering green cloak. Supposedly left behind by the god when he took to the seas, heading east, this fantastic garment was given pride of place in expectation of his return. The base was woven from the finest Cuernavaca cotton into which a rich layer of the extravagantly iridescent green Quetzal feathers was sown. Epaulettes of crimson feathers sprouted extravagantly at the shoulders and the edges of the ensemble were embroidered with gold thread. Even in the half-light of the torches it was radiant, as though suffused with immortal powers.

Either side of Quetzalcoatl's cloak were carved representations of the Feathered Serpent himself. On the left he was depicted forcing back a prisoner's head to catch his blood in a bowl, while the tablet on the right showed him setting out into the sea on a raft made of reeds. The 'bearded one' seemed to stand out from the wall as though he were watching over the assembled throng. Crocodile realised his mouth had been hanging open as he gazed at the images and snapped it shut, hoping that no one had seen him.

The crowd passed through another wide doorway topped with a lintel that looked as though it was made of solid gold and on the other side, everyone fanned out into the vast throne-room beyond. Grey Privy Knights lined the walls of Moctezuma's seat of power. Here, the enormous expanse of ceiling was supported around the edges by regular, trapezoid buttresses of stone that widened as they spread up to meet massive mahogany beams. At the far end of the hall, a large, raised dais supported the icpalli, the tlatoani's wooden throne and six more modest seats positioned around it, none of which would raise their occupant more than a token amount above the floor. Here, the tlatoani ruled supreme.

'Where is your friend?' Two Sign asked over the general hubbub.

'I'm not sure if he'll be here,' answered Crocodile.

'Try over there.' Two Sign pointed to the left-hand side of the throne room where the preponderance of people gathered had neither the finery of the nobility nor the combat costumes of the knights.

'Thanks, father,' said Crocodile and set off through the crowd, ducking and elbowing murderous looking warriors aside as gently as possible. He sustained a sharp punch in the ribs on the way for stepping on someone's foot, but eventually caught sight of Jaguar and clasped his hand firmly.

'You made it then!' said Crocodile.

'Yes. Apparently my father's seat on the Tlatocan entitles me to a place.'

'Mind if I join you?' Crocodile waved over Jaguar's shoulder at Blade of the South, who was deep in conversation with Magic River. He was pleased to have found Jaguar. His father's friends were all warriors, Eagle Knights and some Jaguar Knights and, although Two Sign was well respected among the nobility, Crocodile didn't consider any of them to be friends. Growing up with Two Sign in the barracks, he got on well with the older warriors but found that they had a relentless intensity to everything that they did, which became tiring after a while. Whether it was training or relaxing at the end of the day, they fought, wrestled, repaired weapons, they argued, and played games and practical jokes on each other without letup so that eventually, Crocodile had to escape to a more relaxed environment.

Crocodile envied Jaguar his easy family life. The two exchanged a few pleasantries as the room filled up, people jostling for the remaining spaces.

'How is that lovely fox of yours, Precious Flower?' Crocodile asked his friend with a knowing wink. To his surprise, Jaguar coloured visibly and turned away, hiding his face. He tried to make it look as if he was searching for someone in the crowd but it was obvious to Crocodile that he had unearthed something very interesting. His suspicion grew when, expecting a jovial retort or an abusive response, all Jaguar managed was a feeble reply that he had not seen Precious Flower recently. Crocodile was in no mood to let his friend off the hook without a fight.

'What do mean you haven't seen her lately, you idiot?' derided Crocodile. 'You live in the same house, don't you?'

'Be quiet,' hissed Jaguar vehemently and grabbed hold of Crocodile's upper arm tightly, as if to drive the message home with his finger nails.

'Ow!' exclaimed Crocodile, trying to bat his friend away.

'Please leave it... please!' begged Jaguar, barely audible, adding, 'Look, I'll tell you later, I promise.'

'Alright, alright, Jaguar! By the cursed Skin of Xipe Totec, let go!'

Crocodile rubbed his arm. Although taken aback by Jaguar's outburst, Crocodile could hardly contain a broad grin. Jaguar must finally have seen sense and done something about Precious Flower. The girl adored him. Why was he the only person who couldn't see it?

At last, the palace attendants were able to close the great doors to the throne room. As one, the multitude sat down upon the floor and then, gradually, the din of excited conversation subsided. Taking their cue, a group of musicians on the right-hand side of the royal platform struck up a triumphant tempo on a selection of instruments. Two of the musicians beat out a jaunty marching pace on a pair of huehuetls. Shaped at the base to form three legs, these hollowed out logs with snakeskin covering made a cavernous booming sound that reverberated powerfully through the hall. Gradually, the urgent rhythm of numerous teponaztli, small wooden gongs, could be heard, their volume rising like ambush warriors from a misty forest floor. This overlay rose to a crescendo then faded away to murmur over several cycles, conjuring to mind the ebb and flow of battle. The imagery of war was reinforced when the single, mournful, rallying note of a conch shell rose querulously above the clamour.

While the music played, Crocodile scanned the assembled audience. Two rows forward sat the solid frame of Magic River, the back of his head just as scarred and misshapen as the front. Next to him was Jaguar's father, Blade of the South. Nearer the centre, where Crocodile could have been seated with his father was a phalanx of Eagle Knights.

Crocodile nudged Jaguar and drew his attention to the two famous knights. Worried that he had upset his friend, Crocodile was keen to make some conciliatory overtures.

'Look over there!' Crocodile whispered heavily.

Jaguar craned his neck to see around the person in front. 'Where? The light's not great in here without torchlight.'

'The big men next to my father.'

'I see them,' replied Jaguar. If he was still angry with his friend, Jaguar showed no sign of it. In fact, he looked relaxed and pleased to be at the festivities.

'My father says there's been a big recall from the outlands. Lots of warriors are being brought back for this fight with Chalco.'

Jaguar nodded.

'Well,' continued Crocodile in a low voice. He needn't have worried. The noise level in the room meant it was impossible to hear anyone more than a couple of paces away. 'The one over there with the strap round his head is Rock, a captain in the Eagle Knights, and the one next to him with no hair at all is Wind of Death. I told you about him, remember? He's the crazy one who reckons he's the reincarnation of the legendary warrior Smoking Mountain?' Living in military accommodation with his father, Crocodile heard a lot of stories about warriors and details of campaigns in the furthest reaches of the empire and he regaled Jaguar with these tales of extraordinary adventures, feats of bravery and interesting exotica from distant lands. In return, Crocodile received updates from Jaguar on local intrigue, political wrangling and administrative hiccups that he gleaned from his father's contacts in the Calpullicalli.

'Which ones?' said Jaguar, straining to see over the crowd.

'Over there,' said Crocodile, pointing through the crowd. Rock was a captain in the Eagle Knights, who spent most of his time touring the trouble spots on the border. He was an immense man, at least a head taller than the next tallest warrior in Tenochtitlan, and possessed of incredible strength. Rock's only weapon in battle was a solid oak club, conspicuous for its total lack of blades, with which – it was said – he dashed his enemies aside like so many dried maize stalks.

Crocodile turned to Jaguar with serious expression. 'One day, everyone will know my name.'

'You're almost there already,' observed Jaguar with a wry smile. 'The talk is already all over the city about "the youngest warrior ever to reach the required number of captives".'

Crocodile made a glum look. 'It's about time I achieved some notoriety. I've been feeling overshadowed by the wizard of ullamalitzli!'

The bass drum beat ceased abruptly as the music changed to a delicate, tripping cadence played out on turtle shell drums and cleverly embellished by the trilling of three flautists on pan-pipes. This change announced the arrival of Tenochtitlan's royal family. The majority of the pipiltin were already assembled, but now, the highest of the high-born and Moctezuma's immediate family filed in to take up positions in the innermost semi-circle closest to the raised dais. There must have been sixty members of the royal family present, even without the women and all were dressed in sumptuous, coloured robes and feathers, decorated with strong patterns and animal motifs. Every single one was draped in exquisite jewellery of cast copper, gold, amethyst and jade, some of which Crocodile suspected was the work of Jaguar's family.

Only now were the members of the High Council allowed to step forward and take their places by the throne. Acamapichtli was there and the diminutive Zipactonal strutted up to his seat. Tlacaelel emerged from the far corner of the room to take his place. His outfit was exceedingly simple so that anyone who did not know who he was would have mistaken him for a low-ranking warrior. He wore a single, plain white mantle over his loin cloth and carried a distinctly un-ceremonial sword at his waist. Like all the warriors, he too was barefoot although his rank and his position as the tlatoani's brother would certainly have permitted him to wear sandals in the ruler's presence. Cloud Face was absent, leaving Crocodile to suspect he would make his entrance later. Next the members of the Council of Twelve stepped forward and Blade of the South had to go and take his place next to the dais.

The music stopped and the whole room fell utterly silent. There followed an interval of several minutes before Moctezuma Ilhuicamina, tlatoani of Tenochtitlan, finally stepped through the curtain behind the dais. He was resplendent in the traditional headdress of black and iridescent green Quetzal feathers. His tunic was made from a single jaguar's pelt, beautifully tailored to enhance the ruler's athletic physique, with the big cat's tail hanging naturally at his back. Strapped to his belt was a ceremonial sword whose handle and shaft were swathed in gold braid. Instead of the irregularly shaped black obsidian that usually served as blades, cutting edges of this sword were perfectly symmetrical squares carved from the most exquisite jade. It looked magnificent, but wouldn't be any use in a fight. Jade was too soft and lost its cutting edge too quickly, whereas the black, volcanic glass often sheared off so to leave an edge even more hideous than the one that had broken off.

Moctezuma paused for effect at the front of the raised platform and looked out at his audience. Everyone looked at the floor, it being forbidden to stare directly at the tlatoani. It seemed to Crocodile as though everyone was holding their breath too.

'Greetings to you, my brave people!' Moctezuma's voice rang out across the great hall.

'Hail, tlatoani!' rang back a thousand voices in perfect unison.

Moctezuma strode to the edge of the dais and put his hands on his hips, projecting his voice across the sea of heads.

'Our fathers and our fathers' fathers built this city from nothing! Once there was but a snake infested island. Now, there is Tenochtitlan, the biggest, brightest city in the world!' He raised his voice and shouted the last words so that they reverberated around the pillars and seemed to shake the ceiling. Moctezuma smiled and raised his arms to shoulder height, palms up.

It was difficult to watch the tlatoani whilst avoiding eye contact. Crocodile could see that Jaguar's head was facing the floor in-front and to the left, which allowed him to glance out of the corner of his eyes. Moctezuma paced slowly to the other end of the raised platform, holding his upturned palms steady.

'When our people first came to the valley, we were the weak ones. Now we are strong!' Moctezuma paused. 'We have many enemies, but we will prevail. We will sweep across this land, from the beaches to the mountains. From Tlaxcala to Oaxaca, the people will know the Mexica and shall bow down before us!' Slowly, the broad grin on Moctezuma's handsome features sagged. He lowered his arms and his expression became stern.

'I know that many of you and your families are worried about tonight. The great cycle of the years is done. Fifty-two years have passed and once more, our priests must bind the years so that the cycle may recommence. One Rabbit ends and so we seek the return of Two Reed.' Moctezuma nodded, acknowledging his people's concerns. 'I know also that we have suffered. For four long years we have seen little rain. The crops wither and die and animals turn to bones before our very eyes.'

At last, there was a smattering of murmurs around the room and the tlatoani nodded again. He raised an arm and pointed out into the crowd. Again, he raised his voice.

'Know this, my brave people,' said Moctezuma. 'Know this! Through the efforts of our warriors, most of you here tonight, we have amassed over six hundred people to offer up at tonight's ceremony. With this tribute we will appease the wrath of Huitzilopochtli and Tlaloc. Prayers and offerings will be made to Xipe Totec, he of the Flayed Flesh and to Mictlantecuhtli, the Lord of the Dead. Tonight, every god will receive special tribute.'

Crocodile covertly watched as the tlatoani moved back to the centre of the stage as he brought his outstretched hand to his face and clenched it into a fist. His deep voice boomed out again more stridently. 'More than this though, you know that tonight we have a special sacrifice! Tonight, our priests will take Sacred Stone to

Colhuacan and there, our high priest, Mixayacatl, will light the New Fire. I call upon Sacred Stone!'

There was a roar of approval from the assembled crowd and then from under his eyebrows, Crocodile saw the tlatoani sit down on his throne. As the great hall fell silent again, the massive teak doors at the main entrance swung open once more. Everyone turned to watch as a dozen priests in black robes filed in two-abreast, each carrying a flaming torch. They threaded their way towards the throne, the serried ranks of warriors parting gingerly on either side to give them room. Behind the priests swaggered a young man decked out in a lavish costume of red and yellow feathers over a tunic and breechcloth of shimmering gold and then, bringing up the rear was the high priest of Huitzilopochtli dressed in a dalmatic of dark, blood red.

Crocodile recognised the young man as Sacred Stone, selected one year ago from a group of seventeen high born children whose families had put forward a bearer for the New Fire. Sacred Stone was fourteen and had led a privileged life. His family were of the purest Mexica nobility, who could trace their lineage back to the original exiles from Aztlan. The family had been thrilled when their son, the youngest of five, had been chosen as the carrier for the eternal flame and for the last year, while Sacred Stone had been fed and clothed at the expense of the tlatoani, living in a section of the palace specially set aside for him and attending all the state's most important functions, his mother and father, uncles and aunts had been invited to one party after another, fêted as though they too were deities. Sacred Stone was the living emblem of the Sun God and it was his final duty tonight as the vessel of the New Fire that would release him from his worldly duties.

Crocodile got a good glance of the youth as he lumbered past, smiling benignly at the throng on either side. The lad was rotund as the result of gorging himself on the richest foods all year. His neck had disappeared under two or three bulbous chins. His long, dark hair was tied back tightly giving him a slightly squinty look. Over his rounded cheeks, his dark, liquid eyes had a glazed expression.

The priests took their places on either side of the dais while Sacred Stone waddled up the few steps to the platform with Cloud

Face stalking smoothly behind him, his head gleaming in the light from the high windows. They took their places on the remaining seats and finally the banquet was underway.

Crocodile and Jaguar salivated as an army of palace servants made their way between the seated ranks, placing a sumptuous selection of food in large earthenware bowls on the floor at regular intervals. Much of what was on offer was unavailable to the common citizens of Tenochtitlan, even in times of plenty. Almost all of the dishes were completely alien to the two young warriors.

'What's this?' Crocodile asked his friend, prodding at a salty tasting portion of fish in his bowl.

'Is it from the sea?' asked Jaguar with a puzzled expression.

'But that's several days from here!' exclaimed Crocodile between mouthfuls. 'Why hasn't it gone bad?'

Jaguar shrugged his shoulders. 'When the tlatoani demands fresh fish from the sea,' he said, 'fresh fish from the sea is what he gets.'

Crocodile took a mouthful of a delicious fruit juice cocktail, trying to determine the ingredients. It had an orange hue and smooth texture that suggested papaya, but a predominantly cool, sweet tang that could only have come from pineapples, also brought in from the tropical coast.

'Wow, this is great!' enthused Jaguar, feasting noisily on his bowl, which was laden to capacity with pickings from every dish within reach. It was heaped with tomatoes, tamales and tortillas crammed with succulent dog meat, peppers and chillies.

Crocodile's eyes bulged and he stared in astonishment as he caught sight of Moctezuma, hand-feeding Sacred Stone. 'By the Sacred Skin, will you look at that!' he exclaimed through a mouthful of peppers. 'The boy's a hero even though he barely knows which end to shit through!'

As the banquet progressed, a succession of courses was offered around, culminating, to everyone's delight, with drinks of hot chocolate that Crocodile had never tasted before. He clasped the mug in both hands and savoured the heady aroma. The raucous sounds of the festivities floated away so that they became a distant murmur. The musicians had started up again and Crocodile tuned into the haunting tune. He took a sip of the rich cocoa and rolled it slowly around his mouth wondering when he would next get the chance to drink something as good as this.

The man on the pan pipes held a pure, single note that lingered in the air like a sad memory, a slow drum marked out the passing of time accentuated by the fading light outside. It was getting quite dark inside the palace now without flames or torches of any kind to light it. There was a sudden cacophonic flourish that set Crocodile in mind of the last frenetic moments of battle. Unbidden, Archer Eagle's ghastly death surfaced and Crocodile squeezed his eyes shut for a moment, as though trying to banish the gruesome image.

'Hey!' Jaguar prodded Crocodile. 'Is that a tear in your eye?'

'No!' said Crocodile scornfully and turned away, as though looking for somewhere to put his mug down.

'Funny,' said Jaguar. 'You know, for a moment, I could have sworn you were daydreaming about something.'

Crocodile wiped his mouth and managed to dash the tear from his cheek in the same instant. In a serious voice he added, 'Well, perhaps I was just savouring the moment. We may not have long after all...'

Jaguar gave his friend an odd look, but before he could say anything, the music changed again. This time the instruments were joined by voices as the musicians sang the ballad of Huitzilopochtli, the tale of his famous battle with his sister's army. A baritone voice resonated across the hall like a volcanic eruption of honey.

> Running, slashing, blood abounding,
> Arrows high and shields clashing,
> The falling autumn whirl of leaves.
>
> All the elemental fires screaming,
> As powerless, fleshy mortals flee,
> Darkness come and gather me.

Suddenly everyone was quiet, listening to the ancient song. The singers paused and then rejoined the music, their voices wavering and then rising to the final crescendo. The hair on the nape of Crocodile's neck stood on end.

> Fire serpent breathes a golden flash,
> Leaves a burning, smoking pall,
> The sacred weapon conquers all.

'Hey, Jaguar.' Crocodile thumped his friend's shoulder, trying to lighten the mood. 'That's what we need!'

'Eh?'

'What do you think happened to the Fire Serpent?' insisted Crocodile.

Jaguar gave Crocodile an exasperated look. 'Do you suppose you could handle a weapon that spews lava?'

'Of course I could,' said Crocodile, offended.

'There's a good chance that you'd incinerate your own friends.'

'Ridiculous,' scoffed Crocodile with a good natured scowl.

As the song drew to a triumphal close, everyone rose to their feet and began cheering. Nobles, warriors and even some of the priests clapped and stamped their feet in a roar of approval.

Moctezuma stood up to quieten the guests. He raised his arms in a placatory gesture and waited for the din to subside.

'Good people of Tenochtitlan,' the tlatoani called out in a voice that was crisp and clear. 'I trust you have enjoyed the entertainment tonight!' There was a roar of assent. 'As you know, the main event of the night takes place in just a few hours. I deliver you into the hands of our high priest of Huitzilopochtli, Mixayacatl!' He pointed at Cloud Face who rose to make the closing speech.

Again the main hall fell utterly silent. Behind Cloud Face, Tlacaelel looked unimpressed.

'Times have been hard for our people in the last four years,' said the high priest quietly. He reached up to run a hand over the birthmark on his forehead and over the back of his head. 'Tlaloc has withheld the rains causing droughts drying up the land around us. Frosts ravage maize crops when the summer sun should be warming the growing cobs.' He looked round the chamber at his audience, as though daring someone to disagree.

'For the third time since we founded our proud city, the New Fire is upon us.' His voice was stern and growing in strength. He gathered up the edge of his long cloak and moved to the front of the dais saying, 'In the last cycle the gods have delivered us from the service of the Tepanecs and given us glorious victories over distant peoples. They have shared immeasurable wealth with us for our raids to the south of Oaxaca.'

Cloud Face raised his voice again, screwing up his face and pointing into the crowd gathered before him. First he pointed his finger at the warriors, then the clansmen to the right. Then, his arm made a grand, accusatory sweep that took in the nobility. 'How do we repay them? I'll tell you how we repay them!' This cry was met with an embarrassed silence.

'*We repay them with nothing!*' roared the high priest shaking his fist.

'If you are in any doubt,' he continued, now low and menacing. 'If you are in any doubt as to why we have not been able to bring the rains, look to the sacrifice.'

Crocodile had no reason to feel ashamed. His recent success in the ravine to the east of Texcoco should have been proof of his own contributions to the priests and yet somehow he felt to blame. He did not have to look around him to see that no one was holding their head high.

'Our tributes have been pitiful,' continued Cloud Face. 'Every year the gods give us great treasures and we repay just a fraction of their dues.'

Crocodile noticed Tlacaelel suddenly sweeping from the room. There was no mistaking the contempt in his face as he ducked behind the curtain behind the dais. Sitting on his throne, the tlatoani remained impassive, but a few sharp intakes of breath around the room alerted Cloud Face to the effrontery of Moctezuma's brother.

'I have done all I can for you,' said Cloud Face through gritted teeth. 'Tonight, the grand cycle comes to an end.' Here he bade Sacred Stone stand up. 'What is your name, son?' said Cloud Face to the boy.

'I am Huitzilopochtli,' Sacred Stone chanted the sacred response in monotone.

'What is your purpose?' asked the high priest.

'I am the sun. I am the fire. I am the life, the light in the new world and I am the warmth in your blood.'

'What is our purpose?'

'You must live and see the light. You must pay tribute to keep my path true in the sky. You must breathe and you must die,' intoned the boy.

'Sacrifice shall be made once more,' cried Cloud Face, 'both here and at the altar on Colhuacan.' He pointed around the room again. 'If we are successful lighting the New Fire tonight, and I pray we are, it will be your turn to show your devotion to the gods!'

Crocodile felt chastened. Tenochtitlan was his home and these were his people, had been since his own family were taken from him. The life he had and everything he knew were thanks to Two Sign and the Eagle Knights, who had rescued him as a boy, and now he understood the love of a people who looked after their own.

'*Tomorrow,*' Cloud Face shouted, '*we need to begin again and usher in a new age, a new age in which we pay the debts we owe!*' As one, everyone in the hall got to their feet and roared their tumultuous assent, whistling, clapping and stamping their feet. The deafening noise reverberated for a long while and hardened warriors wept like children. Crocodile felt tears spring to his eyes and wiped his cheek again, glad of the encroaching darkness. The old man gave the smallest of bows, just a hint of a nod, indicating that he was done.

Moctezuma advanced to the front of the platform and put his hand on the high priest's shoulder. He smiled tightly at Cloud Face and embraced him. They exchanged a few words and then Cloud Face escorted Sacred Stone down the steps where they were joined by the remainder of the priestly retinue. It was so dark now that Crocodile struggled to see Sacred Stone waving at the people on either side as he made his way out, smiling like an idiot.

Chapter 7 - Mazâtl

Jaguar and Crocodile emerged from the palace at the faltering trip-step allowed by the crush of people. Twilight cloaked the city and the lack of torches accentuated the deep shadow that sucked hungrily at the city streets. In spite of this, their spell inside the palace without illumination had prepared them and their eyes were already adjusted to the gloom. Overhead, the clouds had an ethereal, luminous quality thanks to the invisible moon hovering above Xochimilco. Jaguar caught himself glancing to the south, looking for the spark of light on the hilltop, but of course the ceremony would not take place until midnight.

A few of the warriors who had families dispersed, heading home to spend these crucial hours with their loved ones, but most of the men made their way to the square at the foot of the Great Temple where they would wait for the ceremony to begin.

'Are you going back to your family?' Crocodile asked his friend.

'They said I could stay out,' said Jaguar. 'My father's going to be there. Arrow One is there too so they'll be fine.'

'Great!'

'Let's go then,' said Jaguar moving to follow the rest of the crowd.

'I've got a better idea, Jaguar,' said Crocodile.

'Oh yes?'

'Follow me.'

'Where are we going then?' asked Jaguar, nonplussed.

'Temple of Tezcatlipoca,' replied Crocodile with a mischievous smile, taking care that there was no one to overhear his suggestion.

'*What?*' Jaguar was astonished. 'We can't go up a temple when there's a ceremony on! Anyway, they won't let anyone just wander around the temple precinct.'

'It'll be fine.' Crocodile shucked his shoulders. 'You'll see. Tezcatlipoca plays no part in the proceedings tonight. You really don't remember your basic religion, do you?'

Jaguar ignored the mocking tone. 'This is a bad idea. What if someone sees us?' His friend ignored him and headed off, past the House of Songs, heading for the south-east corner of the temple complex.

The feeble light that seeped through the clouds was just enough to make out the stucco covered wall that formed the perimeter of the temple complex. Built during the reign of Huitzilihuitl and added to by Chimalpopoca, the Serpent Wall was fifteen feet tall and formed an imposing barrier around the temple complex. Just above head height, the wall was inlaid with ornate friezes along its entire length. Each frieze consisted of a panel ten feet long and two feet high into which a scene was cut in sharp relief. There was too little light to make out the details but Jaguar had passed them a thousand times. Pastoral scenes lay alongside classical feats enacted by the gods. He and Crocodile passed a series of panels that depicted forest animals and birds. The next set showed the twelve levels of the universe, from the underworld to the earth, and through the various strata inhabited by the gods. One panel showed mayeques bringing in the harvest while in the next, a snake-like beast with wings and talons devoured impenitent children by the dozen. The stark shadow below the jutting figures made the silver-grey protrusions bulge from the wall as though they were trying to wrestle free from their silicate prisons.

After a little while Crocodile stopped where a bridge crossed a tiny rill that ran out from a culvert under the Serpent Wall. It was little more than a stagnant drainage channel.

'Look,' said Crocodile, obviously pleased with himself. So saying, he jumped down into the bottom of the ditch and ducked under the bridge. Jaguar checked to make sure no one was around before following. Night soaked into the bottom of the culvert but Jaguar smelled damp slime and rotting vegetable matter and something much, much worse of animal origin and when he jumped in after his friend he felt it ooze out between his toes, cold and gelatinous. He gagged and wished he could see it, then immediately changed his mind.

'I think you've found the entrance to the temple of Tlazolteotl,' hissed Jaguar.

'The goddess of excrement,' chuckled Crocodile from the darkness ahead. 'Lovely! Thanks for that image. Mind your head here,' he added. 'This section is really low. We'll have to kneel down for about eight feet.'

The culvert narrowed as Crocodile had predicted. There was a curious velvety quality to the darkness here. It lay thick and heavy as though its density had caused it to puddle in the bottom of this hole. Jaguar cracked his head on the ceiling in spite of the warning, cursing a dozen gods in turn in the bitterest language he could muster. This was turning out to be one of Crocodile's worst ideas and there was no shortage of competition either, like the time he suggested they vault the enormous chinampa at the north end of Atzacualco using a wooden pole. Crocodile had explained that by charging the canal and planting the pole halfway across, they could carry the twenty foot gap. That had been his theory anyway. Jaguar's pole had sunk so deep into the sediment that he'd pitched head first into the water while Crocodile's had at least hit something firmer before promptly snapping in two with a loud retort. Crocodile had gashed his leg on the splintered remnants of a stick jutting out of the canal.

Jaguar crawled on his hands and knees trying not to breathe for the distance that the drain ran underneath the Serpent Wall. He was glad when they emerged on the far side just at the rear of the temple of Tezcatlipoca. The friends wiped their hands on the masonry first to get rid of the worst of the effluent before resorting to their tunics to clean off the remainder.

Jaguar looked up at the temple at the faint black-on-black silhouette of the ziggurat against the night sky. This temple was not as large as the great edifice at the centre of the complex but it was an imposing structure nonetheless. Tezcatlipoca was Smoking

Mirror, the Lord of the Night Sky. It struck Jaguar as an appropriate place to spend the evening.

'Come on,' called Crocodile, who was off again, scaling the stepped rear slope. Jaguar scrambled up behind Crocodile. They both paused briefly at each of the three wider ledges and listened for voices above or priests on the ground below who might spot the stealthy shadows and raise the alarm.

'We'll be in serious trouble if we're caught,' breathed Jaguar.

'It's the end of the world!' said Crocodile. 'Is anyone going to care if they see us?'

They reached the penultimate step and peered over the edge of the platform. It was, as Crocodile had predicted, deserted.

'We can't stay here once the fire is returned to the city.' Jaguar pointed out the figures below them scurrying through the South Gate, assembling in the temple precinct for the final moments of the fifty-two year cycle. The two would be in full view of anyone from the ground once the temple fires were re-lit, even if they were not discovered by the temple acolytes.

'That's why we're going up higher,' said Crocodile staring up at the temple roof, another thirty feet above them. He was looking for a suitable route to the top where they would have an unobstructed view of the proceedings in the Great Temple itself. 'Look, we can climb up one of the corner statues, and from there the rest is easy!'

There were carvings around the door of the shrine and then a little over head height, the wall was embossed with a rectilinear arrangement of blocks that looked like useful handholds. Within a matter of moments the two friends were crouched on the flat, stone paved roof of the temple, from which they would have had an unrivalled view of the surroundings if there had been any light to see by. Jaguar and Crocodile found they had some difficulty picking out the dull grey of the roof edge against the black backdrop, so they moved about with extreme caution.

'This is great!' admitted Jaguar finally. 'How did you get this idea?'

'You know all the building work that was done to enlarge the Great Temple?'

'Yes, of course.'

'Well, a couple of months ago, I was posted to guard duty in the Cuepopan district. It was an early shift and a group of workmen had stopped there to get breakfast on their way in.'

'There are some stalls close to that workshop that makes swords,' said Jaguar, who had hunkered down with his back to the low wall that formed a parapet around the top of the shrine. It wasn't much protection from the damp that was all around them, condensing out of the night air.

'Yes, that's the place. Anyway, I was close enough to overhear the workmen talking about the view from up on top of the temple. One of them said there was a clear view of Colhuacan,' Crocodile explained. 'Anyway, it wasn't until later when someone – I can't remember who – mentioned that they wanted to see the New Fire being lit that I remembered the temple.'

'What about the drain and Tezcatlipoca?' asked Jaguar. He could see the vague outline of his friend, who was clearing an area of the roof to lie on.

'Archer Eagle,' muttered Crocodile. He put his hands behind his head and gazed up at the mottled, louring underbelly of the clouds. 'We were talking about it the day he died. I said it was a shame there was no way into the temple grounds because this would make a good viewing platform. That's when he mentioned the drain under the wall.' Crocodile's voice seemed to float, disembodied above the small roof.

Jaguar could barely see his friend. The night folded round them, swaddling them in a cloak of midnight, shot through with strands of silver. He wondered what Archer Eagle had been up to when he found the route into the sacred enclosure.

Down in the temple precinct, the murmur of the crowds faded, an unseen cue indicating the proximity of the appointed time. It was impossible to make out the volcanic cone of Colhuacan in the pitch blackness but Jaguar strained his eyes, trying in vain to pick out the hump at the end of the peninsula between Lake Texcoco and Lake Xochimilco. On the rooftops of houses around the city, Jaguar could just distinguish the faint outlines of people who had found less advantageous view points to watch for the first flames.

The small temple at the summit of Colhuacan radiated a ghostly light from its simple, whitewashed stonework, echoing what little mournful moonlight permeated the clouds above. The polished stone floor was evidence of the popularity of this pantheistic place of worship. Last renovated in the time of Chimalpopoca, it was a simple affair rising only one step up from the apex of the hill with a single pristine shrine set slightly back from the centre. An unpretentious altar brooded silently at the front.

Cloud Face waited, as motionless as the sinister trees that crowded in around the little temple. All the preparations for the ceremony were done, completed by his assistants hours ago before the last of the daylight faded. *Last of the daylight*; that phrase set a chill in the old priest's bones and added another knot to his twisted bowels.

He could hear Snake Eyes and Devine Cactus whispering inside the building as they tried to soothe Sacred Stone. It irked the high priest to acknowledge that Feathered Darkness had been right. They should have drugged him more. The Chosen One had been calm all the way to Colhuacan, but as soon as he stepped down from his litter, the fat fool had suddenly got the terrors. They always did. Whether they lived as Sacrifice for a week or a year, whether high born Mexica or captured enemy, they all succumbed at some point or another. This idiot was as bad as any of them that Cloud Face could recall. Sacred Stone's sturdy looking legs had proved anything but, buckling under him so that he collapsed to the ground, keening like a speared coyote. Devine Cactus and Snake Eyes had been forced to manhandle him to his feet and drag him towards the privacy of the chancel to administer one of Snake Eyes' poisonous little concoctions, but only after Cloud Face had made it abundantly clear that if he got the dose wrong and the Chosen One died, Snake Eyes would be forced to take his place.

At last the whimpering subsided and the now docile boy was led up to the altar. Cactus and Snake Eyes still had a firm grip under each of his arms. He was moving but he looked half dead with his head lolling on that impossibly fleshy neck of his.

Cloud Face cursed under his breath, disappointed by the scent of shit. Sacred Stone had soiled himself. Why could the Sacrifice never conduct himself with decorum? They never grasped the magnitude of the honour bestowed upon them. Cloud Face tried to suppress his contempt and conjure up a feeling of wellbeing. This was a crucial moment and he was determined not to poison it with negative feelings.

Fifty-two lucky men stood faceless in the darkness around the temple, one for each year since the last time. Thirteen priests, thirteen warriors, thirteen noblemen and thirteen commoners had all been selected by lottery to witness the glorious rebirth of the world. Even Moctezuma was not present. The tlatoani would observe the ensuing ceremony at the Great Temple and the celebrations afterwards.

The last moments of the year One Rabbit flowed by like thickening treacle. Three more priests attended the altar upon which Sacred Stone had now been placed. Only an occasional snuffle indicated that the boy was still alive. At least he was not struggling. That, reflected Cloud Face, would have made the procedure very difficult.

The three priests stepped up to the altar and helped to pin Sacred Stone down while Devine Cactus looked up to check the stars. There were none in evidence; all cloaked behind a stifling blanket of cloud that threatened to choke the world of life. Relying on some other cue known only to himself, he gave the word and picked up the fire drill, handing it to Cloud Face before returning to hold Sacred Stone's head steady in a bear-like grip.

Cloud Face stepped forward and placed the wooden fireboard on the Chosen One's chest. His throat was dry and he wanted to pee, badly. Instead he felt for the hole in the fireboard and inserted the rounded end of the drill, a smooth and perfectly straight wooden stick, into it. Gripping the drill tightly between his palms, he started rubbing his hands together and began a low chant.

'I summon the Fire,
The Fire is there.
I call on the Gods
To heed my prayer.
I pull on the years
And join them here.'

Sacred Stone's chest was moving up and down rhythmically but Cloud Face was pleased to see that all the practice had paid off and he was compensating effortlessly. The stick whirred in his hands and seconds later he caught the scent of charring wood. The boy twisted. Even with the five priests holding him down, he shifted enough to dislodge the drill from the fireboard. Cloud Face snarled at his assistants who were hunched in charcoal obscurity over the victim and they redoubled their attempts to keep the Chosen One still. Cloud Face quickly replaced the singed plank and slotted the drill into the smoking hole once more, chanting the prayer again. Again he rubbed his palms together tightly, pulling down upon the rotating stick to increase the friction in the tiny notch. Devine Cactus, Snake Eyes and the other priests continued the low chant. Cloud Face was quickly out of breath and was forced to concentrate on the drill, repeatedly shifting his palms back up the stick as they slipped down.

The universe stood poised at the brink and Cloud Face got the feeling that everything had been leading up to this. Everyone on this hill had been drawn here by an irresistible force, condensing into this single hiatus, and if the process worked, they would all flow outward and move on again, restarted and reborn.

Once more, wisps of smoke rose from the tip of the drill and Cloud Face bent to the task with even more determination. The months of preparation would not be in vain. An infinitesimally small orange glow appeared amongst the smoking wood dust. Three more times, Cloud Face's hands rippled smoothly to the top of the drill and susurrated back and forth, the tiny glow pulsing slightly each time. Then with a cry, Cloud Face tossed the drill aside and smoothly pulled fine hay from a bag at his side. Carefully tipping the smouldering dust from the fireboard into the nest of dry kindling, he lifted it to his lips. Cradling the precious bundle between his hands he blew carefully between pursed lips and blew again, long and slow.

Devine Cactus let go of Sacred Stone's head and stepped forward with a life-size replica arm carved from wood, complete with an impossibly bowl-shaped hand. Cloud Face blew again and suddenly, flame erupted from between his steepled hands.

Instantly he dropped his flaming bundle into the wooden hand where the fire bloomed. After the bitter darkness of the last few hours, the light was shockingly bright and strangely alien. The priests' straining faces leered and loomed around the altar, made grotesque by the flickering light.

Now Cloud Face pulled the ceremonial knife from his belt and stepped up beside Sacred Stone again. The boy sensed that something had changed. Through the powerful elixir and his befuddled senses, he understood the threat. He raised his head but it was too late. The spiteful, jagged blade swept down with every sinew of the high priest's body straining behind it. There was no mistake. There was a whoosh of air, expelled unwillingly from the victim's body and a moist popping sound as his stomach opened to his breastbone.

Winded, Sacred Stone was unable to cry out for a moment as his chest spasmed to take in air. Cloud Face plunged his hands into the hot, wet wound and thrust the blade up under the boy's breastbone. The two priests holding Sacred Stone's arms reached forward on either side and gripped the lacerated flesh and held the wound apart. Working swiftly, Cloud Face carved shapely sickles around the palpitating core of the Chosen One.

Sacred Stone shuddered and jerked violently. Suddenly his lungs found air and the boy emitted a short, bubbling shriek.

Cloud Face pulled the knife out and thrust his forearm once more into the crimson carnage where he found the still-pulsating heart, loosened now and almost free. He grasped it firmly and ripped it back from under the ribs with such force that Sacred Stone's heavy body moved on the altar. Blood drops spattered and kissed the upturned faces of the priests like gentle rain as the high priest held the beating heart up high in one triumphant hand. Devine Cactus passed him the flaming receptacle that held the New Fire.

'Oh, Huitzilopochtli!' called Cloud Face. 'God of Fire and of the Sun, take this sacred flame and light the world once more.' With that, he plunged the burning hand on the end of the carved wooden arm into the Chosen One's chest.

The air was cold up on the temple roof but Jaguar and Crocodile were not aware of it. They strained their eyes looking south, hoping to see a spark, a flame, some sign that the ceremony had worked. Jaguar had never known time to move so slowly. Perhaps the priests had already failed and the Fifth World would never come to pass, the earth, instead, tearing itself apart and the fabric of the universe unravelling to the sound of a thousand violent thunderstorms. Jaguar thought of Precious Flower and remembered her gentle caress as the two lay on the canal bank, the feel of her soft skin under his hand and realised that he didn't want to lose her. His throat tightened and he squinted into the night.

The absence of sound from the city spread out below them was unnerving. It was as if the entire population was holding its breath. Moment upon moment passed with no sign of a pinpoint of yellow flame. Had they missed it?

'It hasn't worked!' hissed Crocodile.

Jaguar couldn't answer; unsure of what to say. The appointed time had arrived and passed now, but if it had worked, the fires should be visible by now. The two young men strained to hear sounds from the Great Temple that might explain the delay but there was nothing. Jaguar wanted to scream out loud to break the tension.

Then, just as they began to give up all hope; just as Jaguar was about to suggest they climb back down to the square to find out what had happened, a tiny light could suddenly be seen in the distance. A gigantic bonfire bloomed at the southern end of the lake. Streamers of incandescent, orange flame snaked up into the night. The year Two Reed was underway.

'Yes!' exclaimed Crocodile.

Jaguar could only clutch the edge of the chill stone parapet gazing in disbelief. All at once, the claustrophobia of the last few weeks lifted with the realisation that everyone was safe. He wanted to speak to Crocodile or cheer out loud but couldn't speak. His throat was tight with emotion. Instead he just reached out and patted his friend on the shoulder.

Crocodile rolled his eyes and breathed out a heavy sigh of relief as he lowered himself into a sitting position. 'Mictlan's balls!

I never want to live through anything like that ever again!' he exclaimed.

The crowds in the great courtyard erupted into cheers of delight as the result was made known to them by the priests from the platform of the Great Temple. Jaguar and Crocodile shuffled to the other side of the roof so that they could watch the proceedings, but found it was still too dark to see what was going on. Runners would eventually arrive from Colhuacan, bearing the New Fire for all the city's torches and fires. In the meantime they would all have to wait in darkness.

'You know, we should make an offering,' Jaguar said. 'A ceremony as important as this one demands a sacrifice from everyone.'

'Ah,' said Crocodile, patting the waistband of his loincloth in a futile gesture. 'I didn't bring anything sharp.'

'No. Neither did I.'

'Well that's that,' said Crocodile into the gloom. 'I wonder if the gods will notice. Have you given blood before?'

'Yes,' Jaguar replied.

'What did you do?'

Jaguar shuffled round on his knees until his was facing east. Perhaps re-enacting the offering would be enough to satisfy the deities. He reached up and pretended to slice a deep incision into his left earlobe, pinching it as if to provoke the flow of blood. Penumbrous rafts of militant clouds blotted out what little moonlight there had been so Jaguar wasn't sure if Crocodile could see what he was doing. Nevertheless, he continued, feeling oddly content that it was the right thing to do. He cupped his hand under the imaginary wound and even convinced himself that a warm puddle of blood was pooling there. Next he flung his arm out spattering the blood over the parapet. He heard a low chuckle beside him.

'Feeling better?' said Crocodile.

'Actually, yes.' Jaguar smiled as he settled back against the central stone block to wait for the torches in the temple precinct to be re-lit.

'Thanks,' said Crocodile after a while.

'What for?'

'For being a friend.'

It was too dark to see Crocodile's face but he sounded a little uncertain.

'I may not have brought a blade or needle to make sacrifice but I did bring something else.'

'What's that then?' asked Jaguar. He watched the shadow that was Crocodile reach under his cloak and remove something small which he placed on the floor between them. Jaguar was unable to make out what it was until the relentless march of clouds trailed a thin patch across the lambent moonlight. It was just enough for him to see small squares of cloth lying flat upon the stone. Lying upon an outer layer of maguey cloth and several layers of cotton lay two small nodules that, in the meagre light, could have been pebbles or fat caterpillars. He prodded one of them and found it to be firm but slightly yielding.

'Peyotl,' whispered Crocodile and grinned weakly.

Jaguar was shocked and intrigued in equal measure. 'So that's why you've been acting so strangely tonight.' He looked at the cactus root in amazement. 'Have you got any idea what will happen to us if we get caught with that?'

Crocodile nodded.

Use of peyotl was supposed to be strictly controlled. It was permitted to the priests in religious ceremonies and in a few medicinal cures, but Jaguar knew a number of people who had tried it. Of course there were wild tales of the experiences. Some spoke of inanimate objects coming alive, others talked of the world bending in on itself and demon-shaped dogs that devoured babies whilst explaining the true nature of the universe. Jaguar had been disinclined to take his peers too seriously on the matter.

'Where did you get it from?'

'One of the mayeque in Tlatocan sells it on the quiet,' replied Crocodile. 'Rat Face told me where to find him. Have you ever tried it?'

'No,' said Jaguar. 'What's it like?'

'I don't know,' admitted Crocodile sheepishly. 'Tonight should be a good time to find out though, especially as we've got this great hiding place.'

Jaguar frowned. 'I'm not so sure.' He glanced across at the Great Temple, suddenly remembering Precious Flower's tale that he'd been followed.

'Come on,' insisted Crocodile. 'No one can see us here.'

Crocodile handed one of the thumb sized lumps to Jaguar, who tried to examine it in more detail, turning it this way and that, but to no avail. No matter how hard he peered at it, he could see no more than a pale grey lump.

'What do we do with it?' he asked.

'You're supposed to eat it,' Crocodile answered, 'but you may want to just chew it for a while instead.' He popped the peyotl button he had reserved for himself into his mouth and began chewing, watching as Jaguar followed suit.

The disc shaped cactus top was exceedingly dry and slightly rubbery to begin with, causing Jaguar to grimace in disgust. The fibrous vegetable centre began to break up, mixing with Jaguar's saliva to give a dreadfully bitter taste that made his tongue feel furry. He endured it for as long as he could, but was forced to spit it out after a short while. Crocodile endured for longer but was forced to give up when he began to gag repeatedly.

'Ugh! I hope the effect is better than the taste,' Jaguar said. 'How long do we have to wait?' Before Crocodile had a chance to reply, Jaguar had a thought. 'I wonder if it's dangerous to do this up here?'

'What, you mean we might get dizzy and fall off?' said Crocodile.

'Uh, yeah.'

'I hadn't thought of that,' admitted Crocodile, scratching his head.

The two young men relapsed into silence again, backs to the stone parapet that edged the high platform. A time passed during which time they watched for evidence of the torch-bearers returning the New Fire to Tenochtitlan. Sure enough, after a while, it was possible to make out pinpoints of light, like flashing fireflies, bobbing and creeping their way along the southern causeway.

The noise from the temple precinct below began to build as relief washed over the crowds. They'd seen the flames as well.

Before long, the city would be alight with ten thousand torches and fires burning on street corners, all lit from the same single source. Jaguar could tell that the mood of the crowd was light. There was excited chatter and snatches of laughter floated up to where they were hiding. The good humour was infectious and soon, Jaguar was buoyed up with an intense feeling of well-being. There was no way to tell whether this was the result of the peyotl or the raw appreciation of the importance of the evening's events. Jaguar wasn't sure it mattered. The world was safe from destruction, at least for the time being.

'So what was it you were going to tell me about Precious Flower?' asked Crocodile in cautious tones.

Jaguar's stomach lurched. This time it definitely wasn't the acrid root that was to blame. He wondered if he could avoid the subject again but found instead that he needed to talk to someone.

'Crocodile,' Jaguar began.

'Yes, my friend?'

'I think she really likes me.' Even in the half-light, Jaguar could see Crocodile's expression of mock surprise.

'No! Are you sure?' said Crocodile, his voice heavy with irony.

The world lurched oddly and Jaguar struggled to make sense of what his friend had just said. Crocodile's supine body had swirled oddly and for a moment he appeared to be standing on his head. Jaguar shut his eyes tightly and then opened them again.

'Look, I know this is all very funny to you.' Jaguar was exasperated. 'Everyone seems to think that something's been going on between me and Precious Flower, but I promise you, she's never shown any interest in me until recently.'

'Don't be a fool,' said Crocodile quietly. 'If you take a long, hard look at all the times she's come looking for you or traipsed around after you, you might just change your mind about that.'

Jaguar felt a little odd, lightheaded. The sky looked a bit weird too, odd colours. Perhaps Crocodile was right. Precious Flower had always been close but there had been more physicality about their exchanges in the last year. Jaguar remembered her light touch on his arm. He recalled putting his arm around Precious Flower's slender waist at the Festival of Maize and her happy smile. All of it leading up to the conversation on the pier and then their embrace down by the chinampa. Jaguar told Crocodile how Precious Flower had come and retrieved him after the incident with the vultures and of the tryst in the meadow by the canal. There were a few details he could not bring himself to share with his friend but there was no need. Crocodile understood exactly what had transpired. He already had a large number of female admirers as befitted the most celebrated warrior of his age and Jaguar suspected that his friend had probably bedded more than one of them.

'Sorry, Crocodile,' said Jaguar.

'About what?'

'Back there in the palace,' explained Jaguar. 'I was just scared someone would overhear.'

'Ah,' said Crocodile.

'You remember that story about that fruit merchant from Atzacualco?' said Jaguar urgently. 'How he was found in bed with one of his slaves?'

'Yes, I do,' said Crocodile. The story had been the talk of Tenochtitlan the year before. The merchant had been forced to pay over half his family's wealth to the girl and the following day he had been led up to the Great Temple, naked but for a generous covering of turkey feathers stuck all over his body with pine resin. There, upon the temple, with the population of the city watching, he had been eviscerated and then beheaded.

'I don't want to die,' said Jaguar. 'I'm not as brave as you are.'

'She's a free woman now, isn't she?' said Crocodile. 'You'll be fine.'

Jaguar felt very strange now and his blood was cold as ice. He got to his knees and tried to rub some warmth into his arms. He looked back at Crocodile whose body had somehow merged with that of the slab roof on which he sat, as though the two had melted like hot beeswax and reformed as one. But it didn't stop there. The change was spreading even as Jaguar watched it. Like ripples on the surface of a pond, the melting process spread outwards from the centre of the roof. The stone parapet dissolved, puddling around Jaguar's feet, which in turn began to lose their shape.

'What makes you think I'm brave?' said a disembodied voice.

Jaguar recognised it as belonging to his friend. He smiled vacuously at the malleable shapes that swam and bulged around him. 'Come on, Crocodile. You're a legend already.' Jaguar realised for the first time that he was jealous. 'You're the youngest warrior ever to qualify for the knights!'

Crocodile made a noise that might have been dissatisfaction. They watched as torches and firebrands streamed around the temple complex in slow motion, like lava around a rocky outcrop. Gobs of it spat and lurched up the Great Temple steps until it reached the top where two huge stone urns had been prepared with piles of firewood. Soon, the temple precinct was awash with searing, coruscating light. Jaguar and Crocodile realised with alarm that someone had lit torches just below them on the top of the temple of Tezcatlipoca. They allowed their molten bodies to slump down onto the roof of the shrine that was like an oasis of cool shadow, an island in the fire.

The melting world and everything within it began to sublimate. Jaguar felt his individuality merging with a larger force. It was not a menacing phenomenon but benign and gentle, accepting all seemingly separate entities and showing them how they truly were, all interconnected, joined in one mysterious but undeniable singularity.

Somehow, Crocodile's hand materialised out of the morass and clapped Jaguar on the shoulder. 'I'm going to tell you something,' said his voice.

Jaguar tried to pinpoint Crocodile's face, but the sparks and flying embers that spiralled upwards on columns of searing flame caught his eye. They danced and swirled upwards into the dark night sky. Eventually two of the orange motes resolved themselves into reflections of the temple fires in Crocodile's dark eyes.

'I'm serious,' said Crocodile. 'Your secret is safe with me, and now in turn I'll share mine with you.'

Jaguar had no idea what his friend was on about. He had to concentrate hard to remember what they had been discussing.

'You have to promise not to tell anyone, yes?'

'I won't tell a soul,' swore Jaguar.

Crocodile had some difficulty continuing because he began to say something several times, each time getting no further than opening his mouth. At first, Jaguar thought the peyotl had turned his friend into a fish but gradually he realised that Crocodile was struggling to say the words.

'I'm afraid...' Crocodile finally managed. 'I'm afraid of death.'

'That's alright, we all are,' replied his friend, remembering the way his own stomach churned before battle.

'You don't understand, Jaguar!' Crocodile insisted, shaking Jaguar's shoulder as if to reinforce the point. 'I don't want to die like Archer Eagle did, but a death like his doesn't frighten me. At least he died in battle.' He gestured at the Great Temple and the preparations taking place there. 'That's what scares me,' he cried. 'Where's the glory in that? One in a long line of victims, held down by half a dozen stinking cowardly priests to be butchered without a hope of escape?'

Jaguar was shocked. Crocodile was the archetypal Mexica warrior, fierce and proud in battle and in captivity. That was what everyone believed. 'Crocodile, that is the way of our people!' Jaguar broke away from his friend, lucid and loquacious for a moment. 'It's through our efforts on the battlefield that we earn the patience of our gods. Without our struggles and our sacrifices the sun would cease to rise and the universe would tear itself apart!'

'I know all this,' Crocodile answered calmly, 'but I still don't want to die like that. If I die, let it be with an axe in my skull, fighting to the last, not whimpering and crying like a terrified child asking for its mother.'

'What about what Archer Eagle said?' asked Jaguar.

'Forget that shit!' spat Crocodile. 'He died a noble death back there in the pass. You reckon it would be any prettier getting sliced open on a slab?'

The peyotl was taking hold again. Now everything seemed to be made of rods of shimmering gold that speared skywards in perfect unison. Crocodile's head and shoulders skewered up and pierced the clouds while Jaguar stayed quite still.

Jaguar was running out of arguments. 'Warriors like you don't die anyway,' he said while his friend's face stretched away to infinity. Jaguar blinked to clear his vision but to no avail. 'You'll gain immortality, reincarnated as one of the warrior spirits, the butterflies of the north.'

'Have you seen what happens to the butterflies?' Crocodile asked. 'Every year they swarm here in their thousands and after a few weeks the streams and chinampa become clogged with their lifeless bodies.'

Jaguar gave up. He was finding it increasingly hard to think. His fingers looked like gigantic needles and even his mind spiked out into the surrounding city.

'Do you feel the peyotl yet?' Jaguar asked.

'Colours have gone strange but not much else has changed,' answered Crocodile.

'It's incredible!' cried Jaguar. 'The Great Temple over there is a fulcrum. I can see it, a huge spike reaching up to the heavens. The fabric of the cosmos tilts and sways upon it like a set of scales wherein our lives are weighed by the gods.'

'Ha-ha,' laughed Crocodile. 'You should hear yourself. You're just babbling now. You've never made much sense but this peyotl has turned you into a gibbering idiot.'

Jaguar was unfazed by his friend's insults. A sense of wellbeing and tolerance suffused him. Jaguar wished there were some way he could convey the experience to his friend but it was hopeless. How could Crocodile understand that Jaguar's soul had insinuated itself through every speck of every single person, stone and tree? He was an extension of the universe itself.

A low resonant beat of drums started up as the priests on the platform of the Great Temple completed their preparations for the remainder of the night's sacrifices. Once more the watching crowd stirred in nervous anticipation, although this time it was driven by a keen hunger, not the dread fear of the unknown. The world was saved and the Mexica would now demonstrate to the watching deities that they were worthy protectors of the Middle Kingdom. Soon the blood would flow, replenishing the empty coffers of debt owed to the gods and perhaps soon, the plight of the starving would be addressed.

'The view...' Crocodile never finished the sentence. He gazed, awe-struck at the temple as though it was something entirely new. On top of the imposing pyramid of the Great Temple, the walls of the twin shrines shone with the radiant glow of the two stone braziers and a hundred torches whose flames leapt and guttered in the night breeze, spitting bits of burning debris that shattered and blew away in a million whirling embers. The chacmool basked in the warm glow between the fires and behind it, an ornately carved altar. The crazy, toothy grin of the recumbent statue was visible even from this distance.

Jaguar shook his head slowly. 'Why has no one else found this place?'

Everything was ready for the first sacrifice. Two dozen priests stood in attendance behind the altar and in front of the shrines to Huitzilopochtli and Tlaloc. Their long dalmatics fluttered slightly and the shadows that played across the fabric, between the folds, across the undulating cloth made their garments seem alive, as though the holy men were wrapped about with living spirits.

The two youths watched from their elevated hiding place as the formal dedications to the gods began. The sonorous boom of a single, gigantic drum called out from the courtyard below, down by the skull rack. Jaguar felt the exhilaration of the moment; that point at which the first of the chosen was escorted solemnly to the foot of the steps. It was an excitement born of the visceral terror of death, an overwhelming gratitude that tonight, others would die to sate the gods and also a deep, deep guilt caused by the relief that it was someone else that had to make that payment, not Jaguar himself.

Now the first of the chosen ones was escorted up the temple steps by two burly warrior priests. As they reached each successive flight, another drum joined in the quickening tempo. Stage-managed to perfection, the spectacle held everyone in thrall.

The needle-like manifestations of everything and everyone around Jaguar thickened and coalesced, at the same time becoming translucent. The harder Jaguar tried to resolve them into their individual shapes, the faster they agglomerated until everything belonged to a shimmering, see-through crystal, packed tight against its neighbour and stretching up to the heavens. Behind him to the south, Jaguar sensed the mighty Popocatepetl, box shaped and nestling against a hundred thousand tessellated shards of trees, walls, villages and towns. The temple of Tezcatlipoca, Crocodile and all the people and features in the temple complex were all packed like a celestial puzzle that stretched to the temple of the sun in Teotihuacan to the north and even beyond. Through this attachment with the world about him, Jaguar felt a raw power surge through him. The Great Temple seemed to be the focus, acting as the point of contact between the Middle Kingdom and the Celestial Level; it was the binding place of unimaginable forces that held the universe together.

'Do you feel that, Crocodile?' asked Jaguar. His friend gave no answer, perhaps caught up in his own kaleidoscopic vision.

The sacrifice was greeted on the temple platform by the priest who conveyed him swiftly to the serpent altarpiece. They had to get a move on now. The next of the chosen ones was already being led up the temple steps and a long line of captives waited their turn by the skull rack. Jaguar watched as the priests stretched the first man out on his back on the waiting stone. The drummers worked themselves into a frenzy but they were hardly audible over the roaring, screeching noise in his ears. Jaguar's augmented senses detected a swirling vortex in the sky above the temple that mirrored the one below it and made such a din that Jaguar couldn't believe that he was the only one who could hear it. He saw tendrils of blue energy snake up and down across the gap between the temple and the whorl of clouds that raged and seethed around the temple structure, growing in strength as the priests continued with their incantations. Spellbound, Jaguar and Crocodile looked on as the priest in charge raised his hands high, holding a savage blade of polished stone.

Abruptly, there was silence.

The chosen one lay face up on the serpent altar, limbs held fast by the watching acolytes, eyes transfixed by the gleaming knife. The warriors, merchantmen and nobles gathered at the base of the temple looked up, unable to move lest they break the magic.

Brutally swift, the priest's hands descended in an arc that intersected with the chosen one's breastbone with a thud that

Jaguar and Crocodile both heard across the temple courtyard. Both of them saw one of the acolytes flinch as he was showered with gouts of dark ichor. Distracted momentarily, he lost his grip upon the limb that was his charge so that it thrashed suddenly, sporadically, before it was recaptured. Then suddenly a high-pitched cry rose up into the night sky and the priest held aloft a dark, sodden bundle in his left hand. In spite of the distance, Jaguar thought he could see the pulsing heart, pumping blood in lumpen, glistening rivulets down the priest's arm.

The roaring sound resumed as the vortices of power above and below him moved, inexorably closing the gap until they joined like two enormous drops of viscous liquid. The narrow isthmus through which they touched initially, widened outwards from its centre above the temple until the Middle Kingdom and the Celestial Level merged as one. Jaguar felt nauseous and sat back to feel the cool stone of the parapet against his back.

He heard the drum pick up again, crashing on and on as one-by-one in quick succession, the chosen ones were escorted up the temple steps. He sensed, but did not see, carved scales and fangs of the altar glistening darkly, drenched in coagulating blood as each subject was dispatched with ruthless efficiency. Jaguar tried to count the number of times he heard the drums go quiet but gave up as the toll stretched into hundreds.

Jaguar didn't notice the effects of the peyotl wearing off. At some point, he noticed that the world no longer looked strange, as though seen through amber. The swirling clouds had gone and the wind had abated. He felt only a huge relief and an overpowering urge to drink buckets of water and eat something, anything to clear the acerbic taste of the root from his mouth.

'Crocodile,' Jaguar shook his friend, who was curled up in a foetal position on the roof where they were hiding. 'Come on. We've got to get down from here before the ceremony is over.'

Crocodile groaned and rolled himself into a kneeling position.

Jaguar glanced over at the Great Temple again where the sacrifice continued. Several of the priests had taken turns with the sacrificial blade. Now they all looked tired. Their clothes and hair were heavy and stiff with gore, which dripped from the hems of their cloaks, leaving black puddles wherever they stood. The temple steps were awash with blood that splashed off the altar and oozed over the edge of the temple platform in curtains. Gobbets of human detritus lay spattered down the steps, knocked from the dead as they were hurled back down to the floor below.

'Come on, big man,' said Jaguar. 'Let's go.'

Crocodile groaned. He looked pale as he levered himself up. 'I've got to find that peasant who sold me this rubbish. I've been poisoned.'

'Don't be absurd,' chided Jaguar. 'You're just sensitive. A little blood and you chuck your guts up everywhere.'

'Don't even joke!' cried Crocodile.

Jaguar peered over the edge of the parapet to see if the temple of Tezcatlipoca was still empty. There were several torches on the platform but no one in sight. He was just about to climb over the wall when Crocodile grabbed his wrist, crushing it in his meaty paw.

'Jaguar! You have to promise me something.'

'What's that?'

Crocodile pointed across at the Great Temple. 'If I ever get captured,' he began. 'If you ever see me taken in battle and you're close by...' Crocodile stared into Jaguar's eyes, holding his arm tightly. 'You have to finish me off.'

'What?'

'If I can't get free,' implored Crocodile. 'Hurl a spear! Anything. Just promise you won't let me end up like that.'

Jaguar could tell he was serious. There was desperation in Crocodile's voice, a fervent intensity that was alien to his usual, imperturbable demeanour. 'Alright, I promise, and in that case, you'd better do the same for me. Come on now, we have to go. Are you alright to climb down from here?'

'I'm fine,' replied Crocodile tersely and let go of Jaguar.

Jaguar clambered quickly down the side of the shrine and waited for his friend. This was a new dimension to Crocodile that he'd not seen before. He was obviously in distress. Jaguar put it down to the peyotl, but the memory of Crocodile's ferocious grip on his wrist wasn't quick to fade.

Chapter 8 - Tôchtli

News that the New Fire had been kindled had spread swiftly and all the women and children had come out into the streets, singing and dancing with their men-folk. Great bonfires burned at every street corner banishing the night. Moctezuma had ordered the palace storerooms be thrown open and sent to supplement the makeshift street kitchens that had been arranged by the city council. The class divide seemed temporarily suspended as pipiltin rubbed shoulders with mayeques. The nobility and wealthy merchants danced with gaunt labourers and emaciated slaves. Priests laughed and joked with warriors, poking fun at each other. The aroma of maize fritters, spices, roasting meat and chillies swirled amongst the revellers, pungent and enticing to a population used to years of famine.

Just outside the temple precinct, by a stand of fragrant juniper trees, Magic River, Blade of the South and Fire Mountain sat on a low wall enjoying the spectacle. Fire Mountain was describing what he had witnessed that evening. Both Blade and Magic River had shut themselves into their homes with their families, only emerging when the cries of joy from the street alerted them to the news that the fire had been returned to the city. Magic River had held his baby granddaughter in his arms while his daughter and her husband danced with their neighbours. Magic River's wife held his arm and chattered excitedly with all her friends. Eventually, Magic River had handed his charge over to his wife and had gone in search of his friends.

The three warriors had got around to discussing the battle that was to take place with the Chalca when a lean, grizzled man struggled past the three friends wearing only a loincloth as protection against the chill night air. He stopped and slurped noisily from a rough stone jar. He looked across at the three men on the wall and waved his crude chalice in a cheery greeting.

'Hey, old man!' called Magic River. 'I don't recognise you, sir. Are you pipiltin?'

'No shir, I am not,' slurred the skinny drinker. With the back of his hand, he carefully wiped a pathetic collection of white whiskers that sprouted on his chin. 'The nobles have shervants, and the shervants have slaves. The slaves have dogsh. If the dogsh had servants, and those shervants had slaves, then I might have the honour... of working for those slaves.'

Magic River's scarred face crinkled into a smile that exposed the gap in his front, lower teeth. 'I see,' he said. 'Then, as I do not know your name, I shall call you Dog of the Twofold Slave.'

'Very kind, shir, very kind. It is a fine name and to be sure, I have been called much worsh.' The old man smiled grotesquely and wobbled as he stood. He raised the jug to his mouth again but it was empty. He stared at it in disbelief.

'Dog of the Twofold Slave?' said Magic River.

'Yes?'

'I assume then that you are over fifty,' said Magic River.

The old man took a couple of uneasy steps towards Magic River and reached out to steady himself on the wall. 'Indeed I am,' he replied. 'Everyone knows your name, shir. Magic River is a hero; a fearless warrior and one-time Eagle Knight.'

Blade of the South leaned in conspiratorially. 'You must be really drunk, old man. This stout fellow may look like an uncouth brute, but in reality he's a simpering tailor to the nobility. See here his dainty hands?' He pointed at Magic River's plate-like hands that rested on the walls.

The scrawny old-timer looked suspiciously at Blade. 'No, shir, I believe that you are wrong,' he said. 'Not only is this man a fighting legend but he is a genius too!' Turning back to Magic River he added, 'How do you know my age?'

Magic River laughed and patted the old man on the shoulder. 'I don't know your age, Dog of the Twofold Slave, but you appear to have drunk a large quantity of octli and as we all know, this is forbidden to all but the pipiltin and those beyond the age of fifty. Since you are not a nobleman, it must be your age that entitles you to drink.'

The inebriated man took his hand off the wall and wagged it at the three men on the wall. 'That may be true usually,' he said, 'but shum of the priests over by the temple are giving it out to everyone.' He winked. 'Speshul occashun. Ha-ha!'

'Sounds good,' said Fire Mountain, breaking his long silence. 'Let's go.'

Fire Mountain was a tall man with broad shoulders, impressively muscular upper body and a permanent frown perched on top of a prominent brow. From under his frown, the big man scanned the world through half-closed eyes. The sides of his head were shaved and his long black hair was scraped back tightly in the standard fashion. Aside from the well defined wrinkles on his forehead and a tracework of lively veins, there was little evidence of his age. He fought like a man in his twenties, but Magic River knew Fire Mountain to be nearly fifty years old. Magic River checked to see if he really had spoken. The big man blinked once, very slowly, which Magic River took as confirmation.

Seeing the exchange, Blade agreed. 'Good idea,' he said and eased himself off the wall.

Fire Mountain and Magic River pointed the old man in the direction of the school of the White Lady in Atzacualco. The clan elders, who ran the school, had opened up the doors to the homeless of Tenochtitlan and to those from outside the city who needed somewhere to stay while the celebrations wound down.

The three men sauntered off in search of the handout.

'What were we talking about before that old coot showed up?' asked Magic River.

'I was telling you that the location of the battle with the Chalca has changed,' Blade said to Magic River. The other two listened as Blade described Tlacaelel's speech to the Tlatocan.

'So where do we meet the Chalca?' asked Fire Mountain, finally wading into the conversation.

'Amihuatzin has been told to expect us on the plain to the south-east of Texcoco,' Blade explained.

Magic River cut in. 'Is that a good idea?'

'Tlacaelel persuaded the Tlatocan that the traditional site puts us at a disadvantage.'

Magic River nodded thoughtfully. 'The Chalca have learned our tactics and become much stronger. Colhuacan is like a trap with no room to manoeuvre and no escape. I wonder where he got the idea.'

'It might have been Two Sign,' suggested Blade.

'No.' Fire Mountain's tone allowed no room for disagreement. Blade and Magic River looked at him in surprise but the big man had no more to offer on the subject. Fire Mountain knew Two Sign well and the two of them talked often.

'Fire Mountain spoke the truth,' admitted Blade. 'This has the mark of the Woman Snake all over it. It's ingenious, it's new and it breaks with all tradition.'

'I can't imagine Cloud Face liked it. Didn't he raise any objections?'

'No.'

'I don't like it,' Magic River muttered. 'There's trouble brewing between those two.'

'I agree, but in the meantime, there's other bad news.'

'What's that?'

'Texcoco won't be joining us.'

'What?' exclaimed Magic River.

Fire Mountain raised his eyebrows.

'Yes, I know,' said Blade. 'Nezahualcoyotl told the Tlatocan that he couldn't risk Texcoco being left defenceless if the Chalca won.'

Magic River shrugged his shoulders. 'So the sleeping cur is true to his name. So much for the Triple Alliance!'

Fire Mountain nodded wisely.

By now the three men had reached the square near the House of Songs and they had to pick their way through the revellers and the stalls that had sprung up spontaneously. Three jugglers blocked the path; one was a whirl of flying maize cobs, the second was keeping three skulls aloft, while the third was on his back with an enormous log rotating at high speed above him. There was a fine selection of vendors offering food for sale and some areas had been set up by the priests, serving simple food to the poor, but these were outnumbered by enterprising merchants and market traders who had obtained special licence from the council to take advantage of the celebrations. Mouth-watering smells filled the air near these stalls. Meat hissed and blackened on spits, dripping juices into the roaring fires below. Heady, sweet aromas mingled with the savoury as smiling traders handed over amaranth cake and honey breads.

'Hungry?' asked Magic River of his friends.

'Hungry,' said Fire Mountain with a pained expression.

'I have some savings set aside for this occasion,' said Magic River. 'Let's avoid the free stuff. I'll buy something.' Magic River stopped at a stall selling tortillas. There was only a modest queue and within a short time they were being served. Several large rush mats were spread around them on the ground, upon which stood teetering piles of the crisp maize pancakes. At either end of the mats stood large earthenware cauldrons of stew that simmered gently over smouldering fires. The heady smell of fish and chillies issued from the pot. Magic River realised that he was famished. He fetched a small silver token from his purse and paid the man behind the stall. Cloud Face and Fire Mountain thanked Magic River and were soon biting into a heavily loaded, steaming tortilla. Hot gravy leaked from the ends and scalded their chins but the food tasted so good there were no complaints.

The mood in the square was one of infectious delight. Two peasants made fun of the fear they had seen in each others' faces in the run-up to the ceremony. They mimicked each other and did impressions of doleful expressions, each trying to make out that the other had been more cowardly. Before long they were howling with laughter, pointing at each other and stamping their feet on the ground. Around them, womenfolk chattered happily and sworn enemies clasped each other affectionately vowing to set aside past wrongs. Small children played boisterous games of catch around the forest of legs, somehow managing to avoid being trampled underfoot and dodging the many firebrands that lit the square.

Magic River spotted a commotion up ahead. The crowds parted suddenly, making way for two street urchins who swerved confidently through the crowds, threading themselves neatly through the chaos. A girl in a threadbare shift and a riot of tangled hair led the way, carrying a large discoloured bag over one shoulder. Right behind her was a flighty looking youth with a hunted look. Some way behind them, a short, rotund man was in pursuit. He was purple with rage and a lack of oxygen and when he drew level with the three friends he was forced to stop, wheezing from the effort of the chase.

'What's the matter, Trenchant Breeze?' piped up one of the bystanders who had seen the children rush past. 'Mugged by a fierce hoard of Tarascan bandits, were you?' There was a scattering of laughter from the crowd. The unfortunate victim was about to embark on a bitter reproach of his detractor when he remembered that his foes were getting away. He snarled once before setting off at a brisk waddle, thrusting people aside as he went.

Magic River, Blade and Fire Mountain moved on when they had finished their tortillas, but by the time they reached the gatehouse where the octli was supposedly being handed out, there was no one to be seen. An icy blue tinge crept into the sky behind Popocatepetl and at last the celebrations began to wind down. Many of the torches had burnt out and no one was replenishing them. Here and there, women were gathering up fractious children and leading them home, some still high on the excitement, some rubbing their tired eyes. As the trio made their way back to Harbour Street, there were only a handful of die-hard revellers clustered around the embers of a fire singing unintelligible songs.

'How's that boy of yours?' Magic River asked Blade.

'He seems well enough,' replied Jaguar's father.

'Has he talked about the recent sortie?'

Blade shook his head. 'He's been very quiet. I didn't want to push him.'

Magic River rubbed his chin, running his thumb over the scar on his lower lip. 'It was a messy business. We lost a few good men that day, including Archer Eagle.'

'I heard about that.'

'Your boy did well though. You can be proud of him,' said Magic River. In truth, he had not seen much of the action on Jaguar's side of the ambush, but he did know that the young warrior had been in the front line when the fight had started and he had lived to take a captive. If there was one thing that Magic River knew about warfare it was that innate survival instincts counted for much more than heroics.

'Jaguar is fit and fast on his feet,' said Magic River. 'He's got lightning reflexes too. I have seen him plenty of times on the ball court. He's going to be a fine warrior.'

'Thank you,' said Blade. 'What about Two Sign's boy?'

Magic River looked Blade in the eye meaningfully and nodded. 'He's one to be watched. I've never seen such a natural born killer, except Fire Mountain, of course.' Magic River winked at Fire Mountain who only scowled back from under his heavy brow. 'Did you know we've submitted an application to the Eagle Knights on his behalf?'

'No. Jaguar didn't mention it.'

'I don't think either of them knows just yet.' Magic River grinned. 'He's taken the five captives already. We thought we'd save him the trouble, didn't we, Fire Mountain?'

The big warrior shrugged at Blade and raised one dark eyebrow in acknowledgement.

Fully fledged warriors were usually rewarded with a small parcel of land and the allocation then increased in accordance with their success on the battlefield, but Crocodile was a bit young to run a smallholding with peasant farmers. Magic River wondered what Crocodile would do with it.

Dawn was well advanced by the time the three men reached their homes in Teopan. The clouds in the east flowed like sumptuous lilac coloured drapes. A breeze was picking up, causing small eddies of dust and fallen ash from the now extinct torches.

Feathered Darkness finally gave up the pretence that he would sleep. He lay between the towering buttress roots of a gigantic amatl tree shivering as though at death's door. He was chilled to the bone and had been curled in a foetal position for the last three hours praying for sleep while his teeth chattered. Daylight penetrated the forest canopy and the birds of the forest were in a raucous mood, screeching and hooting to each other exuberantly, heedless of Feathered Darkness' exhaustion.

Groaning, Feathered Darkness stretched out and then hauled himself to his feet, frightening a group of foraging chachalacas who rushed, squawking into the undergrowth. He was alone. The two warrior priests he had taken with him to Tlaxcala were dead; hacked to bits on the order of the brutal leader of the Tlaxcala republic.

He hadn't eaten since fleeing Tlaxcala yesterday evening but he didn't feel hungry. Shock at the savage murder of his companions had shorn him from the need for food; that and the gut-wrenching fear that Xicotencatl had lied about granting him safe passage so that perhaps, even now, a group of the tlatoani's warriors were hard on his heels. Apart from the brief, futile effort to get some rest, Feathered Darkness had been running almost non-stop since leaving the gates of Tlaxcala. The only thing he could think of was making it back to the blessed sanctuary and civilisation of Tenochtitlan. Feathered Darkness shook himself and began walking. There was no question of him running again until the searing pain in his legs and back subsided.

The priest drank copiously from a stream and then relieved himself. He briefly looked to see if he could see anything edible in the forest around him, but it was just an unending sea of brown earth and green plant matter, most of it entirely alien to him. He was not trained like the warriors to forage from the land. Feathered Darkness hated nature. It was all too chaotic and ungovernable. He slapped at something that was trying to bite his neck. Why would anyone prefer this baffling and uncomfortable setting to the city where everything was ordered, planned and one didn't have to scout around for hours on end for the bare necessities?

A creeping sense of worry that Tlaxcalan warriors weren't far behind him overcame Feathered Darkness' hunger and he struck out for Tenochtitlan once more. He didn't know exactly where he was but an occasional glimpse of the peaks of Popocatepetl and Ixtaccuihuatl through the trees showed him the route to take. Cloud Face would be pleased that the message had been delivered, but Feathered Darkness was far from certain that Xicotencatl had any plan to act on the information he'd been given. The ruler of Tlaxcala had been openly hostile from the moment he'd been presented with the three priests from Tenochtitlan. Feathered Darkness, Snow Head and Spirit Man had been captured on the road to Tlaxcala as expected. There was no way for three priests from the Triple Alliance to approach Tlaxcala without raising suspicion. The warriors who captured them were a dour lot and their peculiar dialect of nahuatl made conversation awkward. It had taken all of Feathered Darkness' considerable persuasive powers to convince them that he had a message for their tlatoani and that he would be very angry with them if he ever found out that the message had not made it through.

The three priests had had their hands bound behind their backs and had been manhandled all the way to Xicotencatl's palace. Feathered Darkness had been unimpressed with the absurdly crude building that passed for the palace of one of Tenochtitlan's greatest enemies. The entire building would have fitted inside the great hall of Moctezuma's palace.

The priest's contempt gave way to fear as it became clear that Xicotencatl was in a foul mood. The ruler of Tlaxcala was a young man, slender and effeminate, in spite of the tuft of hair on his chin. His face was dark as thunderclouds as he ranted at the three men from Tenochtitlan for over an hour. It was an impassioned and vitriolic outburst against Moctezuma and his ancestors, Nezahualcoyotl and anyone even remotely associated with the Triple Alliance. Try as he might, Feathered Darkness had failed to interject and explain that he was here to help. Xicotencatl refused to listen. He accused the priests of being spies and when Snow Head stepped forward to lend his weight to Feathered Darkness' pleas to be heard, the tlatoani had flicked one finger casually at his warriors. In an instant, Snow Head was cut down with a vicious blow to the back of his head. Moments later, and without any provocation, Spirit Man was dispatched where he stood. Feathered Darkness felt the wind of the sword pass his own shoulder as it sliced towards the other priest's neck. Suddenly, he was alone before one of the fiercest, most merciless opponents of the Mexica.

Feathered Darkness had been terrified, but his belief that the gods favoured the Mexica gave him strength. It was impossible to concede that Huitzilopochtli could somehow favour these barbarians. So too, Feathered Darkness' loyalty to Cloud Face was like a solid outcrop of rock in the middle of a mountainous landslide of doubt.

The death of two of the priests from Tenochtitlan calmed Xicotencatl down, as though he'd lanced a particularly ugly boil and he finally asked Feathered Darkness why he was trespassing on Tlaxcalan soil.

Feathered Darkness repeated what he had been told to say. The Mexica army was weak. Texcoco would offer it little assistance and so, with a little help from Chalco, the people of Tlaxcala would inflict a famous defeat on their hated enemy. Xicotencatl was immediately interested and wanted to know more. Here Feathered Darkness confided in him exactly as Cloud Face had instructed. The Tlaxcala should look to the centre of the line where the Mexica would be weakest. Here, the combined forces of Chalco and Tlaxcala would drive a wedge through the Mexica and dispatch them straight to the Lord of the Dead.

'It sounds like a trap,' said the diminutive leader.

Feathered Darkness did not consider himself to be an expert in warfare so he had felt distinctly uncomfortable having to ad-lib.

'The Mexica will struggle to make a trap with inferior numbers,' he had pointed out and was immensely relieved to find that Xicotencatl accepted his answer. The lack of detail was disappointing to the ruler of Tlaxcala, who remained deeply suspicious and paced the flagstone floor of the reception chamber they were in, carefully avoiding the pool of blood that was spreading outwards from Spirit Man's corpse and muttering about Moctezuma's treachery.

'Why should I believe you?' Xicotencatl had demanded after pacing for a while. 'How can I be sure this message isn't from that warmonger Tlacaelel trying to lure us into battle at his own convenience?'

Feathered Darkness had drawn himself up and set a severe expression on his face. 'I am a servant of Huitzilopochtli. I do not run errands for the tlatoani, less still that jumped-up brother of his.'

'I only have your word for that.'

It was then that Feathered Darkness remembered the hummingbird pendant that Cloud Face had given him. Reaching carefully into his robes lest he should startle Xicotencatl or one of his guards into hasty action, Feathered Darkness had slowly withdrawn the bundle and passed it reverentially to the ruler of Tlaxcala. There was no other like it in all the towns and cities of the Triple Alliance. No one but the high priest of Tenochtitlan and Moctezuma were permitted to wear the sacred feathers. To be caught with even one such bird, alive or dead, without a special licence from the tlatoani was a death sentence. If the tlatoani possessed such an item, he never wore it, preferring instead to have the iridescent green feathers sewn into regal headdresses or gaudy tunics. Feathered Darkness had been appalled that Cloud Face had parted with the necklace so readily.

Xicotencatl had been thrilled when he had unwrapped the tiny black and green bird and the thin leather cord that was threaded through it. The neat little bundle fitted easily into the palm of his hand. His face had creased into a smile and Feathered Darkness was certain that the little man had been utterly convinced.

The trees began to thin out as the narrow trail wound its way up an enormous escarpment on the northern flank of Ixtaccuihuatl. Feathered Darkness wasn't cold anymore. The exercise had warmed him up, but he was beginning to feel weak with hunger.

He had been so nervous at the banquet in Tlaxcala that he had barely touched the food set out in front of him. Just as in the city of Tenochtitlan, the people of Tlaxcala had been preparing for the transition to the new calendar and the dawn of the new age.

Feathered Darkness was convinced that Xicotencatl would have him added to the ceremonial offerings that night. He had been shown the greatest courtesy by Xicotencatl and his court since presenting Cloud Face's token and he had even been promised safe passage home, but a deeply ingrained instinct told Feathered Darkness that he was in mortal danger. All that afternoon, Feathered Darkness had made polite conversation with the ruler of Tlaxcala and his courtiers, who fawned and grovelled about their feminine leader in a disgusting manner. Feathered Darkness was not bound or restrained in any way, but there was always a corps of warriors just a few strides away. It was only when the pageant of the evening got underway that Feathered Darkness had seen an opportunity to escape.

On the way to the temple in Tlaxcala, Xicotencatl's retinue had detoured through the palace gardens, which, unlike those in Tenochtitlan, were abundantly stocked with a profusion of verdant, energetic, forest plants, interspersed with liana and exotic orchids. The drought that affected the high plains was not in evidence here. The greenery was so profuse that the paths were narrow and quite obscured so that when one of Xicotencatl's twelve wives tripped and fell to the ground, the ensuing pandemonium had allowed Feathered Darkness to step sideways onto a deserted artery through a curtain of aerial roots where his robes blended into the darkness.

Feathered Darkness had waited for a few heartbeats just in case anyone had spotted him so that he could be found, innocently waiting for the poor unfortunate woman to be set on her feet. When it became apparent that no one had noticed, Feathered Darkness turned, his heart hammering painfully in his chest and walked quickly in the opposite direction, expecting to crash headlong into someone coming to find the source of the hullabaloo. Tlaxcala was not like Tenochtitlan, which was hemmed in by water with only a few, well guarded exits and narrow causeways. Tlaxcala was an open and sprawling city, barely half the size of the Mexica capital, which made it relatively easy for Feathered Darkness to slip through the darkening alleys and out into the surrounding countryside.

He had gathered up the hem of his robes and ran like he'd never run since his childhood. Within a few minutes, his lungs had been burning but he plunged on into the forest, crashing through branches and knocking palms aside, all the time certain that Xicotencatl's men would be after him. It hadn't mattered to Feathered Darkness that there was no sound of pursuit. They would be stealthy just as warriors were trained to be and he would never hear them coming.

Last night seemed like days ago to Feathered Darkness. His arms were bruised from pushing through unyielding saplings and his feet were cut and blistered. His robe was torn in many places and it felt as though he'd crossed a thousand miles. As he crested the sparsely wooded ridge at the top of the escarpment, he caught sight of Lake Texcoco stretched out like a glittering jewel in the distance. Feathered Darkness thought he'd never seen such a beautiful sight.

Chapter 9 - Âtl

The start of the new cycle, ushered in by the previous night's activities, appeared to have had the desired effect upon the weather. A light spattering of rain had dampened down the earth of the practice ball court and made it slippery. The previous night's cloud cover had not dissipated. Charcoal coloured stratocumulus clouds trundled heavily in from the east, their bases swirling and curdling in wind whipped strands. It drizzled fitfully without offering the prospect of a decent downpour.

Two Sign had joined up with a few of the regular players who had gathered at the practice court for a knockabout after gaining permission from the authorities. The recent events had disrupted the regular schedule of training so that a lot of the ullamalitzli players had been keen to get back on the court.

In his youth, Two Sign had been a formidable player in his time, but his real skill was on the battlefield and the call of the empire had been too strong to ignore. Games gave way to raids into enemy territories and when the previous commander of the Eagle Knights had perished in an ambush by Tarascan bandits, Two Sign had been elevated to the highest post in the land that a warrior could achieve and now there was never any time. Today was different though, in effect a day of holiday when most people were expected to be giving thanks to the gods and recovering from the party; so when he'd heard about this practice game, Two Sign had seized the opportunity.

Jaguar had turned up, which pleased Two Sign. In spite of the friendship between the young warrior and his own adopted son, Two Sign rarely saw him. Crocodile was not present. He had never shown any aptitude in the ball game and in any case, he had drawn guard duty at the barracks.

In spite of the atrocious conditions, Two Sign lost himself in the game and managed to put warfare and political concerns entirely out of his mind. The players slipped and slid all over the court, often crashing painfully into the bordering walls. Two Sign was fit; military training and action on the borders of the empire saw to that, but his sense of timing took a little while to return. He managed to catch the opposition out three or four times in the early stages with what he reluctantly had to acknowledge were lucky shots. There followed a lengthy spell when he didn't seem to be able to make any good shots and even mistimed a ricochet from the wall that caught him a glancing blow on his already misshapen nose that brought tears to his eyes and took him out of the game for several minutes. He watched Jaguar from the end zone, admiring the youth's speed and agility. He had the ability to jink and change direction in the blink of an eye and an almost magical gift for accuracy.

Two Sign recovered and rejoined the game. His form returned too, so that he began to enjoy himself again. There was no scoring, but that didn't seem to diminish the intensity with which the players set about the game. After about an hour, everyone was caked in mud so that it was hard to distinguish one player from another.

Two Sign turned at the sound of a commotion behind him and was surprised to see the portly Devine Cactus marching determinedly onto the court. A platoon of well armed warrior priests hovered at the entrance to the court. Devine Cactus somehow managed to single out Jaguar through the dun coloured camouflage they were all wearing and spoke to him in a low, urgent voice. Two Sign could not imagine what business the high priest of Tlaloc would have with the young warrior. Two Sign took another, professional look at the high priest's escort at the edge of the court. They were not an impressive bunch, but they were armed, which neither the players nor the scattering of spectators that day were. The big warrior tossed the ball to Crimson Cloud and walked over to find out what the matter was. Devine Cactus spotted Two Sign approaching and before he could say anything, the high priest put his hand out to hold him at bay.

'Stay out of this, Two Sign.' Devine Cactus' voice was honey smooth but the undercurrent of menace was unmistakeable. 'Mixayacatl has sent for Jaguar. I don't want any trouble.'

'What need can Cloud Face have of this young man?' said Two Sign.

Devine Cactus smiled. 'I'm afraid I have no idea,' he replied. 'But I'm sure one of the two parties will advise you afterwards should they feel you need to know.' He placed his hand on Jaguar's shoulder proprietarily. 'Come on, young man.'

Jaguar looked worried. The mud that was spattered all over him from head to toe and matted in his hair only served to make his appearance all the more downtrodden and Two Sign could do nothing to help. The high priests had absolute discretion within the city limits answering only to Moctezuma. Tlacaelel's recent run-in with Cloud Face hadn't helped, stirring up latent tensions.

'Where are you taking him?' Two Sign asked.

'The temple barracks.'

'I'll go with him,' said Two Sign, trying the only thing he could think of.

'No. You won't.' Devine Cactus was adamant. 'You may wait for him at the entrance to the temple complex but you will not be admitted after your recent outrage.'

Two Sign set his jaw angrily as Devine Cactus continued firmly. 'The tlatoani has decreed that you and Tlacaelel are forbidden until further notice, or have you already forgotten?' He turned and swept off the court pushing Jaguar ahead. His armed priests closed around them and Two Sign was left wondering what in the name of Mictlan's teeth was going on.

Crimson Cloud and the others gathered round. They had caught some of the exchange and wanted to know more. Two Sign was unable to enlighten them further and the lengthy interruption proved terminal to the practice session. Everyone was tired and filthy so they collected their cloaks and headed home.

Deep in thought, Two Sign headed for the barracks where he plunged himself brusquely into the cold baths and scrubbed himself clean. He transferred himself to a steam room to warm up and when he was fully dressed, he went to find Crocodile's dormitory. Crocodile had just come off shift, so over a simple meal, Two Sign related the extraordinary event that had just taken place.

'Have you got any idea why the priests would want to talk to Jaguar?' asked Two Sign.

Crocodile looked tired. Without ever once looking at his father, he swallowed a mouthful of savoury maize cake and shook his head. 'Uh, no.'

Two Sign was concerned. Ever since the two friends met as boys, they had been in and out of trouble, but he had always put it down to youthful inventiveness. Two Sign remembered having to refund a fisherman for his canoe once but otherwise their scrapes had been fairly harmless. There was also that time they managed to set fire to a field. Luckily, no one had been injured but again, some recompense to the farmer had been necessary in addition to the three days of hard labour that the courts had imposed on the boys. Two Sign had hoped that the two friends had put their mischievous past behind them.

'Son.' Two Sign paused to get Crocodile to look at him.

Crocodile chewed another mouthful and looked up.

'Jaguar could be in real trouble this time. Cloud Face does not see people without a very good reason.'

Slowly at first, Crocodile began to recount what had happened on the evening of the New Fire. With embarrassed pauses, he told his father how he and Jaguar had sneaked up onto the temple of Tezcatlipoca and how they had taken peyotl.

'But it was the tiniest amount!' pleaded Crocodile.

'You must have been seen on the temple,' said Two Sign. 'It's the only explanation.' He steepled his hands for a while and then added, 'you had better hope they don't know about the peyotl.'

Crocodile was suddenly miserable, realising the danger they were both in. 'I'm sorry, Dad.'

Two Sign looked at his adopted son for a while and then his expression softened, as it had the day he'd seen the orphan standing alone in the remains of his ruined village.

Two Sign reached out to pat Crocodile on the shoulder. 'Look, let's not worry until we know what it's all about, eh? It may be nothing.'

Crocodile exhaled deeply and nodded.

'Good,' said Two Sign. 'I see you've made an application to join the Eagle Knights.'

Crocodile looked up, puzzled. 'Eh?'

'I just heard today that your name has been put forward and you've been sponsored by Magic River and Fire Mountain!' Two Sign was unable to contain the pride he felt. He had raised Crocodile since he was a boy. True enough that as a knight of the Mexica Empire, he had the support of the finest nurses and tutors in the land, but it had not all been plain sailing. Crocodile had been surly and unresponsive for months after his parents had been slaughtered. He had run away several times in the first year. Life in the military barracks was not easy after all, in spite of there being several other children there whose fathers were single parents due to illness or some other misfortune.

'You don't know about this?' asked Two Sign.

'I've got nothing to do with it, father,' answered Crocodile.

'Ha!' cried Two Sign. 'Even better. Magic River must have made the submission on your behalf.' Two Sign pretended to rub his squashed nose in order to conceal his smile. 'You have reached the required tally though?'

Crocodile nodded, seemingly more cheerful with the change of subject.

Two Sign suppressed his instincts to hug Crocodile, managing instead to keep himself to another hefty pat on the arm. 'Just don't get carried away, will you?' He levelled a serious gaze at his adopted son. 'Take care of yourself first and...'

'...and care to take the captives second. I know, I know,' interrupted Crocodile. 'By the Skin of Xipe Totec, Dad! How many times have I heard that?'

Jaguar quickly found himself back in the temple complex, steered by the heavy hand of Devine Cactus that never left his shoulder. Repeated attempts to get the priest to reveal the reason for the summons had proved unsuccessful.

The Great Temple was a hive of activity. A large number of slaves had been drafted in to help the priests clear up the sacrificial remains. Some of the slaves and even one or two priests looked a little the worse for wear, presumably still suffering after the all-night celebrations. A number of acolytes had been set to work severing heads from the corpses of the sacrificial victims that lay in vast piles at the base of the temple. Jaguar had heard that there was a room in the temple that contained large stone boxes filled with maggots used to strip the skulls clean in a matter of hours. There was much to look at, but Jaguar had little time to appreciate it. He felt ill. His abduction from the ball court by priests was frightening enough, but the prospect of being interrogated by the high priest of Huitzilopochtli was cause for real alarm.

Cactus guided Jaguar down a passageway and through a section of the temple complex he had never seen before. There were houses for the most senior priests, squat, ugly dormitories for the acolytes and simple, featureless barracks for the warrior priests. In one doorway, Jaguar smelled the odour of a building shared by a hundred unwashed bodies. From another, Jaguar caught the stench of rancid cooking fat overlaid with a scent of herbs and frying maize kernels.

Soon they came to the door of a large, yet simple building. Its whitewashed stucco finish was utterly devoid of paint work, friezes or decoration of any kind except for a small carving of the Huitzilopochtli glyph either side of the entrance. The entrance opened into a long corridor that lead into a courtyard at what Jaguar supposed must be on the east side of the temple complex.

'This is where the high priests and administrative staff have apartments,' said Devine Cactus. They were the only words the priest had spoken the whole journey.

A light precipitation hazed the sky again as Jaguar was led across the courtyard. The paving slabs were cold and slick under Jaguar's feet. In the centre of the courtyard was a rectangular shaped depression formed by three large steps down to an arena, perhaps twenty feet square and furnished with a single stone plinth, waist high and five feet square. The meagre scattering of rain lent a curious mottled effect to the grey slab.

Jaguar pointed at the slab as they passed by. 'What's that?'

'Altar,' replied Devine Cactus without a glance. 'For training,' he added.

The stepped depression, almost like a temple pyramid inside-out, with the altar at the bottom, formed an ideal place for acolytes to observe the procedure.

Jaguar wished he hadn't asked. His stomach lurched as the danger of his situation really began to sink in.

Devine Cactus pushed Jaguar through a doorway in the opposite side of the courtyard and guided him through numerous poorly lit passageways. Finally, they arrived at a doorway no different to the many others they had passed, except that it was hung with a curtain affording a certain degree of privacy.

Jaguar found himself in a room that would have comfortably contained the whole of his family home. It was dingy and at first glance seemed empty. Half a dozen peculiar contraptions stood neatly in the centre of the room. Jaguar recognised none of them. As his eyes adjusted to the light, he could see that the walls were covered with racks, but he didn't immediately recognise what they held. The box shaped cubicles stretched the length of the room, row upon row from the floor to a ceiling that was twice the height of Jaguar. Devine Cactus stopped Jaguar, giving him a chance to look more closely. Eventually the strange cream and brown things curled up in every one of the hundreds of cubicles resolved themselves as parchments. Jaguar had only seen a handful of parchments before, held reverentially in the hands of tutors at school. This must have been Cloud Face's own personal library. Jaguar had not been aware that so many writings existed in the city, let alone in the possession of a single individual.

Cloud Face was nowhere to be seen. Devine Cactus cleared his throat and then spoke to Jaguar in a whisper. 'You will address Mixayacatl as 'My Lord' or 'Honourable Father', do you understand?'

Jaguar said that he did. The room was oppressively dark and airless. Jaguar found himself fighting for breath. His anxiety rose as a series of noises in the adjoining room heralded the arrival of the high priest. A tall figure in long brown robes stepped through the opening and glided smoothly towards the centre of the room. His burnished scalp gleamed on one side where the light from a small window set into the opposite wall cast a baleful shaft of light across the room. Jaguar had never seen the high priest of Huitzilopochtli close up before. The birthmark on his forehead was dark and ominous, even in the half-light. Although his eye sockets were sunken, the eyes inside them shone with an unsettling intensity.

'Heart of the Jaguar,' said Cloud Face. 'So pleased you could make it.'

The tone suggested that he'd had a choice and Jaguar was surprised at the apparent warmth in the old man's voice.

Cloud Face inclined his head towards Devine Cactus. 'You may go.'

'My Lord.' The high priest of Tlaloc bent his portly frame slightly at the waist, then turned and left the room.

'I am sorry it's so dark in here,' said Cloud Face. 'I have been trying to rid myself of a headache after the recent excitement. Would you like some chocolatl? I have just had a fresh jug of it delivered.'

Cloud Face moved towards one of the strange devices that Jaguar had seen in the centre of the room. It proved to be nothing more than an ornate stand that glowed with an unearthly pale light of its own and acted as a seat for a circular metallic platter on top. Jaguar had never seen anything like it before, but there was one thing about it that he was very familiar with from special commissions his family had taken on; the white material was bone, and Jaguar guessed it was human bone. Cloud Face reached for the jug that stood on it and filled two delicate gold rimmed cups. He handed one to Jaguar and breathed deeply from the steam that rose from his own cup, closing his eyes as he did so.

Jaguar was too nervous to do anything but hold on to the cup and watch as Cloud Face took a sip. The chocolate beverage was scalding hot so Jaguar contented himself with wrapping his hands around the cup. The damp mud that coated him was beginning to cool now that he was no longer hurling himself around the ball court and the warmth from the cup was welcome.

Cloud Face must have noticed Jaguar's rigid stance.

'Don't worry,' said Cloud Face reassuringly. 'You can forget all that military stuff in here. We priests have a great deal of ceremony but we only apply it when it's necessary.' He smiled again, leaving Jaguar perplexed. Any minute now, he felt sure the old man would bring up the subject of Crocodile and Jaguar's visit to the temple of Tezcatlipoca.

Cloud Face gestured at the cup in Jaguar's hand. 'Are you enjoying the chocolatl?'

'I, er... yes, Honourable Father,' said Jaguar. 'It's a little hot though.'

Cloud Face waved his hand dismissively. 'Take your time,' he said and motioned to a modestly furnished seating area.

Jaguar looked down at the mud that clung to his legs and was smeared liberally over his loincloth. Cloud Face noticed his hesitation.

'That's alright,' said the high priest.

Jaguar sank down on a soft deerskin rug taking care to keep his drink level. Cloud Face sat down opposite him.

'You may not be aware of this, but I used to know your mother.' Cloud Face seemed embarrassed.

'Really?' said Jaguar meekly.

'Indeed. Her father and I fought together for the Tepanecs under the great Tezozomoc. Of course, Musical Reed was just a child at the time. She won't even remember me.' There was a hint of a smile, but Cloud Face's expression was wistful.

Jaguar tried to recall his histories. Although the Mexica had been vassals of the Tepanecs, when they had finally toppled their masters, they developed a curious affection for Tezozomoc, perhaps as a reaction against the hated Maxtla. Jaguar remembered the countless times his mother had adjured him to good behaviour, threatening a visit from the evil spirit of the last ruler of their Tepanec overlords.

'My mother told us that Tezozomoc had orange hair and that he would eat our livers,' said Jaguar.

'Nonsense!' Cloud Face retorted. 'His hair was as black as yours is now and mine used to be when I was your age.' He stroked his smooth head and without a trace of a smile added, 'Of course, the stuff about the livers is true though!'

Jaguar did his best to adjust to the high priest's friendly banter but couldn't shake a deep unease.

'Honourable Father, if you and my grandfather were warriors, how is it that you went such separate ways?'

'We were not warriors,' replied the high priest simply. 'We were both training to be in the priesthood. Sadly for me, your grandfather showed real flair in battle, whereas I never distinguished myself.' This last was said without a trace of embarrassment. Cloud Face shrugged. 'So I continued in a lifetime of devotion to Huitzilopochtli... whereas your grandfather became a famous warrior.'

'My grandfather died in battle,' Jaguar pointed out.

'True, true,' acknowledged Cloud Face, 'although that is a worthy end.'

Cloud Face stood up and he took on a serious expression. 'Listen,' he said. 'There is a serious matter to attend to.'

'What's that?' asked Jaguar trying to keep his voice level. This was the moment he had been dreading. He had convinced himself that he and Crocodile had been seen on top of the temple and Jaguar had absolutely no idea what punishment this would occasion.

The high priest started pacing slowly back and forth near the seating area. He loomed over Jaguar adding to his discomfort. 'I'm afraid I must speak with you candidly,' began Cloud Face. 'You see, I think you may be in terrible trouble.'

Fear returned to Jaguar like a hammer blow. He didn't know what to say. 'I'm sorry, but what are we talking about?' he tried.

Cloud Face stopped pacing and assumed a dolorous expression. Feeble light from the single opening cast his angular features into stark contrast. 'You were seen.'

Jaguar felt himself blanch. A strange humming noise permeated his head and blurred his eyesight. He wanted to speak, to say something that would explain the harmlessness of the rooftop vigil, but his mouth was as dry as the Mezquitic hills. Jaguar gripped the cup of chocolate tightly, finally finding a use for it which was to steady his trembling hands. Slowly, Jaguar raised the cup to his lips, hoping the action would appear nonchalant. Perhaps he and Crocodile had not actually been seen on the temple but only in the area, as they slunk into the temple complex or as they made their way out. Perhaps Cloud Face was bluffing, hoping that Jaguar would give himself away.

'Come now,' said the high priest. 'You were both seen and at a moment's notice I can summon someone to testify to this effect. Where, what time and exactly what you two got up to.'

Jaguar decided it probably wasn't a bluff but he was determined to force Cloud Face to reveal what he knew. After all, he and Crocodile had had a few scrapes over the years so this wasn't the first occasion they had had to answer to the authorities. After burning the roof of his mouth and his tongue on the chocolate drink, he decided he could no longer hide behind the pretence of drinking it without sustaining serious injury.

'I'm not sure what you're referring to, Honourable Father,' said Jaguar. 'I don't believe I've hurt anyone, damaged anything or stolen anyone's property.'

Cloud Face's eyes became narrow slits as he realised Jaguar wasn't going to roll over. 'That may be true,' he conceded, 'but you have broken the laws of Tenochtitlan.'

The high priest's voice was still devoid of opprobrium or menace. It was all worryingly matter-of-fact, suggesting that Cloud Face did not need to browbeat Jaguar into a confession. Jaguar decided that an early show of contrition would play well, even without any direct admission of guilt.

'I'm very sorry, Honourable Father,' said Jaguar. 'What law have I broken?'

Cloud Face shook his head. 'Do not play games with me young man,' he said brusquely. 'This business is far too serious for silly pretences. Fornication with a slave girl is an offence that is punishable by death! I am astonished that you try to brush it off or pretend that nothing happened!'

This time Jaguar's heart stopped. He slopped the still hot drink over his hands and yelped in agony as he spilt yet more over his thigh where there was only a thin layer of drying mud to protect him from the lava hot beverage. Jaguar hurriedly put the cup down using the pain to mask his shock. What did Cloud Face know? How did he know that he and Precious Flower had been in the field together? And then Jaguar remembered what Precious Flower had said about the man who had been watching him.

Jaguar closed his eyes and groaned, unable to suppress his anguish as he remembered the conversation with Crocodile about the merchant and the slave girl. He didn't need Cloud Face to point out the seriousness of the offence.

'Good!' Cloud Face drew himself up, haughty. 'I'm glad we've reached the end of that unedifying charade.' He strode to the far side of the room and scanned the shelves of parchment. He made a show of pulling several of them out one at a time and examining them. He had to blow thick dust off one of them and another fell apart as he pulled it from its crepuscular niche. At last he came away from his library with a handful of the amatl parchments and loomed over Jaguar, reading from them one at a time.

Jaguar quickly gathered that these were historical records of trials in which the priesthood had played an active part. The first one detailed the crime of a nobleman who had transgressed with a slave-boy and who as punishment had been cut in two from his crotch to his neck. The second contained the sorry story of a noblewoman who had forsaken her family to run away to Toluca with a slave. The warrior priests, who had been dispatched to hunt them down, caught up with them on a mountain pass and, rather than ferrying the reluctant lovers back to Tenochtitlan, they had tied them with long lengths of rope to two boulders that they had then tipped over the edge of a precipice, watching as the lovers were dragged after them.

For a while, dark broodings crammed Jaguar's imagination like a log jam in a raging torrent, as he thought of Precious Flower's tender embrace. His chest ached with chagrin, tortured by a hundred possible fates that might befall them now. He cursed himself, wondering why he hadn't had the sense to wait a few days. Then he remembered the tiny hairs on the nape of her neck as she'd twisted and writhed under him, moaning in pleasure.

When Jaguar heard Cloud Face once again, he realised that he had missed some further horrific endings and still the high priest had more parchments to read from. The current indiscretion related how a warrior from Chapultepec had fallen for a slave girl belonging to a neighbour and had been forced into gladiatorial combat, tied to a ceremonial stone with only a simple club for defence against a fully armoured Jaguar Knight.

Cloud Face fell silent and looked down at Jaguar.

Jaguar threw himself forward and abased himself at the feet of the high priest, silent in his misery. Perhaps Precious Flower would be safe. Not one of the slaves mentioned in the records had been harmed and Jaguar recalled that the law was designed to protect the most vulnerable members of Mexica society.

'You know what my duty is now,' Cloud Face announced to Jaguar's prostrate form. He didn't wait for an answer. 'The law demands that I report you to the council. Sadly the priests no longer handle such matters.' He paused, adding, 'Your father is a member of the Council of Twelve, isn't he?'

'Yes,' said Jaguar in an anguished voice.

'Do you suppose that he will sway the other eleven members to grant you clemency?'

Jaguar's voice was barely audible as he replied. 'No.'

'So in effect, the father will be signing his own son's death warrant.' Cloud Face mad a sad face. 'It might not go so well for your father either.'

Through his desperation, Jaguar saw his father, disgraced and banished from the council, perhaps from Tenochtitlan as well. Their workshop would certainly be boycotted. Jaguar imagined his mother, Musical Reed, forced to flee the only place she had known all her life and live like a fugitive for the rest of her days. Precious Flower would have nowhere to work. Jaguar's sister, Little Beetle, and her husband, Arrow One, might be able to escape the humiliation if Little Beetle disowned her own family.

'Sit up,' commanded Cloud Face.

Jaguar collected himself and wiped his eyes. He was shivering uncontrollably and his stomach ached and roiled as though awash with acid. His breath came in little shuddering gasps.

'We may be able to help each other.'

Jaguar blinked and stared, uncomprehending. Like a simpleton, his mouth hung slack.

'That's right,' said Cloud Face. 'You need me, and Devine Cactus, to keep quiet about this shameful transgression of yours. Without our silence, your family is ruined and you... well, I'm sure you have an idea how things will go for you.' Cloud Face began pacing slowly, doing a circuit of the room as though working on a complex problem. The high priest stroked his bald head with one hand and then rubbed the back of his neck.

'You know, there is one small matter that you may be able to assist me with.'

Jaguar could scarcely believe his ears. He looked up, hardly daring to breathe lest he miss one syllable.

'You will be fighting against the Chalca tomorrow?'

Jaguar nodded stupidly.

'If this matter of the slave girl is kept quiet, I mean,' added Cloud Face, seeing Jaguar's confusion. 'If you agree to help me with a very minor task, this time tomorrow you will be marching out to battle against Chalco.'

Jaguar nodded, understanding this time. A small corner of his brain began to weigh up what was taking place and wonder just what this minor task could be.

'Excellent!' beamed Cloud Face. He fetched the jug of chocolate drink and returned to top up Jaguar's cup that sat half-full beside him on the floor. He had also brought the second cup with him and proceeded to fill that one as well. He set the jug and the cup down on the floor opposite Jaguar and dragged another rug out so that they were sitting opposite each other.

'Have some drink. Go ahead. It will make you feel better.' Cloud Face sipped from his own cup warily, as if to confirm to Jaguar that it had cooled down. He crossed his legs slowly, wincing at the pain of an old man's bones.

'What do you need from me?' Jaguar asked.

'Where to begin?' Cloud Face spread his hands expansively. There was a pause during which Jaguar felt himself to be the object of scrutiny. It was as if the high priest was trying to decide whether to trust Jaguar. 'I don't suppose you know a great deal about me, do you?'

Jaguar admitted that he did not.

'It's a sad fact that the more important you become, the lonelier you get,' said Cloud Face with a rueful smile. 'I expect that very few people in this city know how hard the priesthood and I work on their behalf.'

Jaguar made a noncommittal gesture, which he hoped would be interpreted as any one of a number of responses that the high priest might have wanted.

'It isn't easy you know.' Cloud Face took a swig from his cup and sighed. 'Our tlatoani does his best, you know, but there are so many things to attend to.

'Of course, we're supposed to look after the spiritual aspects of the people and act as the fulcrum between them and the gods. Sometimes though, we have to do more.'

'More?' asked Jaguar.

'There will be trouble in the battle with Chalco.'

'What kind of trouble?'

'I have reliable information that the Tlaxcala will come to the aid of Chalco.'

'That's not unusual,' replied Jaguar. 'They hate us almost more than the people of Chalco do.'

Cloud Face gave a wan smile. 'Indeed. I look upon it as a measure of our success.' He drank from his cup and then dropped it on the edge of the rug he was sitting on. It tipped on its side and rolled once before settling into a fold of the cloth, a thin trickle of brown liquid creeping gently towards the rim.

'The thing is, I have come into possession of some information that Xicotencatl and Amihuatzin are plotting to encircle our troops with the largest fighting force this valley has ever seen.'

Jaguar struggled to work out what use he could be and told Cloud Face. The high priest urged him to be patient for a while.

'I'm nearly there,' said Cloud Face. 'If these two can field their armies at full strength and catch us at a disadvantage, they could finish off the Mexica once and for all.'

'I still don't understand what you need from me,' said Jaguar.

'My spies tell me that the enemy plans to surround us. We must not allow that to happen.'

'How do we do that and why don't you speak to Tlacaelel? Surely he's the general.' Jaguar regretted speaking the words as soon as the words were out of his mouth. He knew from his father that Cloud Face and Moctezuma's brother did not get along.

'Tlacaelel?' Cloud Face spat contemptuously. 'The Woman Snake? Don't make me laugh! Do you think he cares for his people?'

Jaguar had no answer.

'The tlatoani's brother seeks to glorify his own name through conquest.' For the first time, Cloud Face looked genuinely angry. 'He cares nothing for the gods or for our safety. He is reckless and knows nothing of the way the world works!' Cloud Face turned away from Jaguar and stared into the far distance. After a while, he gathered himself and began rummaging in the pile of rugs on his left-hand side. He casually pulled out two cotton throws the like of which no ordinary family in Tenochtitlan could ever afford. One was red with an ochre coloured sun intricately embroidered in the centre. The other was deep blue with reflective flecks around its edge caused by what looked like a rough weave of gold thread woven through it. Cloud Face rolled them one after another and laid them out in front of his crossed legs. He pointed at the ochre cloth that was closest to Jaguar. 'Our warriors will be lined up on the field like this.' He indicated the blue roll that he had placed in a parallel line to the first one. 'The Tlaxcala and Chalca will make a long line in front of us like this. By placing their own knights and some of their finest warriors here, in the centre, they plan to cut through and draw our Jaguar and Eagle Knights into the middle to defend the line.'

'How do you know all this?' breathed Jaguar.

'It is my duty to know these things, Jaguar,' said Cloud Face. 'Long before the city of Tenochtitlan was founded, the people of Aztlan, our founders, relied on the priests for guidance. We commune with the gods and we see things that the farmers and merchants, warriors and labourers could never comprehend.

Look...' Here Cloud Face pointed once more at the two lines of cloth that lay on the floor between them. He pulled the middle of the ochre cloth into a ball, contracting it. 'When they have drawn the best of our fighting men to the centre, our enemies then will extend their wings out wide and come around both ends to encircle us.' Cloud Face demonstrated by wrapping the ends of the blue cloth around the knotted fabric that represented the Mexica.

It was too much for Jaguar to take in. He felt lost and alone. He had never seen a battle described in advance like this. The ambush in the ravine several days ago had been planned, but that had been achieved with a few simple directives on the spur of the moment. Jaguar tried to comprehend how thousands of men on a chaotic battlefield might be controlled and could not do it, much less guess at what the high priest wanted him to do.

'What do you need me for?'

'Your clan, Island Home North, will be fighting near the centre,' replied Cloud Face gravely. 'Your people will be hit very hard.'

Jaguar looked at Cloud Face expectantly.

'It's very simple,' said the high priest. 'You must hold the centre ground with your lives! It's vital that our warriors are not all drawn into the middle.'

Jaguar put a hand on his forehead and squeezed his eyes shut. 'Isn't Tlacaelel dealing with this? Does he know?'

Cloud Face tried to move and winced. 'I'm sorry, I must stand. I cannot sit like this for long.' He swept up the two throws and dropped them back onto the pile they had come from before easing himself slowly to his feet with a grunt. He put both hands on his back and arched his body as though trying to unfold it.

'Of course Tlacaelel knows. He believes that our line must give in the middle, and that seeing this, the enemy will charge in behind, allowing us to come around their flanks. The trouble is, he doesn't know that the Tlaxcala are coming in strength, which means we won't be able to encircle them and, of course, he just won't listen to me.'

Jaguar stood. He felt tired and confused. His body was covered in flakes of drying mud that made him look like he had a dreadful illness, sloughing skin all over the seating area. 'What makes you think they will come?'

Cloud Face's hand whipped out and he grabbed Jaguar by his hair, twisting it hard and making Jaguar cry out in pain. The high priest held him so he was on the verge of overbalancing. Jaguar reached out to grab the cleric's robes but his hands were slapped away viciously.

'Listen, you little shit!' hissed Cloud Face venomously. 'Don't get smart with me. I've spent a lifetime serving my people.' Spittle flecked his lips and splashed Jaguar in the face. 'It just so happens that I know the plans of our enemies thanks to the emissaries that you so recently captured. It was a good thing I had them interrogated before they were sacrificed or we'd never have known about their plan.'

Cloud Face was inches from Jaguar and stared hard into his eyes. He shook Jaguar's hair violently again. 'Just remember that I know your sordid little secret. If you have any honour and want to protect your family from the shame, you'll do what I say!'

Jaguar tried to nod but the high priest's grip was so tight he could only blink in assent.

'You need to persuade your clan to stick tight and hold the line, do you understand?'

'Yes!' gasped Jaguar, eyes watering from the pain.

'If you fail and our line shrinks to plug the gap our whole army will be destroyed!' Cloud Face let go of Jaguar and wiped his hands on his robes as if tainted. 'Go now. Devine Cactus will escort you out. Know this, Jaguar. I will have people watching you. I have eyes everywhere. You will do as I command, or your death will be just the start of your family's sorrows.'

Jaguar turned to leave, numb and dazed. Devine Cactus must have been listening outside because he slipped into the room and grasped Jaguar by the arm and began to lead him from the room.

'One last thing,' called Cloud Face as they reached the door. 'Your standard bearer will fall. You will pick up the flag. It will be the rallying point for your men. Stand firm and they will stand with you.'

Chapter 10 - Itzcuintl

'I can't understand what got into you, brother,' said Moctezuma.

'And I can't believe you've taken his side,' replied Tlacaelel, annoyed.

'You're usually so meticulous.'

'I did what I thought was right for Tenochtitlan,' said Tlacaelel. 'Cloud Face failed to turn those captives over to us for questioning. Of course, we don't know what they were up to, but if they were headed for Tlaxcala, you can be sure it wasn't to discuss the weather.'

The sun had just begun to stain the early morning darkness in the east. A living orange and cinnamon glow ignited the smeary scattering of clouds beyond the gloomy bulk of the mountains. The previous day's thin drizzle had petered out and Moctezuma and Tlacaelel stood outside the palace where a doorway led into the Marshall Courtyard where the cream of the Mexica warriors waited for the tlatoani's address.

'I've got more important things to do than intervene when you two behave like children?' Moctezuma was angry. 'I've told you before that I can't support you just because you're my brother! If anything, it makes it harder. If there's any doubt at all, I have to come down on the other side.'

Tlacaelel tried to compose himself. 'This isn't about me. This is what I don't seem to be able to explain to you. That meddling high priest is withholding vital information from the Mexica war machine and undermining your leadership in the process.'

Moctezuma rolled his eyes. 'Please! This is nothing like the drama you pretend it is. Firstly, Amihuatzin is bound to have sent for assistance and not just to the Tlaxcala. We can be fairly certain what message was being conveyed. Secondly, even if our warriors prevent this message from getting through, you can be sure that others were dispatched who did make it.'

Tlacaelel gave up. He knew his own brother well enough to know that he would not win this argument. Even when they were young, Moctezuma had been a poor loser. He was, for the most part, a rational man, but Tlacaelel knew that his brother's even handedness was proportional to his detachment from the issue at hand.

'I'm sure that's true,' said Tlacaelel, 'and it doesn't change our plans. We assume that the Tlaxcala are coming anyway.'

'Excellent!' cried Moctezuma. 'Perhaps now we can concentrate on this speech?'

His brother sighed. 'Yes. Fine.' He gathered up some notes he had made that consisted of quite a few sheaves of parchment. 'You're content with the introduction?'

Moctezuma nodded.

'And the middle section consists of the explanation for why we must crush the enemy so comprehensively that they will let us pursue our interests abroad?'

Moctezuma waved him on. 'Yes, yes. That part is easy.'

'Well then,' rejoined Tlacaelel. 'The third part is the heart warmer, the Spirit of the Fire. You've done this many times before. It has got harder of late due to this cursed famine, but this time, we have the recent success of the New Fire to cheer the men.'

'Ha!' exclaimed the tlatoani. 'You see! One minute you berate him as a traitor, and the next, Cloud Face is our greatest ally thanks to his success on the altar. You can't have it both ways.'

Tlacaelel groaned.

'It's all about balance, do you see?' cried Moctezuma. 'I need both of you on my side in order to succeed. This petty squabbling does you no favours... neither of you.'

'Alright,' conceded Tlacaelel with a pained expression. 'I think you're ready.'

Moctezuma looked triumphant. The imminent speech was an added excitement for him. Tlacaelel felt that no one deserved the title of The One Who Speaks more than his brother. Moctezuma was born to be the tlatoani.

They stepped out into the Marshall Courtyard to the concerted roar of approval of four thousand knights of the realm. Four Grey Privy Knights flanked the brothers as they climbed the four steps to the stage from where they could see over the heads of the two thousand Jaguar Knights and the two thousand Eagle Knights who made up the backbone of the Mexica army. As Moctezuma took his position at the front of the stage, the assembled warriors, as one, raised their swords on high and gave a second mighty roar.

Tlacaelel looked out appreciatively at the knights. All were fully clothed for battle in their formal battledress. The Eagle warriors occupied the left-hand half of the courtyard wearing their feathered headdresses. The Jaguar Knights stood neatly in the right-hand half of the courtyard wearing their jaguar skins with the upper part of the jaguar's head as a cap and the beautiful, dappled pelts draped over their shoulders. Tlacaelel could have worn his own jaguar-skin cowl but had opted for a simple black loincloth with red trim and tassels that hung to below his knees. He had a small battle tunic of black fabric that covered his shoulders, back and pectoral muscles and had thin hexagon tiles of a reddish wood close sewn together for his armour.

Tlacaelel wished that the other three thousand knights engaged in operations outside the capital could take part in the operation today, but it was not to be. Sentries posted along the major arteries of the empire could not be withdrawn. Rebellion in Oaxaca could not be paused and restarted at a whim and tax collectors needed protection, which could not be interrupted without depleting the coffers of the Mexica machinery.

The tlatoani raised his staff on high and the knights fell silent. He lowered his staff and there followed a lengthy silence while Moctezuma cast an appraising eye over the men. For a while he scanned the sea of faces, all of which were turned politely to one side.

'I am surprised!' he began in a stentorian voice. 'Only two days after the New Fire and everyone seems to have made it here intact.' He turned to his brother. 'Tlacaelel, remind me not to invite any of this tedious bunch to my next party.'

A ripple of laughter spread through the crowd. The men sounded nervous, hesitant or perhaps still sleepy. The sun would soon top the shoulder of Ixtaccuihuatl and warm them up. Moctezuma would speak and pour fire into their hearts. Tlacaelel smiled and listened as his brother got to work.

'When our ancestors came to this land, three or four generations ago, they were treated like dogs!' Moctezuma's powerful voice rang out across the assembled multitude. He thrust his chest forward in a show of confidence. His handsome features were proud and determined.

'But our grandfathers and their fathers were tough. The dogs bit back!' That brought a laugh from his audience.

Moctezuma resumed when the murmurs died down. He raised both hands in front of him, palms down in a placatory gesture. 'I know that things have not been easy of late. Like you, I have worried about the end of the year and the transition to Two Reed. No one has been unaffected by the famine... and the continuing lack of rains is a source of worry for us all.'

Tlacaelel liked to watch his brother speak. In time, he thought, people would write songs about the man. Under normal circumstances, he was possessed of a quiet magisterial presence, but given a stage, Moctezuma was an oratorial giant.

'Step-by-step,' roared Moctezuma, 'we will put these problems behind us!'

'Thanks to our priests and their ministration, the Binding of the Years is past and we are safe again... for the moment. So we have taken the first step and the gods have shown mercy. Now though we must return their trust. We must redouble our efforts and continue to prove ourselves worthy.'

Moctezuma paced once around the stage as though deep in concentration. Four thousand warriors watched him in total silence. When he returned to the front, he held one finger aloft.

'You know that we are the chosen people. You know that Huitzilopochtli especially watches over us.' Moctezuma had got into his stride. Sunlight crept inexorably towards the stage from the far edge of the training ground and touched the mood of the watching warriors.

'The God of War is not an easy patron,' admitted Moctezuma. 'We must be sure that his will is done and of course we must repay his support in kind. Tlaloc, Xipe Totec, Mictlantecuhtli and all the others must also receive their dues.

'Be certain of this! The drought is our own fault.' There was a collective gasp from the audience.

'Yes! Look inside yourself and you will see that this is true. We have been doing something wrong these past four years. You see?' Moctezuma waved his staff out over the serried ranks.

'I have been in conversations with the priests, the council and Tlacaelel here,' said Moctezuma. 'Many discussions have taken place as to the cause. One thing we all agree on is that we must take more captives. Where there was disagreement, it was on just how to achieve this. Some favour an escalation of the War of Flowers with Chalco. Others believe that this local squabble is a distraction that weakens us.'

'I have decided, along with the council, that we must widen the reach of our domain and to do that, we must settle our scores with Chalco and move on.'

Tlacaelel watched as Moctezuma paused to rest his voice and to let the message sink in. This was the most difficult part of the speech. This was the content, dry and factual, but a crucial part of the foundation upon which the warriors' belief rested. There could be no doubt in their minds as they went into battle. They needed purpose and they needed to understand the consequences of failure.

Moctezuma stepped forward and resumed his speech.

'You need to see, as I have seen, that by extending the boundaries of our empire, we will achieve two aims: firstly, we will have a great many more people at our borders and therefore, be able to take more captives for the gods; and secondly, we would control more land and agriculture and whether the drought lifts or not, we will be able to collect more tributes and gather more food.'

Now Moctezuma crouched low in a feral, hunting posture, one hand on the ground in front of him, the other holding his staff above his head. 'Then my friends...' He nodded, willing the knights to acknowledge this simple truth. 'Then we could put food in the bellies of our families!' He stood upright again and raised his voice once more. 'So you see, step-by-step, we will resolve our problems!'

Tlacaelel nodded in approval as his brother's last words were met with a thunderous response. The hardest part was over.

'So what is our next step?' asked Moctezuma. No one spoke. No one interrupted the tlatoani.

'Are you feeling bold, Mexica knights? Is the spirit of the jaguar within you? Does your heart soar like the eagle? The next step is to make this valley safe for our people so we can come and go as we please.' Moctezuma raised his voice a little louder with each sentence.

'Today, we will teach Amihuatzin a lesson that he will never forget!

'Today, we will rob the womenfolk of Chalco of their husbands!

'Today, my friends, we will send these maggot-ridden Chalca back to Mictlan-tecuh-tli!' The tlatoani bellowed the last words, inviting a response again and this time, the warriors stamped their feet and cheered for several minutes.

Moctezuma winked at Tlacaelel.

Precious Flower crashed through the door from the small room she shared with Arrow One and Little Beetle, stumbled awkwardly across the room and threw her arms around Blade who was perched on a stool preparing for the coming battle. Fat teardrops coursed down her cheeks and splashed down Blade's back.

'Oh thank you, father!' she cried. 'How will I ever repay you for your kindness?' Precious Flower hugged Blade hard, her loose hair tangling in his face.

Jaguar noticed his mother smiling at the scene through the same doorway that Precious Flower had just come through.

Musical Reed had just handed the official document to Precious Flower, the legal proof that her slavery was at an end. She was, henceforth, a free person, all debts to Blade's household paid off. Blade had delegated the task to his wife, knowing full well that he was not suited to emotional scenes. Jaguar also knew that his parents had offered Precious Flower a job in perpetuity in the family workshop. She was too valuable to lose and certainly a better jade worker than he or Little Beetle would ever be.

Blade patted her on the back. 'You have already paid us off a hundred fold.' He smiled. 'I gather you want to stay? Are you sure of this?'

'Of course,' Precious Flower sobbed in gratitude and then gave a little laugh. 'I was so worried you wouldn't want me.'

Jaguar's mother scoffed good-naturedly.

Precious Flower unwound herself from Blade and gave Jaguar a perfunctory hug. Jaguar felt sick. There was nothing he could do to protect Precious Flower from his misery, nor could he find any way to tell her or his family what was wrong. They all believed that he was nervous about the imminent fight and Jaguar saw no reason to correct them because the truth was too terrible to relate.

Jaguar contrived to smile. 'I'm very happy for you.'

Jaguar was wracked with guilt and shame. He had hardly spoken to his family since returning from his meeting with Cloud Face the previous day. Even the basic civilities demanded a superhuman effort that drained him to his core. His mind had been working feverishly, turning and worrying as he wrestled with his predicament. Jaguar had not slept at all last night, at least, not as far as he could recall. He pulled his battle tunic on crossly. The thick, quilted cloth had been soaked in salt water and dried to stiffen the material and make it more resistant to blows and sharp blades. It was itchy and not very comfortable, which only served to increase Jaguar's anger.

Jaguar and Blade picked up their shields, swords and provisions for the day and made for the door. Just then, Little Beetle burst in. She had been outside watching the clansmen assemble for the march. Her husband, Arrow One, had left a short while ago to oversee the clearing of one of the main drainage channels that ran through the city.

'Where is Ja...' she began. 'Oh. There you are. Come outside quickly. There's a woman here and a boy who say they want to speak to you.' She pushed a few loose strands of hair behind her ear and led the way out.

'This had better not take long or we'll be late,' muttered Jaguar's father.

The street outside was busy. Whitewashed houses that gleamed in the piercing, early morning light, disgorged men dressed for war as their families clustered around, chattering with nervous energy and ill-concealed fear. Women shepherded their children towards their fathers to give them what they fervently hoped would not be their last farewell.

Little Beetle pointed Jaguar at a woman and a small child who stood, waiting at a respectful distance. He recognised the woman from the Moyotlan district, Melody, which meant that the boy holding her hand must be Shield of Gold, although Jaguar could scarcely believe the transformation a few short days had wrought. Where the boy's eyes had been closed and crusted with dried mucus, they were bright and clear. Although he was still painfully thin, the boy looked steady on his feet now. His tousled hair that had been filthy and matted at least looked clean now. The clothing that Melody and her young charge wore was pitifully threadbare but something told Jaguar that they were wearing their best clothes. They had made a special effort to come and see Jaguar off.

'Shield of Gold has brought some food for your journey,' Melody said quietly. She urged the lad forward. Blade of the South, Musical Reed and Little Beetle all watched as Shield of Gold held out a package wrapped in amaranth leaves, tied neatly with a piece of string made from woven strips of reed.

'That's very kind,' Jaguar's voice cracked as he replied. 'You didn't have to bring me anything.'

Melody put her arm around the boy. 'It was his idea. He wanted to thank you... for saving his life.' She nudged Shield of Gold, but he was too shy and said nothing.

Jaguar tried to find something to say but could only stare back, still shocked at the boy's condition. Shield of Gold had stick-thin legs that sprouted from bony feet that looked too large for him. His loincloth looked absurd, like a blanket wrapped round a snake. His stomach was slightly distended and twig-like arms hung lifelessly at his side. In spite of this, the boy did look better. His hollow cheeks had recovered so that a healthy brown colour now replaced the ashen yellow complexion Jaguar remembered.

'Are you well?' asked Jaguar.

Shield of Gold nodded minutely.

Melody saw the boy's discomfort and stepped in. 'He was sick every time I fed him for the first two days,' she said sadly. 'The only thing he could keep down was water. The last two days have been much better though.' She smiled at Shield of Gold and ruffled his hair.

Shield of Gold wiped at his nose with the back of one hand and gazed back at Jaguar. 'It's vulture,' he spoke at last.

'I'm sorry?' said Jaguar.

'The food. Mamma hung the bird you killed and smoked it yesterday.'

Jaguar looked down at the package he was holding and nodded dumbly.

'Supplies for you to take to the battle,' explained Shield of Gold.

'Thank you,' said Jaguar politely. His head swam and he was having difficulty concentrating. He looked at the boy and all he could see was a life that had nearly been extinguished at a time when his own life had seemed to be limitless and inexhaustible. Now the situation was reversed. Jaguar's own life was forfeit and he could not see past the end of this day. Once again, the simple effort of speech nearly buried him.

'I'm glad you're both well,' murmured Jaguar.

'Well, and thanks to you well fed too,' the woman said. 'You should have taken one of the vultures we killed. They would have made several meals for your family.' She smiled at Blade of the South, who had been watching the exchange with interest.

'Your need may have been greater than ours,' said Jaguar's father kindly. 'Now, Melody, we must be on our way. The army will not wait for us.'

'Oh, of course, I am so sorry,' Melody said. 'May Huitzilopochtli keep you safe.' Melody took Shield of Gold by the hand and they set off home, weaving through the residents of Island Home North who were all turning out to say farewell to the departing warriors.

Jaguar added the package of food to his shoulder sack of supplies. Food had lost its appeal to him since the meeting with Cloud Face. He knew he had to eat food to keep his strength up but it was a mechanical exercise consisting of a sufficient number of jaw movements to reduce the food to a point that it could be swallowed. Revulsion registered briefly in Jaguar's head as he made a connection between the contents of the parcel and the stinking bird he'd fallen on in Shield of Gold's house. Had he cared more, Jaguar would have thrown the food away, but he was nearly catatonic.

Blade said a warm goodbye to Little Beetle and Precious Flower, reserving his fondest farewell for his wife. Jaguar followed suit but it was a struggle to do more than go through the motions. The feel of Precious Flower in his embrace was an unwelcome reminder of the terrible danger he had put them in. He couldn't bring himself to look into her eyes, scared of what she might see and terrified that she would guess his secret. He knew that he deserved her contempt. She couldn't be allowed to know what had transpired between him and the high priest and it felt like an impenetrable barrier had been thrown up between them. He turned away.

When Blade and Jaguar were sure they had everything, they set off to the appointed meeting place with a great many other warriors from Teopan in tow. They joined the informal march to Mexicaltzingo, which lay at the southern end of the causeway. In one place, so many people were out, lining the route, waving goodbye and praying to the gods for their safe return that the line of warriors had to force a route through.

'That was a noble thing you did, rescuing that boy,' said Blade.

Jaguar could sense his father looking at him, willing him to meet his eye.

'You never mentioned it to us.'

Jaguar shrugged. 'I'm sorry.'

'If it hadn't been for Precious Flower, we'd never have known.' Jaguar's father sounded hurt.

'When did she tell you?' asked Jaguar.

'While you were out watching the ceremony.'

Jaguar grunted. He wanted to shake his father by the throat and cry out to him to change the subject. It was hard enough trying to keep himself from thinking about her without everyone else bringing her up in the conversation. Every time he thought of her, he remembered the way she had run her hands down his back, the way she had looked at him with her smouldering eyes and every time he closed his eyes, the fragrance of her skin sprang to mind. And then, every time he thought of her, the brief reveries were thrust aside by the image of Cloud Face and his ugly threats.

Blade of the South reached across and gave Jaguar's shoulder a squeeze. In front of them stretched a long line of warriors heading to the Amatcamatl gate, which stood between Tenochtitlan and the southern causeway. Behind them, more men joined the march, streaming from their homes and waving their weapons in the air as they passed knots of women and children cheering them on.

Blade dropped his hand to his side and cleared his throat. 'I know you're worried about this battle, son.' He pointed ahead to where Fire Mountain's head bobbed above the sea of people around him. The road crested slightly as it passed through the Matlalatl Gate and over the retractable bridge. Magic River accompanied Fire Mountain at the head of the clan.

'We've got some of the best warriors,' said Blade. 'We'll stick close to them and we'll be fine, eh?'

Jaguar gave what he hoped was a reassuring smile. 'I'll be fine, Dad. Once it all gets started, I'll be fine.' He would have to come up with a convincing story soon as to why he had been summoned by the priests. Two Sign had been present when Jaguar had been led away by Devine Cactus and it wouldn't be long before he made inquiries as to what had happened. For the hundredth time, Jaguar wondered whether he should tell his father the truth. Perhaps they would have an opportunity on the way to battle, some quiet spot removed from the rest of the army where Jaguar could pour out the sorry tale. Jaguar had no way of knowing how his father would respond. Blade was used to his son getting into scrapes, but this was something else entirely. A simple, vital point of law had been breached and no father, however understanding, could take that in his stride. Again, he came inexorably to the same bitter conclusion. He would have to do the high priest's bidding.

Jaguar breathed deeply, trying to draw strength from the warm, morning sunshine that fell upon his face. The clouds that had looked so promising yesterday had dispersed and the end of the drought looked as far away as ever. A flight of geese made an arrowhead in the sky pointing north, away from the battlefield. Jaguar was no soothsayer, but he would have wagered a new cloak that the family priest would have ruled it a bad omen, a thought that did nothing to lift his spirit.

After traversing the length of the southern causeway, flanked on either side by tall, gently swaying reeds, the warriors disgorged on an area of flat, marshy land just outside the town of Mexicaltzingo. The army already looked vast but it swelled further as it was joined by a fighting force of over three thousand warriors from that town. Tlacaelel's change of tactics had left everyone a little more nervous than usual, which meant that the reinforcements from Mexicaltzingo were cheerfully received.

Moctezuma and Tlacaelel, through the council, had put out the call for a maximum strength turnout, meaning that every able-bodied man from Tenochtitlan was required to present himself for duty to his clan elders. The old men and the walking wounded from previous battles would remain behind on guard duty in the city, bolstered by a small crew of Eagle and Jaguar Knights, who were already on the rota.

Tezozomoc, son of the previous tlatoani, Itzcoatl, had been dispatched on behalf of Moctezuma and all the people of Tenochtitlan to entreat Nezahualcoyotl once more to join the fight but he had returned with a long face and fervent desire never to hear any more of Nezahualcoyotl's poetry.

In the wider expanse of the fields outside Mexicaltzingo, the size of the assembling army became apparent. Out to the east lay the woods and marshes that sprinkled the land between Colhuacan and Chalco. At the head of the army, waiting at the edge of this hinterland were the knights. Jaguar caught sight of their standards, but the gentle morning breeze was too benign to stir the cloth and reveal the individual symbols.

'How many knights in the field today?' Jaguar asked his father.

'Four thousand,' replied Blade whose position on the council meant he knew the details and strategy of the day. 'It's a big day, make no mistake.'

Jaguar and Blade could see the nearest knights and it was easy to distinguish between the extravagant white and brown plumage of the Eagle Knights and the sleeker silhouettes of the Jaguar Knights with their fitted jaguar skin uniforms.

Jaguar had always hoped to join the knights that were his namesake. Their ruthless strength and skill in battle was the subject of countless tales on which he had been raised. Only half a year ago, the news had come back from the frontier that a company of two hundred Jaguar Knights had been set upon by an army of three thousand braves from Tarascan. The Mexica had been reconnoitring the tiny outpost town of Acucha high in the mountains on the far side of Toluca when they received word that an army of Tarascan warriors was advancing on their position from the east, effectively cutting off their retreat. With only hours to prepare, the knights had gathered water, requisitioned meagre supplies from the townsfolk and hastily erected fortifications with rough screed and boulders that lay about them on the mountainside. Wave after wave of Tarascan fighters stormed the rudimentary defences for two long weeks. All were brutally repulsed. The besieged men clung desperately to life, licking dew from the rocks in the early morning and cooking the meat of their enemies to bolster their depleted supplies.

Bloody and beaten, the enemy had retreated on the fifteenth day, leaving behind the bodies of two and a half thousand of their comrades. When reinforcements had arrived from Tenochtitlan two days later, they found vultures circling the rocky outcrop where the stones and thin, brown grass lay slick with blackened blood. Bloated corpses crawled with maggots and the putrid air was thick with clouds of flies. Eighty Jaguar Knights greeted the new arrivals. Half of them were too weak to stand but none would leave until they had been reassured that the enemy had truly gone.

The goal of joining the knights seemed impossibly out of reach. Jaguar clamped down on his hopes and tried to concentrate on the mission that the high priest had set him.

On the dew-speckled bunch grass around Jaguar, the working men of Tenochtitlan were gathered in groups representing their clans. The largest part of the Mexica army was comprised of labourers, fishermen, stonemasons, artists, market traders, farmers, porters and others from the rank and file citizens. From the age of sixteen, every young man from every walk of life was compelled to attend four weeks of training and spend a minimum of twenty days a year in military service. Jaguar saw Storm Light holding the standard of Island Home North. The umber coloured cloth hung limply from the pole so that the twelve-fold black feathers and beady gold eyes of Quetzalcoatl could not be seen. Jaguar wondered how the scrawny youth had been selected for the job. He was hardly stouter than the pole he was meant to carry.

Blade tapped Jaguar on the arm. 'Look! The straw men are coming.'

Jaguar smiled at the derogatory term for the fighting nobility. They were streaming off the causeway and fanning out behind the clans. He could just about make out the red and gold banner of the Teopan nobility from his own quarter of the city. There was no mistaking these men for the common people. Their fine quality costumes were decked out with magnificent plumed headgear, items of lightweight battle jewellery and colourful insignia. Jaguar made a sour face at the pretentious outfits. The nobles were not known for their bravery.

'Are we fighting alongside them?' asked Jaguar.

'No,' agreed Blade. 'Tlacaelel has tactfully placed them where they shouldn't be in danger and more importantly, they shouldn't get in our way.'

'Where's Crocodile?' asked Blade. 'I was expecting him to join us.'

'I don't know,' answered Jaguar, suddenly tense again. Two Sign might have told his son about the summons.

With the nobility came the warrior priests and their non-combatant brethren whose job it was to invoke the blessings of the gods and tend to the wounded in the aftermath of war. Every god was represented, no matter how trifling. The holy ministers of Huitzilopochtli were there, as were the priests of Quetzalcoatl, famed for their invincibility. A phalanx of savage warrior priests of Xipe Totec bristled with sharp skinning knives while the sinister, brooding clerics of Tezcatlipoca marched in stony silence. Tlaloc's priests were lightly armed, eschewing confrontation except in dire circumstances, choosing instead to work with the healers of Ixtlilton. The more obscure sects were hard to tell apart.

While the men around Jaguar chattered excitedly, pleased to have the holy men alongside them in battle, Jaguar scanned the newcomers for a sign of Cloud Face. He felt sure that somewhere, that gaunt, cadaverous face would be staring back at him, wordlessly reminding him of their contract. There was no sign of him but Jaguar hadn't forgotten his boast about having eyes everywhere.

The exodus from the city slowed gradually as the appointed time of departure approached, until finally, Moctezuma arrived, borne upon a golden litter and escorted by sixty Grey Privy Knights. The tlatoani and his entourage swept through the multitude of priests and warriors to rapturous cheers. A number of council members accompanied him as did a small army of servants, cooks and the sumptuous imperial retinue, the bulk creating a bow wake through the crowd. The men of Island Home North had to step back to let the party through. Jaguar and Blade caught a brief glimpse of Moctezuma sitting imperiously on his litter as he was transported towards the knights and his brother, Tlacaelel, who waited in the vanguard.

A short while later the order went up for the army to move out. The sheer weight of numbers meant that it was a long time before Jaguar and the men around him could do more than shuffle forward. Morning dew still lay in the thickest clumps of grass, wetting Jaguar's feet.

Jaguar wondered what had become of Crocodile. He missed his friend's unquenchable good humour. For the hundredth time, he considered telling his friend about the meeting with Cloud Face. After all, he had already told Crocodile about his indiscretion with Precious Flower. But then Jaguar reminded himself that he could not reveal Cloud Face's purpose, even if the high priest was correct about the tactics, Crocodile would know that there was something wrong about the story. Why couldn't Cloud Face have spoken to Tlacaelel? Jaguar felt sure that the general would have listened to a well-reasoned argument, in spite of their mutual dislike. Even if that had not been possible, Cloud Face could simply have given a warning to warriors like Fire Mountain or Magic River who would be fighting in the centre of the line. Why resort to blackmailing a young warrior to do his bidding? No, there was something very suspicious about the priest's behaviour, but Jaguar knew he had no options.

The army left Mexicaltzingo behind and followed the southern shoreline of Lake Texcoco. The ground here was usually marshy underfoot and would not normally have been a good route, but the shortage of rainfall had caused the water-level in the lake to drop so that the going was dry and made easier passage for an army than the wooded ground to the south. At this time of year, these wetlands were usually alive with the sound of waterfowl and migratory birds, but the din of the thousands of men on the move drowned out the songs of any birds that had not already fled.

The sun was high and bright and a faint haze was already beginning to accumulate over the expanse of Lake Texcoco. In the distance, the great temple of Texcoco was just visible, rising above the lakefront dwellings. Now and then, the tide of warriors parted to skirt round clumps of willows that had escaped the ever widening quest for firewood. Jaguar listened to his father join in as some of the men sang an old chant said to have originated with the lost civilisation of Tula. Apprehension was mounting and the warriors were doing everything in their power to defray the tension. A group next to Jaguar laughed as they exchanged tales of previous battles and as usual, Magic River had a story to tell.

'...we were in the middle of a pack of motherless Tlaxcalans,' explained Magic River. 'We were thoroughly outnumbered and ready to die in the name of Huitzilopochtli. Just as the dogs moved in to finish us off, Guarded Fist here,' he continued, indicating a short, pinched looking man to his left, 'lashed out and caught one of them under the chin!' His wiry companion grinned and waved his hand in the air in a chopping motion re-enacting the scene.

'By all the skins! You should have seen the blood gush from this man's throat!' Magic River paused to negotiate a large rock. Jaguar wondered how much the original tale had been embellished.

'Anyway,' continued Magic River, warming to the task. 'The new grass was green and slippery, so what with the rivers of blood, the ground was as slick as fish skin.' Even the older warriors were taking an interest in the story.

'Well, two of the mangy curs waded in to avenge their friend's death...'

'Get on with it,' someone called out.

'Speak up!' called another from somewhere in the marching pack. The warrior gave a hideous grin through his missing teeth but ignored the hecklers. 'Two of them jumped on us, but then Guarded Fist threw his sword up in the air!' Everyone in earshot gasped at this development, aghast at this apparently suicidal move. One man trod on another's ankle and caused a pileup. For a while the air was blue with curses and the storyteller had to wait to continue.

'I know, I know. I was convinced the crazy fool had lost his head completely, but these two oafs were so distracted by the sword whirring over their heads, that it allowed me to mash one of them in the face, but that's not the best bit.' Magic River was really enjoying himself now. 'Remember, Guarded Fist didn't have a weapon anymore, so he grabs the nearest Tlaxcalan by his tunic front at about waist level... well, he couldn't reach any higher you see.' There was a ripple of laughter from the marching warriors.

But there was more to follow. 'Before the man understands what's happening, Guarded Fist jumps back, still holding on to the Tlaxcalan's tunic and swings down and through his legs.'

'Ridiculous!' snorted one man in disbelief.

Magic River held a palm up. 'I swear it is all true!' he insisted and then went on to finish the tale. Apparently Guarded Fist's compact body had shot between the legs of his assailant, skidding so far on the slick grass that he ended up behind the converging enemy ranks where he had stood up, snatched his sword from the air as it descended and rushed back into the fray, immediately despatching four of the startled foe from behind. Unsettled by this bizarre wizardry, the outnumbered Tlaxcalan warriors turned and fled.

Magic River bowed at the conclusion of his story and Guarded Fist did a victory jig as he walked. Half of the men listening burst out laughing while the other half howled in protest at the outrageous tale.

A couple of paces away, Blade was shaking his head, though whether it was in astonishment or disbelief, Jaguar could not say. Just then a hand clamped on his shoulder. He jumped, worried that it might be Cloud Face or one of his priests, but when he turned, he could see it was Crocodile, who had shouldered his way through the crowd.

'Don't do that!' Jaguar cried in dismay.

'Hey, you're touchy,' said Crocodile.

'Where have you been?' asked Jaguar testily, changing the subject.

Crocodile said cheerily, 'Why, did you miss me?' His voice was so full of natural good humour that Jaguar found his gloomy mood lifting.

'I'm sorry,' replied Jaguar in a puzzled tone. 'Have we met before?'

Crocodile responded with one of his trademark punches to Jaguar's arm.

'Hey!' cried Jaguar in mock outrage. 'I was going to save your life with that arm.'

Crocodile burst out laughing. 'What do you mean? Can't you beg for mercy with your left arm?' Crocodile saw Blade watching them and winked. 'So, you wanted to know where I've been,' he added.

'Alright,' agreed Jaguar.

'My father dragged me along with him so I could be inducted into the Eagle Knights,' said Crocodile triumphantly.

Jaguar could only stare in awe. It should not have been a surprise since Crocodile had proven himself in combat but they had discussed this moment so often that it seemed like an impossible dream. He reached out and patted his friend on the back.

'You didn't tell me you'd applied!'

'I didn't,' said Crocodile. 'Fire Mountain and Magic River put my name forward.'

Magic River heard his name being mentioned and guessed the subject. He waved, signalling his approval. Others nearby overheard and congratulated Crocodile, as did Blade, who had edged over towards the two young men as they walked along.

'So why aren't you up there with the knights?' Blade pointed towards the front of the army.

'I could fight with them if I wanted to but I have to serve another year as an initiate before I am entitled to wear the uniform so there's no rush. Besides, I feel more at home with you lot.'

It was so typical of Crocodile's easy going manner that for him there was no urgency in being associated with the knights. It was every boy's dream to be selected for the knights and most thought of nothing else throughout their adolescence. Crocodile was now the youngest warrior ever to have been accepted into the Eagle Knights and within a few years he could be a captain with land, power and slaves. Jaguar had always envied Crocodile his easy path into echelons of the warrior caste, unencumbered by the expectations of a family with a business to run. Suddenly it occurred to Jaguar that since Precious Flower had agreed to stay on at the workshop, his own options were suddenly that much more open. Precious Flower had the vision and the skill that Little Beetle lacked. Jaguar's sister was not a gifted artisan, but she was an excellent administrator and knew where to source the best greenstone and gems. The two of them would make a great team leaving Jaguar free to join the knights, secure in the knowledge that his father's business was in good hands.

Then Jaguar remembered Cloud Face and his flight of fancy turned to dust.

Chapter 11 - Ozomahtli

The sun was directly overhead when the army drew up on the flat, brown plain on the outskirts of Ixtapaluca, a few miles north of Chalco. Behind the small town, patches of turquoise water on Lake Chalco shimmered in the midday sun, visible through a gently waving carpet of reeds. Across the expanse of the plain, some five miles wide, dried grasses swirled and swayed a silver-brown dance, soughing in the gentle breeze. Beyond the plain, the land was a crumpled patchwork cloth of emerald green, spring forest, shot through with gold and russet meadows. To the left rose the desolate beauty of triple-headed Ixtaccuihuatl, its rugged, pock-marked slopes covered in pristine white snow, matched only by the silent, snow capped dome of Popocatepetl at the southern end of the ridge. To the right lay the hunched-back hill of Tlapacoya, a place of pilgrimage for the followers of Tlaloc.

Tlacaelel was deep in thought. He rubbed his nose and then tightened the sash that held his black loincloth in place. Assembled opposite his own warriors was the largest army he had ever seen. He was not a man used to worrying, but the sheer size of the enemy forces gathered in a mighty sweep encompassing the southern edge of the plain was daunting. The Mexica were outnumbered, but Tlacaelel refused to consider any consequences until he had facts with which to revise his plans.

'How many?' he asked without turning. Moctezuma was in heated discourse with Two Sign and Last Medicine. Representing the common warriors, Magic River stood respectfully to one side awaiting instructions. Half-a-dozen of Moctezuma's gaudily dressed retinue stood nearby, mute as usual, unless invited to speak by the tlatoani. Two Sign looked fearsome in his eagle outfit, even without the beaked headdress. Last Medicine, the commander of the Jaguar Knights, was a battle hardened veteran of the Azcapotzalco years. With his jaguar-skin cowl thrown back over his shoulders, the old man was distinguishable by the fine, grey stubble on his head and the large scar that snaked down the right side of his face, where his ear had been gouged out some twenty years ago. He had tattoos in the likeness of thorns on his forearms and the skull of a cat on each of his cured hide shoulder guards. Last Medicine was the living embodiment of the Mexica war-machine and his men were fiercely loyal to him. He had a reputation for escaping certain death, a reputation that others mistook for recklessness, but Tlacaelel knew different. He hoped the old man's luck would hold out today. They would need it.

'Fifty thousand?' said Last Medicine.

'What?!' roared Moctezuma in disbelief.

Tlacaelel shook his head. 'No, my friend. There will be heroics today, but I don't think it's that many. Two Sign?'

'My scouts estimate thirty or thirty-two thousand from Chalco and perhaps eight thousand from Tlaxcala.'

'Where did they get so many men?' cried Moctezuma.

'It looks like Amihuatzin has been doing the rounds of his neighbours with the begging bowl,' replied Two Sign.

'Yes, brother,' said Tlacaelel still scanning the distant ranks. 'Xicotencatl has raised an army from his neighbouring states the like of which we've never seen before.' The admiration in his own voice surprised him. They were in for a rough ride today, that much was certain. 'Still,' he said to himself, 'no one sings songs about easy victories.'

'We have four thousand knights,' said Moctezuma. He ran his hands through his hair despairingly. 'How many others?'

Two Sign answered on behalf of Tlacaelel. 'Just over twenty thousand macehualtin from Tenochtitlan, Tlatleloco, Xochimilco and the others, My Lord. We also have four thousand seven hundred more comprised of the nobility, merchant classes and the priests. Just less than thirty thousand all told.'

Moctezuma raged. 'Damn that prancing Nezahualcoyotl for the degenerate fop he is and you too, Tlacaelel! Texcoco would have fought alongside us if we'd stuck to the original plan.' The tlatoani stamped about, flattening the dry grass in frustration, alternately looking south and then casting a hopeful eye to the north just in case the ruler of Texcoco should have a sudden change of heart.

Tlacaelel turned back to face his brother with calm assurance. He'd seen enough of the opposition. 'My Lord,' he said. 'Our plan is a good one. Firstly, our opponents are unused to battles on this scale...'

'As are we!' shouted Moctezuma.

Tlacaelel continued unperturbed. 'Chalco's knights are no match for our own. They have a fraction of the training and no experience beyond this valley. Xicotencatl may have persuaded some friendly allies to contribute to this expedition of his, but they are loosely affiliated with little exposure to the consequences of victory or defeat so far from their borders.' The explanation was delivered with a smooth confidence that Tlacaelel did not entirely feel. Nevertheless, it had the desired effect and he even felt better as he built his case. 'The various factions will splinter when put under pressure. They lack the common purpose that we possess.'

Tlacaelel clapped his hands together and smiled. 'Whether your cousin shows up or not, the day is ours. Two Sign, Last Medicine, Magic River...' Tlacaelel's voice tailed off as he saw the high priest of Huitzilopochtli approaching with Devine Cactus, Zipactonal and a phalanx of warrior priests in tow.

Cloud Face addressed Moctezuma and made polite greetings to Two Sign and Last Medicine before turning his attention to Tlacaelel. He showed no sign that he had even seen Magic River.

'Hail to you, Tlacaelel, knight-commander of the Mexica and Woman Snake.'

'Hail to you, Mixayacatl,' replied the general, ignoring the familiar undercurrent of derision that the high priest applied to his official title. 'May I offer you my sincere congratulations on the successful execution of the Binding of the Years?'

Cloud Face bowed. 'Why thank you.'

'Now,' continued Tlacaelel warmly. 'If you and Devine Cactus could only devise a ceremony to bring back the rains, you would have the whole nation eating from the palm of your hand.'

Cloud Face bristled, but Tlacaelel pushed on.

'Perhaps, now that the God of War is awash with tribute, we should turn our attention to Tlaloc? I am no expert, but do you suppose the God of Rain is feeling a little neglected?' Tlacaelel inclined his head politely towards Devine Cactus and was delighted to see Cloud Face wrestling for composure.

'Your consideration for our travails astonishes me, Tlacaelel,' said Cloud Face, managing a smile. 'Perhaps, if we outlive this day, my fellow priests and I will look to your suggestion.' Here the high priest took in the broad expanse of the enemy on the far side of the plain with a sweep of his arm. 'Would you excuse me if I make a recommendation?'

'You are a member of the High Council, My Lord,' replied Tlacaelel. 'You know that we must always listen to your opinion.'

'We should withdraw. We are outnumbered and the omens are not good. This is not a good day to fight.'

Zipactonal nodded his head. Tlacaelel wasn't surprised. The Lord High Administrator wasn't known for holding his own opinion and had probably been leant on by the high priest on the march from the city.

'This strategy was approved by both councils, Cloud Face,' cut in Moctezuma, who had been watching the exchange coolly. 'You had your chance to vote against it then.'

'My Lord.' The high priest bowed. 'I only have our best interests at heart.'

Tlacaelel could have sworn he saw a ghost of a smile as the high priest turned and moved away to confer with Devine Cactus. He decided that Cloud Face was playing safe, so that whatever the outcome of the day, he could claim to have had the best advice.

'Tlacaelel,' said Moctezuma. 'I believe you were saying something?'

'Thank you, My Lord. Two Sign, Last Medicine, Magic River?'

'Yes, general,' snapped the men in unison.

'You know the plan,' said Tlacaelel. The general's instructions were clipped and precise. 'Jaguar Knights out on the left flank. Last Medicine, this means your men will mainly be fighting Tlaxcala. Eagle Knights on the right.' He turned to Magic River.

'Your macehualtin will hold the centre,' he said. 'Amihuatzin will place some of his best men opposite you so it's going to be tough. I expect you to have to give ground, but you must fall back gradually and draw the enemy in.'

'I understand,' said Magic River.

'Have you all passed on my instructions to your men with regards to captives?'

All three confirmed that they had.

'Good,' said Tlacaelel. 'We need captives, but not until we've routed the enemy. Is this clear?'

'It is clear,' said Two Sign. Last Medicine and Magic River nodded in affirmation.

'Today is the day to remember the words we teach our young men: "First take care of yourself and care to take captives second."

'Go and make whatever final preparations are necessary. The time is upon us. May Huitzilopochtli fight beside you.' Tlacaelel was pleased with the sour face Cloud Face made at the easy imprecation of his god. He watched as the three commanders set off at a trot and hoped he would see them again.

One after another, Magic River checked on the commanders of the four quarters of Tenochtitlan. The warriors in charge of Azcapotzalco and Tlacopan were brash and complained about the instructions for an orderly retreat. The man in charge of Moyotlan was far less ebullient. Both he and Fire Mountain, who was leading Teopan, understood what was required and agreed without hesitation.

Magic River drank in the atmosphere as he made his way through the ranks of Mexica warriors. In hushed tones, exaggerated estimates of the size of the opposing army were exchanged.

'Pah!' spat one warrior. 'What good are forty thousand mewling pups against the mighty fist of Tenochtitlan?'

'Send them away to get reinforcements!' shouted another and everyone cheered at that.

Commanders barked their orders and slowly, the Mexica fanned out along the width of the plain to face the opposing forces. All those who had not yet donned their armour did so now and unwrapped their swords from the protective sacking that shrouded the obsidian blades. Many laced their sandals again, tightening them ready for battle while many more left the ranks and wandered off a short distance to relieve themselves.

Magic River offered some soothing words to one young man who looked ready to shit and run for home. He felt sorry for the young. An image of his granddaughter came to mind, all chubby folds of skin and toothless smiles and gurgles. Although he had lost count long ago of how many battles he had faced, Magic River always felt that cold, prickly fear welling up in his abdomen. He had never managed to make it go away, but he was pleased that he had learned to embrace it rather than fighting it. He thought of his own family, grown up and independent. 'They don't need me so much now,' he thought, 'not even the little one.' That made it all easier. 'Breathe deep and easy,' he told himself. The plain's dust and the scent of the trampled grass mingled with the smell of leather, oiled wood hafts and fresh pine resin used to cement the heavy blades in place. 'Breathe deep and easy,' he repeated.

'Place your trust in the gods,' Magic River said to one man. 'They will protect us.' He dispensed some advice to one man about his shield and then shook hands with another as he traversed the line-up. From the corner of his eye, he glimpsed the same preparations taking place on the other side of the plain. When Magic River arrived back at the very centre of the line, he nodded to Fire Mountain and Blade of the South, who stood shoulder-to-shoulder with the rest of the fighting macehualtin from the Teopan quarter. Slowly, he checked the glass-sharp pieces of vitrified stone sat tightly in his sword. It was a pointless check, born of habit. He'd checked it five times already since he'd woken up.

'Hey, Fire Mountain!' shouted Magic River. 'Where do you suppose those spineless Texcoca have got to?'

Fire Mountain shook his head ruefully, so Blade offered a riposte. 'They heard you were coming and went home,' he said. 'They don't like fighting alongside losers!'

Magic River smiled. The pre-fight banter was underway.

'Oh, is that so?' said another voice from the crowd. 'I heard they didn't want to fight alongside Blade the Brainless in case they got their skulls caved in by their own side.'

'Ha-ha,' said Blade.

Suddenly all the warriors were joking and making fun of each other or placing wagers on their performance.

'I heard your wife never cooks for you while you're away,' said one bandy-legged individual to a stout man whose eyes were obscured by his thick head of hair.

'Oh yeah?' drawled the stout warrior. 'Why's that?'

'She says you're so useless that she never expects you to make it back.'

'At least my woman notices that I've gone,' came the retort.

Those not trading insults or laughing at them adjusted their equipment or silently surveyed the battlefield, muttering prayers to their family god or goddess and calling for strength. Those men that had brought provisions or spare weapons threaded themselves through to the rear of the line and deposited them in communal areas for safekeeping. Some checked the straps on their wooden shields and some just stood transfixed, as though in a trance, waiting for the order to charge.

Magic River could see that the army was ready. The entire regiment Jaguar Knights massed to the east and the Eagle Knights stood out on the west. Between them stood Magic River's own command of two and a half thousand commoners from Teopan. The whole line made a slightly convex bow so that men at either end stood further forward than the warriors in the centre. Two hundred Grey Privy Knights and four thousand seven hundred more men, made up of merchants, noblemen and priests stood in a second line held in reserve.

Someone eager to get started smashed the haft of his club into his shield again and again. Another joined in slapping the flat of his sword on his shield and then, bit-by-bit, the slow beat was taken up by others. Soon, the entire army reverberated with the powerful, pounding noise. Before long, the Mexica heard the answering crash and boom as the enemy ranks joined in.

Everyone was ready but there was still no sign of the battalion of warriors from Texcoco that Nezahualcoyotl had promised. Magic River scanned the battlefield again. Under a piercing blue, benevolent sky, the menacing ranks of warriors looked unearthly. The louring clouds of yesterday had gone, swept up to the high sierras by the stiff south-easterly breeze. The sky was clear and Magic River was glad that the heat of the sun had begun to penetrate his padded armour. 'Good,' he thought. 'At least we won't be fighting in a downpour.'

The wind suddenly picked up, gusting and swirling over the plain, gathering dust and broken grass stalks in its path and dashing detritus in the eyes of the warriors. The veterans narrowed their eyes to slits. Without warning, the sibilance grew to a crescendo and, out of the flying debris, a powerful dust devil sprang into life on the eastern edge of the plain. A column of air and debris thirty feet tall formed quickly, gyrating as it began to move across the broad swath of plain that separated the two forces.

The sonorous beat of weapons against shields subsided on both sides of the plain. The men stopped banging on their shields and watched the whirlwind in awe. Many had never seen such a thing before and some mouthed silent prayers.

Straw and pebbles tumbled into the maelstrom at the base of the vortex and were swept upwards in a whirling torrent of air. Slowly at first, and then picking up speed, the dust devil picked its way between the two armies, its thin end twisting and jumping about between the tufts of grass, like the questing snout of a hungry animal. Debris rained down on Magic River's head as the apparition passed by heading for Lake Chalco.

'Huitzilopochtli!' whispered someone close by.

'No,' breathed another. 'Mictlantecuhtli... come to see who's joining him in the underworld.'

The dust devil passed the southern shoulder of Tlapacoya and then, as unexpectedly as it had appeared, it raised its ragged skirts, leapt upwards into nothingness and quiet descended on the battlefield.

Magic River had never seen an omen like it. He knew the old stories that told of smoking mountains and terrible floods that foretold the outcome of ancient battles, but he had never expected to witness such an event himself. The dust devil had been bound for Chalco. As he was trying to interpret this sign, Tlacaelel stalked out to the front of the army.

Moctezuma's general had evidently given up waiting for Nezahualcoyotl's men and decided not to allow his men to brood on the nature of the extraordinary spectacle they had just seen. Tlacaelel strode confidently fifty paces towards the enemy and turned to face his men, one hand raised on high. He held his hand aloft for ten long heartbeats and then turned to face the Chalca lowering his hand to point the way.

'Forward men!' shouted Magic River.

Jaguar fell into step with the men around him. He felt both numb and full of energy at the same time. His mind raced and the world around him seemed to slow. A few hundred paces separated the two armies. Crocodile and the men of Island Home North kept pace beside him. The world began to coalesce around Jaguar and his mind attained a simple clarity. Jaguar had to stay alive and he knew that he would do whatever it took to protect his family. If Cloud Face wanted the clans to hold the centre of the line then Jaguar would hold the line. If Tlacaelel's plans had put Jaguar's friends in danger then he would hold them together and help them through the trouble.

Storm Light had been granted the honour of carrying the standard of Teopan. Jaguar could see him a little way off to the right. He would have to keep the youth in sight somehow.

The progress was slow at first so that it seemed the armies would never meet across the intervening gap, but details of the enemy forces become clearer. A banner fluttering above the ranks immediately opposite carried the motif of a frog. One to the left a snake, while to the right, Jaguar could see the motif of a white skull emblazoned on a crimson flag.

The veterans took up a chant and it gradually rose in volume as everyone pitched in.

> Like the talons of the eagle,
> Like the teeth of Cipactli,
> We are the wrath,
> Of Huit-zil-opoch-tli.

Jaguar muttered the words through clenched teeth. Rough grass scratched at his ankles and occasionally, sharp stones found their way through his open sandals and under his foot, but he hardly noticed. Suddenly, the yawning gulf between the two armies was a narrow strip of land and at a signal from the commanders, the Mexica began to jog.

> Like the talons of the eagle,
> Like the teeth of Cipactli...

The combined voices of thirty thousand warriors made the chant a deafening, inchoate roar. Now individual faces of the enemy could be seen howling their own battle cry and then, suddenly, both sides were running at each other. Mexica bowmen at a run loosed a cloud of arrows into the sky ahead but only a handful of the charging Chalca pitched onto their faces before being swallowed up in the thundering press of their comrades. If there was an answering salvo, Jaguar didn't even notice it.

At less than a hundred paces, Jaguar saw the first spears arcing towards him. There was a blur above him to the left and the thump of impact somewhere behind him. Jaguar burned with boundless energy and flew at the onrushing Chalca. Countless days of practice on the ball court had given him speed. He felt as though he could run forever. He heard a shrill noise and realised he was screaming.

The enemy swept towards them like a dark and thunderous storm front across a forsaken valley and then the gap snapped shut. Two lines of men hurtled into each other with the crash and rattling sound of an avalanche.

Tlacaelel had arranged for several portable wooden platforms to be brought by a team of porters. The landscape here provided few vantage points and although the ground sloped slightly down towards Chalco, the only way to get a good view was by perching on one of the general's stands. They were simple constructions consisting of four stout branches about a foot long with a collection of rough cut planks strapped to the top and bottom with tough, braided hemp. Moctezuma had no need of one because he was standing on his litter squinting into the distance.

Cloud Face was irritated that he had nothing to stand on, but he could hardly blame Feathered Darkness. His assistant had only returned to Tenochtitlan the morning before, scratched and dishevelled, and after a debrief consisting of half a dozen sentences, he had fallen into a deep sleep from which no one had been able to wake him.

It was no good sending one of his acolytes to request one as the platforms were in demand. Tlacaelel had one and the remainder had been claimed by members of the High Council and relatives of the tlatoani. Swallowing his pride, Cloud Face shouldered his way through the non-combatant members of nobility and the wealthiest merchants who had gathered to watch the battle. He smiled graciously up at Techoponia, the son of Moctezuma's uncle, Acamapichtli. Why the young man was not on the battlefield was beyond the high priest's comprehension. He coughed loudly.

Techoponia looked down at Cloud Face. His frown was immediately replaced with a look of shock and he leaped off the platform offering abject apologies. Cloud Face snatched the makeshift lookout from the ground and prowled back to Devine Cactus and Snake Eyes without a backward glance.

'You'll get a good view with that,' called Devine Cactus.

'It isn't for me,' replied Cloud Face. 'It's for him.' He pointed at the diminutive figure of Snake Eyes and placed the rough-hewn box on the ground in front of the old priest.

The look Snake Eyes gave him was full of mistrust. He clearly still hadn't forgiven Cloud Face for backhanding him during the practice sessions for the ceremony. His cold, hooded eyes were as black as Mictlan's heart.

'Stand on the box,' instructed Cloud Face, losing patience.

Grudgingly, Snake Eyes did as he'd been told.

'The battle,' sighed Cloud Face, as though at a child, and pointed at the melee. 'Look to the standard of Teopan.'

'Quetzalcoatl?'

'Yes, a black motif on a red background. Do you see it? It's near the centre.'

Snake Eyes scanned the dark, writhing chaos of tens of thousands of combatants, who were nearly a quarter of a mile away. The banners bobbed and ducked, their cloth furling and unfurling as the bearers weaved in and out of the maelstrom, trying to remain at the heart of the battle while staying out of harm's way.

'I see it.'

'Good. In a short while, that part of the fight will go badly for the macehualtin. They will be forced to retreat and Tlacaelel will send the reserves up to help. When that happens, the warrior priests will be called in too.'

Snake Eyes twitched an acknowledgement. Cloud Face took a cautious look around to see if anyone was listening, but he needn't have bothered. Everyone was staring in rapt fascination at the battle. Moreover, there was a continuous din from the battlefield. Nevertheless, he beckoned at Snake Eyes so he could whisper. Devine Cactus leaned closer to make sure he didn't miss out.

'Choose two of your most trusted men,' said Cloud Face at the priest of Xipe Totec. 'Make sure they get close to that standard. There's a pale, skinny youth carrying it now...'

'Yes,' interrupted Snake Eyes.

'He goes by the name of Storm Light. He has an oval face with a pointed chin. If he is still holding the standard when your men get there, they are to kill him. Do you understand?'

Some lank strands of hair had fallen across Snake Eyes' face. He pushed at them unhurriedly and glowered down at Cloud Face. 'Why can't your people do this?'

'My esteemed colleague,' began Cloud Face, inviting Snake Eyes to step down from the box. 'You recall our little meeting a few days ago when we discussed what would happen to us if we didn't all pull together?'

Snake Eyes nodded.

'Since then, you'll be delighted to hear that we have all been very busy.' Cloud Face fixed Snake Eyes with his most disarming smile. 'My second-in-command, Feathered Darkness, through his spies, has found us someone we can use to influence the outcome of this disaster. At great personal risk, Devine Cactus caught him and brought him to me for instruction.'

Out of the corner of his eye, Cloud Face saw Devine Cactus raise one eyebrow imperceptibly. He had to raise his hand to prevent Snake Eyes from interrupting again. 'I managed to arrange for some powerful allies to come to our aid. You can be sure that by the end of the day, we will be in a much better place than we are now, but to be absolutely certain, we have need of specialist skills that you have at your disposal.' He paused expectantly but was forced to resume when it became clear that the priest of Xipe Totec wasn't going to speak. 'Snake Eyes, you do recall our, erm... agreement, don't you?'

Snake Eyes swallowed once and looked long and hard at the high priest. 'The standard bearer,' he said.

'Thank you.' Cloud Face shook his head as Snake Eyes sloped off.

'How did you do that?' asked Devine Cactus after Snake Eyes had disappeared out of earshot.

'Devine Cactus, you underestimate me,' chided Cloud Face quietly. He felt pleased and uncharacteristically candid. 'I'm sure that the tlatoani would be very unhappy if he discovered that his aunt had been drugged and sorely abused many years ago by an aspiring priest!'

Devine Cactus' jowls wobbled as he chuckled. 'After all this time, Mixayacatl, I should not be surprised. At last I understand why I've led such a blameless existence!'

'Don't worry,' thought Cloud Face, 'sooner or later I'll discover some depravity that you've been hiding.' He turned his attention back to the battle. It wasn't easy to see what was going on, so he stepped up onto the platform. It creaked under his weight and tipped slightly on the soft ground. He didn't like the sensation. After a quick scan of the plain, he gingerly alighted and offered the platform to Devine Cactus, who eyed it doubtfully.

'Will this young ball player really make a difference?' asked the high priest of Tlaloc.

Cloud Face shrugged. 'Tlacaelel has staked a lot on this one battle. With Tlaxcala fighting alongside Chalco, it might not matter, but if I can use the boy to tip the scales in my favour, it seems worth pursuing. He and his father, Blade of the South, are popular and respected members of their clan. If the boy picks up the standard and stands his ground, as I've instructed him, a large number of the macehualtin will fight alongside them.'

'That doesn't sound like a good place to be,' said Devine Cactus.

'No,' said Cloud Face in a matter of fact tone. 'Not a good place at all.'

Chapter 12 - Malînalli

The Eagle Knights were slightly ahead of the rest of the Mexica army as the two sides came together. Two Sign led his men at a charge into the tide of warriors from Chalco. He picked a target, tightened his calloused, two-fingered grip around his sword and at the moment of impact, swung his shield up high and ducked his right shoulder under it. The shock of the impact rattled Two Sign's teeth as he crashed into the solar plexus of his victim and hurled him backwards into the Chalca behind, bowling them over. Before the man had time to come to a stop, Two Sign was on him and sliced his back open. A flash to his right and Two Sign twisted away, spun round and extended his shield arm out at head height. A wet crunch, but Two Sign had no time to inspect the damage because another warrior was on him. In the fraction of a heartbeat that he had to assess the threat, the commander of the Eagle Knights saw staring eyes and a wide, screaming mouth, but in that pivotal fragment of time, the weapon was the key. An ugly edge of chipped stone loomed under Two Sign's throat as the spear point thrust towards him. Head down, pushes back neck and now twist shoulders away. The spear rushed across his neck and left a shallow graze. The icy grip of battle-fugue clamped tight on Two Sign's senses. Off-balance now but with his shield arm still describing a violent arc, he wrenched the arm down. Shield intersects shaft of the spear and fragments of the shattered pole explode across the ground.

Two Sign staggered and fell back onto one knee, vulnerable, but the spear wielder was still shocked. He recovered quickly and fumbled for the short sword he was clutching behind his shield. Dimly aware of another figure looming beside him, Two Sign lashed out with one foot, kicked the spearman's legs out from under him and flung his shield up defensively as the figure lunged. There was a clatter and lightening jags of pain ripped through his arm. He gritted his teeth and jabbed into the centre of the shadow, heard a groan and jumped to his feet just as the spearman re-materialised. Two Sign chopped viciously and his sword bit into shield. Wrench sword back, ripping shield from spearman. The shield fell away and Two Sign slashed the man again, knocking the short sword from his hand and opening a deep gash in his neck. Two Sign blinked at the fine mist of blood that sprayed his face and checked around him. The tiny oasis of calm he had carved for himself wouldn't last long so he scanned the conflict around him with the eyes of a seasoned campaigner.

The battlefield was a heaving mess of lurching, lunging warriors. Two Sign was relieved to see that he had not become isolated. Large numbers of Eagle Knights were engaged with the enemy all around him. The line was steady and holding firm, even though they had been forced to thin out to avoid being outflanked. Over the heads of others, Two Sign could see a tall figure about four hundred paces away. Standing out in the distance like that, it could only be the giant veteran Rock.

An ululating cry warned Two Sign that his brief respite was over. A hideous Chalca with a face-full of warts and broken teeth rushed at him. He bared his teeth, dropped to a fighting crouch and brought his shield to the fore.

Rock wielded his oak club with ferocious intensity. He felt strong and the massive weapon sat comfortably in his meaty hands. He was part of the squad of Eagle Knights assigned by Tlacaelel to prevent the enemy from getting around the western flank. It was an order that was proving difficult to carry out. Stretching the line out as far as possible had resulted in a dangerous thinning of the Mexica line with the result that Rock found himself utterly surrounded. It was, he admitted, an unorthodox tactic, but distancing himself from his own men allowed him to make the best use of his club and his long reach. Irritated, he tugged a rogue feather from his eagle cowl as it was getting in the way and wished that he could just get rid of it. His trusty leather headband would have done.

'Come on!' the big man urged the Chalca around him. 'Come and die like the mangy dogs you are!'

Stung by the insult, half a dozen Chalca leapt forward, eager to earn the distinction of being the man to kill or capture the famous knight. Their haste was their undoing. Rock's club swept round in a gigantic arc, splintering one man's pelvis as it carried him off his feet and bowled over three more. The two approaching from his shield side could do no more than beat upon the wooden structure. Rock had had his shield specially made for him. It was twice the diameter of a normal shield and nearly twice as heavy. It was painted black and the rim bristled with one hundred and two black turkey feathers that made it seem even larger than it was.

The two new attackers hesitated; with their comrades dashed away, they faced Rock alone. The closest man lashed out again, but couldn't get past his shield and in the next instant the Chalca was pushed back with such ferocity that he fell back on the ground. The second man lifted his own shield just as Rock's club came down. The tree limb hammered down upon the upraised surface of wood and leather with such force that it dashed it into pieces, broke the warrior's forearm and still the shattered fragments of the shield hit his head with enough strength to knock him out.

No sooner had Rock finished with the last man, than a new batch leapt at him, somehow sure of their success where their comrades had failed. Rock swung his club again winding one man and forcing another man's club against his chest, skewering him on his own club. He fell to the ground where he writhed and twitched among the tufts of grass, eyes staring madly as he tried in vain to push the club away.

Still more warriors pressed around Rock and he wondered if this time, he might have pushed his luck too far.

_____

Shouts, shrill cries and the sound of clashing weapons rang out across the plain. A thin pall of dust rose over the entire field and already, a thin haze towered high in the pale blue sky above Lake Chalco. On the far left flank the ground sloped up gently towards the woods where a myriad of low-growing, dark shrubs cluttered the uneven ground, waiting to trip the unwary. This was the ground occupied by Last Medicine and the Jaguar Knights.

It was clear to Last Medicine that Xicotencatl's appeal to the tribal rulers of Tlaxcala had been successful. He counted thirteen banners representing each of the great houses of the federation.

Following Tlacaelel's orders, Last Medicine had instructed his men to spread out. 'We will not be outflanked today,' he resolved. Fifteen small groups of men had been directed to keep back and watch for the enemy breaking through the thin line. It would be their job to step in and strengthen the ranks where it was needed most. Last Medicine had elected to command one of these units as this would give him the chance to gauge the early progress.

He was satisfied that the Jaguar Knights were not in imminent danger of collapse, in spite of the superior numbers they faced. The training regime in the knights was harsh. The weak were ruthlessly weeded out and re-assigned to civic duties in the city watch or carrying messages. Those who passed muster were assigned to increasingly hazardous missions as Tlacaelel prosecuted the expansion of his brother's empire. The result was a brotherhood, an adamantine corps of fighting men who lived at the boundary of death and revelled in it. All along the battlefront, Last Medicine's men ripped through the violent but ill-disciplined Tlaxcalan army and yet there were signs of weakness too.

Last Medicine ran a hand over his grey stubble and surveyed the line. There was a section straight ahead that looked troublesome. He couldn't get a clear view through his old eyes but he didn't need to. He couldn't say exactly what it was. Tlaxcalan warriors had broken through in several other places that perhaps another, less experienced fighter, might have chosen. No; there was an unusual intensity to the struggle in that area, a surge and flow that just felt wrong. The scar tissue that had once been an ear prickled the way it always did before the carnage.

Last Medicine signalled to two of his lieutenants that he was heading into war.

'It's time. Let's do it!'

'Where are we going?' one of the lieutenants asked.

Last Medicine pointed and then picked up his shield and his shortest sword. This was not a good day for a heavy weapon. He gave it a few, quick experimental sweeps and grunted in satisfaction.

The lieutenant pulled his own jaguar cowl up over his head and adjusted it, settling the jawbone with its fearsome teeth around his neck. The second one arrived with five more knights.

'Ready?'

No one complained so Last Medicine loped off, aiming for the spot he had identified.

'Any instructions?' asked the lieutenant.

'Is that Quitzatzatia's standard?' Last Medicine asked, silently cursing his eyesight. 'Thank the gods it's still alright for close up fighting.'

'It is,' the knight agreed.

'He needs help, but we'll avoid all the people at the back. There's a place ahead where the line is thinner. See the Tlaxcala behind?' They weren't far away now. 'We'll cut through there and come in from the other side.' Last Medicine broke into a run.

They slid between the churning crowds and got in deep behind Quitzatzatia's standard before they ran into real opposition. Last Medicine swatted a Tlaxcalan sword aside and penetrated deeper into the crush, leaving one of his men to dispatch the off-balance swordsman. At a glance, he could see no more than half a dozen of the enemy occupying the space between the mass of the Tlaxcalan ranks and the seething melee that surrounded Quitzatzatia. Last Medicine pounced just as they recognised the new threat.

Last Medicine lifted his sword and powered down onto a warrior festooned with human jawbones. 'He doesn't look old enough,' he thought. The youth did manage to get his shield up quickly though and Last Medicine's sword wasn't heavy enough to do more than rattle it. The Tlaxcalan swept his own sword in at chest height, which Last Medicine blocked easily with his shield. He was about to lunge again then changed his mind. He stepped back, lowering his shield as though off balance. The Tlaxcalan couldn't resist and raised his own sword high. Step in. Jab. Its point wasn't sharp but judging from the recipient's gasp, it was painful when poked into his solar plexus. His enemy bent over double and Last Medicine, moving in a blur, drew his sword across the man's throat, releasing a torrent of crimson upon the necklace of jawbones.

Last Medicine glanced up and noticed that their incursion had drawn attention from the main body of Tlaxcalan troops. They would have to work quickly.

He scowled as one of his lieutenants stumbled into him and went down with a familiar sigh. A shame; he had been a good man. Last Medicine sidestepped a ridiculously ornate warrior who rushed in clumsily and he just had time to lift his sword across the man's face as he lurched past. He sensed he'd done some damage but had no time to follow up. Push, cut. Block, and block once more. He turned and danced round one, some distant corner of his mind appreciating the fluidity of the movement. Now one blocked the other's attack for a moment and Last Medicine hooked his shield behind that of his opponent and ripped it aside, following with a chop across the swarthy midriff. The heaving man went down and fumbled for his innards. Last Medicine stepped back, forcing the second man to jump over his fallen comrade. Just then, one of his own men barrelled into the Tlaxcalan and they both went down struggling. The knight quickly overpowered his man and finished him off.

'This way!' Last Medicine shouted. Quitzatzatia's standard was not far away now and the Tlaxcala on this side were oblivious to the threat behind them.

The four warriors were at his side in an instant leaving the remaining lieutenant to fend for himself. They leaped on the backs of Quitzatzatia's assailants, hacked them to the ground and quickly penetrated to the heart of the fighting where a sorry sight awaited them. The Scourge of Oaxaca, Quitzatzatia, stood pale and swaying, his sword arm hanging by a tendon from a ruined elbow. Someone had found time to tie a leather tourniquet below his bicep. On his good arm hung a shield so battered and splintered that there was very little left. His once proud face and hawk-like features smeared with blood and streaked with sweat. Behind him stood his standard bearer, a grizzled warrior well past his fighting prime, untouched but out of breath, a look of desperation on his face. Six more knights formed a loose circle around them, facing outwards, crouched in grim determination. Three or four dozen bodies lay strewn around them in a slick of gore and pressing close around that circle were more Tlaxcala, perhaps another twenty. The stench of blood and faecal matter raked Last Medicine's nostrils and, not for the first time, he wondered if he could trade his sense of smell to improve his failing eyesight.

The besieged group cheered and let them in.

'Quitzatzatia!'

'Last Medicine, what kept you?'

'I don't much like your choice of spot for lunch,' snarled Last Medicine.

The Tlaxcala sensed they were in danger of missing their chance to take this group. There was a clatter of sword on shield and grunts as the Tlaxcala warriors pressed home the attack again.

Quitzatzatia frowned, befuddled and drained from the struggle to survive. Then he got it. 'Ha!' he gave a sparing bark of mirth. 'Have you found somewhere better?'

'No, my friend, I have not, so let's kill these fuckers or we will not eat in peace.' The human shield of men around them was too intent on holding off the opposition so Last Medicine spat his orders. The veteran's steady voice was firm and clear so the men knit tight together, confident again and drew the enemy in.

There was a crisp snap as the stout man's collar bone broke with the force of the blow. The warrior from Chalco staggered, the nerves to his left arm severed and the shield dropping from his lifeless hand. Still he was not beaten. He was thick-set and powerful and he parried Jaguar's next blow easily. The two weapons smashed together in an explosion of razor-sharp splinters. Jaguar cried out as the shock jarred his arm. He switched tactics and moved his shield to a defensive position. The man from Chalco hammered it several times, each time driving Jaguar back a step, but it was plain to see his strength was waning. Jaguar tried another strike of his own but it was met, and then another. With only one arm, the man from Chalco was tiring quickly as the shock of his damaged arm set in. His time was running out and he knew it. With a desperate lunge he struck again, trying to come round and under Jaguar's shield. Instead of blocking it, Jaguar pulled his shield and arched away so that the wicked blades whickered past his stomach. This time, the solid frame and strength of the man from Chalco worked against him, dragging him off balance and exposing his side to Jaguar. Wrenching his sword up from under his shield, Jaguar caught the warrior's ribs with a powerful backhand that punctured deep into the man's chest. The warrior collapsed onto his knees, let out a small keening sound and then rolled over on his side.

Jaguar experienced a moment's nausea and giddiness; was that three men he'd downed? All around him, there was carnage on a scale he'd never seen before. In the dozen or so skirmishes that he had been involved in, there had never been more than a hundred men in total. He'd been too young for the last great battle with Chalco and no one had told him it would be like this.

The combined momentum of the two armies had driven fighters deep inside each other's ranks so that a broad swath of the plain was a seething maelstrom of Chalca and Mexica. Carried through by their momentum, hundreds of warriors were wrestling, stabbing, pushing, slashing and stamping, hard pressed on all sides and everywhere he looked, the clan of Island Home North were trying to stay alive.

Jaguar started as a figure leaped out in front of him.

'Are you alright?' Crocodile shouted over the din.

Jaguar managed to wave his sword in some semblance of an acknowledgement, still trying to get his breath back.

Crocodile was caked in grime and gore. Rivulets of sweat coursed down his neck and chest, cutting channels in the filth; the only place his skin was visible. Jaguar frowned, trying to work out whether any of the blood belonged to Crocodile. His friend's sword had lost two of its obsidian blades, snapped off in the heavy cut and thrust.

'What about you?' Jaguar began.

'Watch out!' said Crocodile suddenly, looking over Jaguar's shoulder.

Someone rushed at Jaguar, but at the last moment, he was intercepted by Magic River, who chopped him savagely to the ground.

'This is no time for a friendly chat,' said the old man, grim-faced. 'Fire Mountain is dead and we're in trouble. Pull back.'

'Fire Mountain is gone?' Crocodile said, disbelieving.

Jaguar was shocked. 'How?'

'Three Chalca knights caught him out in the open.' Magic River's tone was detached, matter-of-fact. 'I tried to get to him...' He shrugged his shoulders, unable to finish the sentence.

'We can't pull back!' said Jaguar. With a lurch, he remembered Cloud Face's instructions.

Magic River looked at Jaguar as though he was deranged. 'Take a look around you!'

Whorls of savage action ebbed and flowed everywhere they looked and, as if to drive the point home, three more Chalca burst out of the human storm and rushed at them. Jaguar raised his shield defensively while Crocodile dropped into a fighting stance, sword overhead. Magic River set his jaw firm and waited, his eyes dark pools of grim determination.

Time played strange tricks as the world stood still and Jaguar gazed spellbound at the attackers. All three were clothed in exquisitely wrought snakeskin armour that draped their shoulders, arms and back in a ribbon of amber scales. On their heads sat caps much like the jaguar cowls but in the likeness of a mighty serpent. Reptilian eyes glowered down from above the wearers' ears and affixed to the peak of the cap, two large, white fangs curved down before their eyes.

'Coaxayacatl!' roared Magic River. 'Close up! Close up!'

There was no time to make a defensive circle, but the three Mexica stood shoulder-to-shoulder as the dreaded Serpent Knights fell upon them.

Jaguar experienced an icy shiver of dread then his world went quiet. The man that came at him was lean and fast, a pure-white bone spiked through his nose. He wielded his twin swords with lightning speed, swinging them in at Jaguar from either side. Jaguar responded with his shield on one side and his sword out on the other. There was a crash and the snake-man barrelled into him, knocking him over. Shocked, Jaguar dropped his shield and sword as he hit the ground. The snake-man fell across him, suddenly ungainly as he tried to get back up. Jaguar reached up instinctively and grabbed the exposed throat, reaching around under its scaly armour at the back. The Serpent Knight still held his swords and Jaguar knew that if he gave the man any space to use his weapons he was dead. He held the man close and dug his thumbs deep into the snake-man's windpipe, watching as the demon's eyes bulged. Desperate, the snake-man wrenched away and struck at one of Jaguar's arms. The flinty, stone-edged sword bit. Jaguar roared in his opponent's face and flung him to one side, rolling the other way and groping for his sword. It had to be there, somewhere amongst the brown grass stalks.

Already the Serpent Knight was on his feet, snarling and Jaguar saw him swing, one-handed. Jaguar rolled, too slow and felt the sword strike his arm. It felt like a caress, a glancing blow, but now he had come upon his shield. He ripped it from the grass and flung it one-handed up into the warrior's face. Its edge smashed the fangs from the cap and crushed the Serpent Knight's nose. Shocked, the man from Chalco put his hands up to his face, his swords dangling from things around his wrists. Jaguar sprang up, bundled him over and pinned him to the ground where he began pummelling him in the face. He caught sight of his own sword lying a few feet away, but before he had worked out how to get a hold of it, another warrior from Chalco hurtled into the fray with a piercing shriek and launched a blow at Jaguar's head. With no time to think, Jaguar threw himself at his sword just as the Chalca's weapon sang through the space where he had been.

He got clear and saw the Serpent Knight impaled accidentally by the new attacker. Still not on his feet, Jaguar swung out in a wide arc with his sword catching the second man's ankle from behind.

'Come on!' urged Magic River, suddenly at his side. The scar down the side of his face was livid and his eyes darted about warily. 'We have to go.'

The veteran grabbed at Jaguar's arm but his hand slipped on the wash of blood that streamed down it. Jaguar saw a flap of flesh hanging, gouged from his upper arm and was suddenly aware of pain. He winced as Magic River hauled him away from the threatening ranks of Chalca. In a flash of anger, he saw that Cloud Face had been right. Tlacaelel's tactics had gone badly awry. The general should have reinforced the centre at the start. Many hundreds must be dead already.

Magic River slashed at the back of someone in his way and as the Chalca dropped to his knees, clawing at his damaged spine, they saw Crocodile standing before them, chest heaving, breath sawing in and out. Crocodile's eyes widened as he saw the hoards massing behind his friends.

'Head for the standard!' cried Magic River. The flag of Island Home North was not far off, but Jaguar, Crocodile and Magic River had become separated from the body of the Mexica army as the clansmen had been forced to retreat.

'Who were they?' Jaguar finally asked. 'Coaxayacatl?'

'Amihuatzin's assassins,' Magic River said grimly. 'I've never seen them before. I've only heard the stories. We did well to survive.'

'Will there be more of them?'

'I don't know,' said Magic River. 'I hope not.'

––––––––––

'Send them in!' cried Moctezuma.

'Not yet,' said Tlacaelel. 'Be patient, just a little longer.'

Tlacaelel tried to ignore his brother, who was practically tearing his hair out in exasperation. A great orator and spiritual leader he might be, but the tlatoani was no tactician.

'Look! Look at that!' Moctezuma was pointing to the middle of the plain where the Chalca seemed to be running rampant.

'Brother, calm yourself. That is exactly what we want,' said Tlacaelel. 'See how our enemies are pouring into the gap. It's like a bag, and when that bag is full, we'll tighten the drawstring around the top.' In truth, Tlacaelel was not as confident as he sounded. Although the Eagle Knights were in control of the western end of the line, the Jaguar Knights were faring less well against the Tlaxcalan units to the east. In spite of their discipline and ceaseless training, the Jaguar Knights were struggling to hold back the sheer numbers and the Tlaxcala were beginning to spill around the edge.

'Our people, Tlacaelel!' Moctezuma was wringing his hands and kept turning away, unable to watch as more and more ground was given up.

'I'll give the order very soon. Look, even as we speak, the Chalca swarm towards the breach and some Tlaxcalans too.' Tlacaelel reached out tentatively and put a hand on his brother's shoulder, an action that, he realised, would be impossible under more formal circumstances.

'Armies flow like water, My Lord.' Tlacaelel switched to the honorific to offset his overly familiar gesture. 'Where there is a hole or least resistance, that's where the fighters go. This is the shape we made to lure the Chalca in.'

'But how much longer can the macehualtin take this punishment?'

'Take heart, My Lord. If everything goes as planned, by the end of the day, Amihuatzin's army will be crushed and trouble us no more. And if we send the reinforcements in too soon we will not trap our prey.'

Moctezuma grunted, unconvinced.

Tlacaelel retrieved one of the wooden boxes from a member of Moctezuma's retinue and found the largest hummock he could to place it on. He stepped up gingerly; it wasn't very steady. Tlacaelel cursed his parents under his breath. 'Taller! Just a little taller would have been useful.'

'Where are Nezahualcoyotl's men?' raged Moctezuma, finding a new outlet for his frustration.

'You know what these artists are like,' called Tlacaelel. 'He'll probably claim it wasn't an auspicious day.'

Tlacaelel watched as the enemy forces succumbed to the lure of an easy victory and poured into the rent in the Mexica line. The general jumped down and signalled to two runners who were waiting nearby. They were initiate warriors, no more than fifteen years old.

'You,' he pointed to the first youth. 'Go to the Jaguar Knights. Find Last Medicine or any of the captains and tell them that Tlacaelel instructs them to close the net.'

'Yes, My Lord,' said the first runner. He hesitated fractionally.

'Go now! That's the message. They'll know what to do.' He turned to the second runner as the first sped off.

'Yes, My Lord?'

'Same message to the Eagle Knights. Find Two Sign or one of his captains on the right flank.'

'Close the net?'

'Indeed, now run because many people's lives depend on your message.'

Moctezuma was still fretting. 'What about our reserves, the nobility and priests? You must send them in now.'

'I'll take that message myself.' The general collected his sword and shield and set off at a jog without a backward glance. Four members of the Grey Privy Knights peeled off from a squad assigned to protection of the tlatoani and his entourage and set off in pursuit.

Chapter 13 - Âcatl

'Too old for this,' thought Blade of the South. 'Too far gone. Exhausted beyond belief, breath rasping in and out noisily. Just as well we're not setting ambush,' he suppressed a small giggle. 'Damn creaky knees would have given us all away long ago. Eyesight's not great either from all that close-up carving work.' He was not ancient, but the years of work, bent over delicately fashioned pieces of jade had taken their toll. A stabbing pain up the whole of his left calf told him he'd pulled a muscle. Mictlan's bones! He was a craftsman and a statesman, not a warrior.

The man who faced him now was probably half his age. Murderous vitality exuded from the youngster's every pore, as though he was somehow drawing strength from the madness around them. Blade's own over-exerted lungs felt like they were on fire, aggravated by the dusty air.

The Chalca moved like a flash, feinted left then came in from the right. Blade admired the move dispassionately and since he had already twitched his sword to counter the bogus move, he had to let the weapon take its course, leaving his side exposed. He pivoted on the ball of his foot and, as the Chalca's sword cut in, Blade's shield slid into place. The jagged sword crash-chopped the wooden roundel, juddering his arm.

With his back exposed, Blade had no choice but to continue turning on the spot. He ground the ball of his foot into the unyielding earth and pushed his shoulder out and round, snapping his elbow in behind it, powering through the arc. It was a large, unwieldy movement and the Chalca had plenty of warning. He ducked under it and thrust his sword up under Blade's ribs.

Blade yelped as the point dug in but he was still rotating and the weapon was turned aside before it did real harm.

The young man paused, perplexed, the flow of his fight upset.

Blade felt as though he was looking at his own reflection. In the Chalca's vigour, Blade saw the youth and boundless energy he had once possessed. The inexhaustible belief that he too had had all those years ago, during the hundred day siege of Azcapotzalco when Itzcoatl had fought back against the tyranny of Tepanec rule and all the warriors had slept rough through cruel spring frosts, eating only meagre rations.

The youth sprang to the attack again and their swords met overhead with a vitreous clatter. Blade lashed upwards instinctively with his shield to counter a possible downward punch of his opponent's sword handle. Blade almost allowed a wry smile to claw its way onto his lips. There was an art to the fight. It had been a while since he'd done anything but practice, but now he began to recall the craftsmanship that made the difference between a nasty brawl and a total war; a thing of real beauty.

Someone barged into Blade from behind but he couldn't take his eyes from his opponent. Had to hope it wasn't an attack aimed at him. Someone bounced off him with a curse then moved away, preoccupied with his own survival. The Chalca saw his chance and pressed home his attack again. He made another feint, this time signalling an attack with his sword but then shoved hard with his shield. Blade managed to step out from behind the thrust, offering no resistance so the Chalca was suddenly up close. He raked at the youth's exposed stomach with his sword in a move that would normally have eviscerated an opponent.

It was said that, after battle, a warrior need not speak of his valour as his sword would speak for him, and so it was with Blade. The eight fearsome cutting edges that had been set into the shaft were broken and jagged, like the teeth of a peasant from Cholula. So instead of slicing the Chalca's belly into ribbons, Blade's sword merely scratched it.

The two continued their exchange, each probing for the other's weakness, trying to find a way in. Blow after blow was traded, but in spite of the youth's inexperience, Blade couldn't find enough speed to get past him to make effective use of his damaged sword. Bit-by-bit the younger man's energy began to pay off and Blade struggled to keep pace.

Suddenly, a fierce chop knocked Blade's raised shield askew and caught him a glancing blow on the side of his head. He reeled and the Chalca hit out again, pressing home his advantage. Somehow Blade managed to deflect it, but his confidence was gone. He knew he was tired and it was getting difficult to focus. The next blow scraped over the top of Blade's shield and smashed into his upper arm, knocking his shoulder out of joint and severing a major artery.

Blade saw the gushing wound in his arm as though from a huge distance. Waves of thick, crimson blood pulsed from the ragged flesh. The Chalca warrior saw the damage and knew the older man was finished. He pushed him over contemptuously, impatient to move on to his next victim.

Blade wondered if Musical Reed was preparing an evening meal. It was all he could think of as he felt the ground rush up to meet him.

'Excellent,' crowed Cloud Face. 'We may not even need Snake Eyes to do his bit!' The high priest was watching as the rearward line of warrior priests and the fighting nobility swarmed into the back of the Mexica line where it was thinnest.

'What bit is that?' asked Feathered Darkness, who had just arrived from Tenochtitlan.

'Some additional precautionary measures,' Cloud Face said enigmatically.

'Would these measures involve the young ball player?'

'Yes, and more, but you need not concern yourself,' the high priest said.

On his return from Tlaxcala, Feathered Darkness had made his report to Cloud Face and had then dropped into an exhausted sleep. When he awoke, he was horrified to find that he had been out for two days and had hurried out of the city to catch up with the army. When he had arrived at the sweeping expanse of the plain, Feathered Darkness was astonished at the sheer scale of the conflict. Last year's battle in the ongoing War of Flowers now seemed like a skirmish.

'And this is going well, is it?' asked Feathered Darkness, pointing at the battlefield. It was, he decided, impossible to establish who was winning. A carpet of grey specks oozed back and forth across the plain, pulling and swirling, easing apart and then coalescing once again. Closer to, the conflict was a sea of churning bodies, largely indistinguishable from each other with the exception of the Eagle Knights. A persistent droning floated across from the battle, interspersed with desperate shouts and cries of anguish.

There was no answer from Cloud Face. He was too busy watching the events unfold.

Feathered Darkness looked around. The tlatoani was there, a short distance away with his brother and the usual hangers-on. They were all staring to the south, unable to tear themselves away from the action. Behind them, several families had decided to break for lunch. Mecatl and his family were grouped around a pot with some tamales and the Administrator General was there too with his three sons and his slaves were setting out baskets of maize cakes and a pot filled with a bean and green tomato compote. Feathered Darkness was unsurprised when he spotted Devine Cactus helping himself to the food that was on offer.

Feathered Darkness decided to see if the high priest of Tlaloc was in a conversational mood. Devine Cactus had eased himself to the ground where he sat in a rather undignified heap. Someone had laid out a cloth and a modest selection of fruits and cakes in front of him.

'May I join you for a while, My Lord?'

Devine Cactus looked up from a succulent avocado. 'Why, Feathered Darkness, of course. Please sit down and help yourself.'

'That's very kind, My Lord, but I didn't mean to... truth to say, I'm not feeling very hungry with all that going on.' Feathered Darkness nodded over his shoulder. He sat down on a hummock. He was still feeling weary from his trip and the various scratches and bites he'd accumulated sleeping rough were itching like a pestilence. He ran his hands through his hair and raked at his scalp.

'Very well,' Devine Cactus looked concerned. 'I'm afraid I was unable to hold out. I wasn't sure how long this battle would last and I've eaten nothing all day. You see I was out here just after daybreak to visit the sacred springs at Tlapacoya.' He waved a hand at the hill behind Feathered Darkness. 'I couldn't resist. I figured the day before a big battle like this would be one of the few times this area would be relatively safe.'

'Really? You thought you'd be safe this close to Chalco?' Feathered Darkness frowned.

The corpulent priest raised an eyebrow. 'Hark at you! Didn't you just get back from Tlaxcala?'

Feathered Darkness winced.

'Don't be alarmed, my friend.' Devine Cactus gave a nonchalant wave. 'My servants either don't care or are doubtless in the employ of Cloud Face anyway. The very gods would have to be asleep for either of us to get away from prying eyes.'

Feathered Darkness shrugged noncommittally.

'Mixayacatl is really fired up at the moment,' remarked Devine Cactus nonchalantly, selecting a moist looking cake from the basket in front of him.

Feathered Darkness looked pensive, wondering whether it was safe to say anything at all. Devine Cactus carried on regardless.

'His idea to fetch Xicotencatl really worked.' The high priest of Tlaloc bit genteelly into the maize cake.

'Was there ever any doubt?' asked Feathered Darkness.

'Now that all depends on the consequences, doesn't it?' mused Devine Cactus. 'It always comes down to consequences. This,' he added, gesturing towards the battle, 'is the kind of thing where even the consequences have consequences of their own.'

'Cloud Face knows what he's doing,' Feathered Darkness said with conviction.

'Does he really, Feathered Darkness?' Devine Cactus asked quietly. He went on in a conspiratorial tone. 'There is a war on, my friend, and what you see here behind you is only a small part of it.'

Feathered Darkness decided he had heard enough. 'Serves me right,' he thought. 'Have to be careful what you wish for.' He thanked Devine Cactus politely and rose to leave. The high priest of Tlaloc called out cheerfully as he left.

'So glad I could be of assistance. Please come back if you change your mind about the food.'

Jaguar inhaled deeply, trying to steady his ragged breathing and wiped at his perspiration soaked face. His hand came away black from a mixture of sweat, dust and blood. He was about to brush it off on his tunic when he realised that it was just as filthy. A transient pocket of calm had opened up around his position. With enough time to take stock of the situation, Jaguar felt the rough edge of despair lurking in the outer reaches of his mind. Although the sun had barely moved in the sky since the battle began, it felt to Jaguar as though a lifetime had elapsed. It was difficult for him to recall a time before the battle. His knees were shaking from exhaustion. The wound in his shoulder burned like a red-hot coal and every time he moved it, fresh gouts of blood leaked from it. He just wanted it all to stop, but the end was nowhere in sight. For every Chalca he cut down, two more tried to take his place.

The clans of Eastward Point and Snake Rock East had been overrun and decimated. Their shattered remnants had been forced to give ground again and again, until they could do no more than seek refuge amongst the comrades of Island Home North. Crocodile and Jaguar, along with the other members of their clan, had retreated to a raised area of the plain, perhaps it had been a sandbar in an ancient riverbed. It was too low to be of any real tactical advantage, but it gave the warriors a sense of security, however tenuous. From this insubstantial fortress, the beleaguered macehualtin had begun a last and desperate stand.

In the momentary lapse afforded him, Jaguar caught a glimpse of a familiar figure being hauled back from the tumultuous battle front.

'No!' he screamed and broke into a sprint to reach his father's side. He swerved to avoid one man and skirted round behind Storm Light, who was still carrying the clan's standard. He ducked under another's arm and pushed one more out of the way to kneel at Blade's side.

'I'm sorry,' said Achcauhtli, the armourer, lowering him gently to the ground. 'I didn't see what happened. He's still alive.'

Jaguar scooped his father up in his arms and held him close. Blade's breathing was shallow. Blood pulsed horrifically from his damaged arm and Jaguar was suddenly aware of the similarity of their injuries. 'Only I got lucky,' he thought.

Achcauhtli shouted at Jaguar. 'We need to move him further back. We're not safe here.'

Together they pulled Blade out of reach of the Chalca and the surging, stamping feet of the Mexica warriors. It was hard to get a good hold because his skin was slick with blood. A dozen yards away they stopped. Jaguar laid his father's head down gently and tore a strip off Blade's lacerated tunic to apply a tourniquet to his arm. He tried to find a place to tie it but the wound was too high up, too close to his father's shoulder. Blade was slipping in and out of consciousness, weak from massive blood loss. Jaguar felt powerless. Achcauhtli put a sympathetic hand on Jaguar's shoulder and then headed back into the fray.

'Don't worry,' said Jaguar softly. He knelt down and tried to wipe the filth of battle from Blade's pale face. His lips were blue and his eyes rolled haphazardly under drooping lids.

'I'll get you home,' Jaguar choked, his throat taut with emotion. He turned his face up to the sky. The placid, cloudless blue was starkly incongruous with the ravaged bodies on the plain below.

Jaguar looked down again upon his father's ashen face. His father's eyes were open and he was trying to say something. Jaguar bent closer to hear but a fit of coughing seized Blade and he wheezed weakly for a while. Eventually he tried again and Jaguar strained to hear against the shouts and screams that rent the air around them.

With a huge effort, Blade of the South lifted his head fractionally. 'Take care... of your mother... for me,' he whispered.

His head dropped back onto Jaguar's lap and his eyes closed one final time. He looked so peaceful.

A tear rolled down Jaguar's dusty cheek and he closed his eyes in anguish wondering whether he would get to bear that message home. Cloud Face wanted him to rally the warriors and hold the centre ground, but he had failed. Jaguar looked about him at the plight of his clansmen, hard-pressed by the Chalca onslaught. There seemed to be no end to it and nothing that one man could do to turn the tide. He said a small prayer to Quetzalcoatl, the family's chosen deity and asked for peace on behalf of his father. He laid his father's head upon the ochre grass stalks and pushed a lock of hair from his forehead. Jaguar was just getting to his feet when he was struck by a heavy object that knocked him sprawling across his father's outstretched legs and pinned him to the ground. Indignity fuelled the savage rage that blossomed in his heart. Jaguar wrenched himself free and sprang up, ready to wreak vengeance.

A young Mexica lay in an untidy heap, draped across Blade's body. Jaguar recognised the fallen youth but could not place his name. It did not look like he would ever rise again. Jaguar's attention flicked to the young man's assailant whose red clothing indicated that he was a priest of Tezcatlipoca. By dispatching Jaguar's kinsman, he had broken through the dwindling line of men and stood upon the shallow rise. If any more broke through like him it would surely presage the total rout of the macehualtin. There was the briefest pause as the two parties weighed each other up.

A distant corner of Jaguar's mind registered that once again, he had nothing but his bare hands to defend himself with. It hardly seemed to matter. Cold fury consumed him and a rushing, roaring sound filled his ears, but in the instant before the priest from Chalco struck, fear and anger fled and left an empty space where everything was razor sharp. He stood firm as the priest bore down on him, watching as the Chalca raised his sword. Sunlight glinted on its scintillating teeth. Detached and disembodied, Jaguar felt himself flow to one side as the weapon carved its downward path. With the priest in reach, Jaguar lashed out and his palm connected with the priest's jaw, smashing it aside. There was a crunch of gristle and bone. The crimson clad priest screamed and fell to the dirt, clutching at his broken, dislocated jaw.

Yet more Chalca piled in, trying to cut the line in two. All at once there was a commotion from behind and a wave of Mexica warrior priests and assorted noblemen came charging in. Fresh and eager for the fight, they surged through the flagging warriors on the bank and broke upon the enemy. Jaguar found himself alongside a pipiltin warrior resplendent in a headpiece of shimmering aquamarine plumage and a thousand tiny sea shells woven into his tunic as armour. This handsome noble was no man of straw. He plunged into the roiling mass ahead. The yells of Xipe Totec's devoted followers reverberated all around as they leaped headlong over fallen bodies, slipping on the blood-soaked grass in their hurry to do their holy work.

A cry to Jaguar's left drew his eyes to the clan's standard, ten short strides away. Island Home North's flag toppled as Storm Light was brought down. This was the moment Cloud Face had predicted and so, decided on his course of action, Jaguar darted over. Storm Light's guards were scattered, fighting for their lives. A burly warrior with pale skin and bulging muscles stood over the young Mexica, raising his sword for the killing blow. Jaguar decided the warrior was from Tlaxcala as he bounced off the big man's shield, forcing him back a step. Still weaponless, he crouched, staying low and out of reach. The man from Tlaxcala sneered contemptuously, his shoulders bunching ominously and the sinews in his neck standing out like thick lianas as he prepared for his attack.

But it was all too obvious. Jaguar felt sharp and revelled in his lack of weapons, unencumbered. The Tlaxcala lunged. Deadly blades flew at Jaguar's face, but he was white hot, ablaze with a deadly, instinct-driven speed. Head tipped back and as the sword fizzed past, Jaguar sprang in behind it. He strained every fibre of his body. Calves honed to perfect fitness in long hours of practice on the ball court contracted and launched him at his opponent. Jaguar lowered his head in-flight and it punched into the enemy's solar plexus. The stocky man's midriff caved in and he let out an explosive grunt then crashed back to the ground. Jaguar rolled out and reached for a fallen sword. He snatched it up and clove the Tlaxcalan's purple, wheezing face in two.

Storm Light lay face down on the ground writhing. One hand was bent up behind his back, clawing to reach the arrow that jutted from below his shoulder blade. He glanced up at Jaguar uncomprehending.

'Lie still,' said Jaguar. 'Rest now and I'll be back.'

Jaguar retrieved the fallen standard, but he had a feeling he was too late to satisfy Cloud Face's plans. The time to hold the Chalca back and make a stand had long since gone. The section of the Mexica army between the Jaguar Knights and the Eagle Knights had caved in. The fighting men of the clans had simply been outnumbered. Where they had stood five or six deep, the enemy had nine or more. Superior Mexica training had evened the odds, but in the end, the constant pressure of fresh and ready Chalca could not be held at bay. The line had buckled, reformed and buckled once again. Jaguar cursed and wished he had taken action earlier. This is what the high priest had wanted to avoid and now it was too late to make amends. Never mind, Jaguar knew that he must hold the standard now no matter what. His clan must have a rallying point. The red cloth unfurled as he raised it skywards and unveiled Quetzalcoatl's reptilian face surrounded by dark feathers.

Someone cheered.

'To me!' Jaguar shouted. 'To me,' his cry rang out again.

One of the standard bearer's guards was free and rallied to the call. Magic River too had seen the standard fall and was already on his way. He had extricated himself from another desperate skirmish and within moments was at Jaguar's side.

Now Jaguar held the flag aloft with one hand on the wooden pole. In the other hand he held the sword he had picked up moments earlier. It didn't feel familiar, but at least it seemed well made and still had several cutting edges.

Magic River's scarred face contorted. 'Move forward!' he roared at Jaguar. 'We have the reinforcements now and I'll watch out for you.'

Jaguar strode into the thick of the struggle with Magic River just ahead. On his left-hand side, one of Storm Light's last remaining guards trudged with them then Achcauhtli joined them on the right. Feeling less exposed, Jaguar's eyes swept up and down the length of the plain and saw that the knights had fared less badly. They had contained the broad expanse of the enemy's attack and funnelled it into the centre, but they had not been able to close the net. The combined strength of the Chalca and Tlaxcala made such a feat impossible. Jaguar never thought he'd see the day when he'd be grateful for the nobility taking arms beside him. This then was that day and, with the warrior priests alongside too, it looked as though their fortunes might just be reversed.

Then Jaguar recognised Two Sign wading towards him through the frenzied action and felt a sudden thrill. Far out on the flank he must have seen the plight of the macehualtin and, knowing that his knights were in control, he'd left them to it, electing instead to help the common warriors. Through the ducking, wheeling crowds, Jaguar watched Crocodile's adoptive father carve his way towards them.

A tall man came at Two Sign, all teeth and spittle, long arms wheeling. The Eagle warrior took the first blow on his fast disintegrating shield and parried the next with his own sword, turning it aside. Quick as a flash the tall man launched a backhanded blow. Two Sign nudged it safely up and over and then had to dance back as the rangy man jabbed at him with his shield. Jaguar saw Two Sign wait. A thrust with the shield, and then another. The Chalca used the length of his arms to keep Two Sign on his back foot. Suddenly the Eagle Knight hooked his shield behind the other as it came at him again. He wrenched the man towards him and calmly inserted his sword into the space between shield and neck. Gangly arms dropped the sword and shield as the stricken warrior clamped his fingers to his jugular in a futile attempt to staunch the wound.

Jaguar rapped an enemy fighter on the head with his sword as he got too close, tangling with Magic River, then he turned back in time to see two more Chalca launch themselves at Two Sign. The Eagle Knight had now reached Jaguar's clan and his presence instantly lifted everyone's spirits. Now it was the turn of the Chalca to baulk and falter against the newly strengthened Mexica front. A wiry man, who looked like an administrative clerk, hesitated as he stepped into Two Sign's path. The Eagle Knight's feathered cowl hung in tatters around his neck and his shaven head was streaked with gore. Numerous cuts about his arms and thighs oozed gentle rivulets of dark ichor. Gobbets of nameless filth clung to the knight's ragged loincloth and, hanging loosely at his side, the chipped stone teeth of his sword and battered shield told a tale of a day of violence.

With the wiry Chalca was a swarthy, muscular warrior, who reminded Jaguar of a dark-haired tapir, all shoulders and no neck. The tapir man moved first. Two Sign blocked him with his shield, but the now frail structure flew into a hundred fragments at the brutal impact. The wiry man darted in but Two Sign swatted him away. A rattling jolt forced Jaguar to defend himself. An evil looking Chalca with a necklace full of human jawbones had slashed at him, narrowly missing his arm and clattering into the standard. Jaguar poked at him with the sword, frustrated at the loss of freedom now that he held the flag. He needn't have worried. Crocodile appeared briefly on one side and swung a heavy blow that smashed one of the Chalca's legs out from under him. The warrior screamed and fell upon his rattling string of jawbones. Crocodile rapped the flat edge of his sword on the downed man's skull and rendered him unconscious.

'Thanks,' Jaguar called out to his friend, who had already danced back into the melee. Suddenly, Two Sign was by his side. His last two adversaries were nowhere to be seen.

'Good work,' rasped the Eagle Knight. Then he called out to everyone around him. 'Stand here! Do not advance!'

Inspired by the presence of Two Sign in their midst, the clan, together with several members of the nobility, drove the enemy off the shallow slope they occupied. Magic River, who had begun to flag, found some untapped reserves of energy. There was something strange in the way the two veterans moved. Jaguar saw that while the younger men around them leaped and darted in and out, Two Sign and Magic River's movements were almost lazy. They stepped deliberately between their fallen comrades, fluid, almost graceful and always lethal.

The mood had changed across the plain. Somehow the din of war had taken on a different tempo. Jaguar sensed the end was not far off. Disheartened by their inability to capitalise on the break, the Chalca were falling back and even the Tlaxcalan attack was petering out as the Jaguar Knights stood, unbroken. There was a moment in every battle that the old men called 'the eagle's claw' that described when killing switched to capture. That time was not far off. With every passing moment, Jaguar felt the apprehension grow as the warriors tried to get the timing right. Make a move too soon and the catcher would be caught. Wait too long and lose the chance to take a victim as the enemy melts away. Everyone was wary, testing each engagement.

Rock sensed the change in timbre of the voices around him. He staggered forward, pushed two enemies over backwards and swiped at a leg that protruded from the pile. A knee shattered and the injured man howled in agony. Rock stamped on the other man's stomach. 'Won't be getting up soon,' he thought. His arms were leaden. Two more men jumped on his back, but Rock flipped his club over his shoulder and one fell senseless to the floor. A flicker at the corner of his vision, an arrow. He spun away and heard a groan as the man holding him round the neck, trying to choke him dropped off, breaking the arrow from his own back as he rolled onto the ground.

Rock was bleeding from a dozen cuts and his eagle cowl had long since been torn from his shoulders. He flicked the trailing end of his leather headband out of his eyes and stepped back, bumping into a tattooed warrior called Red Horizon who had managed to fight his way alongside him. A dozen more Eagle Knights were close behind him, ferocious in their feathered headgear and covered in enough blood to make the God of War proud. He nodded once in thanks.

The smile on Rock's face died and he hissed in pain as an arrow suddenly protruded from his arm. He scowled at it and lifted his head to see the archer thirty paces away, reaching for another arrow. Rock lodged his gnarled club in the space between his shield and left forearm and snatched up a spear that lay discarded upon the ground, owner already treading the dark path to Mictlan's world of shadows. He hefted it back and flung his arm forward with a grunt. The archer had notched his arrow and looked up, just as Rock's spear punched through his ribcage and bore him to the ground.

A brief lull developed as the opposing forces in this part of the field drew back a little to assess the situation. The Eagle Knights had held their own out here, but the Chalca still seemed so numerous.

'Have you been cowering at the back again?' Rock rasped at Red Horizon. He gripped his familiar club again and tried to draw breath.

'What are you talking about?' Red Horizon shot back. 'You wandered so deep into the Chalca army you were practically fighting the women and children at the back!'

'Pull this out will you?' asked Rock glaring at the arrow. 'We've got more work to do and this is just going to get in the way.'

At the eastern end of the raised area, Crocodile was praying fervently for the battle to end. He was exhausted, needles of pain shot through his calf muscles, his shoulders ached intolerably and his arms felt as heavy as mountains. It took an immense effort of will to rise to each new encounter. He no longer noticed the thick, gelatinous layer of blood, sweat and dust that caked his skin and clothing. The brief rest he had taken just a few moments ago felt like a lifetime ago. He spat, and spat again, trying to clear the grit from his mouth, but he could make no saliva. He was as parched as the cracked, sun-baked plain beneath his feet.

The sun had been a little to the east of the city of Chalco when they arrived that morning and now it was just to the west, above the lake, less time than it took to row a war canoe across Lake

Texcoco, but an eternity for a pitched battle. Crocodile allowed a small smile to crease one corner of his mouth. They would sing songs about this day. The raw, feral terror that had threatened to consume him at the day's first charge had faded to a dull ache in the base of his stomach as he had settled to the butchery. He had lost count of how many Chalca had fallen beneath his sword. Ever since the murder of his real parents, Crocodile had sought solace in warfare. It didn't matter to him that the real killers had been from Oaxaca. Each enemy faced might be his father's killer. Every raiding party interrupted was like the one that tore his village apart and dragged his mother off to slavery. But although the death toll mounted, the dull ache never left him.

Now, as the tide of battle turned, Crocodile's fear returned. The threat of capture loomed. Indiscriminate vengeance had given him nothing, left him empty. There was no absolution in the service of Mictlantecuhtli. The Lord of the Dead cared nothing for the living.

A knight from Chalco stood before him with a leer and Crocodile stared back at him edgily.

'Come on, boy,' goaded the knight, waving his club in a figure of eight. 'Come and get me if you can.' He carried no shield – perhaps it lay broken on the field somewhere – and his finery marked him out as a captain. He was handsome with a cruel nose and an easy swagger. This was a man who was used to war. He stood a few paces away, safe with his men around him. Up and down the line the story was the same. Each side had pulled back a little with no one willing to be isolated behind enemy lines.

Crocodile said nothing.

The captain switched his club smoothly from one hand to the other, attempting to distract Crocodile with its movement. 'Run back to your mother's skirts, boy!' the captain taunted.

'I would do,' Crocodile replied at last. 'Only I chopped her head off and ate her brains for breakfast!'

The corner of the captain's mouth twitched upwards in amusement, then he lunged forward switching his club neatly to his left hand. Crocodile batted his opponent's weapon aside with a deft movement then shifted his stance to compensate for the ambidextrous attack. Again the Chalca warrior lunged, and again it was on the left. Crocodile swung his sword to intercept, but the lunge stopped short as the captain flicked his wrist back and aimed higher at Crocodile's shoulder. It wasn't a complex move, but it was fast. Crocodile was its equal, twisting his body and arm back to block the shot. As the two swords smashed together, one of the blades on the captain's club snapped off in the impact and flew at Crocodile's face. Crocodile sensed the movement and looked away instinctively but too late. The stone shard lodged above his eyebrow, which instantly ran red, partially blinding him.

For once, Crocodile was slow to react; slow to step back into the safety of the Mexica ranks. Crocodile desperately tried to blink away the blood from his eye in time to put up a defence. He wiped it with the back of his hand, but that only made it worse. He only succeeded in depositing an agonising load of grime into his eye. The next moment the captain had his sword arm in a crushing grip and twisted it violently around. Crocodile cried out and dropped his weapon.

Unlike the captain, Crocodile had no aides fighting close at hand. Magic River and Two Sign stood in defence of Jaguar and the flag of Quetzalcoatl, too far away to help. Achcauhtli was engaged in a fierce struggle of his own.

The captain got his other arm around Crocodile's neck and tried to drag him back among the grasping hands of his own men. Crocodile struggled and twisted like a frenzied snake, trapped at the end of a forked stick. He kicked and thrashed and tried to bite his captor's arm. Stark terror fuelled his animal violence. An image sprang unbidden to his mind. The top of the Great Temple on the night of the New Fire and a triumphant priest beside the sacred altar with a sodden, grizzly prize held high. Crocodile choked back vomit and lost control of his bladder, splashing pungent urine down his loincloth and his legs. Frightened and ashamed, Crocodile broke down and sobbed, suddenly spent. His captor barked triumphantly and hauled him back behind the Chalca lines.

Crocodile felt a shockwave crash through his head and he fell, poleaxed, face-first in the grass.

Chapter 14 - Ocêlôtl

The cries of wounded and dying men floated across the wide expanse of the plain, but compared to the clamour of war a few minutes earlier, it sounded peaceful. The pall of dust was clearing fast and high above the desiccated grasslands, above the detritus and viscera, in a painfully innocent blue sky, fifty or more vultures glided like ghosts. In pairs or threes they wheeled in tight circles over Tlapacoya, gaining height in the thermals before setting out on a broad reconnaissance around the perimeter of the battlefield. Now and then, a plaintive cry rang out as the creatures called to each other, eager to begin the feast.

Tlacaelel gazed up at the circling specks with disgust; at least Tenochtitlan would be rid of them for the next few days. Wherever he looked, the ground was strewn with corpses; some recumbent as though peacefully asleep without a mark upon them. Others lay ripped apart as though by some rapine monster. A few were slumped in awkward, unnatural positions. One wretch lay face down in the dust, his shoulders prone upon the ground while his gleaming buttocks pointed at the sky, loincloth not much use at this angle.

Moctezuma's disappointment hung in the air like the odour of month-old carrion.

'Is this your crushing blow against the Chalca?' the tlatoani gesticulated. He paced up and down, while his litter was being prepared. Tlacaelel had one ear for his brother; with the other he was listening anxiously for the messengers that came in from every clan and unit. The Chalca were pulling back to their city, heading for the safety of the walls and in the far distance, the Tlaxcala were regrouping in the lee of Ixtaccuihuatl, readying for the journey home.

Tlacaelel's thick eyebrows tried to meet in the middle of his frown. 'It did not go as well as I had hoped,' he said.

'Well?' Moctezuma's voice rose a notch. 'Brother, that word in no way describes what happened here today!' He pointed a finger at the retreating enemy. 'We needed to annihilate them. You promised me that we would deal them such a blow that they would never trouble us again.'

'We slew many Chalca today,' Tlacaelel said quietly.

'Have you seen how many we have lost?' Moctezuma raged. He swept his arm across the landscape from the mountains to the lake. 'No need to count them! They are scattered everywhere you look.'

He was right of course, thought Tlacaelel. The numbers, in the end, had been too many. And yet something was wrong. Tlacaelel had been in a hundred battles of every size and almost as many had fallen under his command. He had studied every strategy and martial tactic of great Tezozomoc and he knew in intimate detail every battle and major skirmish that had ever taken place between his people and the Chalca since the reign of Acamapichtli. The plan to draw the Chalca into a trap had worked almost exactly as he had intended. Tlacaelel had known that the clansmen would be forced back and yet they had not fallen back far enough or quickly enough. The gaping maw of the Mexica had not expanded enough to swallow the enemy warriors and surround them. Something else was nagging him.

Tlacaelel was turning the evidence over in his mind when Cloud Face moved into view. The high priest looked serene as he picked his way towards them through the tlatoani's advisors and family.

'My Lord, we repelled a larger force than ours,' replied Tlacaelel, forced to defend himself.

'But at what cost, brother?' Again the disappointed tone. Moctezuma's litter was ready now. Eight slaves in simple loincloths stood beside it, waiting for the command to take the tlatoani back to his palace. The courtiers and nobility already looked bored of the proceedings and looked keen to head back to the city. Some had their own litters but etiquette dictated that they could not leave until Moctezuma did.

Cloud Face was closer now. The odious Snake Eyes was trotting along beside him and as always, Feathered Darkness followed on behind. Cloud Face had a friendly hand on Snake Eyes' shoulder and the high priest of Xipe Totec appeared to have much to say.

Suspicion bloomed and then was gone, leaving behind a small kernel of certainty. 'I think, My Lord,' Tlacaelel said quietly, 'that we have been fighting more enemies than we supposed.'

'How many then?' demanded Moctezuma. 'I thought Two Sign said forty thousand.'

'No. Um...' Tlacaelel wasn't really listening anymore. 'I'm sorry, My Lord, can we discuss this later? There's something urgent I must attend to. Would you excuse me while I go and check on our troops?'

'You may go, Tlacaelel, but I want a full report tomorrow in the Hall of Truth. Make sure you bring one of your commanders in case I need more detail of what happened out here today. Oh, and one other thing... send a messenger to Texcoco right now. I want to know what that useless shit Nezahualcoyotl has been doing while our people have been dying on his doorstep!' Moctezuma's voice rose to a crescendo.

'And that,' thought Tlacaelel, 'is why it is not me but my brother who is the tlatoani. There was some ghostly imprint of Huitzilopochtli in the man that he would never have.' Tlacaelel felt a burden of responsibility for the Mexica, but to his brother they were more; they were his children. For all his love of plans and for attending to meticulous detail, Tlacaelel had failed his brother and so he was angry with himself.

'Of course, My Lord.' Tlacaelel turned to go but found Cloud Face blocking his path.

'What's this?' asked the high priest silkily. 'Going so soon?'

Tlacaelel stared up, unblinking, straight into Cloud Face's eyes, trying to see some tangible evidence of wrongdoing in those black, impenetrable depths. Tlacaelel was almost a head shorter and noted the high priest's posture, leaning over him to intimidate, head slightly on one side as though puzzled by the actions of a wayward child. He tried to find some shred of empathy in the man before him, tried as he had before to establish a human connection on any level, but there was nothing. Tlacaelel wondered if this was the price a man must pay in order to be a vehicle for the gods. In his time the general had fought and killed perhaps a hundred men himself, but always in the heat of battle. 'Maybe ten thousand sacrifices might reduce me to a cold, uncaring husk,' he thought.

'Has the day gone well?' Cloud Face finally broke the silence.

Still with his eyes fixed firmly on the high priest's face, Tlacaelel replied coolly, 'I don't know yet. Why don't you ask Huitzilopochtli?'

Cloud Face addressed Moctezuma. 'My Lord, do we have news of casualties yet or how many of our men were taken in return?' Tlacaelel decided that he wanted no further part in the conversation and stalked away. Over his shoulder he heard the tlatoani reply.

'No, we do not, Mixayacatl. It's still too early.'

'Is this a victory?' asked the high priest doubtfully.

Tlacaelel didn't hear his brother's reply, but he was too annoyed to listen anymore. The high priest would stir up trouble and he would have to undo it all at the meeting tomorrow. Tlacaelel collected four members of the Grey Privy Knights and set a brisk pace towards the centre of the field where the macehualtin had made their stand. He had known that the common troops would pay a price for his strategy, but in his plans, the retreat should have happened earlier and tempted the enemy further from their own lines, instead they had held out too long. Their own resilience had been their own undoing as it had forced Tlacaelel to delay the reinforcements. He clicked his tongue in irritation.

Jaguar sat on a tuft of bunchgrass, knees drawn up under his chin, shivering uncontrollably. He didn't notice the corpse that lay beside him. A cloud of flies swarmed about the body, dancing excitedly about the black, syrup-like puddle it lay in. Several flies had settled on the wound in Jaguar's arm that still oozed darkly. Now that the fighting was over it was agony, but worse than that, he was wracked by bouts of trembling that set his teeth chattering. He tried to clench his muscles to bring it under control. He shut out the world and focused on the stalks of grass in front of him. He tried to relax and breathe deeply, but nothing seemed to work. When each fit passed, Jaguar felt drained and hollowed out, like one of Xipe Totec's skins with black holes where the eyeballs used to be. Then, when he felt he might be able to get up and rejoin the world, the dreadful tremors returned and all he could do was hug his legs tightly.

News of Crocodile's capture had spread quickly. Everyone in Jaguar's clan knew him and treated him as one of their own.

Achcauhtli had come to give Jaguar the bad news immediately after the battle ended. The armourer had been beside him only narrowly avoiding a similar fate. 'You would not believe how bravely he fought!' he exclaimed. 'He was as good as his name.'

Jaguar had gone numb when he had heard the news, at first telling himself that Achcauhtli must be mistaken. Crocodile would surely swagger into view any minute wearing his idiot grin. Achcauhtli was forced to repeat the tale again for Two Sign who listened to it all with a stolid expression, arms crossed. At the end, the big knight had embraced Achcauhtli saying, 'Thank you. We can all be proud of Crocodile. He was a true warrior to the end.'

Jaguar had watched in disbelief as Two Sign wandered off and began to organise work details. This was the man who had adopted Crocodile and raised him single-handedly. This was the man who had found lodgings for the boy in the barracks and made him go to school. Two Sign had patiently put up with Crocodile's mischievous side, calming the victims of his pranks when he, and later Jaguar too, had got into trouble. The knight had turned his back and got on with his duties, as though his adoptive son had never existed.

All across the plain, the gruesome task of sorting and collecting the dead for burial was going on. Jaguar was vaguely aware of the work going on around him. Here and there, in groups of twos and threes and accompanied by a priest, weary men turned corpses over, looking for their clansmen and neighbours and hoping to find more survivors. In the aftermath of war, every casualty had to be inspected by a priest skilled in the art of medicine. It was one of the edicts issued by Tlacaelel after a story had spread around the lake about Hand of the Warrior, who had returned home three days after the rest of the raiding party. Hand of the Warrior had been an experienced fighter, ten years in the Jaguar Knights. The raiding party had been dispatched to exact vengeance on a rebellious town on the banks of the Mizteco River. After a savage fight on the outskirts of the town, Hand of the Warrior had been left for dead. Three days later, he had stumbled in through the door of his family home in the early hours of the morning, streaked with mud and filth, clutching at the stump of his dismembered left arm and collapsed on the earthen floor in front of his own hearth. The unfortunate man had drifted in and out of consciousness for another day before he finally succumbed. He had been the talk of Tenochtitlan and the subject of endless disputes as to whether he would have lived if he had been carried home by the raiding party.

Resurrection was not likely for the carcass next to Jaguar. Two warriors came and examined it. One of them moved on while the other hunkered down next to Jaguar briefly, muttering words of encouragement. He ended by patting Jaguar gingerly on the shoulder and joined his comrade, who was stooping to inspect another victim.

Jaguar was just wondering whether the Chalca would return to retrieve their dead when another fit of shakes took hold of him, this one less violent than the ones before. When the rattling of his teeth subsided, Jaguar decided that he had to take some action, do anything to occupy his mind and give his muscles something else to do but shiver. Feeling light-headed, he staggered to his feet, gritting his teeth against the waves of pain in his arm. The world swam in and out of focus.

'Sit down before you fall over,' said a firm voice.

Achcauhtli had returned to check on him.

'I'm going to clean your wound. I brought some water and some clean cloth to bind it with.'

Jaguar sat down heavily and the armourer opened a gourd he had with him. He doused Jaguar's shoulder and bicep and used a small section of cloth to wipe it gently, moving up against the direction of the flap of flesh that hung open. The movement provoked the welling up of fresh blood and Achcauhtli made satisfied noises. He took another length of cloth and wound it several times around Jaguar's arm before tying the ends together.

'The wound is clean now, but this is going to slip,' said Achcauhtli. 'You'll have to get someone to retie it for you if it does. Try not to move it for a few days.'

'Thanks,' said Jaguar. The bandage made him feel better. 'I need to find my father. Have you seen him?' Jaguar asked.

'That may be where they've taken him, over there.' The armourer pointed to a pile of twenty or so bodies that lay a short distance away, one of perhaps a hundred that were growing across the width of the plain. Scores of warriors who were still fit enough to dig were scraping out shallow graves, assisted by slaves who had been brought from Tenochtitlan for that purpose. 'I'll come with you,' he added.

The two of them went over to inspect the bodies. Next to it, dozens of men, sweating profusely had managed to excavate an area about twenty feet square, knee deep. After moving around the pile, Achcauhtli shifted one man whose cheek and jaw had been hewn from his face. There, beneath him, was Blade of the South. Jaguar wasn't sure what he would do when he saw his father. Whatever it was, Jaguar felt nothing now. The man he knew was gone. A greyish, shrivelled shell was all that remained of Blade of the South. Jaguar looked up into the sky and wondered what he would tell his mother and then he remembered that he could not return to the city. Rage and frustration welled again and mingled with self-pity. For a moment, Jaguar was sure that another trembling fit would overtake him but then he noticed someone familiar on top of the pile. Storm Light. The boy hadn't made it. The last time Jaguar had seen him, he had been wriggling on the ground like a worm. The arrow that had finished him off was still protruding from his back.

Achcauhtli followed Jaguar's gaze and gasped. 'I don't believe it,' he said, crestfallen.

'What?'

'This arrow is one of mine.'

'One that you made?' asked Jaguar. 'How do you know?'

Achcauhtli reached over. With an effort, he broke the arrow and held it out. 'Blue fletching, see? And the red string that binds it.'

Jaguar took the broken wooden shaft and rolled it between his thumb and forefinger. Two of the feathers were black while the third was brilliant blue. 'You all have different colours?'

Achcauhtli shrugged, 'All the noblemen insist on their own designs and so do many of the clans, but I remember them all. I made these. A Chalca must have picked it up and fired it back at us.'

Jaguar was doubtful. 'And hit Storm Light in the back?'

'Why not?' retorted Achcauhtli. 'It's a battle. Everyone is running in all directions.'

'Not the standard bearer,' said Jaguar, inexplicably angry again.

'You two!' barked a short man who appeared beside them. He wore a black loincloth with red tassels. His tunic was armoured with flat, wooden pieces sewn in. Behind him stood four Grey Privy Knights with stern expressions.

Jaguar and Achcauhtli recognised Tlacaelel immediately and inclined their heads.

'Did you fight with the macehualtin?' the general asked abruptly.

'Yes.' Jaguar answered for both of them.

'What happened?'

Jaguar and Achcauhtli looked at each other.

'You.' Tlacaelel pointed at Achcauhtli. 'What's your name?'

'My Lord,' the armourer began. 'My name is Achcauhtli and this is Ocelotyolotl.'

'I know your name,' said Tlacaelel. 'You make weapons, don't you?'

'I do, My Lord.'

'You go first. Tell me what happened during the battle. But wait!' Tlacaelel turned to the Grey Privy Knights and waved at the wide hole that had been dug and then the pile of bodies. 'You, help get these bodies buried.' The knights placed their weapons on the ground and began to help the slaves and other members of the burial party.

Tlacaelel listened as Achcauhtli explained how he had been near the back when the battle commenced but that, within a short time, the line had fragmented, hurling him into the thick of the fray.

When it was his turn, Jaguar recounted the events as well as he could remember them. Now that he tried to piece the action together, he found it very choppy, a series of engagements, each consisting of a few memories of split second decisions and frozen images. His recollection of the broad developments around him during the battle was a crude sketch rather than a coherent narrative. He told the general how the warriors of Teopan had begun well enough but had then been swiftly overwhelmed by the Chalca. He remembered being joined by Magic River and Crocodile and how the three of them had fought off the Serpent Knights and how Magic River had led their retreat. Finally, Jaguar described how he had picked up the fallen standard and how the clansmen had rallied around the flag, eventually joined by Two Sign.

Tlacaelel listened impassively to the two warriors as they gave their own version of the battle.

'You should have fallen back,' said the general. 'Didn't you get the order to retreat?'

Hearing an accusation, Jaguar lashed out, forgetting who he was addressing. 'We would have done better if our own side hadn't been shooting arrows at us!'

Achcauhtli put a hand on Jaguar's arm to hold him back, but Tlacaelel wanted to hear more.

'What are you talking about?'

Jaguar pointed at Storm Light's corpse on the pile. Two of the slaves on burial duty were already collecting bodies from it and carting them over to the shallow grave. Jaguar had to prevent them from moving Storm Light.

'Look, see?' Jaguar showed Tlacaelel the broken arrow shaft embedded between the boy's shoulder blades. 'He's been shot in the back by one of our own warriors!'

Tlacaelel frowned. 'How can you be certain?'

Jaguar handed the broken end of Achcauhtli's arrow over and pointed at the armourer. 'He made this.'

'Is that true?' said Tlacaelel, inspecting the feathered end.

'Yes,' acknowledged the armourer.

'That doesn't mean anything,' argued Tlacaelel. 'A stray shot from one of your clansmen could have done this.'

'Ah,' Achcauhtli interjected. 'Actually, these are specials, not standard issue to warriors. These have to be purchased and they're expensive. Unless someone picked up a fallen one...'

'So one of the pipiltin fired at the enemy and missed. A warrior from Chalco or Tlaxcala picked it up and shot it back,' suggested Tlacaelel.

'No!' cried Jaguar. 'I just explained this to Achcauhtli. Storm Light was the standard bearer. He would have been facing forward the whole time. That's what he was supposed to do.'

Tlacaelel frowned, suddenly thoughtful. 'Achcauhtli, do you sell many of these arrows?'

'No, but enough that I can't tell you who purchased this one just now. Perhaps one of my craftsmen will recall the commission.'

Tlacaelel rubbed the bridge of his nose once and then seemed to come to a decision. 'Right,' he said. 'I may need to speak to you two later on. Where do you live in case I need to send for you?'

'White Lady Bridge,' said Achcauhtli.

'Harbour Street,' said Jaguar, thinking as he did so that he would probably never see the place again. 'Blade of the South's workshop.'

Tlacaelel smiled. 'Are you the jade carver's son? Tell me, how is your father? I know my brother rates his work very highly!'

'My Lord,' said Jaguar through gritted teeth. 'He died today. That's him behind you.' As he said the words, two of the Grey Privy Knights arrived and took hold of Blade of the South's arms and legs to begin carrying him towards the communal burial pit.

Jaguar made to go and help them but Tlacaelel stopped him.

'Your father's spirit is gone.' The general's hold on Jaguar's forearm was firm, but his voice was kind. 'Let them do their work.

I will speak of your father at the next council meeting so that everyone there will know he died a hero's death.'

Jaguar hung his head.

'Now I must go and speak to others. Do either of you know where Magic River is?'

Neither Jaguar nor Achcauhtli had seen him since the battle ended, so Tlacaelel collected his escort and set off to find him.

For a while, Jaguar stared after the departed general. If he thought the clans had held their ground then perhaps Cloud Face would see it that way too. Standing next to the now crowded burial pit it seemed a forlorn hope and then Jaguar remembered his retreat from the Chalca with Crocodile and Magic River, just after their struggle with the Serpent Knights and his heart sank. The high priest would see things differently to Tlacaelel so it was impossible to contemplate a return to Tenochtitlan.

'Hey!' interrupted Achcauhtli. 'I have more work to do,' he said. 'I'll stop by your home tomorrow to check up on you, alright?'

Jaguar thanked the armourer for his kindness and stalled for time. 'I'll be fine. I need to go and pick up my provisions,' he added. 'See you tomorrow.'

Achcauhtli set off in search of other wounded men and Jaguar went looking for his pack that he had deposited behind the army earlier in the day. He circumnavigated the burial pit. The slaves had finished piling the bodies into it and were covering it over once again. Clods of dust and ochre-coloured earth were flying through the air and showering the remains that lay there. Tangled roots and broken grass stalks lay jumbled in the mix and, although they had not been working long to fill the hole, already there was precious little to be seen that looked remotely human.

Suddenly Jaguar latched on to something Tlacaelel had said. 'He died a warrior's death', was how the general had described Blade's final moments. Now Jaguar knew what he had to do. As Archer Eagle had lain dying in the narrow pass, he'd used his final words to tell the Chalca to choose sacrifice; a quick and worthy death as an offering to the gods, but that had not been Crocodile's wish. Crocodile was a fighter and would have preferred to die in combat and that, realised Jaguar, was what Tlacaelel had been talking about and so he vowed to fulfil the promise that he made to Crocodile. He would seek his friend out in Chalco and find a way to bring him out so he too could die a warrior's death. Jaguar did not allow himself to think beyond that moment. He would see Precious Flower again one day, but he could not dwell on when or where that might be. Everything felt better when he focused on the immediate task.

The sun was sinking in the sky when Jaguar found the spot where he and others in his clan had left their provisions. Most had already been claimed by their owners or by the owners' friends who knew that dead men have no need of snacks, spare swords or arrows. The plain that earlier had seethed with clashing men and arms lay silent as the last Mexica finished up their duties and left the field of battle to the scavengers, the looters and the Chalca dead. There was no one left to see Jaguar pick up his simple cloth bag and set off for the wooded slopes of Tlapacoya. His legs wobbled, unsteady with exhaustion and in spite of Achcauhtli's ministrations, his upper arm was agonisingly painful.

'Get into the cover of the woods,' decided Jaguar. 'Then you can rest and eat something.'

Chapter 15 – Cuâuhlti

The gathering twilight was darker here beneath the stands of tall pine, where the gnarled branches made weird and twisted shapes against the glowering sky. A thick carpet of pine needles made a dry susurration under Jaguar's feet and added to the heady scent of pine resin on the cool, refreshing evening air, so welcome after the parched air on the plain. The guttural 'haw-wow' call of a potoo rang out across the echoing forest, answered only by the gentle chirruping of cicada and the melancholy hoot of a solitary screech-owl up on the slopes of Tlapacoya. For a while Jaguar was under the impression that something was wrong and he couldn't work out what it was, but then he noticed that there were no insects. Tenochtitlan was rife with flies this year, mosquitoes and scores of other biting insects, so the crisp clear air in the wooded hill above the valley floor came as a welcome change.

A tiny stream bounced and tumbled down a shallow channel, sluiced out from pine needles and the thin soil of the hill. Jaguar sat down by the stream and dipped his hands into the frigid water, washing them again and again. When his hands were clean, he scooped water over his arms and legs, scratching with his nails at the dirt that felt ingrained into his skin. A scab of dried blood lifted easily from a wound in his leg that he hadn't even noticed before. Jaguar dared not remove the cloth that Achcauhtli had bound around his upper arm. It ached constantly and hurt whenever he had to move it. Jaguar finished scrubbing the rest of his body well, remembering the lectures on cleanliness he had had to sit through in telpochcalli. When he was satisfied that his body was free of grit and grime, he rinsed his face and stubble covered head.

Jaguar was standing up when a sudden noise from between the dark trunks behind made him start. He crouched down instinctively, squatting over the gurgling rill and looked back the way he had come. For what seemed like an eternity, he held the uncomfortable position, motionless, hardly daring to breathe, and then a whirring rattle of wings marked a bird's flight through the pine branches. Jaguar relaxed and picked up his bag, his sword and shield and went in search of a place to bed down for the fast approaching night. He wished he could have cleaned his filthy clothes, but the night would be cold and they would not have dried.

Soon, a natural clearing in the forest appeared and as the land sloped steeply here, at the highest point, Jaguar could see clear across the valley that had been the site of the battle. The first stars had begun to appear above Popocatepetl's ghostly snow-capped peak. Vestigial evening light reflected on the cloud that hung perpetually over the volcano's summit, giving it a rose-tinted silvery glow. Below and to the south lay Chalco, a million motes of firelight against the dark waters of the lake. Although it was too far away, Jaguar imagined he could hear the sounds of the townsfolk celebrating their victory. 'It will be alright,' Jaguar told himself, hoping he would be in time to save his friend. The proper rites had to be observed so it was possible that the ceremonies wouldn't start for a day or two and that set him wondering how he would sneak into Chalco. Surely the gates would be well guarded in the aftermath of battle.

Jaguar crossed to the centre of the clearing, where a massive fallen oak, the cause of the cleared area, lay rotting, surrounded by a miniature, knee-high forest of assorted weeds, pine and oak seedlings. A generous canopy of spring foliage on the downhill side of the reclining oak demonstrated its obstinate refusal to die. Jaguar dropped his sword and shoulder bag to the ground and crawled under a large branch where he collapsed to shelter from the falling dew.

Jaguar lay on the ground looking up at the myriad stars through the dark tracery of the leaves and tried to make sense of the events that had led him to this place. He felt good, now that he had decided on a course of action. He needed to fulfil his promise to Crocodile, however low his chances of success, and anyway there could be no prospect of a return to Tenochtitlan, at least not for a very long time.

Jaguar tried to work out how he could slip into the city. After a while, when he had come up with several ideas and discarded them, he began to wonder how he would establish where the captives were being held. It occurred to him that the captives would be held near the temple, much like Tenochtitlan. Then of course, he would have to free Crocodile and both of them would need to escape without drawing attention to themselves. The more he thought of the endeavour, the less certain he became that it was possible.

Jaguar's stomach grumbled noisily, reminding him that he hadn't eaten since the morning. He rummaged through the scant provisions he'd packed in his bag, it being too dark to see the contents clearly. To his surprise, Jaguar felt the rough contours of the straw effigy that Precious Flower had made for him and realised that she must have placed it in there when he wasn't looking. He pulled the figurine of the ocelot out and held it in his hands, wrestling with his emotions. He remembered the feel of Precious Flower's soft skin, beaded with perspiration and swallowed. He could clearly picture, as though it was only yesterday, the veins in her neck standing out as she arched back and let out a long slow sigh of contentment. He hoped it was a sign that Precious Flower had forgiven him for his surly mood of the past couple of days. She didn't know about his meeting with Cloud Face and would have attributed his terse responses and lack of warmth to his worries over the impending battle. 'If only we had been more careful,' he thought.

Reaching into his bag again, Jaguar located the carefully wrapped parcel that the boy, Shield of Gold, had given to him that morning. He got it out, pulled at the string and exposed the contents of the package. It was impossible to see whether it was edible so Jaguar sniffed cautiously at the vulture meat. There were definitely two tamales in the palm of his hand, stuffed with a generous quantity of something indistinguishable, and since it all smelled distinctly edible, Jaguar's hunger got the better of him. He took a bite and chewed at the dry contents for while. It wasn't great, but it might just see him through until the following day.

There were more faint sounds from behind the trees not far away. Jaguar tried to chew without making any noise. Stories abounded of men and women disappearing in mysterious circumstances, particularly around old temple sites like Teotihuacan, and Jaguar knew that Tlapacoya was a special, spiritual place and forests too were notoriously dangerous places. Jaguar recalled a story of a small lake in the hills behind Chapultepec that even now made his flesh crawl. One summer, before the drought, a party of four boys and five girls had sneaked off to the lake for a swim, away from the bustle of the city. None of them told their parents where they were going for fear they would be stopped and because the lake was a couple of hours distant, no one went looking for them there when it was discovered that they were missing.

A frantic search of Tenochtitlan and the miles of chinampa that surrounded it followed, assisted by the entire clan, all to no avail. It was well after nightfall when one of the boys stumbled back into the city, babbling incoherently, tears coursing down his cheeks. A long time later, the boy, apparently the oldest in the group at thirteen, calmed down enough to give an account of what had happened, interspersed with prolonged bouts of gut-wrenching sobs. According to the distraught child, he had left the little hollow that held the lake to defecate a little way into the woods. He had been on his way back when an ominous rumbling sound echoed around the tiny, tree-lined lake. Five of the children had been playing in chest-deep water, but two of the girls and one boy had yet to venture into the limpid pool. He had watched as the lake turned from blue to a greenish, foaming white around them, as though it was boiling over. He demonstrated with actions how his friends had become extremely agitated, thrashing as they struggled to stay afloat and get back to the shallows.

'A boiling lake?' repeated the adults, exchanging worried glances and scratching their heads.

The boy went on to say that very quickly, the children in the lake had stopped struggling and had sunk back into the lake.

Convinced that they had been dragged below by some fiendish demon, the boy had been unable to move, rooted to the spot and screaming at the remaining three to run towards him up the slope, away from whatever monster lurked below.

Here the distressed child broke down in tears again, shaking and clinging to his mother for several minutes until the other parents became impatient. Some of them set off for the lake immediately with a large, armed escort of volunteers, unable to wait for the conclusion of the story. It was only after they had gone that the frightened boy concluded the chilling tale.

The story was etched clearly in Jaguar's mind because he had nearly gone with the swimming party, but the others had refused to let him come when they learned that he was going to invite Crocodile, who had something of a reputation for being difficult. Four Hummingbird, for that was the boy's name, told of how the three children had started up from the hollow but one-by-one they had wobbled, tripped and fallen over. Again and again, Four Hummingbird had called out to the two girls and the boy as their struggles slowed to nothing and then, unable to endure the horror any more, he'd finally turned and fled. He was so petrified that he didn't care which way he ran and soon became lost, only finding his way back to the valley the following day.

Jaguar was just finishing the first of the tamales when, without warning, a large shadow jumped down from the tree trunk behind Jaguar and landed with a heavy crunching sound. He started in alarm and bit his tongue and then scrabbled frantically around in the leaf litter, looking for his sword. This must surely be a demon from the blackest recesses of Mictlan's ghoulish realms that had come to spirit him away.

A black silhouette moved with impossible speed and pinned Jaguar down by his throat. He cried out and punched uselessly at the trunk-like arm that held him to the floor.

'It is you, Jaguar,' said a gruff voice that could only be Two Sign.

Jaguar felt the two-fingered grip on his neck that confirmed his attacker as the Eagle Knight.

Two Sign loosened his grip. 'I nearly missed you under this log.'

Jaguar scrambled to his feet with his heart still hammering in his chest. His fright gave way to anger. 'What in the name of the Creator Pair are you doing here?' Jaguar shouted at Two Sign's silhouette.

'I could ask you the same question.' White teeth hovered, disembodied against the inky forest, reflecting the faint light of the night sky. 'Alright,' sighed Two Sign. 'I was worried about you, you know, with the death of your father and Crocodile's capture.'

'And you followed me here.'

'I tracked you here,' corrected the Eagle Knight. 'I was keeping an eye out for you and saw you head this way, but I was too busy at the time to head you off. I saw the line you were taking and the rest was mostly guesswork.' The faint, silvery glow of the big warrior's shoulders shrugged.

'What are you going to do, now that you've found me?'

'That depends on what it is you're doing.' Two Sign's voice was suddenly full of warning.

Jaguar said nothing.

'Are you a spy for Chalco?'

The suggestion was so preposterous that, exhausted as he was, Jaguar burst out laughing.

'This isn't funny!' Two Sign's voice was menacing. 'I have no idea what you're up to.'

'I'm going to rescue Crocodile,' said Jaguar matter-of-factly.

It was the Eagle Knight's turn to snort in disbelief.

'It's true,' insisted Jaguar. 'I'm going to go to Chalco, find a way to get in and work out where they're keeping Crocodile, then I'm going to get him out.'

'You make it sound easy,' scoffed Two Sign.

'Well, alright. I haven't got it all worked out yet.'

'It's a ridiculous story,' said Two Sign angrily. 'You're a spy for Amihuatzin. At least that would go some way to explaining the poor outcome in the battle. Why else would you be striking out for Chalco?'

Jaguar ground out the words. 'I just told you! I'm going to get Crocodile out. He doesn't want to be sacrificed.'

'What makes you say that?'

'He told me so,' Jaguar shot back.

In the darkness, Jaguar could see Two Sign shake his head. 'Whatever he told you, that's not the way. Crocodile is sacrifice now. He knows this. We all know how it works.'

'Maybe you know how it works, but I made a promise to Crocodile to make sure he was never captured. He even said that I should kill him if I couldn't stop him being taken captive.'

Two Sign snapped. One moment he was a shadow, listening to Jaguar, and the next, he had Jaguar by his bad arm and was spitting fury.

'Even if this nonsense is true, I won't let you rescue him!'

Jaguar tried to squirm out of the big man's grasp, but the pain from his wounded arm was excruciating and his vision swam with a thousand stars.

'Do you understand the dishonour you would bring on Crocodile and on me if you managed to get him out?' Two Sign was shaking Jaguar. 'Suppose you succeeded in thwarting the will of the gods, do you think that Crocodile could live with that? He would be an outcast!'

Jaguar had nothing to say. There was nothing he could do to make Two Sign understand.

'You're coming back to Tenochtitlan with me,' snarled Two Sign and began to drag Jaguar down the hill.

'What then?' cried Jaguar, digging his heels in to no effect.

'I'll work that out along the way.'

'I can't go back!' Jaguar shouted. He tried to pull his arm free and sent another spike of pain through his bicep that made him cry out again. In desperation, he aimed a kick at the big man and got lucky. Two Sign released his grip just fractionally. Perhaps those missing fingers were a weakness after all. Jaguar twisted, broke free and scrambled back up towards his pack and sword but Two Sign was lightning fast and shockingly strong. He pounced on Jaguar again and forced his head down onto the soft earth and fallen leaves. A pine needle skewered Jaguar's cheek.

Hot tears of frustration sprang to Jaguar's eyes.

'Why can't you go back?' hissed Two Sign in his ear. 'Is it because you're a traitor?'

Two Sign had to understand the consequences for him and his family if he returned to the city and back into Cloud Face's sphere of influence.

'Cloud Face will kill me!' Jaguar shouted into the musky soil under his face.

'What?'

'The high priest will have me killed and bring dishonour to my family.'

'Why?' asked Two Sign, still not letting go.

'I cannot tell you. Please, just let me go.'

Two Sign sat down on Jaguar's back and made himself comfortable. 'Mictlan's bones!' thought Jaguar, scarcely able to breathe. 'He's not going to give up.'

'See it from my point of view,' said the big warrior, who had calmed down a little. 'A battle doesn't go well. One of our warriors is heading for Chalco and that same warrior admits that the high priest is after him, but won't tell me why. It doesn't inspire me with a lot of trust, how about you?' He deliberately shifted his weight again.

'Arrrrhh,' groaned Jaguar.

'Jaguar,' said Two Sign. He sounded concerned. 'Let me tell you a story. Will you let me do that? If I let you up, will you sit still and listen to a story?'

Jaguar agreed and Two Sign let him get up. He spat out a leaf and brushed himself down.

'Let's sit in that shelter you found for yourself,' Two Sign suggested.

The pair found their way back to the fallen oak and ducked under the branch. Jaguar sat with his back against the tree trunk and listened as the Eagle Knight talked. Night was absolute beneath the foliage and the only cue that Two Sign was there was the sound of his deep, steady voice.

'This story begins with a happy child and a loving family who live in a peaceful village in a clearing in the woods. This child has two older sisters and an older brother.'

Jaguar guessed that the story was about Crocodile even though his friend had spoken very little of his life before he came to the city.

'One day, while many of the men were out hunting and only the frail old men and the youngest warriors – like this boy's older brother – were left to guard the village, a fearsome tribe of warriors swoops down upon them. The leader of this band of warriors was called Stone Monkey, a thin and evil man with one white eye and a lust to kill.'

Jaguar listened intently.

'Stone Monkey questioned the eldest of the village wanting to know the whereabouts of the fighting men and older women. The eldest told them they were all out, but refused to say anything more, so Stone Monkey beat him and still the old man held his tongue. Now the boy saw nothing of this. He was out, dutifully collecting firewood when these foreigners descended on his village.'

Two Sign let out a deep sigh.

'Stone Monkey grew angry and stuck a spear in the old man's stomach and then made him watch while he killed one of the boys who had been left on guard duty, the little boy's brother as it happened. "I'll kill another if you do not tell me where the rest of your people have gone!" he said. "And then I'll kill another, then another." The old man knew that nothing would spare the people who had been rounded up so he said nothing, concentrating instead on holding down the pain that burned in his belly. He knew Stone Monkey wished to see him suffer and refused to give him that satisfaction.'

Here Two Sign took out a gourd and drank a sip. Jaguar felt a nudge and realised that the Eagle Knight was offering him some water. He took a swig and passed the container back. There was a noise of the plug being turned in the neck of the gourd and then Two Sign began talking again.

'The boy heard the commotion and the screaming from his village. He wasn't far away. Returning cautiously to the edge of the clearing where the trees were thickest, he watched as his own brother was cut down. He saw Stone Monkey give the word to his men to burn the houses and watched as his sisters were tied up in a line with anyone else who was fit enough to run. Babies, toddlers and the infirm were butchered in the centre of the village or pushed into the flaming huts.'

Two Sign's voice was hushed, but clear and steady.

'A long time later, when everyone had gone, the boy crept out and went to see the old man who was still not dead. "Run and hide, little one!" he wheezed. "They may yet return. You must wait until your father returns with the rest of them." So the boy hid beneath the remains of the only house that had not been utterly destroyed. The old man died later that day, one single moan towards the end the only sign of the agony he endured. For two days, the boy waited in hiding without food or water, but the rest of his family and the other villagers never returned.

'On the third day, another war party entered what was left of the village and they found the boy in his hiding place. He was scared because he did not recognise these people either, but they gave him food and said kind words to him although he would not speak. Eventually, after they buried the remains of the villagers, they took him with them. One of the warriors carried him on his back.'

Jaguar closed his eyes and shook his head. It was no wonder that Crocodile had never told the full story before.

'The warriors took the boy back to a big city, the like of which he'd never seen before. Although he was safe and everything was wondrous, the boy was sad and lonely. Everything was unfamiliar. He went to school and the other children made fun of him because he spoke differently. As he grew up he became tough and learned to fight and so eventually the others left him alone. Still he had no friends.'

There was a long pause this time; so long that Jaguar was able to pick up the tiny background noises of the trees at night. A gentle creak, a soughing of the undergrowth in the clearing and a rustle in the treetops as some roosting fowl moved restlessly on its perch.

'One day the boy picked a fight with you, Jaguar,' Two Sign started up again. 'I remember the day he came back from school, blood dripping from his nose. Neither of us knew it at the time, but that proved to be the best day in his life.'

'Why is that?' Jaguar asked.

'Because he made a friend.'

Jaguar began to say something but Two Sign interrupted.

'I know it took a while, but you two did make friends and Crocodile changed. He began to smile again. For a long time after I took him away from his village, I worried that I had done the wrong thing. He was miserable and took very little interest in the things around him. I thought perhaps that I had defied the will of the gods. Perhaps his destiny was elsewhere than with me. You changed all that. You gave him his life back and through you he made friends with others too.'

Two Sign cleared his throat. 'So now I will repay you for the kindness you showed Crocodile. If you have done something so terrible that the priest will pass a death sentence on you, I will let you run away. I owe you this on behalf of my adopted son, but I must know the truth. Also, I warn you that if you are acting on behalf of Chalco, you must take care that I never see your face again. I shall not be responsible for my actions, do you understand?'

When Jaguar spoke, his voice was scratchy. 'Yes,' he said. 'I understand.'

Two Sign sat quietly while Jaguar told his tale. Jaguar told how Precious Flower had warned him that he was being followed and that they had seen no one. He explained that after leaving the boy, Shield of Gold, behind in Moyotlan, he and Precious Flower had come across a meadow and, unaware that they were being watched, they had embraced.

'That's why Devine Cactus came and fetched you from the ball court?' interrupted Two Sign. 'You must have done a lot more than just embrace!'

Jaguar felt his cheeks flush and was glad of the darkness. He offered no more detail but pressed on, describing how he had been taken to the high priest's rooms and threatened with execution for intercourse with a slave girl.

'These rules are there to protect slaves from abuse,' said Two Sign.

'I know,' breathed Jaguar. 'But I think she loves me.'

'That may be so. What did Mixayacatl say next?'

Jaguar related the high priest's instructions and his claim that Tlacaelel's tactics were flawed.

'Wait! He told you that the standard bearer would fall?' asked Two Sign.

'And he told me to pick it up and stand my ground.'

'That directly contradicts what Tlacaelel wanted!' Two Sign was incredulous. 'What was he playing at?'

'Well, he was right,' said Jaguar. 'We were driven back and we lost.'

'Jaguar, the clans weren't supposed to hold out. You were supposed to lure the enemy into a trap. Anyway, you did what the high priest asked of you. I saw you holding the standard. Why would Mixayacatl carry out his threat if you did as he asked?'

'I don't know,' Jaguar said. 'The whole day seems like a disaster to me. Maybe Island Home North and the clans wouldn't have suffered such a defeat if I'd got to the standard earlier. It's just what Cloud Face said would happen if we didn't hold the Chalca back.'

Two Sign didn't sound convinced. 'I'm not sure about that. Everyone knows the high priest and Tlacaelel despise each other, but Cloud Face wouldn't have put the whole army at risk just to settle a personal score. Are you sure you understood his instructions properly?'

'I'm sure,' said Jaguar. 'What makes you so sure that Cloud Face wasn't trying to undermine Tlacaelel?'

'The high priest, a traitor? It's not possible.'

'Really? Storm Light had an arrow in his back. One of ours.'

'That means nothing. It could have come from anywhere.'

'No, it couldn't,' Jaguar insisted and he proceeded to tell Two Sign what he had told Tlacaelel that afternoon. Storm Light would have had no cause to turn around.

Two Sign didn't agree, but the two of them were so exhausted that they couldn't argue any longer.

'It's too late to return home tonight,' said Two Sign after a while. 'We'll have to sleep here and make our way back in the morning.'

Jaguar had no intention of returning to Tenochtitlan, but decided not to provoke a new argument, so he stretched himself out and pulled his cloak over his shoulders. The dull, insistent ache in his arm kept sleep at bay for a while so he watched the stars through the tangle of foliage overhead. He picked one and watched it until it progressed smoothly out of sight behind a leaf and then switched his attention to another one. His last thought, before he fell asleep, was of the children dying so mysteriously at the lake behind Chapultepec. When the search party got there, they had found eight bodies, five floating in the shallow lake and three lying beside it, and not a single one had any mark or sign of what had caused their deaths.

'Congratulations, My Lord,' said Devine Cactus. 'Everything seems to have gone very well.' Tlaloc's most senior earthly official had found himself a seat.

'It is a triumph!' Cloud Face agreed. 'The last time I saw the tlatoani that angry was when Amihuatzin had two of Moctezuma's own cousins killed and dragged around the streets of Chalco by a pack of dogs.'

'We only took four hundred captives,' said Snake Eyes, who remained standing.

At Cloud Face's invitation, all three priests were back in the reception room with the silver-plated skulls and the stone carving depicting the defeat of Huitzilopochtli's sister. Another cloudless day was dawning and breakfast had been set out to celebrate the previous day's events.

From his own seat, Cloud Face gave Snake Eyes a pitying look. 'We'll find other ways to boost the next ceremony. The God of War at least will understand that some battles require a little ground to be given up in order to achieve much greater goals.'

Feathered Darkness put his head in at the entrance to the chamber.

'Two acolytes to see you, My Lord.'

'Show them in,' said Cloud Face.

Two acolytes trouped in and stood at a respectable distance.

'What of your mission?' inquired the high priest.

'Ocelotyolotl did not return, My Lord.'

'Is that so?' exclaimed Cloud Face. 'Are you sure you didn't miss him?'

The two acolytes shook their heads vigorously. 'Oh no, Cherished Father!' they chimed in unison. Cloud Face looked at the boys, trying to work out whether he could trust them. The calibre of entrants into the priesthood seemed to have plummeted lately and the recent batch was no exception.

Recognising the doubt in the old priest's face, one of the boys piped up. 'We went to Harbour Street and waited all day, just like you said, right up until it was dark. We saw no one fitting the description you gave to us. Some other warriors did go into that house and they must have delivered bad news.' Here the lad turned to his accomplice. 'We heard a lot of crying after that, didn't we?'

'Yes, we did,' said the other. 'Ocelotyolotl died and maybe his father too. We overheard some neighbours talking shortly after that and it didn't sound good.'

'Well,' Cloud Face clasped his hands together. 'I heard that Blade of the South had died, but I'd heard nothing of his son.' He frowned slightly. 'That's a shame. I could have found more use for that one. Still,' he added. 'I suppose it's another loose end tidied up. You may go!'

The two acolytes scurried out.

'As we were discussing, my friends, Blade of the South and Magic River of Teopan are gone, Ueman of Azcapotzalco is dead as well as, if my reports are accurate, two more council members.' Cloud Face made an open gesture with his arms. 'As a result, the Council of Twelve is somewhat short and it will take time for them to rebuild it. Why the selection process alone will take months!' Cloud Face added with a brittle laugh.

'What do we do now?' Cactus asked.

'Moctezuma will denounce his brother,' said Cloud Face. 'He needs to place the blame for this disaster on someone's head.'

'What of Nezahualcoyotl?' Cactus asked. 'Surely Tlacaelel will blame our neighbour.'

'He may try, Cactus, but I doubt that this will save him. Yesterday's battle was run to Tlacaelel's plan, with or without Texcoco. He could have changed his plans when they did not appear.'

Devine Cactus chipped in. 'Moctezuma only tolerates his brother's sacrilegious nature because of his supposed skill in warfare and politics. Tlacaelel's public devotion to Huitzilopochtli is nothing but a facade, everyone knows this, and the tlatoani cannot be seen to support it unless the military campaigns are a success.'

'It is good to see our plans advancing,' Snake Eyes said. He brushed a straggling strand of hair from his face and began pacing back and forth. 'So with Tlacaelel out of the way and the power of the council diminished, your influence over Moctezuma is sure to reassert itself.'

'Let us hope it does, Snake Eyes.' Cloud Face had an inkling of what was coming but played along anyway. 'The old order will be re-established and with it, the divine authority that set our people on the path to glory.'

'The priesthood back in power?'

'Indeed.'

'That is wonderful, of course,' said Snake Eyes. 'A general principle reinforced and, since you are the high priest of Huitzilopochtli, your star will shine the brightest in the heavens. But, ah... what of more specific gains for those who helped to put you back where you belong? Devine Cactus and I have been loyal servants to this cause.'

Cloud Face was pretty sure that Snake Eyes hadn't even the faintest idea what loyalty meant but he smiled all the same. It was, after all, a good day and he was in the mood for concessions.

'You are quite right, Snake Eyes,' the high priest conceded. 'I was just about to explain all this in answer to Cactus' question when you interrupted.' Cloud Face enjoyed driving this last point home. 'The subject of your reward is the very reason that I called this meeting.'

Devine Cactus raised an eyebrow, perhaps a touch nervous, decided Cloud Face, as well he should be. Snake Eyes rolled his eyebrows down lower in suspicion.

'I wish you'd sit down,' the high priest said to Snake Eyes. 'There's a great deal to discuss.'

Snake Eyes gave him a stony look, which he studiously ignored by pouring himself some octli.

'Very well, here's what I have in mind. We priests have a duty to guide the tlatoani and, through him, this nation.' As he spoke, he poured two more cups. 'We have the knowledge of the stars and of the heavens. We have the insights to the will of the gods and we have the deep understanding of tradition that goes back to before Tenochtitlan was founded.' Cloud Face took a drink from his cup. 'The Mexica need our help. This dependency on woolly-minded administrators must be curtailed... and yesterday was the first step back onto the right path.'

Cloud Face levered himself up and handed one cup to Snake Eyes and the other to Devine Cactus. Neither drank.

'The next step is to replace those administrators on whom the tlatoani has come to rely and I have therefore decided to propose to him that the now vacant posts on the Council of Twelve be filled with priests.'

'Us?' said Snake Eyes.

'Mictlan's bones!' Cloud Face snatched the cup out of Snake Eyes' hand and took a long swallow then handed it back brusquely. 'You're no use to me if you're dead, are you?' He reached out for Devine Cactus' cup but the priest stared back at him and refused to give it up so Cloud Face continued.

'Why not?' said Cloud Face turning back to Snake Eyes. 'We don't want the council disbanded. The smooth operation of a city this size requires a body of well meaning people to decide on the day-to-day issues. We just need to make sure that they agree with us on the wider matters.'

Devine Cactus took a swallow from his cup. Seeing this, Cloud Face raised his own and took another drink. He wiped his mouth with the sleeve of his black gown.

'Don't you see? It's perfect symmetry. I will continue in my role on the Grand Council while you and one or two other priests perform the same checks and balances on the Council of Twelve.' Cloud Face raised his cup again.

'With a firm hold on both governing bodies, we should be able to restrict the power of the clans,' offered Devine Cactus with a twinkle in his eye.

Snake Eyes' perpetual look of despondency only deepened. 'What do we know of drainage and watch duties, disposal of the dead and such nonsense?'

Cloud Face dismissed him with a laugh, unable to contain his good humour now. 'You won't need to know anything! Just listen to a handful of macehualtin bickering for half a day and then lend your backing to whoever is most loyal to our cause. It's pathetically simple!'

The three of them fell to discussing other consequences of the battle, speculating as to what punishment Moctezuma would exact on his brother. A little while later, Snake Eyes interrupted. He was still standing but had begun to sway a little with the effect of the octli.

'Wait,' he said.

'What's that?' asked Cloud Face.

'Well, your young lads said Jaguar never came home last night.'

'So?' said Devine Cactus. He didn't look comfortable. He had never looked particularly healthy, reflected Cloud Face, but the folds of skin around his neck and jaw looked especially pallid now.

'Jaguar was alive at the end of the battle,' Snake Eyes said to the high priest, not even turning his gaze to his seated colleague. 'After I shot the standard bearer, I kept my eye on the clans like you asked me to, My Lord. When the fighting ended, Jaguar was there. He wandered around for a while like he was lost and then sat down.'

'Was he injured?' asked Cloud Face.

'No!' insisted Snake Eyes. 'Well, I didn't want to get too close but I would have known if...' His voice trailed off as Devine Cactus groaned.

'I don't feel well,' he said. Beads of perspiration spotted his brow. He tried to get to his feet but the effort was too much. He closed his eyes and sank back onto the seat. 'I'd better take myself off and lie down,' he managed, listlessly.

Feathered Darkness came into the room.

'May I fetch anything for you, My Lords?'

'Our friend has been taken ill,' said Cloud Face. 'Would you be so good as to fetch him some water.'

'Of course,' said Feathered Darkness and moved towards the door. Before he had time to cross to the door, Devine Cactus turned on one side and vomited violently. Everyone stood where they were. Cloud Face moved back and crossed his arms. Devine Cactus vomited a bilious green fluid again, doubling up and sliding off his chair. He managed to look up at Cloud Face, tears running down his cheeks. Strings of snot hung from his nose and stretched onto his voluminous robes.

'Poison?' he said, his voice hoarse.

'Mine,' said Snake Eyes, unable to let anyone take credit for his work.

'How?' The high priest of Tlaloc's voice was hoarse. 'You drank as well.'

Snake Eyes couldn't conceal his delight. 'Not the drink,' he cackled. 'It was the cup.'

Devine Cactus curled up and retched, a dry and rasping sound.

Cloud Face, who had watched impassively, broke his silence. 'I'm disappointed,' he said. 'I thought you were cleverer, possessed more cunning.'

'Urgh.' It was a small and hopeless sound. Cactus clawed feebly for the chair. With a superhuman effort, he hauled himself to his knees.

Cloud Face snapped. He stepped in and lashed out, the back of his hand catching Devine Cactus across his jowls. 'Why?'

Devine Cactus crashed back to the floor. He lay in a puddle of his own puke with a pained expression.

Cloud Face loomed over him. 'Why did you go to Tlacaelel?'

Devine Cactus croaked, 'You're mad. Do you think this is the way to run a city?'

Cloud Face kicked savagely at the fallen priest.

Devine Cactus shuddered and coughed. He was barely audible now. 'Do either of you have any idea how to resolve a boundary dispute between two clans?' he said. He retched again, briefly, turning purple in the face. 'Do you...' he wheezed. 'Do you imagine that the people will be overjoyed to see the priests in charge again? When we've done such a good job of bringing back the rains?'

Cloud Face kicked him in the stomach.

'That was your job, you fool! I bound the years and ushered in the new cycle. It is you who has failed us all. Priest of Tlaloc? Bringer of water? Ha!' Cloud Face vented his fury at the body on the floor, lashing out again and again until the sweat poured from his marked forehead. Eventually, he stepped back and wiped the spittle from his chin. Devine Cactus had curled into a ball and was lying quite still, his face stretched in a silent scream, unblinking eyes protruding in the final rictus of death.

No one spoke for a while until Snake Eyes broke the silence. 'I always wondered if my priests could make two skins from him.'

'Take him away then,' said Cloud Face. 'Both of you, go on!' He turned to Feathered Darkness. 'When you've disposed of him, come back and clean this place up and then go and find those two grinning idiots who were in here earlier. Get them to go straight back and watch Jaguar's house until further notice.'

'Through the night?'

'Yes! Through the night, you imbecile! If he's not dead I want to find out where he is. If he doesn't put in an appearance soon we'll take the rest of his family to the cells and strip their entrails from their living bodies until they tell us where he is.'

'Yes, My Lord,' said Feathered Darkness.

Chapter 16 - Cozcacuauhtli

A night of sleeping rough on sharp twigs and leaves did little to take the edge off Jaguar's exhaustion and there was a foul taste in his mouth, which he blamed on the buzzard meat. He felt cold and damp, but his left arm was hot and throbbed painfully under the bandage. In his dreams, Crocodile had been standing before an altar wearing a gore-spattered ceremonial robe.

'Your heart!' he had grinned, beckoning to Jaguar and pointing at the blood-stained block. 'We need your heart. The sun's power is waning and every year the rains come later!'

Jaguar groaned and glanced at the spot twenty feet away where Two Sign lay fast asleep. The Eagle Knight was obviously used to sleeping on the ground, inured to damp, uncomfortable conditions by countless campaigns in distant lands.

Lack of sleep had not diminished Jaguar's resolve to go to Chalco. He had had no luck, trying to work out how to gain access to the cells where captives would be held. He would just have to get into the city and see where the gods led him. A return to Tenochtitlan was a distant dream. Jaguar wondered who would console his mother in her grief. Arrow One wouldn't be much use. Then he tried to imagine the city streets without the ebullient, swaggering Crocodile and that hardened his resolve. He would fulfil his promise to Crocodile and try to get him out of Chalco. He could think of nothing else beyond that.

Oak leaves fluttered down between the overhanging branches, swirling on a skittish breeze. Jaguar was surprised to see grey, pendulous clouds pressing down upon the land. They jostled each other, roiled, overlapping greedily as they lumbered across the valley. Tree tops swayed and Jaguar wondered if the south-easterly wind would bring moist air from the distant coast.

'Perhaps at last the rains will come,' he said to himself. 'It is time.'

The last real downpour that Jaguar could recall had taken place so long ago that it must have been in his first year at telpochcalli, two years after his family had taken Precious Flower in. That year the lake level had risen dramatically and chinampa had overflowed, flooding parts of the city. Jaguar remembered the thrill of seeing water lapping at the door of their home in Harbour Street and the excitement as he and Precious Flower rushed out onto the streets, stamping barefoot at the water until it splashed through people's windows.

Children had emerged from all the houses and joined in, much to the irritation of the adults, charging up and down the street and churning its surface to a morass of mud. They whooped and hollered and burst into peals of laughter and when they had tired of simply running up and down, they played tag, chasing each other as far as they dared into the deeper water towards the harbour end.

Precious Flower had found a tightly woven reed basket and had filled it until she could hardly carry it, staggering this way and that, threatening to empty it on one person and then the next. Strangely, although the children were already soaked and most had discarded all their clothing by this stage, they were all reluctant to let Precious Flower get close, shrieking and darting away as she approached. The game had ended abruptly when Jaguar snuck up from behind her and pinned her arms as they held the basket, whereupon he had folded them upwards, tipping the basket so that the water cascaded out down Precious Flower's own front. To Jaguar's surprise, instead of being cross, Precious Flower had simply collapsed into his arms, giggling uncontrollably.

Jaguar smiled at the memory of the warmth of Precious Flower in his arms. He stood up, determined to find a way to see her again, but first he would find Crocodile and see what Chalco had in store.

Two Sign woke at the sound of Jaguar gathering up his possessions.

'Where are you going?'

'I told you, I'm going to Chalco.'

Two Sign was sitting up with his arms resting on his knees. He shook his head gently and then it sounded to Jaguar as though the big man had something caught in his throat and was snorting to dislodge it. Two Sign was laughing.

'What?' said Jaguar.

'And I thought Crocodile was stubborn! Are you really going to stroll in there, walk up to the temple guards and persuade them to hand him over?'

'I'll think of something,' Jaguar said defensively.

'Come on then. What's your plan?'

Jaguar made a show of checking the few items he had with him. 'Once I'm inside, I'll hide somewhere close to the temple and wait until it gets dark. If I can create a diversion while he's being escorted there, I might be able to get to him without anyone noticing.'

Two Sign sighed. 'Well it's not the best plan I've ever heard, but at least you've got something there.' He stood up. 'Come on then, let's get going.'

Jaguar looked perplexed. 'Are you coming too?'

The Eagle Knight picked up his sword and examined it with a sour expression. The once razor-sharp stones had been reduced to shattered stumps and two were missing altogether. He tossed it aside with a shrug. 'We won't be able to take our weapons with us anyway,' he observed before continuing. 'Yes, Jaguar, I'm coming with you. It sounds like you're going to need someone to create that diversion, preferably some distance from wherever you happen to be hiding.'

Jaguar grinned.

Two Sign gave him a warning look. 'Don't get me wrong. It's more likely that maize cobs will rain from the sky than this plan actually succeeds.'

'I know, so why are you really coming?'

It was Two Sign's turn to look embarrassed. He paused. 'I'm going to miss him you know... and I decided I won't be able to live with myself knowing that you saw him one last time and got to say farewell.'

'You don't think he's going to come with us,' said Jaguar.

Two Sign shrugged. 'I'm not sure any of us will make it out alive.'

It was late morning when Two Sign and Jaguar joined the queue of people at Chalco's imposing North Gate. Porters and labourers from the surrounding villages joked good-naturedly together as they waited patiently in line. Two Sign even spotted a few poorly disguised beggars, hoping for rich pickings in the market. He hoped that their own disguises were more convincing than the man in front of them who had draped a cotton cloak around his shoulders. The cloak itself was fine, it was just doing a poor job of concealing what lay beneath. Open sores covered the exposed parts of the beggar's limbs and he reeked like one of Xipe Totec's priests doing a month-long penance.

Two Sign checked the baskets that he and Jaguar were carrying. They were filled with firewood that they had purchased from labourers near Ixtapaluca. Two Sign was grateful he had brought a purse from which he produced some coffee beans and several twists of thread in the commercial colours of Chalco by way of payment for the props, which included a pair of mayeque loincloths, their own war cloths being too distinctive to wear into Chalco, especially as they were covered in dark stains from the day before.

'Knights are required to carry something to barter with,' Two Sign had answered when Jaguar asked about the transaction. 'You'd be surprised how many times war parties run into situations that can be resolved with just a little something to bargain with.'

Two Sign decided he wasn't impressed with the disguises. He didn't think either of them would pass for labourers. His scars could conceivably have been caused by defective tools or fights between rival labour teams, but his muscular shoulders and torso looked as though they were honed for battle. Jaguar's own frame, though wiry, didn't have the scrawny, malnourished look of the mayeque.

If the disguises didn't inspire much confidence, Jaguar's plan was only a little better. The basic idea wasn't bad, but on the walk from Tlapacoya, neither of them had come up with an idea for a diversion that would allow Jaguar to extricate Crocodile from the priests who would be escorting him to the altar. Two Sign had recommended a fire, but Jaguar pointed out that timing would be critical and creating a huge blaze would take too long. Jaguar proposed that one of them should attack the head of the convoy escorting captives to the temple. Although they both agreed this was the best idea, neither was prepared to commit to it and the fact that it was almost certain suicide for one of them was left unspoken.

Jaguar didn't seem concerned. 'We'll think of something,' he said with a shrug.

Two Sign had seen this sort of behaviour before. He had seen warriors undertake the most perilous journeys or charge into battle as long as the flimsiest of plans existed; yet even mundane tasks could provoke unhappiness among the men without some sort of grand design.

Two Sign marvelled at the richly carved wooden gates as they shuffled towards the massive portal. On the left, Tlaloc reigned supreme, gazing out across the nearby lake. On the right, Tezcatlipoca squatted, looking stern with his arms crossed. The entrance to the city was a peculiar affair. The ornate gates were set into a stout structure, whose walls looked set to withstand an all-out assault from the most determined of enemies, but a few yards from the doorway, the wall was built from nothing more robust than the backs of people's houses and in some places it disappeared entirely.

'You again?' the guard said to the beggar with the ill-concealed sores. 'For a moment I mistook you for Amihuatzin!' A humourless smile creased his face.

Two Sign and Jaguar watched as the beggar pushed something into the guard's hand and was immediately waved through. The guard turned a casual eye on the two of them and Two Sign readied himself for flight. The guard scarcely glanced at them, but he did ask them to lower their baskets so he could get a look inside.

'On your way,' he grunted.

Two Sign and Jaguar slung the baskets back onto their backs and headed into the city. The streets were busy and it proved to be hard work steering through the crowds. The overall mood was one of celebration. The people of Chalco were jubilant at their victory over the Mexica, but there were mourners too. Everywhere Two Sign looked he saw sombre-looking families threading their way through the stalls and street entertainers heading for the temple bearing small tributes, small plates of food and flowers and, in some cases, the body of a loved one killed in battle.

Two Sign scratched at the unfamiliar loincloth, seriously worried now that it was home to more occupants than the one who had so recently traded it up.

'Where to now?' whispered Jaguar.

'Follow the mourners,' Two Sign replied. 'They'll be heading for the temple and the captives will be nearby.'

'To the right?' Jaguar pointed down one of the side streets.

'Yes, but keep to the main thoroughfares. We'll be fine as long as we're part of the crowd.' Two Sign was pleased with himself. He was on unfamiliar territory and it had been a long time since he had carried out insurgency of this kind, but his confidence was growing.

'Crocodile's going to be surprised to see us!' said Jaguar.

Two Sign could only snort.

'Look!' exclaimed Jaguar. Two Sign had to kick him discretely to stop him pointing at the temple that was now visible over the rooftops. The young warrior would have to curb his enthusiasm if he wanted to avoid drawing unwanted attention.

The pyramid of Chalco's principle deity was perhaps half the height of the spectacle of the Great Temple in Tenochtitlan, but what it lacked in stature, it made up for in sheer, radiant beauty. Where the fierce competition between Moctezuma and Nezahualcoyotl to build towards the sky had produced towering structures of stone topped off with decoration, the steady, insular approach in Chalco had resulted in a small, but breathtakingly ornate building. The temple of Tezcatlipoca was resplendent in brilliant paintwork that shone with an unearthly light. Shades of blue, aquamarine, rich crimsons and gold had been lovingly applied to every nook, every step and every carving.

Two Sign had seen many things during his travels as an Eagle Knight, but nothing could have prepared him for this vision. It was as if the gods themselves had descended from the heavens and bent their own divine craftsmanship to the building. Two Sign had to kick Jaguar again because his mouth was hanging open.

Jaguar found his voice again. 'It's amazing!' he whispered. 'The statues match the best of my family's carvings except they must each be as tall as I am.'

'Try and stay focused on your mission, Jaguar,' hissed Two Sign. 'We need to try and work out where they're holding Crocodile.'

Jaguar opened his mouth but Two Sign never heard his response because he was struck violently on the back of his head. He reeled, pitching forward in slow motion and saw his basket of firewood cartwheel to the ground. Then everything went black.

Tlacaelel was late for a special hearing that Moctezuma had convened to discuss the battle. He hurried through the great hall and turned into the Hall of Truth, one of the four large rooms that ran along the left-hand side. He had to hitch up the hem of his formal white cloak that was rubbing on the inside of his knees. The friezes on either side of the entrance depicted the Creator Pair, while the lintel was reserved for a life-size carving of Ometeotl holding the sun in one outstretched hand and the moon in the other. Tlacaelel nodded at the two members of the Grey Privy Knights as he passed underneath the Lord of Duality and into the Supreme Court. Instead of the Tlatocan, Moctezuma had chosen the room normally reserved for trials that involved the nobility and decisions on the highest laws in the land. It was a clear message that he was in charge of the proceedings.

Tlacaelel silently cursed Two Sign and wondered what the commander of the Eagle Knights was up to. As far as Tlacaelel could recall, the big warrior had never been late before, so he had gone to the barracks to seek him out. The fact that none of the other men knew his whereabouts was odd and irritating to Tlacaelel because it had delayed him so that he was the last to arrive at the meeting.

Cloud Face was already there and engaged in an animated discussion with the tlatoani. Moctezuma had donned an outfit of sombre brown and black feathers cleverly arranged to look like a snake skin. His loin cloth was large, stately and richly embroidered, and he was carrying a favourite staff made from the wood of the pocotl tree. He was staring down at the room from the height of his throne. He looked as haughty as Tlacaelel had ever seen him. This was going to be tough.

Three tiers of benches ranged along the opposite three sides to the tlatoani's seat, interrupted only by the doorway through which Tlacaelel had just entered. Scribes and administrative staff from the priesthood sat in the front row while the next was reserved for the Council of Twelve, their advisors and family. The back row was usually held in reserve for visiting dignitaries and the family of whoever was on trial. Today it was filled with high-ranking warriors of the various orders of knights. The rear wall behind the throne had two small windows whose baleful light had been supplemented by four large fire urns arranged around the central area where the members of the High Council had their seats. Today, four additional stools had been provided because Moctezuma had requested each of the members of the High Council to bring a witness. Snake Eyes was seated beside Cloud Face, Zipactonal had brought Mahuizoh as his witness, while Acamapichtli was accompanied by another relative of Moctezuma's. The general walked to his place and bowed towards the tlatoani.

Moctezuma let the silence hang while the bone-dry wood in the urn nearest Tlacaelel crackled and popped. One of the members of the palace staff was already having to replenish the logs. Tlacaelel put down the loose cloth sack he'd brought with him.

'Where is Two Sign?' the tlatoani said when the fire had been topped up.

'I am not sure, My Lord,' answered Tlacaelel.

'Is he dead too?'

'No, My Lord. I saw him immediately after the battle and he looked well enough to me.'

'So you have no second in this?'

Tlacaelel nodded towards the commander of the Jaguar Knights, who was sitting on the back row. 'I'll call on Last Medicine if I need help,' he said.

'Fine!' snapped Moctezuma. 'I expected the high priest of Tlaloc to be your witness,' he added, looking at Cloud Face.

Cloud Face rubbed his face vigorously with both hands and then looked up in despair at the audience. 'I'm afraid I must deliver the sad news that Devine Cactus has passed into the next realm. Apparently he has been unwell for some time, something he nobly hid from all of us, and has even been undergoing treatments at Tlapacoya.'

The news was met with a stunned silence so the high priest continued.

'Although I can scarcely imagine replacing a man of Devine Cactus' intellect, I am lucky to have a man with a wealth of experience and a lengthy track record in the service of our people to take his place as my second and my advisor here today. I believe you all know Snake Eyes.'

Snake Eyes bowed as Tlacaelel watched him impassively. Devine Cactus had not been ill, of that the general was certain. He would have said something. This new development reeked of murder and Tlacaelel felt sure he was staring at the culprits.

'Let's get on with the proceedings,' cried Moctezuma and then slowly and clearly he began to address the room. 'Traditionally, Tlacaelel has been in charge of investigations into martial matters. However, due to his role in the planning of yesterday's battle, I shall ask the questions this time.

'Tlacaelel, when everyone who wants to speak has done so, you will answer for your part. The High Council will have their say, but at the end, I shall rule on whether the Woman Snake has served us well. Do you understand?'

'I do, My Lord,' replied Tlacaelel.

'My Lord?' ventured Cloud Face.

'Mixayacatl, I'll caution you not to interrupt. You'll have your say.'

'My Lord, I just wonder since Tlacaelel is your brother...'

Moctezuma jumped up, pushing his chair back so that it tumbled from the platform and clattered to the flagstones. 'You dare question my impartiality?'

Cloud Face lowered his gaze to the floor. Someone scurried to retrieve the tlatoani's seat.

'Good. Now listen to this.' Still standing, Moctezuma recounted the events leading up to the battle of the previous day. He explained how Tlacaelel had broken with tradition and persuaded him and the two councils that a new approach was needed.

Tlacaelel listened as his brother gave a fair account of his argument for an all-out war against the Chalca. The general had no need to interject as the tlatoani explained that the War of Flowers was sapping the fighting strength of the Mexica. Tlacaelel loved and respected his brother, but that same respect told him that Moctezuma would not go easy on him just because they shared the same mother. He did not have to wait long for his suspicions to be confirmed.

'So now we must look to the battle that we fought yesterday,' said Moctezuma. He motioned impatiently to the man charged with stoking the fires to get on with it.

'Having taken us away from the traditional approach, Tlacaelel's role was to pick the venue and the strategy, the date and time have long been set as you all know.' Realising that his chair had been returned, Moctezuma sat down, still holding his staff that was planted firmly on the floor beside him. He explained that the change of location was a definite risk and invited the assembly to question whether this was the right decision. Next the tlatoani gave a lengthy account of the layout of the field and why Tlacaelel had wanted the centre-ground to be less strongly defended. Finally, in solemn tones, he summarised the key developments on the battlefield, how the knights had prevented the enemy from outflanking the army and how events had appeared to go so badly wrong for the clans.

'Mixayacatl. You wish to speak,' said Moctezuma.

'Thank you, My Lord,' said Cloud Face.

'Last year we took five hundred and only lost three hundred of our own. Yesterday, two thousand seven hundred of our finest warriors perished and in return we captured less than five hundred enemy warriors.' Cloud Face paused, allowing his words to sink in. He wiped a hand across his bald head that had begun to bead with perspiration. Like Tlacaelel, he was next to one of the fires that lit the room.

'Is this what we can expect from the new strategy?' Cloud Face looked about the room. 'Two years ago, an army of two thousand Jaguar and Eagle Knights took three villages in the Oaxaca heartland. They brought back three hundred and thirty-nine captives and only lost one man... and he fell over a cliff!' Cloud Face waited for the muted laughter to die down before continuing. 'Was it not Itzcoatl who freed us from the tyranny of Maxtla, leading the siege against the Tepanecs? With his stratagems we dispatched two thousand savages to Mictlantecuhtli's realm and brought four hundred more back here as captives! There have been many other famous victories. Need I repeat them all?'

Tlacaelel rubbed his nose while the murmuring in the room grew louder. There was nothing he could do until his brother invited him to speak. Cloud Face had planned his speech well. It was devoid of personal animosity towards Tlacaelel himself and had so far stuck to the facts, a selection of them anyway. There was no doubt that he had the audience in his thrall, but he hadn't finished yet.

'My Lord, my friends...' resumed the high priest. 'For four long years our people endured drought and famine the like of which has never been seen before.' He mopped the birthmark on his forehead again. He was working up a good sweat whilst making his case. Moctezuma had not stirred at all. He was as motionless as the lizard on the branch.

'If you take account of our tribute to the gods these last five years, you will find a marked decline in our offerings of appeasement. I have spent my life in service of the people and can only offer you my humble opinion, which is this... we neglect the gods at our peril.'

Tlacaelel would have burst out laughing but for the seriousness of the situation. Cloud Face's show of humility was preposterous, yet still he wasn't done.

'Huitzilopochtli brings us light and fire. Tlaloc brings us the rains and life and every aspect of the universe turns upon the merest whim of Tezcatlipoca, Xipe Totec, Ehêcatl and all the rest. We count upon their blessings and although the New Fire is safely relit, we should not stand back and think we have done enough. Look to your souls and see if you feel safe with a new strategy that puts conquest before tribute to the gods.' Cloud Face's impassioned speech reached a crescendo. He pointed a finger skywards. 'Ask yourselves this question as you go to sleep tonight: have we done enough to earn their love so they will raise the sun again?' Cloud Face nodded graciously as he thanked the tlatoani and took his seat.

An enthusiastic hubbub met the end of the high priest's argument. Moctezuma waited for the noise to recede but eventually had to intervene. He stood once more and that was enough to stop the chattering. Slowly, he turned the great wooden staff in his hand and pointed it at his brother on the floor below the dais.

'Tlacaelel, your purpose as Woman Snake is to advise the tlatoani. Your job is to help me build the Mexica empire and safeguard the future of our people. I have heard Mixayacatl speak and he condemns our strategy. Do you wish to make your case?'

Tlacaelel was relieved to hear his brother use the word 'our'. It was a lifeline. The tlatoani had not made his mind up yet, but he would need a strong rebuttal to rescue the situation. Tlacaelel wished, not for the first time, that he had his brother's oratory skill. He took a deep breath.

'Yes, My Lord, I do. Yesterday did not bring the victory I had hoped for that is true, but before we turn to that, there are a few points I would raise in answer to some other of the high priest's words.'

Tlacaelel turned his back on the tlatoani and addressed the benches.

'Mixayacatl looks back upon the days of Itzcoatl fondly. Those days were good, he says and claims that everything went well. I expect we all look back upon those times and see an age of plenty. Perhaps that's how you see it, so let me remind you how it really was.' Tlacaelel's voice was flat as he sent out his challenge. 'Those times were bleak and savage.

'The Tepanecs were cruel and vicious overlords under whose rule we lived for many years in spite of the wisdom of my cousin, Itzcoatl. Need I remind you that they treated us like slaves? Surely you recall the countless disappearances from our outlying villages as Maxtla and his evil priests took our citizens for their own ceremonies?'

That stirred up more murmurings around the room. 'Good,' thought Tlacaelel. 'Perhaps I've got some tlatoani in me after all.' He coughed politely and all eyes turned back to him.

'Itzcoatl it was, helped by Nezahualcoyotl, who overthrew the tyrant of Azcapotzalco. Mixayacatl is correct, but what he forgot was that it was I who first went to Maxtla as the ambassador for our cause when no one else would volunteer. It was I who begged for peace and, when Maxtla refused, it was I who anointed him, placed a crown of feathers on his head and a shield and sword in his hands to make our declaration of war.' It was Tlacaelel's turn to pause and let his words sink in and then he turned his gaze to the priest of Xipe Totec.

'Snake Eyes!' he said. 'You are a veteran of those times.' Whilst the words were true, the sentiment was fabricated. Tlacaelel knew, if none of the nobility or warriors present did, that Snake Eyes had played no part in the siege of Azcapotzalco. The scheming priest had been too busy poisoning his way to the top of his own order.

'Remind us all who it was that Itzcoatl and Nezahualcoyotl turned to for a plan.'

Snake Eyes shook his straggly hair and licked his lips nervously. He spoke reluctantly. 'It was you, My Lord.'

'Just so, my friend, just so,' replied the general, allowing himself a smile for the first time since the previous morning. 'Now to my next point. In order to make the correct decisions, it's important to be well informed. I'm sure you're all familiar with the long-standing arrangement that any captives who are believed to possess useful information are interrogated before they are sacrificed and even, in certain cases, released into the custody of the tlatoani.'

Tlacaelel watched Cloud Face jump to his feet.

'I interrogated those captives myself!' cried the high priest.

'Sit down!' Moctezuma spoke from his vantage point.

'But, My Lord, the two captives he refers to had nothing to tell.' Here Cloud Face pointed at Tlacaelel. 'He insulted me by barging into my quarters.'

'*Sit down!*' Moctezuma was on his feet now and pointing his staff at Cloud Face. 'You have had your say and if we wish to hear more from you we will ask! Is that clear?'

'Yes, My Lord,' said Cloud Face and resumed his seat.

The room was utterly silent when Tlacaelel resumed. 'The two captives to whom Mixayacatl refers were members of the nobility in Chalco. The warriors who captured them established that they were on a mission to recruit the Tlaxcala states to their cause.'

'If you know all this, why did you need to interrogate them?' complained Cloud Face.

'I shall not warn you again, Mixayacatl!' growled Moctezuma.

'It would have been useful to establish exactly what message they were carrying,' pointed out Tlacaelel. 'I don't suppose you managed to extract this information from them, did you?'

Cloud Face scowled.

'Also, they might have been able to tell us whether other parties had been dispatched to ensure the message got through.'

'Of course they did,' spat Cloud Face. 'The Tlaxcala came to their assistance.'

Tlacaelel closed his eyes and hung his head as though summoning up great patience before looking up again. It was hard to gauge the mood of the room to see whether he'd won them round yet. He caught a dour look from Zipactonal amongst the faces of the nobility. The Lord Administrator was not a fan of his. The fourth member of the High Council was also present. Acamapichtli was better disposed towards Tlacaelel; at least he understood that the growth of his commercial enterprises depended on Tlacaelel's plans to extend the empire. The general was pleased to see Last Medicine nodding in approval from the back row of seats. He had a blood-stained cloth tied around his forehead and looked a little pale but his tacit support was invaluable. What was going through Moctezuma's mind was anybody's guess.

'Yes, Mixayacatl. We all know this now, after the event.' Tlacaelel made a dismissive gesture. 'We'll never know how that battle would have gone if we had been able to prevent Tlaxcala joining up with Chalco.' Tlacaelel ploughed ahead. This would be the hard bit.

'My Lord,' said Tlacaelel, turning to his brother once again. 'There is another disturbing piece of evidence that's come to my attention.'

Moctezuma raised an eyebrow.

'Someone on our side was killing our own people.'

There was a collective gasp from the audience.

'Two clan members were shot from behind and maybe others too. Storm Light, a young warrior from Teopan, was one and Ueman of Azcapotzalco another.'

Snake Eyes indicated that he wished to speak.

'Yes,' agreed the tlatoani.

'Strange things can take place in the chaos of war, My Lord,' he croaked. 'Surely accidents like this take place frequently.'

'So you don't dispute that these two warriors were killed by arrows made in Tenochtitlan?' Tlacaelel cut in.

'I...' Snake Eyes began. 'Well, were they? Isn't that what you said?' He pulled determinedly at a lank strand of hair.

'No,' said Tlacaelel. 'I did not, but it's interesting that you did not quibble that they had been killed by a Mexica archer though. Everyone else I've spoken to has argued that these men could simply have been facing the wrong way.'

'That is what I meant!' shot back Snake Eyes. 'Arrows get reused in battles all the time.'

'No,' said Tlacaelel again. 'That wasn't what you meant at all. That wouldn't have been an "accident".'

Snake Eyes twisted his hair and glanced at Cloud Face who was busy inspecting his nails.

'Enough!' said Moctezuma from the dais. 'Tlacaelel! Do you have any proof of this?'

'I have one of the arrows, My Lord.' Tlacaelel reached into the sack he had brought with him and produced the broken end of the arrow shaft with the distinctive blue-edge flights. 'An armourer called Achcauhtli and a young warrior gave this to me and showed me the body of the young man called Storm Light.'

'It's not much to go on. Can you produce these two men?'

'Yes, My Lord. The armourer lives in White Lady Street and the younger one down by the harbour.'

'We will look into this matter, but a couple of stray arrows have no bearing on your strategy, which is what has been called into question here. Have you more to say?'

'I am nearly finished, My Lord.'

'Be quick about it then,' said Moctezuma and leaned back on his chair.

Tlacaelel appealed to the assembled nobles and warriors.

'Yesterday we fielded thirty thousand brave Mexica warriors against an enemy that outnumbered us by nearly ten thousand and still we were victorious. If there was error in my preparations, it was to assume that Nezahualcoyotl would lead his army out to stand beside us. I should have taken extra steps to ensure Texcoco would come to our assistance.' Tlacaelel turned and bowed low to Moctezuma who bade him continue with a wave of his hand.

'Yes, we lost two thousand seven hundred men yesterday and took just five hundred captives, but we also sent four thousand more to Mictlan's cold embrace!' There were a few cheers. Tlacaelel tried to project his voice authoritatively for the final part of his defence.

'But here's the thing, My Lord, my worthy friends and noblemen... if you stood in Chalco's streets and courtyards and listened to them speak today, the sound you'd hear would be the sound of fear. Yes, there will be parties in the streets and Amihuatzin will make a victory speech, but listen closer to their tripping heartbeats. Listen to the women and the children wailing in their houses, wondering how they will manage now their men are gone.'

Everyone was sitting forward on their benches and the scribes had stopped their scribbling to watch the general.

Tlacaelel drew another deep breath. Nearly done now, he thought.

'Chalco are used to fighting the Triple Alliance, but yesterday, with outside help, they fought two thirds of that alliance and only just survived the day. They'll think again before they take us on, you mark my words and this is what we need, for if we cannot subjugate them, we must lock them up inside their walls so we can travel far and wide without their interference. Nation states should not toy with one-another; they must make peace or war, there is no in-between.'

The general turned to his brother, bowed and sat down.

The room was completely silent for a long while. Everyone watched Moctezuma with bated breath while Tlacaelel glanced at Cloud Face who returned his stare with thinly veiled hatred. The fire-stoker chose that moment to return, sweating under a fresh load of wood to replenish the dwindling light. Moctezuma waited, watching as the man gingerly added logs to the piles of white ash and glowing embers in each of the four urns. They crackled quickly into life again, splashing light around the walls. Then Moctezuma rose.

Tlacaelel felt the hairs prickle on the backs of his arms. His brother was a master showman; born to rule. With the fires burning brightly again, Moctezuma had chosen the perfect moment for his summing up. The bright flames cast a harsh light around the room and forged a giant, angry shadow on the wall behind.

'Does anyone else wish to speak?' Moctezuma asked the room, knowing there would be no answer. Tlacaelel half expected Snake Eyes to speak, convinced that Cloud Face had put him forward for that purpose, but the old priest just pushed his lank hair from his eyes and stared at the floor.

Acamapichtli stirred and Moctezuma invited him to speak.

'What of Nezahualcoyotl? He said he would send some men.'

'He claims the omens were not good,' said Tlacaelel.

There was a long pause while this news was digested.

Moctezuma collected himself and gazed sternly down at his brother. 'Here is my judgement on this matter, Tlacaelel. You know we must pay tribute to the gods. This comes before all else, even conquest, because our very lives depend on it.'

Cloud Face had a smug look again.

'The next time we fight, whatever plan you put in place, you must ensure we take more captives. I ask you as the tlatoani, but also as your brother. Do not disappoint me.

'Furthermore, your claim that there is some kind of treachery at work is hard to believe,' the tlatoani's face was severe. 'But, if you can prove that this is true and bring whoever is responsible to me, I swear by all of Huitzilopochtli's power vested in me that vengeance will be mine. I give you two days to bring me proof or the matter will be closed.'

Moctezuma banged his staff on the stone floor twice. 'This session is closed!'

When Jaguar came to, he found himself being half-carried, half-dragged between two Chalca warriors. His face throbbed with an icy pain, as though a large splinter had been driven up through his front teeth and nose and there was the taste of blood in his mouth. He ran his tongue gingerly over the teeth in his upper mouth and found a gap in the front where one had broken off below the level of the gum.

Ahead of them, several Chalca led the way, two of them struggling with Two Sign's slack form and the noises from behind indicated that several more were bringing up the rear. Perhaps twenty Chalca in all. Too many to break free. Jaguar's captors let him walk unassisted but held black daggers at his back. Still groggy, he slipped in a smear of fresh blood that had leaked from Two Sign's head and only just managed to keep from falling over.

It occurred to Jaguar that they might be heading for the holding cells that they were keeping Crocodile in. That would be embarrassing, thought Jaguar. His friend would not be impressed with the rescue attempt.

'Where are you taking us?'

'You'll see soon enough!' snapped one of the warriors.

Jaguar's stomach gave a lurch as he realised that the warriors were Amihuatzin's Serpent Knights. They weren't wearing the fanged cowls but glistening snake skins draped their shoulders and hung down to below their waists. The group passed several minor temples and rounded a corner and there, stretched out before them, was Amihuatzin's palace. It was built around a quadrangle with an elegant watchtower at each corner. Lush trees grew within the courtyard and beyond them the main building backed upon Lake Chalco, so that the upper chambers of the palace looked out across the Xochimilco basin, across to Huipulco and the hazy mauve hills beyond. Rising up behind the palace to the south, also on the lakeside, lay the great temple of Tlaloc.

Two Sign stirred and the warriors dragging him along came to a stop. They stood the big man on his feet and two more stepped forward to bind his wrists with twine. Two Sign swayed dangerously but a few well-timed nudges from the Chalca kept him upright. The warrior to his left said something guttural that Jaguar didn't hear, but it made his fellow on the other side let out a laugh.

'Yes, that's it! Too much cactus juice. Ha-ha!'

They chuckled and shoved Two Sign in the back to make him walk on.

After two dozen paces Two Sign seemed to recover. He glanced over his shoulder and gave a small nod of recognition to Jaguar then turned to look where he was going. Jaguar was appalled at the mess on the back of the knight's head where a flap of scalp hung loose, ragged around the edges.

The procession continued down a shallow incline towards the palace and marched through a set of outer gates into a beautiful courtyard garden, complete with trees and ornamental maguey. A giant fig tree stood against one of the high walls, its topmost branches only just level with the top of the stonework that supported it, but elsewhere, the walls were festooned with carefully manicured creepers. Iridescent hummingbirds hovered fleetingly to sup at trumpet-shaped orange flowers that sprouted from the greenery, before darting away on whirring wings. Meandering through the garden was a stream, which tumbled musically over cleverly placed boulders and slid silently beneath ornate wooden walkways. The whole effect was so exquisitely peaceful and at such stark contrast to the surrounding, drought-stricken countryside that Jaguar did not know whether to laugh out loud or cry.

They walked through stands of lush green grass and underneath nodding fronds of fern until they reached a short flight of stairs on the far side of the courtyard. There, a doorway led to a series of corridors where the feet of the warriors slapped and echoed. Two Sign was walking more confidently and they were making good progress so that before long, the pair were ushered into a spacious room, sumptuously furnished with cotton drapes and rugs.

Two Sign said nothing, so it was Jaguar who broke the silence again.

'What are we doing here?'

'You will wait here for now,' said a pot-bellied warrior, who must have been the leader of this little pack. He scratched his back nonchalantly. 'Later, Amihuatzin will see you. He doesn't like spies. I heard he wants to pronounce the death sentence on you in person.'

Chapter 17 – Ollîn

Two Sign sat down heavily on the rugs and gently oozed blood onto them.

'Is that water over there?' Jaguar asked the Serpent Knight with the rotund stomach. The warrior nodded and stepped aside to allow Jaguar to fetch the stone jug and bring it back to Two Sign. He knelt down, removed his tunic and tore several strips from it with which he began to clean the wound on Two Sign's head. The big man hadn't uttered a word since he'd come round and Jaguar was beginning to get concerned. Finally, his inexpert swabbing provoked a response.

'Ouch!' said Two Sign.

'So you are alive after all!' exclaimed Jaguar. 'Listen, I'm going to bind this up. There's a flap of skin hanging off, but it should heal if it's held in place.'

The Eagle Knight just grunted so Jaguar set about winding cloth around his head. When he was done, he removed the bandage from his arm and prodded the wound gingerly. It was swollen and the area surrounding it was an angry red colour but it didn't smell bad, so Jaguar began rebinding it, holding one end of the cloth in his teeth while he used his free hand to loop and tie the dressing. Two Sign watched him but only volunteered to help when it was already too late.

'Thanks,' said Jaguar. He took a drink, wincing at the shock of the cold water on his broken tooth and then passed the jug to Two Sign. All the while, six of the Serpent Knights remained with them in the room, silent and motionless.

Two Sign lay back and closed his eyes. Jaguar sat with his back to the cool stone wall and watched motes of dust drifting in the shaft of daylight from the small window. Eventually, a young messenger put his head into the room and spoke quietly to the potbellied man. After a brief exchange, he bade the two Mexica warriors follow him and their escort followed close behind. Jaguar was pleased to see that Two Sign looked firmer on his feet.

They jinked through a couple of corridors and then stepped through a door that let out halfway along a cavernous, gloomy hallway lit with a handful of torches that sputtered fitfully in stone sconces on the walls. The ceiling was almost lost in sepulchral darkness above and there was an intense dank, musty aroma that reminded Jaguar of moss.

'This way,' said the leader and turned towards lights at one end of the hall.

Someone scuffed a pebble that clicked away into the murky recesses, its sound replicated and magnified by the cold stone walls into a short-lived clatter. When Jaguar and Two Sign reached the far end of the hall, where two guards stood stiffly at a door, warmed by the light of four more torches. The guards stepped aside for their colleagues who swept the two Mexica through with them.

In the next room, light from six windows set high up around the room illuminated the polished stone floor, while the vaulted archways that lined the room remained stubbornly beyond the pool of light. Jaguar was just wondering if the effect was deliberate when he sensed a change in the room. There was a subtle change in the air and the quality of the deep shadow on the far side of the room changed. The Serpent Knights pushed their captives forward into the light and bowed low. Jaguar's eyes began to make sense of the sharp contrasts in the room and he noticed, between two black, misshapen, man-high candelabra, the largest man he had ever seen wallowing in a chair of starkly striped mizquitl. The enormous cinnamon-coloured cloak did little to disguise the vast bulk beneath it and rolls of flesh quivered at the man's neck. Pudgy, plate-like hands protruded from the sleeves of the cloak and draped themselves over the arms of the chair.

Jaguar knew this must be Amihuatzin but could only risk the briefest of glimpses. He bowed low but noticed in alarm that Two

Sign hadn't followed suit. Whether the knight was unaware of what was happening or whether he was being deliberately insolent, Jaguar could not tell.

'Two Sign!' the vast bulk boomed in a cordial fashion. 'I heard you were a man of honour, and yet, here you are creeping about my city like a spy and failing to pay respect to the ruler of Chalco!'

Jaguar waited for Two Sign to reply, but seconds passed without response.

'Come, Two Sign, do not try my patience,' said Amihuatzin. 'I have it in my power to stretch out your death, make you scream until your lungs burst.'

Seeing that Two Sign wasn't going to answer, Jaguar spoke up. 'Please, My Lord!'

'Speak young one, since your companion is either deaf or dumb. Who are you?'

'My Lord, my name is Ocelotyolotl,' began Jaguar. He hesitated for fear of interrupting Amihuatzin but realised that the ruler of Chalco was waiting for more. 'I'm sorry about Two Sign. I'm afraid one of your warriors nearly killed him. He's not spoken a word since he came to.'

Jaguar could just make out a frown from the shadows and was filled with an uncomfortable sense of foreboding. The world had shifted subtly in an unexpected direction so that nothing seemed to fit together anymore. It was extraordinary that he was here, standing before the ruler of Chalco, somehow responsible not just for his own destiny but also for Two Sign's. Jaguar felt as though he was caught on a precipitous mountaintop in the dead of night with certain death on every side. If only there was some safe way down, some cunning route he could explore with tentative, trembling, outstretched feet.

'I see,' replied Amihuatzin. 'So perhaps you can answer in his place. Are you with Two Sign?'

'My Lord,' said Jaguar, deciding he should account for their presence in Chalco since it was his idea. 'It is I who brought Two Sign with me rather than the other way around.'

'Extraordinary!' cried Amihuatzin. 'Did Moctezuma send you here to spy on us?' he added. 'Or perhaps he sent you here to assassinate me!' Amihuatzin shook his pendulous jowls sorrowfully.

Jaguar stole another glance, mesmerised by the sight of the man's corpuscular body oozing over the edges of the throne. Whenever he moved, the more remote parts of his body had trouble keeping up, only setting off after a small delay. His jowls reminded Jaguar of the wattles on a turkey. Two tiny, sunken black eyes stared out accusingly from under a comically small mop of hair.

Something about the candelabra on either side of Amihuatzin caught Jaguar's attention once again but his brain refused to understand what he was seeing. He looked again. Each of the twisted candle holders was made from the remains of what had once been humans. The emaciated, desiccated bodies were naked and their skin looked like charcoal-coloured leather. On the floor beneath each of them, lay the base of a wooden truss lying flat on the floor that supported a vertical pole about the thickness of a man's wrist. The pole disappeared between the victims' legs and, Jaguar supposed, through the anus and up to their heads, thus keeping them upright. Empty eye sockets stared, as though the dead men were transfixed by Mictlan's dark, eternal realms, and the dried out skin was pulled tight over their screaming mouths. Among the wispy remnants of hair atop each head, a clay pot sat neatly in a specially cut hole and in each a candle guttered fitfully, mocking the very soul it had displaced.

'Ahh!' exclaimed Amihuatzin. 'I see you like my friends?' he added. He made an expansive gesture taking in the grisly props. 'You see... this is what we do with unwelcome Mexica in this city. These fine specimens are two of Nezahualcoyotl's sons who came here eleven years ago with a proposal for an alliance. As you can see, it was not a very good offer.' The ruler of Chalco laughed. 'So tell me please, before I add you to this special collection, what is your business here in Chalco? Why has Moctezuma been reduced to sending his most illustrious knights to skulk about the streets like filthy mayeque?' Amihuatzin's voice rose to a crescendo. 'Does the fearsome hummingbird suppose that he can march across the land eating up towns and cities until there's nothing left?'

Was it Jaguar's imagination or had the Serpent Warriors crept away? Two Sign still hadn't moved or given any indication that he understood what was going on. Jaguar saw that he wasn't going to get any help, so if the two of them were to stand any chance of getting out alive, it would have to be him who found a way to make it happen. The ruler of Chalco had started off in an almost jovial mood, but that had utterly evaporated. At another time, Jaguar might have been afraid, but his predicament with Cloud Face and the scale of death he had witnessed the day before, of which his own father had been a victim, had left him cold and diffident. Meanwhile, the ruler of Chalco was working himself into a quivering frenzy.

'We won't stand for it! Do you hear? Since the dawn of the Creator Pair, the people of this land have lived in harmony, working and playing side-by-side. But in the handful of generations that your itinerant ancestors and their worthless descendants have lived in the valley, you have done nothing but stir up trouble!'

Behind the bluster, Jaguar heard real fear and knew instinctively that it might get them killed. What he needed was to divert Amihuatzin's attention before he lost his temper entirely. Nothing came to mind.

Jaguar watched as Amihuatzin hauled himself to his feet and carefully negotiated the three steps down from his throne. He moved slowly and waddled, legs apart to prowl around the back of Jaguar and Two Sign.

'You think that you're untouchable,' sneered Amihuatzin. 'You and that dreamer Nezahualcoyotl. Tlatleloco, Tenochtitlan and Texcoco; the fabled Triple Alliance?' He circled Jaguar and Two Sign menacingly. 'Bah! Where were your allies yesterday? Nezahualcoyotl never even showed his face and he's on our very doorstep! Did you see how Chalco's allies came from far and wide? Tlalmanalco and Amecameca and a host of others rallied to our cause.'

Amihuatzin spat at Two Sign's feet, but the warrior only stared back vacuously. The ruler of Chalco curled his lip and stopped in front of Jaguar instead. He leaned in, his face inches away and Jaguar had to fight to keep from lifting his eyes, even when the ruler poked him in the chest.

'You think you're so superior? I'll take your arrogance and turn it back against you.' Spittle showered Jaguar's cheeks. 'I'll rally every enemy you've ever made across the land and forge an army to send you to oblivion! From Oaxaca and Tarascan to Tlaxcala and the forests of the Yucatan, they'll come swarming in their thousands, all bent on vengeance.'

Amihuatzin withdrew and set to circling around them again so that Jaguar sensed the beady eyes boring into his back. He had never felt so vulnerable. He wanted to turn to face the threat, but knew that such insolence would have meant instant death. His spine tingled.

'Do you imagine this is just a game?' the voice menaced from behind.

A game! That word gave Jaguar an idea. He looked at Two Sign, standing mute but solid next to him. The knight saw him looking and tilted his head quizzically. Whatever was wrong with him, Two Sign hadn't entirely lost his wits.

'What is this?' demanded Amihuatzin, who had noticed the exchange and emerged once again in front of the two Mexica warriors.

'I'm sorry, My Lord. I was hoping Two Sign would speak for himself but it seems your men have reduced him to the state of an imbecile.'

Amihuatzin shook his head irritably but Jaguar pressed on, not wanting him to resume his diatribe.

'My Lord, I...'

'Speak one last time,' said the ruler of Chalco. 'I tire of you and this broken man. Why are you here and what message shall I send to Moctezuma with your severed heads?'

'My Lord, it is common knowledge that the Chalca like a wager just as much as the Mexica.' Jaguar paused to gauge the man's reaction but there was none so he pressed on. He had that distraction that he needed. The pitch was all-important now so Jaguar talked quickly. 'You want to know why we are here in Chalco and this is the reason. I came here to rescue my friend,

313

Obsidian Crocodile, who was captured in the battle yesterday. Two Sign is his father and I persuaded him to come along with me to get his son. Now that you have the reason, I shall make you a wager.'

In the puzzled silence that followed, Jaguar risked a glance at Amihuatzin's eyes, hoping for an insight to their owner's thoughts.

'Wait,' said the vast man, ignoring the breach of conduct. 'Wait. Slow down! You're talking nonsense. What do you mean by rescue?'

'I mean, My Lord, that we intended to find Crocodile and take him back to Tenochtitlan.'

Perplexed, Amihuatzin raised his hands in despair. 'You came to Chalco to find this friend of yours and persuade him to leave with you?'

'Yes, My Lord,' said Jaguar firmly.

Again there was a puzzled silence while Amihuatzin mulled this over, unable to comprehend.

'You would ask your friend to escape from Chalco to avoid being sacrificed?'

The repetitious questioning annoyed Jaguar. 'It would be difficult for him to escape after he's been sacrificed,' he blurted out.

The monarch snorted, a deep and rumbling wet sound, and then snorted again. The snort became a booming laugh and soon Amihuatzin had thrown his head back and was roaring with delight, his hands clasped to his waistband of snakeskin and gold braid as though to prevent it from becoming dislodged from his massive, wobbling stomach. He struggled to control himself and, after a while, he finally managed to speak.

'Why would he do that?' he said.

Jaguar was certain he'd been lucky that his insolence had been overlooked so he answered more carefully this time. 'Because he doesn't want to die.'

This sent Amihuatzin into fresh paroxysms until it really looked as though he'd hurt himself. The laugh became a strangled sort of hooting sound as he fought to control the pain. In the end, he was forced to summon help and two of the Serpent Knights steered him back to the throne where he collapsed, helpless for a while. Jaguar waited patiently.

'Young man,' said Amihuatzin eventually, wiping the tears from his great cheeks. 'No one wants to die, but the warrior who dies with honour goes to paradise. Children know this from an early age.'

'There's no honour in being hacked in two on an altar, My Lord,' Jaguar said simply. 'Besides, it doesn't matter what the children think, I made a promise to my friend that I intend to keep.'

Amihuatzin gave no answer to this but stared at Jaguar, observing him through narrowed eyelids.

'What's this wager then?' he asked.

'I heard someone say that Chalco's ball game players are the best.'

Amihuatzin beamed broadly. 'A wise person indeed. Chalco's ullamalitzli players are the finest in the world.'

'Do you care to put that to the test, My Lord?'

'What do you propose little man?'

'Set up a game tomorrow, Chalca against Mexica.' Jaguar glanced at Two Sign who simply raised one eyebrow. 'The famous warrior, commander of the Eagle Knights and his team play the pride of Chalco! Four players on each team. We'll need Crocodile on our team and another warrior who we will hand pick from among your captives. We'll play your team and, if we win, you let us all walk free.'

Jaguar could see that Amihuatzin was interested. Two Sign looked upset but Jaguar's attention was on the ruler of Chalco.

'And if you lose?'

'Then the gods have had their say... and you offer us to them.' Jaguar spoke the words boldly but they felt like ashes in his mouth. Again he looked at Two Sign, but this time there was no response. The warrior stood at ease, a tranquil look upon his face as he stared straight ahead. Jaguar wondered what he was thinking.

Amihuatzin had regained his composure and a cynical smile tugged at the corner of his mouth.

'You know, Ocelotyolotl,' he began. 'I gain nothing from this wager that I don't already have.'

'Is that right, My Lord?'

'It is.' The overweight ruler waved a hand languorously at a slave who emerged from the shadows with a drink and a bowl of oddly shaped morsels of food that he set down on the wide arm of the tlatoani's throne. 'Why shouldn't I instruct you to play the game anyway, it just so happens we have one scheduled as part of the celebrations tomorrow, and then have your heart cut out whatever the outcome?'

'You could do that, Exalted One,' replied Jaguar, 'but where would our incentive be to play our best? You need to know your team played us at our very best or else you'll doubt the outcome until the end of time.'

Amihuatzin smirked and shook his head. 'Come now. You don't stand a chance, do you? A scrawny lad, an imbecilic knight and a rag tag bunch from the temple's holding cells! Do you have any idea who you'll be up against?'

Jaguar shrugged.

'Ha,' Amihuatzin laughed again, a disbelieving bark. 'Have you not heard of Necuametl, the Fleet of Foot, or Cuetzpalli, who's never been on a losing team?'

Jaguar shrugged again. The man was a pompous fool to think his precious players mattered outside Chalco. Amihuatzin looked astonished. 'You said that our players are famous and yet you haven't heard of any of them. I'm sure you'll find that the lowliest mayeque in Tenochtitlan has heard of Amoxtli the Brave who played half a game with a broken leg, and Nellipatli!'

'I heard of one called Hopalong, could he be one of those?' Jaguar asked innocently.

'Argh!' cried Amihuatzin and tore at his tiny mop of hair. 'You'll meet them soon enough!' he said in a disgusted tone. 'You have your wager, little man, with one exception. Choose two players from the cells, but this friend of yours, if we even have him, will not be one of them. Also, I'll not allow him to watch the game, but if you win, then you have my word that he'll walk free with you.'

Jaguar prostrated himself in thanks and saw that Two Sign was copying him.

'Enough. Go now. I shall ensure you are well attended to.' He beckoned to the Serpent Knights who moved silently back into position around the two Mexica. 'Ocotzonamaca!' said Amihuatzin to the leader. 'Take these two to Atexcalco's old guest quarters and make sure they don't wander off. Send Good Song to them and then go and check if we have a captive by the name of Crocodile, son of Two Sign, in our cells.'

Ocotzonamaca looked Two Sign up and down.

'Yes, My Lord. Shall I double the guard?'

The ruler of Chalco levered himself back out of his chair and waved a hand dismissively. 'Whatever you think best. Be careful though. He may not look as though he even knows his name just now, but don't forget that he's the commander of the Eagle Knights and Tlacaelel's right-hand man.' He clicked his tongue. 'It is a shame,' he told Jaguar. 'When I heard we'd caught this demon, I set my heart on putting him in a ritual fight. The whole of Chalco could have watched the infamous Two Sign being cut to pieces and Xicotencatl would have liked it too.' With a last, disappointed glance, he added, 'My medicine woman will tend your wounds. I need you at your best tomorrow. My people won't be pleased if the game is one-sided.' Amihuatzin turned and lumbered around his throne, heading for an exit in the gloom beyond.

The packed Hall of Truth had been heated to the point of airlessness, which had made it hard for Tlacaelel to breathe. Back in his own cool, uncluttered rooms, he at last began to relax. He placed both hands on his lower back and stretched to relieve the tension.

'Are you well, My Lord?' asked Rock in a voice like distant thunder. His forearm was bandaged where the arrow had been and the fingers of his right hand were swollen. It didn't seem to trouble him, except as a concession he'd decided to do without his trusty club.

Tlacaelel had collared the big warrior after the meeting and asked him for his help. He would need someone in the Eagle Knights to help track down their commander.

'I'm fine,' replied the general. 'I'm not a natural speaker like my brother, so anything like that gives me backache.'

Rock nodded and Last Medicine, who stood beside him, even reached for his own back in sympathy. Tlacaelel had asked Last Medicine to stand in as his second-in-command until Two Sign's whereabouts were known. Of course, there would be politics to contend with. It was inevitable with an appointment of this sort and more so in this case where the post was changing hands between the two principal orders of knights. Difficult discussions could be deferred by making it clear it was a temporary arrangement. Two Sign had not died. He and the young man had just gone missing and Tlacaelel was determined to get them back, especially the young man who had been so sure of treachery during the fighting yesterday.

'Are you sure Two Sign wasn't captured?' asked Last Medicine.

'Yes!' said Tlacaelel, frowning. 'I saw him afterwards talking to survivors.' Last Medicine was a solid replacement for Two Sign. Tlacaelel knew him to be a resourceful fighter and almost as devastating too. He had already heard the story of Quitzatzatia's rescue by Last Medicine and how, whittled down to just three men, the encircled knights had held off a hundred of Tlaxcala's veterans. Quitzatzatia had lost his right arm, but it seemed Last Medicine had saved his life.

'He came to see me as we were heading back,' Rock confirmed. 'He said he had something to check.'

'He didn't say what?' asked Tlacaelel.

'No, My Lord.'

Two more Jaguar Knights trooped into Tlacaelel's quarters with the armourer Achcauhtli in tow.

'Where is the other one?' he asked. 'I told you to fetch the one called Jaguar as well.'

'He wasn't there, My Lord,' said the knight. 'His family were in a terrible state. His mother said he never returned and neither did her husband, Blade of the South.'

'Excuse me, My Lord Tlacaelel,' ventured Achcauhtli. 'Someone broke the news to her that she'd lost her husband and her son so she was distraught. I tried to reassure her by telling her that I'd seen Jaguar safe and well, but he's not been home so now she doesn't know what to think.'

Tlacaelel looked puzzled. 'Two warriors are missing and yet we know they both survived. What does this mean?'

'Maybe they were both taken on the way home,' suggested Last Medicine. 'It sometimes happens to the stragglers.'

'Two Sign ambushed?' Tlacaelel sounded sceptical.

'It would have taken quite a force,' Last Medicine admitted.

'That's true, my friend. We can't find them, yet we know they both survived the battle. It sounds crazy but maybe that's it. Perhaps they were held back for some reason and were set upon by Chalca.' He stared intently up at the large cloth map high up on the wall as if it would reveal the missing men.

'I need information.' He shook his head. 'Rock!'

'Yes, My Lord,' said the warrior evenly. He flexed the fingers of his swollen hand, willing them to work again.

'I'm sorry, I know you've been wounded but this is important. I need someone with your experience to do this. Pick sixty men and scour the battlefield for signs of Two Sign and Heart of the Jaguar. I want you back here at first light tomorrow to report.'

'Yes, My Lord.'

He turned to the warriors who'd brought Achcauhtli in. 'Tlacpac!'

'Yes, My Lord,' replied the taller of the two.

'Go at once to Quimapiqui's house. You know the one?'

'The big house at the water's edge near the Conmina storehouse?'

'That's the one. Quimapiqui has trading partners everywhere and he still owes me favours. Tell him that the Woman Snake needs news from Chalco. Describe Two Sign and the ball player, Ocelotyolotl, and make sure he understands we need to know their location by tomorrow.'

'Yes, My Lord,' the knight replied and set off at a trot.

Tlacaelel cursed himself for not being better prepared. He had a contact within Chalco but no means to get word back from him at such short notice. They had a system that involved an exchange of messages scrawled on stones in a copse near Mixquic, but the location, south of the lake, meant that it took several days to get an answer.

At last the general remembered Achcauhtli and thanked him for coming. The armourer was neatly turned out in a clean tunic and even his stubby fingers, gnarled from his work with tools, were spotlessly clean. The man has a good wife, concluded Tlacaelel, but there was nothing she could have done to disguise the man's exhaustion. He looked pale and drawn. Tlacaelel walked over to the man and put a hand on his shoulder.

'You did a fine job yesterday. It's thanks to men like you that we beat the Chalca back.'

'Thank you, My Lord.'

Tlacaelel released him and stepped back. 'I'm sure your wife is pleased to have you back.'

Achcauhtli's eyes sparkled beneath his permanent frown and he smiled broadly. 'Yes, she is, My Lord. She never complains, but she worries, just like they all do.'

Tlacaelel smiled back and then turned to the reason he'd invited Achcauhtli.

'What was the name of the standard bearer?' He clasped his thumb and finger around his temples and jumped in before Achcauhtli could reply. 'Storm Light, that was it! Moctezuma must hear what you have to say, but first, have you remembered who you sold that arrow to that killed that boy?'

'I have checked, My Lord.'

'Excellent! What news?'

'Well, I knew they looked familiar, but there are so many special orders that I had to check with my assistant. This design of arrow with the blue feather is made for just one order of priests.'

'The priests of the Flayed Flesh by any chance?' asked Tlacaelel.

It was the armourer's turn to look confused. 'Yes, My Lord.' He looked crestfallen, his purpose blunted. 'How did you know?'

'Just a guess.' Tlacaelel winked knowingly. 'You've done well, Achcauhtli. Will you accompany me to see the tlatoani now?'

'Of course, My Lord,' said the armourer, beaming proudly. 'It would be an honour.'

—————————

The Mexica were taken to another room and Jaguar was caught off guard as the big man finally spoke.

'That was a fine performance!' said Two Sign.

'You're back!' he said, so delighted that he ignored the sarcastic note. 'I wasn't sure you'd ever speak again.'

'Neither was I,' said Two Sign. He glared at Jaguar.

'I thought you'd lost the power of speech!' exclaimed Jaguar. 'Why didn't you say anything in there?'

'I'm not sure. Maybe I saw no need to speak.'

'No need to speak?' echoed Jaguar in astonishment. 'He was going to execute us... probably still is.'

'I'm sure he will. What are you playing at?'

Jaguar glimpsed real anger in the man. Two Sign's lips were pressed into a thin line and his hands were clenched tightly at his side as he glowered down at him.

'What do you mean?'

'What is this nonsense about the ball game and a wager?'

Jaguar blinked, becoming more indignant as he tried to work out what the knight objected to.

'It's a wager, plain and simple. What don't you understand?'

Two Sign pointed out of the window. 'We're going to be the laughing stock of Chalco!'

Jaguar frowned. 'Why?'

'Have you lost all reason?' Two Sign gesticulated impatiently. 'Maybe you took a worse knock on the head than I thought. It's that or you've allowed your own arrogance to get the better of you. You're good, Jaguar, but not that good! Do you really think we stand a chance against Amihuatzin's best players? Amihuatzin's favourites do nothing else but play ullamalitzli, you know this!

They're not allowed to get married or go to war and they're on the court so much that they barely get to sleep!'

Jaguar grew more irate with every word. He jabbed a finger in Two Sign's chest. 'Fine!' he said. 'You heard what Amihuatzin said. He wants you in a gladiatorial contest. Why don't you send word to him and tell him you're in?'

'I might just do that!' shouted Two Sign.

The two guards standing just inside the entrance to their chamber weren't sure what to do. They stepped forward as though they were going to intervene but then stopped a few steps away. It occurred to Jaguar that they might have orders to prevent any harm from coming to his two prize exhibits.

'You know what will happen, don't you?'

'Yes,' replied Two Sign. 'If I'm lucky, they'll tie me to a large stone and give me a wooden sword to fight four Chalco warriors...'

'...each equipped with armour and the finest swords in Chalco,' Jaguar finished. 'It's not going to have a happy outcome.'

'At least it will be honourable.'

'Honourable?' exclaimed Jaguar. 'How is there honour in a ridiculous contest like that? There might be honour in it if it was a fair fight!'

Two Sign struggled for an answer. 'Maybe that's the will of the gods,' he said lamely.

'If that's what the gods willed, why did they allow Amihuatzin to take me up on my wager?'

Two Sign scratched his ear thoughtfully and backed off. He found a bench and sat down heavily and Jaguar decided to press home his advantage.

'At least this way we stand a chance! Alright, I admit it's very unlikely, but if the gods have allowed this game to come about, maybe one of them is on our side.'

Two Sign shrugged. 'Even if all the gods are on our side, we'll still need Amihuatzin to keep his word.'

'Are you saying he lied about letting us go?'

'He probably didn't think it would come to that and neither do I. I've heard of some of those players.'

It was true. Anyone with an interest in the sacred game kept their ears open for news of talented players from across the valley. He had heard of all of the names Amihuatzin had mentioned.

'Look, I'm sorry,' Jaguar began hesitantly. He couldn't meet Two Sign's gaze. He fell silent as the big man waited and at last looked up. 'It wasn't supposed to happen like this. It hasn't gone at all according to plan.'

Two Sign grinned. He seemed to have forgiven Jaguar. 'Don't worry. The old plan wasn't exactly great, was it?'

Jaguar's head hurt. The encounter with the ruler of Chalco had drained him. He sat down heavily in the corner and allowed his eyes to wander around the room they were confined to. The room's stone ceiling stretched out unsupported over an area that Jaguar decided would easily enclose his own home back in Tenochtitlan. The masonry of the walls was so precise that it wouldn't have been possible to insert a cactus spine between the big stone blocks. The room was opulently furnished too. There was a large sleeping area of rush matting piled three deep and drapes of the finest cotton hung from the walls, and Two Sign was occupying one of a number of benches. All of the cotton fabric looked as though it had come from the south, probably Cuernavaca, from before Huitzilihuitl's conquest of that area fifty years ago. Most striking though were the dozen jaguar pelts laid out on the floor.

Two Sign saw Jaguar staring at them. 'From captured Mexica knights,' he offered. 'You know,' he added. 'That was a brave thing you did back there.'

'What was?'

'Come on. You know what I mean.'

'No, really.'

'Why did you keep goading Amihuatzin like that? You were trying to provoke him into accepting the challenge?'

'I suppose so,' answered Jaguar and then snorted with amusement.

'What?' asked Two Sign.

'You really fooled him with your dumb act, didn't you?'

Two Sign laughed. It was a good sound and for the first time that day, Jaguar dared to hope. He closed his eyes and felt sleep clawing at him from the darkness. He couldn't understand why his ears were ringing until he remembered he had also been struck on the back of the head. A dull ache persisted where his arm had been sliced open. Jaguar groaned and slid back down until he was stretched out on the floor with only a saffron-coloured rug between him and the flagged stone floor. 'I'll rest my eyes for a while,' he said, more to himself than to Two Sign.

'Hello?' A soft voice intruded.

Jaguar struggled to the surface, feeling sick and disoriented and tried to work out what the interruption was. As the fog of exhaustion cleared, Jaguar noticed a tall, strikingly beautiful woman at the entrance to the room. She had an aquiline nose and full lips. Two of Amihuatzin's men accompanied her and they nodded at the warriors already posted at the door, joining them, one on either side. The woman wore a dun-coloured skirt and shawl and a large, loose bag slung over her shoulder. Jaguar guessed this was Amihuatzin's physician. She had long, radiant black hair that reminded him of Precious Flower. That was where the resemblance ended though. This woman was curvaceous in a way that suggested she had never wanted for food the way Precious Flower and her family had.

'You must be the Mexica,' she said, deciding she would get no answer. 'Amihuatzin sent me to take a look at you. My name is Good Song,' she added.

She moved confidently over to Two Sign, who had fallen mute again.

'May I treat your head wound?'

Two Sign nodded. Needing no further encouragement, Amihuatzin's physician carefully unwrapped the makeshift bandage that Jaguar had applied earlier, making dissatisfied sounds as she worked. Jaguar watched her examine the ragged scrap of scalp that had come loose and then bark at one of the guards to fetch a bowl of water. The alacrity with which the man scurried off to do her bidding was interesting. She might be the healer to the ruler of Chalco, but the way she moved and the way she spoke to the guards suggested her standing in court was much higher than that. There was something about her that put him in mind of Precious Flower. The turn of her shoulder or the way she swept her hair back when it got in the way. Good Song turned and caught Jaguar staring at her. His face burned suddenly. He got up and crossed to the window to avoid watching her at work. The window was small but afforded a magnificent view over Lake Chalco.

The lake was grey, reflecting the colour of the sky overhead and gusts of wind played over its surface, creating dark patches of ripples. Reed beds along the southern shore swayed; whipped into a frenzy by the strengthening wind that channelled underneath the ominous cloud base. Jaguar could smell a change in the air, that sweet earthiness that presaged rain. He hoped it would hold off until after the game.

The game, thought Jaguar sourly. What hope did they really have? As if she had read Jaguar's mind, Good Song piped up.

'Amihuatzin told me that you're going to play for your lives.' It was hard to tell whether she was impressed or just incredulous. 'A game of ullama?'

'Yes,' Jaguar acknowledged.

'Are you the best of the Mexica?'

Jaguar knew where he stood in the rankings. Rainbow of the West was unquestionably the best player in Tenochtitlan. He was an experienced player who rarely lost. Even when he was placed with a weaker team, he somehow seemed to be able to inspire them to victory. Jaguar had played against him twice, his own team made up of veterans and had lost both times, though only by a narrow margin. Tecolote was next best, a player of speed and endurance who wowed the crowds with daring lunges and extravagant tricks. Tecolote, The Owl, was fallible though. He was more entertaining than Rainbow of the West because he took risks, but they often landed him in trouble. Jaguar had played him five times and had been on the winning team twice. Two Sign had been on the team to celebrate one of those victories.

'No, Good Song, we're not the best, but we might have a chance if we can find a couple of half-decent players from amongst our people who have been taken captive.'

'Who treated this man's wound?' interrupted Good Song.

'That... was me,' replied Jaguar awkwardly.

'Well I hope you're a better ball player than healer!' she retorted. 'Call this clean?' She was swabbing the blood-encrusted hair around the patch of skin on the back of Two Sign's head.

Jaguar found the energy to laugh. 'I had just been hit on the back of the head myself, you know. Under the circumstances I was rather pleased.'

Good Song huffed to show she was unimpressed. She produced a pot from her bag and from it, scooped a couple of fingers of a brown poultice onto the knight's head. It had a powerful minty aroma that immediately filled the room. Two Sign was so indifferent to the woman's ministrations he might just as well have been carved of stone. The healer finished by tying a new strip of cotton around his head and stepped back to admire her handiwork.

'You don't seem like the fearsome knight I've heard tales of,' she said.

Jaguar wondered why Two Sign had retreated into silence again.

'He's not been feeling great since one of Amihuatzin's thugs dropped a tree on his head,' Jaguar explained.

Good Song came over to examine Jaguar but he waved her away. 'No, no thank you, I'm fine, really!'

'You don't look well,' she countered. She put a hand on her hip and stared at him defying Jaguar to disagree. 'You look pale. I should look at your arm in case it's been treated as badly as his head.' She jabbed a thumb back at the knight and then had to sweep her hair back again as it slipped over her shoulder.

Jaguar winced as the memory of Precious Flower sprang to mind, unbidden. Maybe she would leave Tenochtitlan to be with him, if he and Two Sign could just win the game and... Jaguar stopped. It was absurd. He had to concentrate on the game. That was the only certainty in his life now.

'I just need food and some rest.'

Good Song beamed at Jaguar. 'Excellent! Food is on its way and you've plenty of time to rest before the games tomorrow.' She pointed at Jaguar's arm. 'May I?' she added.

'All right.' As Good Song worked, Jaguar looked out of the window. The reeds in the lake whipped back and forth, bent this way and then the other in the strengthening gale. It was as though they were bowing down in supplication to the clouds that rolled on overhead, beseeching them for water before their roots became stranded, high and dry above the level of the lake. With every passing minute the louring sky dropped lower. It looked like an ominous premonition of things to come. The next day would be a struggle, like none before. Even the battle on the previous day had held less terror. Somehow, the sheer variety of outcomes diminished the fear of any one of them. The game tomorrow was a different matter. Tomorrow, Jaguar and Two Sign would step onto the sacred ball court and from that moment there could only be two outcomes. If they triumphed over Amihuatzin's players, they might keep their lives and maybe Crocodile's too. If they lost, it was certain death. The only unknown factor left was the nature of their execution. A chill gust blew in through the narrow opening and raised goose-bumps on Jaguar's arms.

Chapter 18 – Tecpatl

First light on the morning of the games found Jaguar awake. Outside he could see that although the wind had eased off, the sky was as grim as ever. Jaguar lay curled up on his side on the floor. Sleep had been patchy so he found contentment in the quiet of the morning, eyes closed and breathing deeply until some slaves brought breakfast. Jaguar couldn't eat and Two Sign didn't wake until much later when an elderly priest scurried into the room. He announced himself brightly as Sands of Eternal Gold, assistant to the high priest of Tlaloc. His youthful enthusiasm was in stark contrast to his stooped frame, hooked nose, white, wiry hair that stuck out in all directions and the proliferation of wrinkles that gathered themselves around his eyes, as though readying an assault upon his nose.

'I will be your sponsor for your game today,' the old man explained. 'I gather you volunteered?'

Two Sign, who looked as though he was surfacing from the bowels of the earth, pointed groggily at Jaguar.

'Excellent! Excellent!' the elderly priest enthused, smoothing down his robes of office. 'You're mad, quite mad. You know that, don't you? Still,' he added without waiting for an answer. 'I admire your pluck.'

Without further ado, he organised the Chalca guards to reform and beckoned to the two Mexica to follow him. Jaguar noticed that the watch had been relieved overnight with the exception of the one Amihuatzin had called Ocotzonamaca who had slipped back into the room moments before the old man had arrived. Sands of Eternal Gold was almost at a canter as they left the guest quarters, his long robes flying behind him. Two

Sign managed to collect a couple of maize cakes and ate them on the way.

'You're in the second game,' the priest called over his shoulder. 'The first one starts any minute now. We should have time to select two more members for your team and get you prepared, but of course the game could end in an instant if someone hits the ring so we'd best hurry.' He led everyone out of the palace and across to the Temple of Tezcatlipoca. A loud cheer went up somewhere off to the east as they left the confines of the palace.

'That'll be it getting underway now,' Sands of Eternal Gold announced with evident delight.

'Are you taking us to choose team members?' asked Jaguar.

'Oh, yes. Our victory yesterday provided us with three hundred and seventy Mexica warriors. Amihuatzin says we can spare two of them to join your team.'

The priest explained that a good many of the captives had been injured. 'We've sorted out those who said they could play the ball game and those who could not,' he added. 'The fifteen warriors who admitted to being able to play have been moved to another cell adjacent to the ball court, so that's where we're headed.'

'Do they know the stakes?' asked Two Sign.

Sands of Eternal Gold said that they had been told that their lives depended on the outcome of the game. 'As you can imagine,' he added. 'They were all keen to win the honour of a place on the team.'

The roar of the crowd grew as Jaguar and Two Sign approached the temple. It swelled and broke into a ragged cheer in response to what must have been a crucial point. The party entered a low building that backed up against the exterior walls of the ball court and followed a narrow corridor all the way to its end where two warrior priests stood beside a stone slab that had to be slid out of the way to gain access to the room behind. A sour odour of sweat and urine burst from the doorway making Ocotzonamaca wrinkle his nose as he ducked inside. The rest of the party followed him. When Jaguar made it into the room, he found it impossible to see anything while his eyes adjusted to the gloom.

From the meagre light that permeated the cell from an opening no larger than a man's fist set high into the rear wall, Jaguar eventually made out the fifteen Mexica to which the high priest's assistant had referred. He mentally wrote off six of the players who lay propped against the walls, indifferent to the new arrivals, and was just beginning to weigh up the remaining nine when Two Sign let out a cry.

'Magic River!' bellowed the knight. 'What in the name of Coyolxauhqui's icy teats are you doing here?'

Magic River looked tired and drawn but he was unable to resist a smile. 'It seems I'm auditioning for a place in your team, big man.'

Two Sign put aside all decorum and embraced Magic River warmly. 'Not my team.' He jerked a thumb at Jaguar. 'Go plead with him.'

Jaguar stepped forward and clasped hands with his fellow clansman. Magic River's grip was as firm as ever, which didn't quite make up for his acrid body odour. He had no tunic and was still dressed in the loincloth he had fought in two days previously. It was filthy and daubed with mottled russet stains.

'I might have known this was your crazy idea!'

Jaguar grinned.

'We're going to get Crocodile out!'

Magic River smiled ruefully. 'He doesn't think we can do it,' thought Jaguar and decided to change the subject.

'What happened to you? I lost sight of you at the end.'

Magic River shrugged. 'I got careless. One of those Serpent Knights got close to me and I waded in too deep trying to finish him off. It was right at the end when everyone started taking captives. Before I knew it, four of them jumped me and pinned me to the ground.'

'I'm sorry,' said Jaguar. 'Sorry I didn't see you.'

Magic River snorted. 'Don't be. I was stupid. Anyway, you're here now,' he added.

Meanwhile, Two Sign had been greeting the other captives. He wandered back over to Jaguar and drew him aside.

'We should take Magic River,' he whispered. 'The only player here better than him is Motonameyotia, do you know him?'

'I've played against him a few times,' said Jaguar. He glanced over at the warrior who was a few years his senior. Motonameyotia looked nervous. He was ringing his hands and every so often he'd scratch the back of his head. Jaguar remembered him for his thick eyebrows that met in the middle, but also for his turn of speed. 'He's fast and fit, but he doesn't play enough.'

Two Sign looked apologetic. 'Speak to the others then. See if there's anyone else more suitable. You're the best of us at this game. You need to choose.'

Jaguar did as Two Sign suggested. He spoke to the players who looked most promising and almost decided one of them would be better than Two Sign's choice until he persuaded the man to speak to him on the far side of the room. He noticed that the man was trying to hide a limp and was forced to rule him out. Jaguar even spoke to one of the lads, who was sitting on the floor, who he remembered from practice sessions. His Path is Straight stared listlessly at the far wall and answered Jaguar's questions in monosyllables.

Jaguar and Two Sign conferred with Magic River and together they decided that Motonameyotia was the best of the candidates.

'He's got the jitters right now, but he'll be fine once he gets going,' Magic River agreed.

While Two Sign conveyed their decision to Sands of Eternal Gold, Jaguar realised that in choosing two of the men from the room, he was condemning the rest to death. He felt sick and had to fight to stay objective. These men were all tribute to the gods from the moment they'd been captured. Jaguar also had to remind himself that being chosen to play the ball game was by no means a certain reprieve. They were going to have to play a game to a level they'd never played before and then, even if they won through, there was no guarantee that Amihuatzin would keep his word.

Ocotzonamaca ushered the four Mexica from the cell. Realising that he'd missed out on selection, His Path is Straight leapt to his feet and clutched at Jaguar, beseeching him to reconsider. His cellmates looked askance at his undignified appeal. When the four Mexica were assembled outside the cell and the stone door had been slotted back into place with a sonorous grating noise, Sands of Eternal Gold led them all to a large washroom furnished with a stone bench and an urn hewn from solid stone that held enough water to sink a small canoe. Six acolytes stood in attendance, their faces set with sombre expressions. There was a seventh man present, who had the darkest skin Jaguar had ever seen. He wore a ceremonial outfit of white cloth, the neck and hemline of which were decorated with thousands of tiny pearlescent beads. In one hand he held a sea-shell horn inset with gold and a red, porous stone that Jaguar knew also came from the sea.

'It's the referee,' said Sands of Eternal Gold. 'He's come to check that you're suitable. Please cleanse yourselves ready for the game,' he added. 'You'll find new loincloths and leather padding over there.' He pointed to a pile against the wall.

The Mexica removed their clothing. As Jaguar discarded his loincloth and tossed it onto the floor, the small cloth bag that had been tied around his waist went with it, hit the floor and a small, straw figure of an ocelot bounced out of it and came to rest against Two Sign's foot.

'What's this?' asked Two Sign, picking it up.

Jaguar hesitated.

'Is it a toy?' asked Magic River with an amused expression.

'No,' scoffed Two Sign. 'It's a lucky talisman, isn't it?' He looked to Jaguar for an answer.

'I suppose it is,' said Jaguar guardedly, unwilling to reveal its provenance. 'It fell into a fire and came out unscathed...'

'A thing made out of straw fell into a fire and didn't burn? It doesn't get much luckier than that!' exclaimed Magic River. 'We should adopt him as our team mascot.'

Jaguar shrugged his consent. Two Sign held the model out for Jaguar who took it back and then found he had nowhere to put it since he was utterly naked. He placed it on the stone bench with the clean clothing and returned to the urn. While the four men washed themselves thoroughly, the priest began a ritual dedication of the game of ullamalitzli to the gods.

'Deities of the Thirteen Celestial Planes, we pledge our game to you,' he began. 'We give our hearts to the game that mirrors the heavenly conflict between Quetzalcoatl and Tezcatlipoca. Through our game we recognise the eternal struggle of good and evil, the sun and the moon, day and night.'

Sands of Eternal Gold rushed the remainder of the dedication as a huge clamour sounded from outside, signifying the end of the first game. Jaguar imagined their opposition in a room close by undergoing a similar ritual.

The Mexica towelled themselves dry with cloths provided by the acolytes and then went to put on the ceremonial maxtlatl, a loincloth specially designed to be worn during the game. Jaguar tied his round his waist and adjusted the quilted, cotton-packed cod-piece to make sure it was properly in place.

When they were all ready, the captain, Ocotzonamaca stepped forward. Jaguar realised that this was why he had returned this morning. He had captured them so it was his duty to formally hand them over to the priest. He turned to address Sands of Eternal Gold.

'My Lord, accept these gifts as sacrifice.'

The Chalca warrior turned to the Mexica who bowed their heads in submission. 'Honourable sons,' he said solemnly. 'Your father bids you speak with Tezcatlipoca, Tlaloc and the other gods on behalf of the people of this valley. I commend you into the care of his priests.'

'Father, I am your son,' said the four Mexica in unison. Jaguar's mouth felt dry and his tongue swollen as he repeated the traditional farewell that they all learned at telpochcalli.

Sands of Eternal Gold shooed the Chalca guards from the room and bade the team kneel for the final dedication. As they knelt down, Jaguar noticed that Motonameyotia was shivering. He fervently hoped they had not made the wrong choice. His own stomach was churning in the usual attack of pre-game nerves although the importance of this game hadn't really sunk in yet, something he attributed to a general numbness in the wake of the battle of two days ago.

'We humbly offer these, our players, up to you, Our Lords, as a token of our love and respect. May they do justice to the game and to you. In the name of the people of Chalco, I ask for your mercy. For four long cycles we have suffered greatly. The land can no longer feed all the mouths that depend upon it. The lakes are empty of fish and seed withers on the dry ground. I therefore beg for your intercession and hand these players into your safekeeping on the court and pray for their success.'

Prostrating himself upon the floor along with the others in his team, Jaguar swept the three middle fingers of his right hand across the floor, licked the dust from them and then rested his forehead lightly onto the cold stone slabs.

Jaguar prayed. He prayed to Quetzalcoatl as he had never prayed before. He asked for strength in the game and he pleaded for victory and Crocodile's release, but more than anything he prayed that Two Sign was wrong about Amihuatzin's promise.

Muffled cheers from the ball court shattered the temporary peace.

'Come on, it's time,' said Sands of Eternal Gold.

Jaguar, Two Sign, Magic River and Motonameyotia rose and followed the priest out of the room. Jaguar had nowhere to put the figurine Precious Flower had given him so he hid it in the palm of his hand. They all traipsed through a short corridor and out onto the ball court where they were met with a roar from the crowd. The light from the overcast sky was painful to their eyes after the dingy cell and ceremonial room. Jaguar had to hold a hand up to shade his eyes from the glare in order to take in the surroundings. He was curious to see how the ball court differed from those in Tenochtitlan, but in fact it followed an almost identical design. Chalco's ullamalitzli court did look older and its walls, especially near the centre line, were smooth from many years of impact from the heavy rubber ball. As in Tenochtitlan, each end consisted of a small, dead-ball zone terminated by an end wall. The earthen floor between the two ends was compacted so hard that it might as well have been stone, so a thin layer of earth had been laid down to provide some measure of protection to the players. A slave was busy scraping up a puddle of black mud, or something that looked very much like it, while another was scattering new earth over the same spot.

Above the high sided walls of the court on the six tiers of stone benches, Jaguar reckoned there must have been over eight hundred spectators. He caught sight of the mountainous bulk of Amihuatzin in the front row on the left-hand side. He was dressed in an extravagant costume of red plumage with epaulettes each topped off with three long, black tail feathers. Sitting either side of the ruler of Chalco were two, somewhat less extravagantly attired, men. With the exception of these three, every single member of the audience was on their feet, hurling their contempt at the Mexica warriors. Some of them stamped, some shook their fists and made obscene gestures at Jaguar and the team, but all of them were shouting. Eight hundred Chalca roared and cursed the Mexica scum, damning their ancestors to an eternity in Mictlan's darkest realms. Even the weather railed against the visitors as menacing thunderclouds rolled in from the west.

Jaguar scanned the sea of faces in the hope that Crocodile had after all been brought out of confinement to watch the game, but he was nowhere to be seen. Amidst the sea of angry gestures, a movement on the topmost tier caught Jaguar's attention. A man was leaning over the wall. It looked as though he was hollering a report to someone on the ground outside. Jaguar reminded himself that half of Chalco would be camped outside the ball court, anxious to hear a running commentary of the proceedings.

The ruler of Chalco raised his arms, requesting silence. The people inside the ball court instantly fell silent, but still Amihuatzin had to hold his arms aloft, waiting for those outside to get the message. The man on the top tier semaphored to the crowd outside and the din gradually subsided. Utter silence followed and the monarch lowered his flabby arms to his side. As though connected to their ruler's hands by unseen strings, the spectators sat down.

'People of Chalco!' exclaimed Amihuatzin. With the experience of a master statesman, he waited and his audience imperceptibly leant forward, hanging on his words.

'*People of Chalco*!' This time he bellowed. 'We are the chosen ones!' Amihuatzin paused again, waiting for the words to sink in. He turned slowly to face the rows behind him and wherever he looked, people lowered their eyes to avoid his gaze, giving the impression of a ripple on still water.

Driven by the storm clouds overhead, a gust of wind plucked at the monarch's imperial cloak, ruffling its crimson feathers and making the ends flap where they hung below his ample frame.

'Our struggle with the Mexica is nearly over,' Amihuatzin resumed. 'The Triple Alliance is broken and, with help from good neighbours such as Xicotencatl,' he said, indicating the small man to his right, 'Tenochtitlan will soon fall.

'Later this afternoon, we will have the usual ceremonial games with gladiatorial combat between brave men of Chalco...' Amihuatzin paused as the spectators cheered. '...and a number of these perfidious, scab-ridden dogs.' More stamping of feet and hissing accompanied this last statement. 'But for your enjoyment, here and now, I present to you a fascinating contest, one that has no precedent in all the records of our fair city.'

The crowd cheered.

'Yesterday, we apprehended two more of Moctezuma's knights sneaking into our city!' There was a chorus of disbelieving, outraged voices to which Amihuatzin held up one chubby arm again.

'I know, I know,' he said in a paternal tone. 'They should be put to death as spies. But...' Amihuatzin paused theatrically and looked from one end of the court to the other. 'I have decided to set them a test. They will play Chalco's finest ullamalitzli players and... if they lose, we will sacrifice them here upon the hallowed earth of the ball court.'

The crowd cheered once more and Amihuatzin was forced to wave them all to silence.

'But if they win, we will set them free!'

This announcement was met with a puzzled silence by the people of Chalco, while Jaguar glanced at Two Sign and clenched his fist triumphantly. Two Sign raised an eyebrow by way of acknowledgement. Amihuatzin smiled benignly at his people and signalled for the final preparations to commence.

One-by-one, Sands of Eternal Gold announced his players to the hostile crowd and Jaguar was surprised that when he was done, a rag-tag cheer went up. At that moment, the Chalca team sponsor, a stocky man with bushy eyebrows and a long wooden staff, emerged at the other end of the court and marched to the centre of the court to introduce his team to the spectators.

'I present to you... Cuetzpalli!' he announced in a deep voice that carried clear across the court. 'The only man who's never lost a game!'

The crowd bellowed their approval as a muscular man swaggered onto the court with an insolent wave at his fans. His gilt-edged loincloth glinted in the sunshine and he wore similar padding to Jaguar's team members. He had perfectly black hair, which was scraped back into an immaculate queue that seemed to twitch with a life of its own.

'Winner of the tlatoani's birthday tournament, Necuametl!' cried the sponsor.

The spectators whooped joyfully. Necuametl trotted out onto the court, alert, with eyes that darted from side-to-side. He was tall and lean, but stooped as though he was leaning into a constant, personal headwind. Jaguar recognised the name from tales of epic games and was pleased to see his hooked nose fitted with his name.

'All the way from Ixtapaluca... Nellipatli!'

A ripple of amusement greeted what must have been a well-worn joke, the town of Ixtapaluca being only a stone's throw away. There was a generous round of applause. Nellipatli wore what looked like a permanent scowl. He joined his predecessors on the centre of the court without ceremony.

'Finally, I give you, Amoxtli!' The team's sponsor smiled smugly and retreated under his eyebrows as the last player sauntered on and smiled at the din that greeted him.

'Looks like Hopalong's leg has mended,' Two Sign whispered to Jaguar with a mischievous expression.

'Worst luck!' Jaguar replied.

The famous player showed no sign that he was favouring one leg. As Jaguar watched, Amoxtli grinned cheerfully and waved back at some contingent of the crowd on the rearmost benches, family perhaps.

All four wore the same matching outfits and Jaguar had to admit that they looked heroic, if perhaps a little too well fed. He decided to see how helpful Sands of Eternal Gold was feeling.

'What are they like?' Jaguar asked their own team sponsor.

'They are the best,' the old man said apologetically. 'Amihuatzin's finest. You haven't got a hope. I would have chosen Necuametl over Nellipatli,' he added. 'More stamina, but then perhaps the tlatoani feels this game will not last long.'

'Do they have any weaknesses?' asked Jaguar, wondering if the old man knew enough about the game to provide a useful answer. Everyone plays with their own particular style, he reminded himself, and personal styles often lead to predictability, which can be exploited.

Sands of Eternal Gold stroked his silvery hair for a while.

'Well,' he said slowly, after he'd given the matter some consideration. 'I don't recall ever seeing Cuetzpalli attempt a subtle shot, but his power means he doesn't really need to. Amoxtli spends too much time at the centre line, which was probably how he got his leg broken last year.' The old man looked up at Jaguar. 'I hope you can find a way to use the information, because it's all I've got.'

The twinkle in the old man's eye told Jaguar he wanted them to do their best, but he certainly wasn't making encouraging comments.

'What about the court?' asked Jaguar. He decided that the priest was something of an expert on the game after all. 'Are there any peculiarities about the way it plays?'

Sands of Eternal Gold looked at his protégés as though trying to work out how much they'd understand and in that instant, Jaguar knew that the old man had been one of the top exponents in his day. 'Watch out when the ball lands close to the centre line,' he said at last. 'The ball doesn't bounce well because the new soil is not well-trodden. And don't even bother going for the hoops!' he warned. 'The last time anyone managed to get a ball through was before the famine began. Best to play safe, eh? Oh, and one last thing,' he added. 'Remember that this is "Tlatoani's Rules".'

This was new to Jaguar. 'What does that mean?'

'Here in Chalco, it means that you need sixteen points to win.'

Jaguar just nodded. It would be a long game. He hoped the Chalca players weren't as fit as they looked.

The court fell silent as the elegant figure on Amihuatzin's left stood to make a dedication to Tlaloc. Must be the high priest, thought Jaguar, the man to whom Sands of Eternal Gold reported.

When the formalities were over, the referee in the sparkling costume tossed the ball at the home team and followed the sponsors who had left the court to find their seats in the tiers above the wall. Jaguar crossed to the edge of the court and placed Precious Flower's gift on the dusty earth in the shadow of the wall. The little, straw cat looked fiercely at the opposition. Jaguar wished it was the real animal with his name, all rippling muscles, razor sharp claws and a mouth full of teeth designed for carnage. That might have unnerved the opposition.

From the moment the Chalca team took possession of the ball it was obvious that Cuetzpalli was the captain, the way he moved and the way the others looked to him to take their lead. In fact they needed no direction. They took their places on the court with the precision of an exotic dance troupe from Xaltocan. What little hope Jaguar had nursed that they could win this game was all but gone. He had played on teams with Two Sign and Magic River and against Motonameyotia, but they had never played together as a team before and Jaguar knew that tight-knit teams were strong and hard to beat.

Cuetzpalli began the practice session by throwing the ball down the middle of the court as was the custom. Jaguar moved forward to intercept it before it bounced for the second time and struck it with his knee. His knee pad cushioned the impact of the heavy ball, which sailed lazily down the left-hand side of the court where Amoxtli was waiting. The Chalca returned the ball with ease, sending it in Two Sign's direction. He caught it on his thigh and sent it back with a lazy sweep. The rally continued in this casual manner for a handful of exchanges until Cuetzpalli suddenly sent the ball cross-court where it bounced against the wall and dropped too soon to make an easy shot. Jaguar tried in vain to reach it, hurling himself forward to reach the ball before it dropped again but slipped on a patch of loose soil. He sprawled in the dirt as the ball bounced past him. The spectators laughed and jeered and Jaguar just felt cross, annoyed that he'd made the effort since this was only practice.

Two Sign retrieved the ball while Jaguar sprang to his feet, embarrassed by the mistake. The Eagle Knight restarted the warm up, which continued for a while until the referee was satisfied that everyone had got their eye in.

In the brief pause, before the game commenced in earnest, Jaguar heard the spectators jabbering excitedly, pointing at them and gesticulating at each other. It looked like a last-minute flurry of betting activity. 'Probably doubling their bets against us,' Jaguar thought darkly.

Magic River sidled up to him. 'What positions do you want us to play in?'

'You usually play at the back, don't you?' asked Jaguar, who was keen to play in a forward position where he might have a chance at hitting the hoops.

The scarred warrior looked at him ruefully. 'I'm happy at the back, Jaguar. My reactions aren't as fast as they used to be.'

'Alright, you and Two Sign are at the back. Your power will come in handy from that distance. Motonameyotia!' called Jaguar. 'You and I are at the front. The old men can rest themselves at the back,' he added with a wink.

Motonameyotia nodded meekly, but Magic River grinned and patted him on the arm. 'You're in charge now.' The two older men had deferred to his authority unquestioningly and their trust redoubled Jaguar's determination.

'Thanks,' said Jaguar. 'Let's see if we can humiliate the captain! He's too smug for my liking.'

Magic River agreed with a sour look. Cuetzpalli was prancing about the court soaking up the admiration of his supporters. Amoxtli was an entirely different proposition. He had set about the warm-up with an intensity that immediately earned Jaguar's respect. He would be dangerous.

The referee eased himself into his perch above the left-hand hoop and signalled for the game to commence.

Cuetzpalli started the game off with an underhand lob aimed at the wall with just enough strength to clear Jaguar's reach. It was a typical opening throw, designed to be difficult to return because of its proximity to the wall, but Two Sign was ready for the ball to rebound off the stonework, which it did, giving him just enough space to swing his thigh at it. The awkward trajectory meant that the ball sailed high into the air, giving Necuametl, playing in the forward position, plenty of time to get behind it. The Chalca shuffled backwards, tracking the ball as it arced back to the ground. He let it bounce once and rushed at it, swivelled his waist aggressively to catch the ball on the side of his buttock. Necuametl's timing was impeccable. He managed to redirect the plummeting ball into a horizontal shot that bisected Motonameyotia and Jaguar and was travelling too low for either of them to reach. The ball struck the end wall and rolled back towards the players.

'Chalco, one point!' called the referee when the cheers from the gallery had abated.

Two Sign apologised for setting the opposition up.

'It's just one point,' said Jaguar as he rolled the ball back to the Chalca for the restart.

Cuetzpalli served the ball again with an almost identical throw to the last. Again the ball was too long for Jaguar.

'It's mine!' cried Magic River who was well placed. He turned sideways at the last instant and managed a good return, deep into the Chalca end, forcing Amoxtli's first contact in the game. He rushed to his right and hit the ball with the outside of his knee, a barely legal shot. He was travelling at such an oblique angle to the court that the ball struck the wall just below the first row of seats. It wasn't a good shot and Motonameyotia was under it, suddenly coming alive. The youth swivelled and deftly sent the ball back down the centre of the court. Cuetzpalli scuttled sideways and got the padding on his upper thigh behind the heavy ball. It looped high into the air and bounced over Jaguar. Two Sign tried to reach it before it bounced a second time, but the ball leapt off an uneven patch of ground right in front of the knight and skipped out of his reach, heading for the end zone.

The spectators showed their appreciation loudly.

'Chalco, two points. Mexica, none!' the priest kept score. A voice from the top row of benches could faintly be heard, describing the progress to the crowd outside.

On the next two turns, the Chalca gained more points as Jaguar's team struggled to read the undulations of the unfamiliar court. Motonameyotia had fast reflexes but often struck the ball too early. Magic River had all the power and accuracy, but lacked outright speed. Two Sign had a long reach and steady concentration, but his lack of practice showed itself in the simple mistakes that he made early on.

When the ball was next in play, the team managed a rally that lasted several minutes. The ball went back and forth as each team probed for weakness in their opposition. First the Chalca tested Motonameyotia. He was the edgy one. Then Nellipatli had the ball several times in quick succession as the Mexica sounded him out. Again and again each recipient passed the test and kept the ball in play. The crowd sensed that the outsiders had finally got their eye in, but Magic River, frustrated at their inability to score a point, stabbed impatiently at the ball when it came his way. He only managed a glancing blow that skipped off his thigh and bounded into the end zone, netting the opposition team another point.

'Chalco, five points,' announced the priest. 'Mexica, zero!' The referee's evident relish was accompanied by gleeful cries from all around the court. Two Sign collected the ball from the end zone and approached Jaguar.

'You need to get a grip of this,' he said patting Jaguar on the shoulder. 'We haven't got long for this world if we don't get some points soon.'

The voice was calm, but Jaguar caught an undercurrent he'd never heard in Two Sign's voice before; was it fear? Jaguar had never led a team so he tried to remember what he'd heard before; the words of encouragement that Magic River and others like him said when they were in charge. He drew a blank but gathered the others round, hoping for inspiration as they drew close.

Motonameyotia had a fierce gleam in his eye, slightly crazed but focused on the game. Magic River's expression was unreadable.

'We can beat this team,' Jaguar tried. 'That last rally was good and long,' he added earnestly. 'Maybe we've got the measure of this court now and the bounce of the ball. Cuetzpalli is too smug for his own good. Amoxtli is steady but unimaginative and Nellipatli isn't great. Necuametl is the one to watch, so let's see if we can keep the ball away from him.'

It wasn't the stirring speech Jaguar had hoped for. He looked at his players in turn. Two Sign smiled his approval, but Motonameyotia's nod seemed automatic, while Magic River just set his scarred jaw more firmly, suggesting disappointment. Desperate, Jaguar ploughed on.

'Motonameyotia, you've got a gift. You're a natural, but you're too tense. You need to relax and take the ball when it's right. You're snatching at it.' Jaguar recalled something he'd heard one of his teachers say. 'Picture the eagle swooping on his prey... that's right, you know this image. He only arches his talons up in the final instant... don't rush it.'

Jaguar turned his attention to Magic River, many years his senior, who had mentored him in many games. 'You're the most experienced one of us,' he said firmly. 'I need you to put pressure on Cuetzpalli and Nellipatli. You're the steady hand. Don't get emotional. By all the bones! How many times have you told me that?'

Turning his attention to Two Sign, Jaguar was suddenly struck dumb. What could he say to Crocodile's father? What words were there to inspire the man who had decided to let go his son. This was Moctezuma's greatest warrior, a man who, on his capture, had resigned himself to die. There was no sentiment or exhortation that Jaguar could think of to make the game count.

Impatient for the game to start again, the crowd began to make their displeasure felt. Anxious to avoid any penalties for delaying the game, Jaguar was about to dispatch his players back to their positions when he remembered the dedication to the gods that Magic River used before each fight. Every commander had their own technique but Jaguar had none as yet and so he borrowed from the man who stood before him. Ignoring the rising protest from the Chalca, he motioned for Magic River, Two Sign and Motonameyotia to get down on one knee.

'What?' began Magic River.

'Do it!' snapped Jaguar, surprised by the authority in his own voice. All three got down on one knee facing him. He joined them on the earthen floor with the ball between them, hung his head and extended his clenched fist to the sky. 'Sturdy souls, we raise our arms in battle once again,' he said in a sure and steady voice. 'Huitzilopochtli, we call on you for courage, O Lord! Send us the power of your rage and fire our souls with vengeance so that we may purge the world of our enemies!'

Magic River had a look that said he finally understood. The ragged corner of his mouth twitched in a partial smile. The spectators sensed that something unusual was up and had fallen quiet, craning their heads to see what the outsiders were up to.

'This is not a game,' Jaguar explained. 'This is a battle, just like the one we fought two days ago and as we fought for our lives on that dusty field, so we must fight again today. Every ball that comes towards you is a sword-stroke or club that must be parried. Every time the Chalca score a point, another wound opens in us that will never heal. We didn't die that day because the gods saved us for this.'

From the corner of his eye, Jaguar could see that the referee was getting to his feet. They didn't have much time.

'Do you understand?' he asked.

'Yes,' his team chorused.

'This may be the last stand we ever make. Let's make it the finest game we've ever played!'

There was a glow and fervour in the faces that Jaguar had not seen in his team before. He dismissed them hoping he had done enough.

The referee issued a stern rebuke and with that, the game got underway again. This time Amoxtli restarted with a low ball. Jaguar managed to get underneath it returning it diagonally across the court towards Nellipatli. The Chalca scrambled to get in position and just managed to swat it back. Sliding and twisting, each team kept the ball in play. Two Sign hurled himself at a cross-court shot and succeeded in wrong-footing Cuetzpalli, who hadn't moved, expecting it to be a winning shot. To everyone's surprise the ball trundled into the Chalca end-zone.

'Chalco, five points. Mexica, one!' the referee called out.

Motonameyotia took the restart and tried to pile pressure on Cuetzpalli with a shot close to the wall but the referee deemed it a foul and made him start again. This time Motonameyotia sent the ball out on the other side. Necuametl dispatched the ball disdainfully back into the Mexica half, but Magic River got to it easily. Jaguar's confidence grew with every passing shot. The ball changed ends several times and then Magic River targeted Nellipatli. The Chalca's scowl remained fixed in place as he intercepted it and put a weak shot back at him. The stocky knight directed the ball straight back at him so that Nellipatli nearly fell over trying to get into position and only just managed to get his thigh behind the ball. As it crossed the line, Jaguar pounced on it to keep the Chalca youth under pressure. It was a classic shot that dropped too close to the wall for Nellipatli, already out of position as he was. Necuametl was also unable to recover it after it bounced awkwardly and rolled across the opposite dead-ball line. The Mexica had won their second point. Another short exchange later and it was three. The cheering from the seats was less exuberant now.

Cuetzpalli put Jaguar to the test in the next long rally, making him stretch out to the left where he nearly collided with Motonameyotia and then sending him back close to the wall. The next time the ball caromed into the Mexica end, Two Sign lobbed it back over Jaguar's head. As he followed the trajectory, Jaguar's eye was caught by the sight of Amihuatzin arguing with Xicotencatl. It looked like the ruler of Tlaxcala wasn't pleased. It was probably a disagreement over a wager. There was a shout from nearby and before he had time to work out what was going on, the heavy ball struck him in the shin and brought him crashing to the ground.

Some of the spectators laughed as Jaguar collapsed and lay on the ground, clutching at his lower leg. He gritted his teeth until the waves of pain subsided, only dimly aware of the feet and ankles gathered round him. The referee took pity on Jaguar and called for a break for water, which was overdue anyway.

Sands of Eternal Gold came back onto the court bearing a couple of water-skins. He was even more excited than he had been that morning. He explained that the betting had reopened and many of the spectators and the crowd assembled outside the court were making contrary bets to their initial ones, now genuinely concerned that they might have staked too much on their own team. This was also, the old man assured them, the cause of the argument between the two tlatoanis.

During the brief stoppage, Jaguar recovered sufficiently to apologise to his team for his mistake.

'Don't worry,' reassured Two Sign. 'We know we can beat them now.'

The big knight's confidence was misplaced. The Chalca set to with renewed determination after the restart and it proved impossible to force them into any errors. Amoxtli won them their first point with a searing shot down the middle.

'Chalco, seven. Mexica, three!' called the referee accompanied by a collective sigh of relief from around the court.

Cuetzpalli and Amoxtli reigned supreme and took the next few points. It seemed that the captain had a right to be smug after all as he treated his fellow citizens to a dazzling performance, sending the despised Mexica frantically from one side of the court to the other. The spectators were enthralled by the display, eager to see their enemy humiliated at their very feet. They clapped and cheered and laughed at every point that their team won. Soon the tally stood at eleven points to Chalco and only four to the Mexica and the fourth point had been costly. Magic River had taken the ball awkwardly and was limping. Jaguar wasn't in great shape either. His chest heaved in and out from the exertion and his lungs felt like they were on fire. Shards of pain shot up and down his shin. The bandage had come off his arm and the gash had opened up again. White-heat speared the sliced muscles with every movement that he made.

Once more the Chalca team restarted. It was another low and fast shot from Amoxtli, designed to land near the centre line where the new soil had been scattered and the ground was softer. Seeing where the ball was going to bounce, Jaguar sprinted over and slid along the ground, shredding the skin from his thigh in his effort to get behind the ball. He managed to return it but the referee blew on his horn to halt the game. From his seat above the court he docked a point from Jaguar's team.

'Use of the knee!' he cried. 'Eleven points to three.'

Jaguar was incensed. 'Hey!' he cried, staring towards the referee.

Two Sign caught hold of him and shook his head.

'But it was a fair shot!' protested Jaguar.

'There's nothing you can do,' the big man warned him.

Cuetzpalli restarted the game and tried to exploit Jaguar's distress by aiming the ball at him before he'd returned to his position. Jaguar was still smarting from the injustice of the lost point and hobbling from his various wounds and failed to react in time. Two Sign rushed across the court to cover for him but didn't make it so another shot rolled into the end zone. Cuetzpalli was delighted but the crowd unexpectedly took against his underhand tactics, showing their disgust, some even spitting at the court. Jaguar realised that the underdogs had finally earned some support.

Cuetzpalli was unrepentant and, in a show of defiance, he attempted a shot at one of the stone rings the next time the ball came his way. A wayward deflection from Motonameyotia allowed the captain of the Chalca team to position himself perfectly. He brought his knee up in a precise jabbing motion, carefully striking the ball with the meat of his thigh and propelling the ball straight towards the target. The spectators gasped and time juddered to a halt. Jaguar watched the flight of the ball, horrified because it looked so good. If it cleared the stone ring, the game would be over. Amihuatzin would have his bloody prize and Crocodile would die, never even knowing that Jaguar had tried to rescue him. He saw three flecks of dust ejected from the spinning projectile begin their own graceful arcs towards the ground. Meanwhile, the rubber ball tracked upwards, until eventually it hit the inner edge of the ring, rattled off the opposite edge and rebounded back towards the Chalca.

The crowd groaned. Cuetzpalli shrugged nonchalantly as the referee awarded a point to the Mexica. Jaguar knew that with a healthy lead, there was nothing to prevent the players from Chalco trying again and cutting the game short at a stroke. Time was running out. Amihuatzin's team could either play conservatively, chipping away the five points more they needed, or go for glory. Jaguar wondered if he dare attempt a shot. Sands of Eternal Gold had warned them against it and every failed attempt would put the opposition further out of reach.

Jaguar restarted this time with a high, looping ball that forced Amoxtli to scurry back to intercept. The sturdy player twisted aggressively. His upper thigh and buttock struck the ball in a classic move and pushed the ball over to Motonameyotia. The Mexica youth staggered under the impact but got a weak shot back over the line. Necuametl looked dangerous as he smacked it down between Jaguar and Motonameyotia so fast that neither of them could reach it, but Two Sign had anticipated it. The big man lunged, striking with every ounce of strength he could muster. Cuetzpalli tried to deflect the ball back at the Mexica, but he misjudged the power with which it had been struck and its momentum nearly knocked him off his feet.

There was a ripple of good-natured laughter but the star player wasn't amused. He picked up the ball and hurled it back at the Mexica for the restart. In the next exchange, Necuametl stepped in and steadied Amihuatzin's team. With a series of well positioned plays, he managed to push all the players from Tenochtitlan deep into their own half before dropping a shot gently over the halfway line. The ball made a couple of half-hearted hops before continuing along the ground. Jaguar could not help but be impressed. The Chalca had blocked the ball, skilfully soaking up its momentum and targeting the newly scattered patch of earth no larger than a child's cloak that had cushioned its landing.

'Chalco, twelve, Mexica, four!' proclaimed the referee, straining to make himself heard over the delight of the spectators.

Another break was called and Jaguar put on a brave face, hoping to inspire his team for one last effort. He had to fight down his own frustration. He felt like he was suffocating. Every time they played a good shot, the opposition seemed to raise their game and keep the ball in play and every time Jaguar's team made a mistake, the Chalca were able to capitalise on it. Jaguar began to sense despair creeping up on him. When he looked at the others, their thoughts were etched clearly on their faces. Magic River hobbled towards the others, his expression black as Mictlan's armpit. Two Sign showed no emotion but it was plain his early optimism had faded. Both of the older men were gasping for breath. Motonameyotia just looked increasingly angry.

In between ragged intakes of breath, the players drank copiously from the water-skins their sponsor brought out. Sands of Eternal Gold pulled Jaguar aside with furrowed brows as soon as he had a chance.

'You're playing it all wrong,' he complained and then pushed on, not noticing the look of mild annoyance on Jaguar's face. 'You're not making the best use of your players,' he whispered urgently.

'Old man...' Jaguar began angrily and received a vicious slap in the face. 'Ow!' he cried. Two Sign tried to restrain the old man by the neck but he danced out of reach with astonishing ease.

'Ow? I'll give you "Ow"!' the priest cut in. 'A few more careless plays and you lot will meet the business end of a sacrificial knife and then you'll know what real pain is!'

Startled, Jaguar shut up and let the old man speak, remembering his insightful observations before the game commenced. His poise and sprightly reactions made it plain. This man had been a champion in his day.

'So you'd have us believe you're on our side, would you?'

'I don't want you to crash out with only four points!' the priest shot back. 'I know you're a better team than that and this score doesn't reflect well on me.'

'What do you propose?' asked Magic River.

Sands of Eternal Gold jabbed a finger at him and then at Two Sign. 'Look at you two! You're dead on your feet,' he said. 'You younger players need to be at the back.' He slapped Jaguar vigorously on the thigh. 'There's more running in these legs and you, the tall one.' He pointed at Two Sign. 'You're a big bastard. Put it to good use up at the front and block everything that comes your way.'

'What about me?' said Magic River with a sour look that puckered his scar up and exposed his missing teeth.

Sands of Eternal Gold stared back at him frankly. 'I've never seen such an ugly brute in all my days,' he said. 'Just stand at the front and you'll frighten the other team half to death.' He cackled briefly, swept up the water bags and disappeared.

Magic River stared, wide-eyed at the figure as he bustled off the court. He blinked a couple of times, looked at Two Sign and then burst out laughing. Two Sign laughed too and pretty soon Motonameyotia and Jaguar joined in, making faces at each other and then at the opposition.

When he managed to wipe his eyes, Two Sign asked Jaguar if he wanted to rearrange the team as the priest had suggested.

'Let's do what he says.' Jaguar grinned. 'I think the crazy old fool knows what he's talking about.'

The players changed positions so that Motonameyotia and Jaguar covered the back of the court. When the ball was put back in play, the shared moment of merriment seemed to have lifted the team's spirit. Jaguar barely noticed his injuries as he and Motonameyotia hared back and forth across the dusty ground swatting back everything that came their way. Magic River and Two Sign held the forward positions, dutifully blocking and feinting left and right when the Chalca were trying to place their shots.

The game seemed to flow of its own accord and Jaguar briefly recalled the peyotl induced vision on top of the temple of Tezcatlipoca; crystalline honeycomb structures he had seen connecting everything in the world. He watched Necuametl steer the ball artfully between the two big Mexica warriors, but knew exactly where it would land and, without conscious effort, predicted its onward flight. Jaguar made perfect contact with his upper thigh, just at the base of his right buttock and the ball soared on a perfect trajectory that struck the opposite wall of the corridor too low and too deep inside Chalca territory to be returned.

Jaguar hunkered down, waiting as Magic River served. The play was short and Nellipatli had to scramble to get under it. Again, Jaguar was in the correct position and swung his knee forward and through the path of the heavy ball. It dropped between Cuetzpalli and Amoxtli who nearly collided in their desperation to make the shot. Cuetzpalli held his nerve and swivelled his hips in behind the ball, but he wasn't prepared for the spin Jaguar had given it. His attempt misfired and arced high into the first rows of spectators who were forced to hurl themselves aside to avoid the heavy projectile.

The referee's voice rang out. 'Chalco, twelve points. Mexica, six!'

A cheer sounded from the excited crowd as it occurred to everybody watching that the strangers had begun a second fight-back. This game might prove to be the talk of the city for weeks to come.

In the chill of a storm-swept breeze, Jaguar and Motonameyotia were dripping sweat, wiping it from their eyes after every play and all of the players were blowing hard between the rallies now.

An awkward rebound from the wall took Motonameyotia by surprise and smashed him in the face so that when he was persuaded to his feet again, blood was streaming from his nose. The fixed look on his face was even fiercer now. He spat blood and saliva and slapped at helping hands aggressively, looking to get back to the game.

With three points between the Chalca and a victory, Cuetzpalli looked keen to press on too, but the men from Tenochtitlan had other ideas, hurling themselves from one wall to the other, stubbornly refusing to let any shots through to the end zone. Eventually, it was Amoxtli who made a rare mistake and mistimed his pirouette. He took a glancing blow to his ribs before the ball rumbled out of play.

'Thirteen points to Chalco. The Mexica have seven.'

Jaguar was barely aware of the score. Every inch of his body was an agonising blaze and his breath came in ragged gasps, but he played as though possessed. He ran and hit, and charged and blocked. Time and again Jaguar struck the ball, hardly noticing the passage of time. Jaguar's attention was fixed on subtle nuances of the ball court's surface and tiny imperfections in the outer coating of the rubber ball. The slightest changes in Cuetzpalli's stance signalled his intentions as he went to strike the ball. Jaguar understood it all. Blood thundered in his ears, but bit by bit the roaring changed. A shriller note intruded on his senses and gradually he became aware of the spectators in their finery, jumping up and down and shrieking in their frenzy.

'Chalco, fourteen points,' croaked the referee hoarsely, trying to make himself heard. 'The Mexica have nine points!'

Fingers of cold despair bloomed in Jaguar's stomach. Amihuatzin's team needed only two more points to hand him victory and Jaguar's wager would be lost. The noise of the crowd was deafening. They were all on their feet, some shaking their fists in defiance and others hurling encouragement at their team to sink the outsiders for good. Amihuatzin was the only one still seated. A small smile played across the ruler's broad face as he looked down at Jaguar over a huddle of chins. Jaguar glared back coldly until a hand grasped his shoulder.

'Time to go for the hoops,' said Magic River.

'I'm too far away from them at the back,' said Jaguar. 'Anyway, the old priest said it was impossible.'

'Of course he did,' replied Magic River. 'He didn't want us frittering points away in the early stages of the game.'

'You want me to give it a go?' asked Jaguar.

Two Sign overheard. 'You've got the best chance,' he said. 'Crocodile told me that you never miss.'

'That's nonsense,' protested Jaguar.

'It's our only hope.'

'If I miss, they'll be one point away from victory,' said Jaguar.

Two Sign looked at Magic River and Motonameyotia to see if they had any objections. Neither of them spoke. The spectators were growing impatient. The referee hadn't signalled a formal stoppage and with the game approaching its climax, no one was in any mood to wait.

Jaguar spoke to Motonameyotia. 'You're going to need to cover for me at the back. I need to get closer to the halfway line to have a chance.'

The youth nodded and wiped stoically at the blood that was congealing in his nostrils.

'Try and keep the play simple and steady. Don't take any risks and sooner or later an opportunity will present itself, alright?'

If the four players from Tenochtitlan had entertained any hope that the Chalca would offer up an easy chance to aim for the stone hoops, they realised how wrong they had been over the course of the next rally. With a win so close they could almost reach out and touch it, the Chalca piled on the pressure. Jaguar had to be careful committing himself to the centre of the court for fear of warning their opponents of the imminent attempt.

Amoxtli met the ball and sent it across to Magic River. Magic River dropped it over the halfway line for Cuetzpalli to scoop up which he managed with contemptuous ease, dispatching it at Two Sign. The big knight had to double back on himself but twisted at the ball before it reached the wall. Again Cuetzpalli had it and this time sent it long to Motonameyotia, who was its equal. A flurry of shots, exchanged between him and Necuametl, ended when Nellipatli intercepted one and sent it diagonally across the court. Seeing his chance, Jaguar sprinted midfield and lined himself up for a shot at the hoop that sat directly below Amihuatzin. As one, the assembly rose to their feet as soon as the ball left Jaguar's right thigh. They knew where the shot was headed and those on the left-hand side all craned to see over the heads of the people in front who were blocking their view.

From the instant the shot left Jaguar's thigh, he knew that the attempt had failed. In spite of that, he clenched his fists and twisted his head over to the left as though trying to steer the ball. It was no use. The ball struck the underside of the ring and ricocheted back at Magic River. A cry of relief rang out around the court as they realised that Jaguar had failed and it was some time before everyone had quietened down enough for the referee to announce the score.

Jaguar felt ill. It was Magic River who came over to him on his way to roll the ball at the opposition for their restart.

'That was close,' he said. His tone was conversational, as though he was commenting on practice tournament instead of being one shot away from a sacrificial knife. Jaguar goggled at him.

'Do it again,' he called over his shoulder. 'Only this time, don't snatch at it. You made the same mistake that Motonameyotia was making in the early stages.'

Necuametl launched the ball back into the game and it was immediately obvious that the Chalca team were wise to this last-ditch attempt by the Mexica and they had no intention of making things easy for a similar attempt. A quick team talk had taken place at the far end and Jaguar sensed that Cuetzpalli was keen to have another go himself.

The ball changed ends a dozen times before Jaguar's suspicion was confirmed. Cuetzpalli stepped lightly into the path of a tired response from Two Sign and launched his hips at the ball. Once more, the excited spectators rose to their feet to see if their hero would be successful. The ball hit the upper edge of the stone ring and bounced up over the wall and into the crowd. There was a heartfelt groan as the Chalca realised they had been deprived again and moments later it was echoed by the throng outside the court as the news was passed on to them.

'Fifteen points to ten!' croaked the referee.

It was Jaguar's turn to put the ball back into play. The game was edgy for a dozen shots or so, both sides playing conservatively, anxious not to give away any easy opportunities. The Chalca could afford to bide their time, while Jaguar knew his own team were fading fast. All four of them had taken part in the recent battle, but Magic River and Motonameyotia had been forced to endure two days of captivity as well, while Amihuatzin's star team would have been rested and well fed in the run up to the game.

Drawing reserves from somewhere deep inside, Jaguar rushed and jinked to keep the ball in play. Moments later and it was back, bounding over Two Sign and heading for the right-hand wall. Jaguar was out of position and made a monumental effort to reach it but slipped as he drew near. He lurched, got one foot down to steady himself and then hurtled into the wall. Lightening pain skewered his shoulder as his collarbone snapped. He slumped to the ground, unable to see, but sensing the ball's progress off-court by the delirious reaction of the crowd, but the noise did not last long. As Two Sign and Motonameyotia levered Jaguar to his feet, it became clear that the referee had called a foul shot. This time it was Cuetzpalli who had been adjudged to have used his knee. There was a tremendous uproar and, through tears of pain, Jaguar could see the look of malice that Amihuatzin fixed on the referee.

Motonameyotia was astonished. 'It's not over!'

'You don't look very well,' said Two Sign. 'Can play the next point?'

Jaguar gritted his teeth and exhaled sharply. He tested his right arm to see if it would hang comfortably but it would not.

'Sit it out,' said Motonameyotia. 'We'll play what's left without you.'

Jaguar shook his head. 'Three people can't cover this area.'

'Come on, Jaguar,' said Magic River. 'You can't play on.'

'Back to where you were,' Jaguar shouted, suddenly angry. 'We'll stick to the plan, now go!' He closed his eyes as his team mates returned to their positions and tried to balance the pain of his bruised shin and the bone-deep ache of the gash in his arm against this new injury. There could be little left to the game now. He would see it through.

Two Sign lobbed the ball down the court and the players summoned their fading reserves. In the ensuing rally, the Chalca exploited Jaguar's injury to the best of their abilities but Two Sign protected him heroically. The Chalca also tried to keep Motonameyotia out of the play as he was playing better than anyone. Jaguar was cheered to see him chasing almost every ball and grateful to Two Sign for selecting him. Amoxtli took a turn and predictably aimed the ball at Jaguar's feet. Jaguar managed to backpedal fast enough to send the ball straight back but the shooting agony that speared his shoulder nearly made him pass out.

It was then that the overconfident Cuetzpalli made a mistake. In his eagerness to keep the pressure on the wounded player, he chose a difficult shot instead of the straightforward reply along the wall to Motonameyotia. The captain of the Chalca team failed to get behind the ball properly and it looped high, dropping back to earth in front of Jaguar where it bounced neatly and predictably.

It was the perfect setup shot, so perfect that it occurred to Jaguar that he was being lured into the shot. It hardly mattered now. His senses shut down on the world around him as he focused on the only thing that mattered. There were no crowds. There were no players. Even the court ceased to exist and, for a fraction of a second, there was no pain. The universe consisted of Jaguar and the ball that reached its zenith and dropped back towards the ground a second time. Jaguar let his right arm go and flung his left arm round, pivoting on his heel. In a single sweep, he whipped his whole body round and smacked the ball with the meat of his upper thigh.

If the crowd made a noise, Jaguar did not hear it. He watched, transfixed as the ball headed for the opening in the stone ring at Amihuatzin's feet.

Chapter 19 – Quiyahuitl

Pandemonium broke out on the terraced seating as the ball touched the inside of the stone ring and leapt through. There was shouting and whooping and, almost before the ball came to rest, the people of Chalco were climbing down into the court where they converged on the players.

Two Sign was still trying to comprehend what had happened when he was surrounded. Lords and merchants, courtiers, landowners and their sons were all clamouring to see the Mexica prodigies up close. Everyone wanted to touch the players from Tenochtitlan. Two Sign saw them patting Magic River on the shoulders and grinned in manic delight. Those closest to Motonameyotia took his hands in theirs and thanked him with tears in their eyes. Others reached out tentatively to touch Two Sign on the arm and he could see over the sea of heads that Jaguar was trying to shield his damaged shoulder from the crush around him. The young man looked up and saw him. He looked exhausted. Two Sign fought his way through the press of admirers to offer Jaguar some words of encouragement.

'That was astonishing!' Two Sign had to shout to make himself heard.

'You didn't think we'd do it, did you?' replied Jaguar.

'No, that's not true,' said the knight ruefully. 'It just seemed like the wrong thing to do... at first. It just seemed disrespectful to the gods. Like we were trying to exert our own will over the fate they'd set out for us.'

Jaguar turned to put his bad arm between them. 'Maybe they don't want us to behave like pieces on a patolli board. Maybe they want us to fight back.'

Two Sign grinned. 'Do you know what?' he said. 'You may be right.'

The crowd jostled the two warriors towards the centre of the court where they were crammed together with Magic River and Motonameyotia and hemmed in on all sides by excitable spectators. A set of broad wooden steps had been carried in by two dozen slaves and placed close to the stone hoop through which Jaguar's winning shot had gone. They creaked alarmingly as Amihuatzin lumbered down them, closely followed by members of his family and Xicotencatl. The ruler of Chalco stopped two steps up from the bottom and favoured the sea of radiant faces with a paternal look. The tlatoani's retinue lined up behind him and four sturdy-looking warriors stood guard at the base of the steps. The excited chatter died.

'Sands of Eternal Gold!' Amihuatzin called. 'Present your team.'

As if by magic, the old priest appeared at their side and the crowd parted to allow them all to get to the front.

Amihuatzin barked at the sponsor of the Chalca team. 'Fire Lizard! Bring your team here.'

The players from Chalco had to be brought from the far end of the court before the vast man continued. He licked his lips and spread his arms out in a welcoming gesture.

'Brave ullama players,' he began. 'See how happy you have made my people? What a game! I hardly know where to begin in praise of your performance. I have never seen such an extraordinary game. Poems and songs will be composed in your honour, yes?'

There were scattered murmurs of agreement around the packed court. Two Sign and the rest of Jaguar's team stared at the base of the steps to avoid giving offence.

'Heart of the Jaguar,' resumed the tlatoani. 'It seems as though I shall have to let you and your men go free if I am to honour our wager.'

'And Obsidian Crocodile, My Lord,' said Jaguar firmly.

'Ah yes,' sighed the ruler graciously. 'We shall see him in good time. He is being prepared for tonight's ceremony.' Here, the chubby ruler waved a voluminous arm behind him in the general direction of the lake. Xicotencatl was forced to duck adroitly to avoid being swept from the steps. 'You and your friends will have to accompany me to the proceedings and we will have him brought to us there.'

Amihuatzin fixed his star player with a steely glare.

'Cuetzpalli! You've never failed me before.'

'I am truly sorry, My Lord,' said the captain.

It was the first time Two Sign had seen him looking less than smug. Covered in dust and stoop shouldered, he and his team members looked utterly dejected.

'You've presented me with a grave problem,' said Amihuatzin seriously, his eyes no more than slits. 'I promised our Lord High Priest of Tezcatlipoca that our sublime deity should have an offering at the end of this game.'

Cuetzpalli must have known this was coming, thought Two Sign. The player from Chalco gave the meekest of nods.

Amihuatzin turned to the high priest, who was behind him. 'My Lord,' he said. 'Cuetzpalli is the brightest star in the firmament of our players and, on his own, surely a fitting tribute to our god, is he not?'

The high priest agreed.

'It seems your team will be spared, Cuetzpalli, but you must pay the forfeit.'

Two Sign watched the proud captain closely and noticed a faint trembling of the man's knees. His team looked ashen as Amihuatzin snapped his fingers.

Four priests materialised beside Cuetzpalli and pinioned him. These were muscular men of the order of Tezcatlipoca in short cloaks and cruel daggers at their waists. Their high priest negotiated the tlatoani's bulk to arrive at the base of the steps where he produced the most exquisite knife Two Sign had ever seen. It's finely honed cutting edge was a translucent grey crescent the length of Two Sign's own forearm. The reverse edge was intricately carved and, where the glassy black shaft of the knife merged with the handle, an ornate binding of gold, silver and copper shone like a handheld beacon. The crowd surged

359

outwards, leaving a circle of the dusty court empty, save for the priests and their victim. The rest of the players found themselves at the edges of the circle looking on while Amihuatzin and Xicotencatl surveyed it all from their makeshift platform.

Cuetzpalli did not struggle, but his eyes were wide and glassy.

Amihuatzin dipped his head, which was the sign for the priests to throw Cuetzpalli on his back and hold him down. The high priest began his supplication.

'Mighty Tezcatlipoca! Lord of the Darkness and the Void. All Powerful Omecatl and Bringer of the Mighty Winds! Look down upon your slaves with peace and love in your heart for we are but small and frail.' Two Sign had hung his head in prayer and wasn't able to see the high priest, but it sounded as though he was turning on the spot, projecting his voice out across everyone who had stayed to see the concluding chapter of the game.

'We give you thanks for the daily cycle and your leave, by which day follows night. Accept this humble offering as a token of our love for you and of our unending devotion.' With the last of these words, the high priest knelt down beside Cuetzpalli who showed no intention of struggling. Holding the blade in two hands, the high priest lined up with the player's breastbone, raised his arms up sharply and brought the blade back down in one fluid movement.

Two Sign watched, appalled and fascinated as Cuetzpalli heaved once, a reflex reaction to the savage blow to his chest, and almost hurled off the restraining hands. There was surprisingly little blood until the high priest reached into the cavity inside Cuetzpalli's chest. He made a few deft slashes with the vicious blade and blinked as the player's crimson ichor sprayed his face. The high priest stood up and held the heart aloft for everyone to see. The organ pulsed feebly, ejecting a sudden wash of blood down the high priest's arm and splashing his ceremonial gown. On the ground, Cuetzpalli convulsed again and gasped once, his lips already blue from lack of oxygen. His eyes rolled up inside his head and his ruined body gave up its fight for life.

Someone in the crowd made a retching sound and several others, presumably close by and caught in the spatter, muttered in annoyance. The high priest pretended not to hear and cried out at the heavens.

'Great Lord, I offer you this man's spirit. Guide him into the afterlife and spare him from the deepest realms of Mictlantecuhtli!'

There was a respectful silence while the hundreds of people jammed into the narrow court and those still occupying the seating above gave thanks to the departing soul and made their own special prayers. Two Sign was forced to retract some of the uncharitable thoughts he'd had about Cuetzpalli. The captain of Amihuatzin's team may have been vain, but he had put in a valiant performance at the last. He had not screamed or struggled, nor had he even let forth a single groan. It was impressive, conceded Two Sign.

Amihuatzin broke the spell. He thanked the high priest then turned again to Jaguar. 'According to tradition, you may now pass among those present and help yourself to whatever prizes you wish to claim as your own; clothes, jewellery and any other trinkets. Remember,' he added with a warning. 'You may only take what you can carry.'

There was a rustling sound from the spectators and Two Sign had to hide a smile. Some miserly lords were trying to hide their precious jewellery out of sight.

Jaguar coughed politely, still keeping his eyes fixed firmly on the ground at Amihuatzin's feet. 'Topiltzin, I cannot speak for my friends,' he began. 'They may wish to take up your offer, but I just want to collect my friend Obsidian Crocodile.'

Amihuatzin nodded and looked quizzically at the others. Magic River and Motonameyotia shook their heads, but Two Sign spoke up. Something interesting had caught his eye.

'My Lord,' the big warrior said. 'There is one item that I should like to claim.'

'Take it. It is yours,' said the fat ruler. 'Is it one of these?' He swept his own gold chain from his neck and held them out magnanimously.

'Gracious Lord, you honour me too much, but no. It is the necklace that hangs around Xicotencatl's neck that I respectfully request.'

There was a shocked silence as everyone tried to digest what he'd said, but Two Sign felt confident. The tradition was absolutely clear in this matter, so much so that the richest members of the ruling classes sometimes had copies of their favourite accessories made to wear to competition games in case they had to give them up. Xicotencatl was no ordinary spectator from Chalco though and it wasn't clear whether Amihuatzin would force the ruler of Tlaxcala to comply.

Amihuatzin was lost for words. He turned, easing his bloated frame around to see what Xicotencatl made of this extraordinary demand. Two steps up behind him, Xicotencatl stood, thin-lipped and eyes like cold fury. Clouds whipped by overhead and the breeze plucked at the small man's finery. Eventually, he reached up to the tiny bundle of iridescent feathers at his throat, untied it and tossed it down at Two Sign's feet.

'Take it,' he said dismissively. 'There's more of a market for hummingbird feathers where you come from.'

Two Sign picked it up carefully and placed it round his own neck as light raindrops began to fall from the roiling sky above. Gusts swirled around the ball court and Two Sign shivered. The combination of the chill wind and the sweat drying on his body was making him cold.

'We are done here!' Amihuatzin announced with a cautious look at the sky. 'Heart of the Jaguar, your friend is being prepared for the ceremony. Sands of Eternal Gold will take you and your team to the lakefront after you have changed. You will stay as my guest at the ceremony tonight. You may leave in the morning when I shall arrange for you all to be escorted back to Colhuacan.'

The slaves who had brought out the wooden steps returned with woven canopies on poles, which they held aloft. Amihuatzin eased himself down the last two steps and took refuge under one of them. Xicotencatl and the high priest took another while members of the tlatoani's retinue fought for the remaining ones. Without waiting for the others, Amihuatzin swept from the court.

'By all the powers!' thought Crocodile. He felt strangely light. The priests had given him something; he had no idea what it was, but it was good. He felt warm and contented in spite of his ruined face. He couldn't see through his left eye and the whole side of his head felt swollen and bruised. He didn't need to see the damage to know that it was a mess. It was still seeping a clear fluid three days after the savage blow with which his captors had put an end to his resistance. Every time he remembered that moment, a profound sadness tugged at him, something to do with failure, but now the spiced drink softened the edges of his sorrow.

'Just look at this place!' He wasn't sure, but he might have spoken that aloud to the two heavily armoured priests who led him out onto the spacious waterfront. The whole harbour was aglow with the light of a thousand torches and fire urns set along the quay and out on the myriad of jetties. The last of the day's light had faded from the looming clouds so that an impenetrable blackness blanketed the sky in all directions. In contrast to the relentless gloom of his erstwhile cell and the ominous darkness of the clouds above, the lake was on fire, its surface alight with the orange glare of fires and torchlight.

The gusty wind stirred up the water, so that all around the shore where the flickering torches burned brightest, the lake's inky surface was churned to a shimmering incandescence made lively by the slapping of the waves against the quayside. A few frigid drops of rain splashed fitfully against Crocodile's exposed skin and made him shiver.

'Come on, this way,' said the guards, getting impatient with Crocodile's unhurried gait. Soon they were confronted by a covered observation deck raised to head height above the dock. The platform was made of roughly hewn pine logs, panelled and roofed with decorated reed mats. Rough-hewn slabs of volcanic rock had been assembled to make a grand staircase to the entrance where four more warriors blocked the entrance. Music, voices and the sound of laughter came from within.

One of Crocodile's guards spoke briefly to the men on the steps and one of them then pushed at the heavy drapes and disappeared inside.

This was not what Crocodile had expected. He had expected the ceremony would be well underway before he was called out to meet his fate. Instead, he could see that preparations were still underway. All up and down the length of the long, stone pier that jutted out into Lake Chalco, he could see priests, some scurrying to and fro, relighting torches, while others clustered round what looked like an altar.

The guard who still had a hold of Crocodile's arm saw him look that way.

'They moved the sacrificial block from the top of the temple,' he volunteered and rolled his eyes as though the merest idea of such an undertaking was pure madness.

'It took three days to get it down and one man lost a leg, crushed when the stone slipped off its sled.'

'Why?' said Crocodile.

'With the Feast of Toxcatl gone and still no sign of rain,' the guard began, 'Amihuatzin threatened to have all the senior priests executed unless they could come up with plan.' The guard scratched at a prominent mole that sprouted from his neck. He had a pot-belly and didn't look as though he did much fighting these days. It occurred to Crocodile that he could probably down this man and reach the lake before the warriors on the steps realised he was trying to escape, or perhaps not. Whatever he'd been given was clouding his judgement.

'They decided to conduct a special, one-off ceremony for all the gods together,' the guard was rambling on. 'Tezcatlipoca and Tlaloc are to be specially honoured tonight.'

'And all this?' Crocodile waved airily at the room on stilts and the preparations at the end of the jetty.

'Just temporary. It will all be dismantled tomorrow.'

Crocodile's head spun. Perhaps it was the after effects of the blow to his head or maybe it was that drink he had been given but everything felt disjointed. In the confines of the cell with thirty other captives packed into the available space, Crocodile had never felt so lonely. Most had been strangers to him, but he had recognised one or two of them from Tenochtitlan's busy streets.

Several of the inmates had not handled their captivity well and were huddled in the corners or curled up on the floor. One was jabbering to no one in particular, but the others kept themselves to themselves, withdrawn, almost lifeless. There was something in their eyes he recognised from that day he'd seen his village burned to the ground and had watched the headman dying in the dust. Only now did Crocodile realise that that was what he'd seen in the village elder's eyes. The look that had haunted him all these years had been nothing to do with the agony in the dying man's gut as the flies crawled over the bitter juices that mingled with the blood and settling ash of burning dwellings. It was something else, a sadness borne of the things he'd never done, sunrises that he would never see or perhaps it was the things he'd never said to those he loved.

'Why am I here?' Crocodile asked, surprised he hadn't asked before.

'The tlatoani summoned you.'

'Why me?' Crocodile wondered whether he'd been chosen to go first; the one whose blood would grease the altar.

'How should I know?' shrugged the guard.

There was a commotion at the door and Crocodile's second guard scurried back down the steps.

'Come on,' he said. 'Amihuatzin wants to see you now.'

They climbed the four stone steps and ducked inside where Crocodile was momentarily dazzled. As his eyes adjusted to the change in light level, he saw that the height of the tent-like building allowed the Chalca to light a hundred torches up and down its length without fear of setting light to the pure white cotton that lined the walls and ceiling. The cloth ceiling flapped and bulged as though the fickle wind was trying to tear it from its mountings. It should have been warm with so many flames and a dozen stone braziers blazing along its length but for the fact that there was no lakeside wall, so that the makeshift room was open, Crocodile reasoned, to the ceremony on the jetty.

The room was full of wealthy citizens and the high-born people of Chalco, some of them lounging on the sumptuous handcrafted rugs that lay in profusion all around the room or around the tables that were piled high with a selection of fine foods and jars of drinks. Nowhere was the crush of people thickest than around the grotesque throne of twisted driftwood upon which Amihuatzin sat. Crocodile had never seen the ruler of Chalco before, but his huge bulk and the braying sycophants around him left him in no doubt.

Amihuatzin's piggy eyes swivelled; he'd seen the tent flap move. He beckoned to Crocodile's guards who pushed a way through the teeming throng. When they reached the tlatoani's throne, they pushed him to the ground where he kneeled in the shadow of the gnarled, bleached wood that reached up and around Amihuatzin like a monstrous, skeletal hand.

The room fell silent and everyone waited to hear their ruler speak.

'Crocodile!' a familiar voice rang out.

'Jaguar?' said Crocodile, astonished, turning his good eye towards the voice.

He felt a hand on his shoulder and suddenly Jaguar was kneeling on the floor beside him. His friend's hair was tied back neatly and he was dressed in fine clothes that didn't suit him. He looked tired, but his eyes blazed with an intensity that Crocodile had never seen before.

'Mictlan's bones! What have they done to you?'

'It's alright,' said Crocodile. 'It doesn't matter.'

'Does it hurt?'

'No. They've given me some octli or something. I can't feel anything.'

'But you need stitches and a poultice.' Jaguar turned to Amihuatzin and addressed him angrily. 'Why hasn't his wound been dressed? Where is your healer?'

Amihuatzin wasn't listening. He was sharing a joke with two members of the nobility who sat close by on smaller chairs. One made a high-pitched yapping sound as he laughed at every word the tlatoani said.

'Leave it!' Crocodile hissed and hauled on Jaguar's arm. 'I said it doesn't matter. What are you doing here anyway?' he added, suddenly realising how odd it was that his friend was here in Chalco.

Amihuatzin heard Crocodile and spoke in a mocking tone of voice. 'Yes, brave Jaguar, please tell your friend Obsidian Crocodile why you're here!'

'I've come to get you out,' Jaguar said eagerly. 'Your father is here too. We've come to take you back to Tenochtitlan.'

Crocodile noticed Two Sign for the first time, standing back at the edge of the space that had formed at the foot of the tlatoani's great pronged chair. 'What? How...' His voice tailed off, bemused. He shook his head slowly, trying to clear it. Whatever it was he'd been given made it hard to think straight. Other familiar faces stood beside his father and for a moment, Crocodile really wondered if he was home already.

'We won a bet, Crocodile. Your father, Magic River, Motonameyotia and I played ullamalitzli and beat the team from Chalco. The tlatoani promised we could go free and take you with us.'

Crocodile smiled to see Jaguar so excited and was about to speak when the fat ruler spoke again.

'That's right, Crocodile,' he said. 'Your friends have accomplished an extraordinary victory and earned the favour of the gods. They risked their lives and showed great courage at the sacred ball game.' Amihuatzin's voice took on a patronising tone as he continued. 'So now they wish to leave and take you with them. Remind us who it was that nearly stove your head in.'

Crocodile tried to remember. The days of his incarceration were a blur and he remembered only fragments of his journey from the battlefield to the cells beneath the temple. His captor had been strong and confident. Crocodile recalled the man had had a broken nose and that he was a captain.

'The Dagger...' he said uncertain. 'No, wait! The Hand that Holds the Dagger,' the name came back to him in a rush and so did the shame of his defeat.

'Just so,' said Amihuatzin. His eyes narrowed further and gazed hard at Jaguar. 'I discovered who had captured your friend,

Crocodile. I wanted to know what was so remarkable about this warrior that you would risk everything to rescue him and so I spoke to The Hand that Holds the Dagger. Do you know what he said to me?'

Amihuatzin didn't wait for an answer and Crocodile could only groan as the truth came out.

'Your friend tried to escape after he submitted! That's why The Hand that Holds the Dagger had to crack his head open.'

The fat ruler sat back in his chair and gloated as the Chalca cried out in disbelief. There were angry looks and several of them shouted abuse; one even threw a handful of eel stew at him. Crocodile hung his head. There was no greater dishonour than cowardice. No alcohol or drugged ceremonial drink could dull the pain he felt just then. He would rather have shouted his own humiliation to the whole world than have his adoptive father know the truth.

'Heart of the Jaguar,' Amihuatzin said in a silky voice. 'Why don't you ask your friend if he will accompany you back to Tenochtitlan?'

With his good eye, Crocodile watched Jaguar try to understand. His friend paused and studied Crocodile for a moment and then shrugged. Crocodile knew that Jaguar had forgiven him and that only drove the spike of guilt in deeper. He looked over Jaguar's shoulder and looked at his father. There was nothing to read in Two Sign's face, not a trace of emotion betrayed his feelings and yet Crocodile saw it all. Two Sign had raised him like his own son and, although the big knight had spent much of his time away on duties for Moctezuma, Crocodile knew the way he thought and that honour meant everything to him. There was no way he could go back to Tenochtitlan where he would be a pariah. The Eagle Knights would never have him now and he would be lucky if he was allowed to work the fields with the mayeques. Even slaves would not deign to speak to him.

'I'm sorry, father. I'm sorry,' he repeated. 'I'm so sorry, Jaguar, but you'll have to leave without me.'

Jaguar opened his mouth to protest, but Crocodile cut him short. The warmth of the priests' drink had gone, leaving in its place an ice-cold certainty that held its own brutal comfort. Crocodile's soul had been forfeit to the gods since his capture on the battlefield. Nothing he or Jaguar could have done from that moment on would have made any difference. It had been stupid and disgraceful to try and break free.

'No! I know I made you promise, but now I am at peace with the gods. Their will is mine. Go now and take my blessings with you. You earned your freedom, Jaguar, but I have not earned mine. Tezcatlipoca and Tlaloc and the others wait for me.'

Amihuatzin began to clap slowly. 'Well done, Obsidian Crocodile,' he drawled. 'Perhaps the gods won't be disappointed with you after all!'

As Crocodile turned to go, he clearly saw a single tear run down his father's cheek. Perhaps it was forgiveness, thought Crocodile and wondered where his own tears were. There was still sorrow, but it was swamped by a gathering mountain of determination to make amends for what he'd done.

Suddenly Two Sign crossed the gap in two large strides, folded his arms around him and hugged him fiercely.

'I... you... I give you my strength,' he said. He let go and stepped back. 'I am proud to call you my son.'

Jaguar came forward too and grasped Crocodile's arm. He held it tightly, not needing to say anything. Then, with a brief nod to Magic River, Crocodile allowed the guards to escort him back outside. In the cold night air, he breathed deeply, trying to relax. The smell of Lake Chalco and the ash from the burning torches felt as real as anything he'd ever smelled before. After a brief conversation with three of their colleagues, the guards marched him towards the stone jetty. As they approached, Crocodile could see that the ceremony was getting underway. Hundreds of people of Chalco were massing all along the waterfront and out onto the firmest of the reed beds, trampling the rushes to get a ringside view of the proceedings. Many more canoes and boats were out on the lake, their occupants hardly daring to dip their paddles in the water for fear of making a noise.

Crocodile was led up to the front of a long line of captives that ended where the jetty began. It seemed as though he would be the first to die after all and somehow that felt good to him. There would be no delay. As soon as he reached the water's edge, the guards handed him over to the six priests who waited to take him the rest of the way. He knocked their hands away contemptuously and set off along the smooth stone promontory holding his head high. He would not kick or scream or sob. He needed to redeem himself.

The six priests hurried after Crocodile, dalmatics flapping in the breeze. A light drizzle was falling once again. The wet stone felt slick under his bare feet but he strode on regardless. At the end, the structure looked as though it had been widened on both sides to make more room for the altar and the priests who would conduct the ceremony. Where the stone wall ended, a wooden ramp had been constructed, which descended at a gentle angle into the lake. This had been built so that the bodies could be taken down the ramp and offered to Tlaloc and the spirits of the lake.

Crocodile reached the altar and stopped. He gazed down at that cold black slab surrounded by unsmiling priests and felt the black worm of fear come crawling back inside him. He closed his good eye and breathed deeply once again. He heard his father offer him his strength and then he saw, as clear as the day it had taken place, the old headman, sitting quietly amidst the swirling ash of his village as his lacerated bowels lay coiled in his lap. Then at last, Crocodile found that he was crying, not for himself, but for the old man. He understood at last that the village elder, whose name Crocodile could not even recall, had chosen to use his last hours on earth to share his wisdom with a frightened boy. 'My time had come,' those eyes had seemed to say. 'Dignity in death, for that is how you will be remembered.'

Teardrops squeezed from Crocodile's eyelids and rolled down his cheeks to join the frigid raindrops on the jetty. He dashed them aside as the six priests caught up with him and threw him on his back. They pulled him tight until his shoulders threatened to dislocate and the cold, hard edge of the altar cut painfully into his calves as the priests bore down on him.

Crocodile heard the murmuring of the crowd, eager for the offerings to commence and a great skin drum began to boom its mournful call across the water. One of the priests began the prayers.

'Great Lord Tezcatlipoca, Protector of the Weak and Emissary of Nightfall,' he began. 'We entreat you to bear witness to the misery of your people who have suffered four long years of drought. We beseech you to cast your far-seeing eyes across the land and help us in our hour of need...'

The opening supplication was long and Crocodile found himself thinking of banal things that he had neglected to do. On the morning of the battle, he had left clothes strewn untidily amongst his bedding in the barracks room that he shared with nine other men. Maybe Two Sign would let the household slaves know that it could all be cleared away. Amongst his meagre possessions were two simple necklaces; one with gaudy stones for beads and the other with fifteen, tiny wooden figures of the principal deities of Tenochtitlan. He wished he had got a message to his father, instructing him that these should pass to Jaguar and to Precious Flower as his closest friends. He still owed a final payment to Rat Face for that tattoo that Jaguar had mocked.

'...sweet rain for the crops of beans and maize,' the priest's voice droned on. 'Bring soothing rain to freshen the water in the stagnant lakes and rivers so that fish might thrive again.'

The priest's tone changed and it was clear that he was uttering the final dedication. The words were lost on Crocodile who searched deep inside himself to find the fear that should have been there. He found nothing. Someone wound an arm around his neck and held it still and an evil-looking blade appeared above him, ripples of yellow firelight reflecting off its edge. At last the final words were said. There was a brief pause and then the razor edge ripped down and smashed Crocodile in the chest.

Winded, Crocodile fought to draw a breath and groan all at the same time as the pain began. Like a lightning bolt, the agony seared his heart and lungs, scorched the spine in his neck and hammered at the base of his skull. He felt his back arch and his legs spasm uncontrollably and then something broke inside him. Some mortal tether snapped and Crocodile was free. He stared up at the sky. A drop of rain splashed wetly on his upturned face and then another. He felt himself lifted from the altar and carried down to the water. There was only darkness now and the sounds around him were just a distant murmur. The cold waters of the lake folded themselves around him and, as the priests pushed him out into the lake, the rain began in earnest.

Chapter 20 – Xôchitl

Tlacaelel had just finished his midday meal when a messenger brought news of Cloud Face's movements. The general was staring out of one of the windows of his Spartan quarters, gazing at the sheets of rain that lashed the buildings in the temple precinct. It was absurd; twelve hours of continuous rain and already the drought didn't seem like such a bad thing.

The deadline Moctezuma had given him expired today. Unless he could find some evidence of the high priest's wrongdoing, his brother would refuse to give him a second hearing. To date, all he had to show for his efforts was a sworn statement from a master armourer in Tlacopan. The arrow that had killed Storm Light had been ordered by the warrior priests of Xipe Totec, but frustratingly there was no direct linkage back to Cloud Face. Tenochtitlan's rules provided no means to forcibly extract the truth from Snake Eyes and Tlacaelel had no other leverage to coerce it from him. The high priest of the order of Xipe Totec was the worst kind of scum, but most of his crimes had been committed so long ago that they had little relevance today.

Tlacaelel was sure that Devine Cactus had been murdered by Snake Eyes, but nothing he could say would persuade Moctezuma to order the priests to hand the corpse over for inspection. Cloud Face must have guessed that Devine Cactus had been spying on him. On Tlacaelel's own request, a polite answer had come back from the priests stating that they had been forced to dispose of the body for fear that it would spread disease.

The messenger sneezed, reminding Tlacaelel of his business. The general snapped his fingers at one of his slaves, who was hovering in the background, and bade him fetch a cloth for the man to towel himself dry with.

'What news?'

'General, two of the guards on duty at the Matlalatl Gate report that Cloud Face has left Tenochtitlan along the southern causeway with twenty well-armed men.' The words tumbled out in a breathless stream. The young lad must have run the entire way through the torrential rain. He took the cloth from Tlacaelel's man and rubbed his hair erratically.

Tlacaelel picked up a bowl of fruit and picked tidily at the contents.

'Did they say where he was going?' he asked without looking up.

'No, My Lord.' The messenger looked crestfallen and the puddle of water at his feet spread out as the water dripped from his mantle. His hair was sticking out in all directions and his teeth began to chatter.

Tlacaelel pushed his bowl aside. 'Thank you. Go and get a steam bath; oh, and on your way out, tell Tlacpac to come straight in.' He had seen the warrior through the window and guessed he would be at the door by now. The messenger handed the damp cloth back to the general's man and left.

'My Lord,' said Tlacpac as soon as he stepped inside. 'I have good news!'

'Quimapiqui?'

'On your request he sent a runner to a merchant in Chalco who owed him a favour and the man he sent out just got back this morning.'

'Mictlan's bones!' The general smacked the table in frustration. 'How do they do it? Why can't we assemble the communications networks that these traders always seem to have.'

'They have an unassailable cover story,' Tlacpac reminded him.

'You're right, of course. Well, come on, out with it then!'

'Quimapiqui's contact says that there are two warriors in Chalco now who match the description that we gave. Not only are they guests of Amihuatzin but they played a game of ullamalitzli.'

'What?' cried Tlacaelel, jumping to his feet.

'Yes, it's true,' the warrior added. 'Apparently, they met up with two more Mexica while they were there and they're all heading back to Tenochtitlan this morning.'

'What are they up to!' shouted Tlacaelel. 'Whatever it is, Cloud Face is going to head them off before they get here. Why am I always last to find out what's going on?' He turned and looked at the sheets of rain outside his window, trying to work it out, and then he spoke to Last Medicine who had been waiting patiently all morning.

'Go and fetch a squad of Jaguar Knights, twenty of the toughest men you have and make sure that they're quick runners too. We've got a lot of ground to make up.'

'Where shall we meet you?'

'The Matlalatl Gate. If I'm not there, assume that I've gone on ahead and follow on down the causeway,' Tlacaelel added as an afterthought.

Last Medicine left briskly. Tlacaelel shouted at his slave to fetch a waxed cloak and followed the warrior down the stairs. Rock and the other guard, who should have been stationed outside the building, were huddled in the narrow hallway, sheltering from the rain. Tlacaelel would have to let Rock return to the frontier before long; the big man didn't look as though he was enjoying his time in the city. His scouting party had returned just before dawn that morning to report that the search for Two Sign and Jaguar had proved fruitless. Rock would have had very little sleep since then and yet he was back and standing watch. The giant started to apologise, but Tlacaelel waved him to silence.

'I don't care, but I need you to follow me now.'

Rock and the other man picked up their weapons and fell in behind him and the three of them marched for the southern causeway. Guardsmen posted at the Matlalatl Gate confirmed that a phalanx of warrior priests had recently passed by, including the high priest of Huitzilopochtli, but that he had not yet seen the knights. Tlacaelel reasoned that Last Medicine would have needed a little time to assemble his men, so after a brief discussion with the guards, he set off down the causeway, certain that the knights would catch up before too long. They were nearing the place where the causeway forked when they heard the sound of heavy footfall splashing through the puddles. Last Medicine caught up with them, emerging through the torrential rain with a squad of determined looking Jaguar Knights.

Together they took the left-hand track that led to Colhuacan, the route that the army had marched a few days earlier. Tlacaelel picked up his pace and they all ran together, matching strides and along the flooded roadway, sending spray in all directions.

Ahead, the causeway was only visible for a short distance through the downpour, so as they approached its end, Tlacaelel motioned for everyone to stop. The water of the lake disappeared into the mist and rain on either side and, ahead, the causeway vanished eerily behind a wall of spray. He peered forward, but could only just make out a few trees and bushes looming out of the grey landscape, but there were muffled voices close at hand.

Tlacaelel and Rock ventured a short way onto the path that led around the south side of Colhuacan and rounded a copse with Last Medicine and the Jaguar Knights close behind. On a bare patch of ground between clumps of trees, Cloud Face and his warrior priests confronted a second group of indistinct grey shadows.

The atrocious weather made it impossible to tell what was going on so Tlacaelel eased his party forward cautiously. Although his force were more than a match for Cloud Face and his men, Tlacaelel didn't like the idea of fighting both the parties at the same time. He tried to do a headcount and guessed at fifteen or sixteen men, but who could say how many more were lurking in the gloom.

Eventually, Cloud Face's men noticed the new arrivals squelching through the mud so Tlacaelel gave up all pretence of stealth and marched up to the gathering. The high priest's robe clung wetly to his skeletal frame. Big drops of water rolled down his pale scalp and his purple birthmark stood out like a livid injury in the peculiar half-light.

'What's going on here?' demanded Tlacaelel.

'Tlacaelel!' exclaimed the high priest. 'How convenient. You may actually be of some use to me.' The acerbic tone was not lost on the general. Cloud Face's assistant stood beside him. Feathered

Darkness' mane of dark hair was plastered down his back and from beneath his dripping eyebrows he watched Tlacaelel with a glacial calm.

'How so, Mixayacatl?'

'I've caught these spies trying to infiltrate Tenochtitlan.' Cloud Face indicated the group of men confronting them. Tlacaelel looked again. Closer to, it was easier to see the figures through the murk and he realised that he'd underestimated the size of the party. There were perhaps two dozen Chalca warriors spread out in a line, six of whom were Serpent Knights who had arranged themselves in a protective cluster around four more men, one of whom Tlacaelel instantly recognised as Two Sign, in spite of the cotton wadding wrapped around his head. A more careful look revealed that he was accompanied by the redoubtable Magic River and the young warrior called Jaguar, who was also heavily bandaged. The fourth member of the group was unrecognisable, with heavy bruising all around his eyes.

'Two Sign!' Tlacaelel called out. 'What is the meaning of this?' The erstwhile commander of the Eagle Knights was dressed in a fine grey cloak hemmed in a repeating red and gold pattern of interlocking squares and with the goggle-eyed glyph of Tlaloc on one shoulder. The other three Mexica were similarly well attired but none of them carried any weapons.

'We'd like to come home,' Two Sign said simply.

'Mixayacatl says that you're spies,' said Tlacaelel.

Two Sign cocked an eyebrow at the heavily armed knights of Chalco on either side. 'An armed escort doesn't strike me as the best way for spies to infiltrate their enemy.'

'Do you deny that you've been in Chalco?' asked Tlacaelel with a severe look.

'No,' was Two Sign's answer.

'A guest of Amihuatzin, too, if my sources are correct.'

'I suppose that's true,' admitted Two Sign.

Tlacaelel noticed Cloud Face smirking, but vented his irritation on the Eagle Knight for playing into the high priest's hands. 'What in the name of the ghosts of Teotihuacan were you doing there? I demand an explanation!'

Two Sign wiped the raindrops from his forehead and his eyebrows. His fine clothing was drenched and heavy with water that dripped around his feet where they were planted in the mire. He opened his mouth to speak, but Jaguar beat him to it.

'My Lord Tlacaelel!' cried the young warrior, pushing his way through the Chalca. The young man was pale, the binding around his left arm was crusted in dried blood and his right arm hung in a sling. He looked wrung out and utterly exhausted, but there was a stony determination in his voice.

'It is my fault that we were in Chalco. I went there to free Obsidian Crocodile and Two Sign followed me because he thought I was deserting.'

This outburst was greeted by a stunned silence, so Jaguar pushed on.

'I promised Crocodile that I would prevent him from getting captured if I could, but I failed him and so, after the battle I left for Chalco to try and put things right. Two Sign caught up with me and tried to stop me, but I persuaded him to come with me instead.'

'This is absurd!' raged Cloud Face. 'I've never heard of anything so ridiculous.'

Tlacaelel ignored the high priest. 'What happened then?'

'Well... we were captured and taken before Amihuatzin and I made a wager he could not resist.' In spite of the seriousness of the situation, the young man grinned. 'I bet him we could beat the best ullamalitzli players in Chalco and he promised to free us, and Crocodile too, if we won.'

Tlacaelel was astonished. 'You won?'

'We did.'

'And all this finery, this honour guard, was granted to you by the tlatoani?'

'It was, Lord Tlacaelel.'

'So where is Crocodile now?' scoffed Cloud Face.

'My son chose not to come,' interrupted Two Sign, his voice heavy with emotion. 'His destiny lay with the gods, as Jaguar should have known.'

Tlacaelel did not know what to say. He shifted his weight from one foot to the other, but couldn't shake the mud that oozed around his sandals. The steady downpour showed no sign of stopping. Bushes nearby sagged under the watery onslaught and all the branches in a copse of willow trees sagged with the accumulated weight of raindrops. Squalls came and went, reducing visibility to a few yards, so that at times the three groups seemed to stand in a tiny, grey netherworld. Tlacaelel was just trying to work out his next move when the sound of a strident horn cut through the air. Everyone turned to watch as a battalion of Grey Privy Knights materialised through the driving rain and marched up the path behind them, closely followed by Moctezuma's covered palanquin and personal cortege. The warriors from Chalco began to look distinctly nervous.

Moctezuma unfolded his tall frame from the litter as it settled into the mud. In a brief sweep, his gaze took in Cloud Face's warrior priests, Tlacaelel's knights and the increasingly inadequate huddle of Chalca and their protégés. Everyone cast their eyes to the ground.

'What's going on here, Tlacaelel?' he demanded. 'Someone has arranged a party and neglected to invite the tlatoani!' His mouth arranged itself into a smile while his eyes spoke heavy disappointment.

'I apologise, My Lord,' said Tlacaelel, annoyed that he had forgotten to notify his brother. 'I should have sent word to you.'

Before Moctezuma was able to respond, Cloud Face approached the tlatoani. 'My Lord! These men are spies and should be put to death. They have told us about a game, preposterous nonsense about a bet in Chalco where they have, in fact, been fed and entertained by our sworn enemy. Look how richly they have been clothed!'

'Mixayacatl, I did not address you,' growled Moctezuma. 'It's not the first time I've had to warn you.'

The tlatoani asked Two Sign to repeat the story, which the Eagle Knight did, beginning with Jaguar's flight from the battlefield and ending with the sacrifice of his son, Crocodile, in the waters of Lake Chalco. Moctezuma listened dispassionately as the tale unfolded.

'Touching as this story is, I'm not inclined to give it any credence.' Moctezuma's eyes bored into Tlacaelel. 'Unless there's any reason to delay we should strip these four men of their fineries and take them back to the city as prisoners. The High Council should convene in the normal place and pass judgement on their crimes.'

The Chalca heard the exchange and began moving away carefully, trying not to attract attention. Tlacaelel supposed that their instructions had been to escort the Mexica home and that they considered their duty done. He sought his brother's permission to call them back.

'My Lord,' said the general. 'You gave me until today to find some evidence to support my claims of treason, so before those men leave, we must hear their testimony and decide whether it supports the story we've just heard.'

Moctezuma gave his consent so Tlacaelel shouted at the Chalca and instructed the leader of the Serpent Knights to stand before them.

'What is your name?' Tlacaelel asked him.

'It is Ocotzonamaca, My Lord.' The Chalca held his head up proudly and kept his gaze high to avoid direct eye contact with Moctezuma.

'Were these men captives or guests in Chalco?'

'They were captives at first. My men and I apprehended them.'

'Did they play ullamalitzli in a bet with Amihuatzin as they claim?'

'They did, My Lord.'

'And why were they set free?' demanded Moctezuma.

'They won,' Ocotzonamaca answered simply, still staring at the clouds.

'So Amihuatzin never met these men before this year Two Reed began?' said Moctezuma, taking over the questioning.

'Topiltzin Moctezuma,' Ocotzonamaca began respectfully, 'I serve as Amihuatzin's eyes and ears in Chalco and beyond. I brought these men before him three days ago and I can assure you that he'd never set eyes on them before.'

Moctezuma stared at the man for a while and then dismissed him. 'Pass on my warmest regards to your tlatoani,' he added.

Ocotzonamaca nodded once, collected his warriors and disappeared into the sheets of rain. Tlacaelel's brother fixed him with a piercing gaze.

'Perhaps these men are innocent after all,' he said, 'but you still have nothing to substantiate your claim of a conspiracy.'

'My Lord, as I have said, several of our clansmen died with Mexica arrows in their backs. Heart of the Jaguar saw his own standard bearer perish in this way.'

'What of it?' snapped Cloud Face. 'The arrows were poorly aimed, presumably by some ill-trained acolyte of Xipe Totec.' The high priest flicked his arm dismissively. The Woman Snake's attempts to implicate me are utterly absurd!'

'Yes, Tlacaelel,' rejoined Moctezuma, 'What possible motive could Mixayacatl have?'

'He wants to crush the clans and restore power to the priesthood.' Tlacaelel spoke the words he knew he could not substantiate. Without Devine Cactus' testimony, there was no evidence to support the claim.

Moctezuma asked Jaguar whether he had seen the man who fired the arrow at Storm Light.

'No, My Lord.'

'So your claim that the standard bearer was killed by one of our priests is only guesswork?'

Tlacaelel almost groaned out-loud but held himself in check. As usual, his brother had cut to the heart of the matter. There was nothing solid they could use to implicate Cloud Face. The high priest would survive and all Tlacaelel's plans to contain the Chalca, so as to allow the Mexica armies to concentrate on the expansion of the empire, would be undermined, his credibility in tatters.

'It's more than that,' said Jaguar. For a moment, he seemed reluctant, as though wrestling with some inner question, but then he spoke again. 'Mixayacatl told me that our standard bearer would die. How could he have known this if he hadn't planned it all along?'

'What new outrageous lies are these?' spat the high priest, his face a mask of rage. 'You cannot take his word for this!' Cloud Face jabbed a finger at Jaguar. 'He's no jaguar. He's a little snake who fucked his slave girl!'

There was a collective gasp from the onlookers, especially from Moctezuma's own retinue. No one liked salacious gossip more than the nobility.

'Is this true?' Moctezuma's voice was low and menacing.

Tlacaelel felt sorry for Jaguar. He found himself wanting to believe the story of the trip to Chalco to rescue his best friend. There was a certain nobility about it that some of the old stories alluded to. Whatever the truth of it, it would not go well for him if Cloud Face's allegation of sexual misconduct with a slave was true. Tenochtitlan's laws did not look favourably on such abuses. The young warrior looked as though he had endured much, but the shock disclosure seemed to have strengthened his resolve.

'My Lord Moctezuma, I can't deny that accusation. I know it will not matter that Precious Flower was only two days from her freedom...'

Cloud Face snorted in disgust. 'No doubt arranged by your family in an effort to get you out of trouble!'

Jaguar carried on regardless. '...so I will take the consequences of my crime, whatever they may be. I don't care anymore,' he said and pointed at the high priest. 'Just make sure you question him as to why he tried to blackmail me into preventing the clans from retreating. He knew this was not what Tlacaelel's plans called for. Ask him how he knew that Storm Light would die, because I think he had a hand in that, a plan that involved a priest of Xipe Totec and a quiver-full of arrows.'

'This is intolerable!' Cloud Face shook with righteous indignation. Tlacaelel saw Feathered Darkness place a cautionary hand on Cloud Face's arm, but the high priest dashed it away and shook his fist at Moctezuma. 'Why are we standing here listening to this drivel? Look at them standing there in their fine clothes, earned with the blood of honourable Mexica. We can't allow them back inside our city gates where they can spy on us and send reports back to their friends in Chalco.'

'Tlacaelel!' Moctezuma snapped at his brother. 'You pride yourself on your information and yet your version of events depends on a weaponsmith whose evidence has no material connection with Mixayacatl and a young man who can't keep his cock inside his loincloth. Is this the best you can do?'

Tlacaelel cursed himself again for not putting Devine Cactus before his brother when he'd had the chance. Cold rain trickled down his neck as he grasped for inspiration. He wiped his face and his nose. It was hopeless. There was nothing else.

'Wait!' called Two Sign suddenly. The big knight squinted as a heavy squall drove across the clearing. 'Tlaxcala's army didn't come to Chalco's aide because of any message sent from Chalco. We stopped their men from getting through. Mixayacatl knew this because he interrogated the men we caught, so he sent his own message to Xicotencatl and persuaded him to side with the Chalca.' The accusation cut across the dank, grey landscape like a knife.

Cloud Face's mouth dropped open and worked soundlessly so Tlacaelel knew that Two Sign had the truth, but how could he have known?

'Do you have any proof?' Tlacaelel asked, afraid what the answer might be.

'I do,' said Two Sign simply. 'Cloud Face dispatched someone he trusted to Tlaxcala to beg for their assistance.' He reached into a pocket sewn into the inside of his borrowed cloak and gently extracted a sorry, wizened looking bundle on a leather thong. Tlacaelel struggled to make out what it was through the squally weather. Two Sign approached Moctezuma who took the object and turned it over in his hand. It was a minute ball of turquoise feathers, the scarcely recognisable remains of a hummingbird.

'Where did you get this?'

'We won our share of spoils from the ball game and I claimed this. The ruler of Tlaxcala did not leave for home with the rest of his army. Xicotencatl stayed as Amihuatzin's guest of honour. He had it around his neck.'

Moctezuma was astonished. 'Cloud Face, this is yours,' he said to Cloud Face. 'You're the only person I permit to wear the sacred feathers of the quetzal.'

The priest looked irritated. 'Clearly Xicotencatl does.'

'Well if this is his, where is yours?'

The high priest reached up to his neck and then dropped his hands. 'I couldn't say. I took it off a few days ago to use the steam room and never saw it again.'

'No,' insisted Two Sign. 'You lie. I spoke to Xicotencatl after the ball game, before my son...' his voice tailed off, but then he gathered himself. 'I asked him where he got it from because it looked like yours. He confirmed that it had been a gift, conveyed to him by one of your priests.'

Tlacaelel had to check. 'Did he say who?'

Two Sign pointed at Feathered Darkness and Tlacaelel realised that this was the final piece of proof they needed. Here was the direct link between the high priest and his treason.

'So it was you who stole it!' Cloud Face was quick with the rebuke. 'Why would you do such a thing, Feathered Darkness, after all I've done for you?'

For a heartbeat Feathered Darkness looked shocked and Tlacaelel understood the sacrifice that Cloud Face was demanding of his assistant.

'Tell the truth, Feathered Darkness,' urged Tlacaelel. 'You do not have to pay the price if this was his idea. You were just following orders. Believe me when I tell you that you do not want to be found guilty of treason.' He turned to his brother. 'What is the punishment for treason?'

'For conspiring with Tlaxcala? Persuading our enemies to side with Chalco in a war against our people?' The tlatoani shook his head. 'Death comes in many forms, brother, but this is something new. What manner of death befits a crime of this magnitude?'

The use of the familial connection told Tlacaelel that Moctezuma had decided to believe his version of events. Cloud Face was at the root of the conspiracy and Feathered Darkness held the final key, but would he implicate his master? Cloud Face seized the initiative, while Feathered Darkness hesitated, and ordered his men to restrain the younger man. Two of them took hold of him and forced him to his knees; one of them had a snaggletooth and greasy hair down to his waist while the other had bloodshot eyes and a thin line of anger for a mouth.

'Confess your crimes and Huitzilopochtli will be your judge.'

Feathered Darkness opened his mouth but Cloud Face motioned to the men who held him down and the one with the jutting tooth twisted his arm until he cried out.

'Open your heart and take your punishment in this world so that you may pass blameless into the afterlife,' advised the high priest.

Feathered Darkness was kneeling in the mud and though the raindrops splashed upon his upturned face, he never took his flinty eyes off the man who stood poised above him. Tlacaelel hoped the young priest valued his own life.

Feathered Darkness exhaled loudly. 'It was me,' he agreed. 'I went to Tlaxcala and begged Xicotencatl to help the Chalca. I took Mixayacatl's necklace as a token of goodwill.'

Tlacaelel could only shake his head as Cloud Face smiled down warmly at his assistant, put a hand on his shoulder and then pulled out a knife. Feathered Darkness spoke again, addressing Moctezuma.

'I took Mixayacatl's necklace because he asked me to. It was Mixayacatl's plan to seek help from Tlaxcala so that Chalco would win the battle and bring shame upon the Woman Snake.'

Cloud Face whipped round and dug the point of his blade into his assistant's throat. 'Recant your lies, Feathered Darkness!'

Tlacaelel drew his dagger and, beside him, Rock held his war club high, but neither was in striking distance. 'Stop!' Tlacaelel called in vain.

'You cannot listen to this worthless piece of shit!' Cloud Face fumed. 'He is a traitor and a liar. He stole the necklace while I was washing.'

Feathered Darkness spoke again, loudly so that everyone could hear above the thrumming of the rain. 'Mixayacatl means to restore the old traditions, force you to give power back to the priests.' He looked unflinchingly at Cloud Face all the while.

'Why?' Moctezuma asked the high priest. 'What possible reason could you have for bringing defeat on your own people?'

For a moment, Tlacaelel thought the high priest would deny it. His white knuckles clenched about his dagger and the tendons in his neck stood out like cords as he fought to control his anger. Then it was as though a dam had burst.

'For over fifty years I've watched, as one-by-one the rulers of Tenochtitlan have let this city sprawl and grow beyond control, and piece-by-piece, they neglected their responsibilities and handed them to weak and godless sons of peasants!'

'What are you talking about?' said Moctezuma.

'There is no law, no fear to bend the people to your whim. Sure, the Mexica empire spreads its mighty wings, but in the city, thieves and criminals roam the streets and in broad daylight too. The clans, whose job it is to maintain law and order stand idly by and watch. Weak men, who know nothing of the gods or the workings of the world, are called to stand in judgement and advise you.' Cloud Face spat. 'These fools know nothing. They have earned nothing, unlike the priests who helped to build this nation. The priests, who speak to gods, the very men who guided the hand of Itzcoatl, Chimalpopoca, Huitzilihuitl and the others before them, each year you hear us less and every year we pay less tribute to the gods whose protection we all depend upon.'

Cloud Face stuck out a hand and grabbed a handful of Feathered Darkness' hair. He pushed the point of his dagger into a fold of skin beneath Feathered Darkness' eyelid.

'Now I'm going to make you pay for your betrayal,' he hissed.

Tlacaelel was powerless, too far away to stop him, only Moctezuma stood closer. Just then a voice cut through the sodden air.

'If you think the clansmen know nothing, then you know nothing of the people over whom you claim to watch!' Jaguar shouted.

Tlacaelel watched, amazed as the young warrior pushed past Two Sign and stepped between Cloud Face and his assistant, forcing the blade aside. He still looked pale, but his eyes blazed up at the old man.

'My father was one of those godless sons of peasants that you so despise. He worked every day of his life for twenty-five years.

As a boy, he started in the fields, harvesting food that went to the stalls in Tlatleloco and fed the people of the city. At every call-to-arms, he did his duty as a warrior and fought for the glory of our people, no matter that he risked his life and bore many injuries along the way. My father was Blade of the South. He buried two of his own brothers who died to make this nation what it is, now thanks to you, he and countless more like him are dead.' Jaguar shook with fury. Rivulets of rain that coursed down his face sprayed into the air with every syllable he uttered.

'When he had earned enough,' continued Jaguar without a pause, 'my father built his own business, and I mean built it, starting with the walls that were to become his workshop. Then every day when dawn broke, this so-called godless man prayed at our family shrine, then worked until the sun went down.' Jaguar raised his cloak-clad arm and pointed at Cloud Face. 'So don't you tell me that my father knew nothing of Tenochtitlan. My father *was* Tenochtitlan, just like so many others appointed to the council.'

Tlacaelel and all the others gaped and Magic River actually cheered.

'Well, your father may have dragged himself out of the slime,' sneered Cloud Face, 'but you haven't. I've had enough of this madness and I've had enough of all of you! What I have done was for the good of the Mexica and was done on his authority. You feeble mortals have no power over me,' he snarled. 'I am answerable to Huitzilopochtli and no one else.' Cloud Face raised his knife to strike, but Moctezuma shouted suddenly.

'It is not you!' the tlatoani cried and thrust Jaguar aside. He grabbed the priest's hand as it held the knife on high and twisted the old man's arm back, wrenching the blade free and drawing the priest toward him. Cloud Face fought back but the old man was no match for Moctezuma. The tlatoani stared into the priest's eyes and dragged him closer until they were in a tight embrace.

'You forget yourself, priest.' Moctezuma's voice was breathy. 'I am the hand of destiny. I am the hand and will of Huitzilopochtli. The tlatoani is ruler by divine authority and you... you're nothing but a messenger.'

Cloud Face made a pained expression and tried to pull away again. This time Moctezuma let him go and with a sucking sound, he withdrew the blade from the priest's belly.

Cloud Face clutched at his stomach and dropped to his knees.

Tlacaelel watched as Moctezuma reached out and ran the jagged blade around the high priest's neck. A spray of crimson splashed across the tlatoani's cloak and quickly dissolved to a cloudy pink on the soaking cloth. He tossed the blade aside as the priest fell, face-down in the ochre quagmire, writhed briefly and then lay still.

The rain was drumming on the rooftops of the houses along Harbour Street when Jaguar and Magic River finally made it home. Cataracts of water poured from the rooftops and lively streams tore across the paths, finding channels between the flagstones. The countless drainage channels criss-crossing Teopan that had, for so long, been nothing more than stagnant ditches, were full to overflowing, sweeping months of effluent away.

Moctezuma, Tlacaelel and Two Sign had insisted on accompanying Jaguar home and, although the tlatoani had dismissed his Grey Privy Knights, an honour guard still flanked him as they negotiated the narrow streets. The group had to thread their way through crowds of people standing in the driving rain, joking and laughing with each other. Some shared out bowls of hot food with their friends and neighbours; many pointed, smiling at the roiling, misty clouds that scudded overhead.

Children ran and dodged between the grownups, splashing and stamping through the puddles and shrieking with delight. Some of the younger ones had never seen it pour like this before.

'It's a party,' Magic River said to Jaguar, laughing and waving at a friend.

Jaguar scanned the faces, looking for Precious Flower and his family, but Moctezuma's arrival had caused pandemonium. The street became more and more choked with every passing step. Everyone wanted to see the tlatoani and find out what he was doing in Teopan. In the end, it was Arrow One who spotted Jaguar first and stared at him in mute astonishment. Beetle followed her husband's stare and cried out when she saw her brother, then elbowed her way through the throng to throw her arms around him. Jaguar ground his teeth at the pain in his shoulder.

'Jaguar! Jaguar!' she repeated over and over again as she clasped him tightly in her arms. 'Mictlan's bones,' she swore uncharacteristically, laughed at herself and then began to sob.

By the time Arrow One managed to cut a path through the crowds, Beetle had recovered slightly. She let go of him and wiped fat tears of joy from her cheeks.

'We thought that you were dead!' Arrow One took one look at the bandage on Jaguar's arm and the sling that held the other one and decided to hold back. Jaguar smiled his appreciation. Behind Arrow One came Jaguar's mother. Musical Reed looked gaunt and tired from lack of sleep and much smaller than Jaguar remembered.

'Welcome home,' was all she said as she embraced her son.

Jaguar wondered whether she would ever be the same again and struggled to find some words.

'I was with him at the end.'

'He would have wanted that,' said Jaguar's mother.

'He said to say he loved you.' Jaguar almost choked on the words. The emotion of the homecoming almost overcame him.

'Don't try to make me believe those were his final words,' scolded Musical Reed. 'I'll bet his last words were instructions on looking after his workshop.'

'No,' said Jaguar remembering then, his father lying in the dusty field with a dark and ugly pool gathering beneath him. 'It was you.' He laughed and cried all at the same time, setting his mother off. 'He told me to take care of you.'

'I don't know how you're going to manage that. Just look at you!'

When at last his mother pulled away, Jaguar saw Precious Flower hanging back uncertainly. He looked down, ashamed. He knew that Moctezuma, Tlacaelel and Magic River were a short way off, all watching him. They knew his secret and now they'd seen Precious Flower too, a reminder of his transgression. The whole street was silent now and everyone was waiting, wondering what was going on. Magic River smiled his cracked and broken smile again. Moctezuma stared implacably. Tlacaelel glanced at the tlatoani, then looked back at Jaguar and shrugged. It seemed as though they would overlook his crime.

The gap between Jaguar and Precious Flower felt like a chasm and Jaguar remembered the way he had avoided her after his meeting with Cloud Face. Regret and sorrow filled his heart.

'Go to her!' someone cried.

'What are you waiting for?' another shouted gleefully, unaware of Jaguar's pain. He looked up and saw her gazing at him with her dark brown eyes and the sweep of hair coiled wetly on one shoulder. His heart ached as he wondered how to tell her of the things that he'd been through. She smiled then, a small, shy smile that he knew so well and suddenly it didn't matter. He had a sudden thought and rummaged in the bag he carried on one shoulder, a new one that Amihuatzin had given him to replace the filthy maguey sack he'd had before. He pulled out the straw figurine of the ocelot that Precious Flower had made for him and held it up to show her that he'd taken care of it. Rain damped the straw, soaked the tiny threads that bound it all together and dripped off its fire-mottled body. Jaguar noticed for the first time that its tiny whiskers had not survived the fire.

The crowd had left a gap allowing Jaguar to walk up to Precious Flower and take her in his arms. She pressed her face into his chest.

'I'm sorry,' said Jaguar. He held her tightly. 'I'm so sorry about the way I treated you.' Jaguar wasn't sure if he could ever tell her about the high priest's threats. 'I was so nervous about the battle,' he explained. At least it was partly true.

'I understand,' said Precious Flower in a voice that overflowed forgiveness.

She turned her face up to him and Jaguar kissed her. The crowd cheered its approval.

Jaguar noticed Moctezuma whispering to Tlacaelel and then discussing something urgently with Two Sign and Last Medicine.

Then Tlacaelel addressed the crowd. The children had to be hushed as they'd resumed their play.

'Our Lord Moctezuma, Father of the Mexica and tlatoani of Tenochtitlan, wishes it to be known that a new knight shall be made today!' The crowd cheered again. 'Step forward, Ocelotyolotl.'

Jaguar let go of Precious Flower and protested. 'My Lord, I have not taken sufficient captives.'

Moctezuma tapped Tlacaelel on the shoulder. There was a hurried exchange of words before Tlacaelel grinned at Jaguar.

'The tlatoani begs to differ. He distinctly recalls seeing you earlier today leading twenty or so captives back to Tenochtitlan.'

Jaguar looked across at Magic River with a quizzical expression. The veteran's grizzled face twisted horribly. 'It will not go well for you if you argue with the tlatoani,' it seemed to say.

'You may not all have heard yet,' began Tlacaelel, 'but I predict that this tale will spread across the land and, many years from now, when your children are old and grey, they will tell their grandchildren of the day a young Mexica warrior played ullamalitzli against the best team in Chalco, and won.' The general held his hand up to defer the jubilation. 'In addition, for his courage in the War of Flowers, I, Tlacaelel, commander of the Mexica, holder of the office Woman Snake, with the sponsorship of the commander of the Jaguar Knights, Last Medicine and with Two Sign as his second, hereby promote Ocelotyolotl to the Jaguar Knights.' Tlacaelel finished with a flourish.

Jaguar rejoined his family who all wanted to hear about the game. When Two Sign came over to congratulate him, he asked whether he could transfer to the Eagle Knights in honour of Crocodile, as that had been his choice, but Two Sign scoffed.

'With your name? Don't be absurd,' the big man said. 'No, don't you worry. Crocodile would have been pleased for you.'

Someone came around offering bowls of steaming soup, which they gratefully accepted. Jaguar held the bowl in one hand and lifted it to his lips. The broth was insubstantial, but the salty tang of fish tasted magical to him. He drank it hurriedly to avoid it cooling in the rain and, as he did, he saw Magic River further along the street. The stocky warrior was holding his infant grandchild in his arms and laughing with his family.

Excited cries alerted Jaguar to some new development that was taking place. A ripple spread through the crowd and people could be seen peering at their feet. Two Sign and Precious Flower looked down and Jaguar followed their lead, then stared in amazement. The ground was carpeted with frogs, their mottled brown skin glistening in the rain. They were hopping and clambering between people's legs, leaping through open doors of houses, all the while croaking boisterously at each other. One landed on Jaguar's foot. For a moment, it sat there with a look of intense concentration on its face. It gulped once, as though trying to swallow something twice its own size and then slowly wiped its eye with a clumsy foreleg and then leaped back onto the flagstones.

'Where are they all coming from?' laughed Precious Flower.

'I don't know! I thought there were none left,' remarked Jaguar.

'Wherever they've been hiding they're coming from the lake and the chinampa now,' said Two Sign, pointing. 'Look.'

Frogs were still arriving, jumping or hauling themselves ponderously from the ditches onto the paths and Arrow One said that they were all over the dock.

Two Sign laughed at the spectacle. 'I don't think anyone will go hungry tonight!'

Precious Flower clapped her hands together. 'Roasted frog for anyone?'

'Yes please,' said Jaguar. 'That's if anyone can light a fire in this weather.'

THE END

Epilogue

Little Maize lay on her side, cold and empty. She shivered and hugged her arms as tightly as she could, trying to keep the rush matting of her tatty palette from rustling, anxious to avoid waking any of the fourteen girls who shared the same room in the sleeping quarters of the Sisters of Penitence. This had been her home since she and Clawfoot had been recaptured.

Every day was the same. Every day was like another day of torture in the cloying realms of Mictlantecuhtli. Dawn came, and with it a whole morning of hard labour, washing clothes, scrubbing flagstone floors and enduring Mother's bottomless well of rage. Nothing that Little Maize did was ever right and hardly a day went by when she did not collect a beating. Even now, three months after her capture, when she'd learned to avoid the obvious mistakes, Mother still found fault although the causes were more and more trivial.

After a midday meal of thin stew, Little Maize would join the other girls for lessons. There was no end to the lectures on the gods and all the proper observances on every special day of the calendar, They all had to learn the history of their people, the founding of Tenochtitlan, the rulers and their great deeds. All the girls learned how to speak in front of nobles although they never saw any. Little Maize learned that if they were lucky, some wealthy, childless merchant might adopt them or a bereaved member of the nobility might choose a new, obedient wife from among them. The greatest honour they could hope for, so Mother told them constantly, was to be chosen as the bride of one of the gods. Then, they would be feted like a queen for a year and paraded around Tenochtitlan, before being sacrificed to spend an eternity with their appointed deity.

As bad as the days were, it was the night that held the greatest terror for Little Maize. Three of the girls she shared with were spiteful, vengeful individuals, mistreated from an early age and no better off since their adoption by the sisterhood. White Moon was their leader. With her gang, White Moon terrorised all the girls, pulling their hair, kicking them and urinating on their beds to make them cry but she reserved her worst treatment for Little Maize, whose quiet determination enraged the older girl all the more. Little Maize's time on the street had made her tough, so she weathered the daytime torment better than most, but in the dead of the night, after the others had gone to sleep, White Moon came to her. She was older and stronger, holding Little Maize down and violating her, with fingers to begin with, but lately with a stick that hurt so much it made her bleed.

Little Maize hoped she'd be left alone tonight and did what she always did when she needed to escape. She wondered what had become of Clawfoot. She hoped he'd be alright. She dreamed of him and the life they would have had together. She dreamed of escape from the city and of a home surrounded by golden crops. Clawfoot hunted for food while she tended to the fields and in the evening, they'd sit by the fire and eat what they'd caught and grown and then they'd watch the sun go down. This tiny, fading kernel of warmth was the only thing that nurtured her and kept her sane. She prayed it would not go out.

Nahuatl Names

Achcauhtli	Leader
Amoxtli	Book
Coatlixtli	Snake Eyes
Cuetzpalli	Lizard
Huitztepoztli	Blade of the South
Ihhuitlayoaya	Feathered Darkness
Itzcipactli	Obsidian Crocodile
Mixayacatl	Cloud Face
Motonameyotia	He Sends Forth Rays of Light
Nahualatoyatl	Magic River
Necuammetl	Edible Maguey
Nellipahtli	True Medicine or Real Cure
Ocelotyolotl	Heart of the Jaguar
Ocmiquiztli	Wind of Death
Ocotzonamaca	It Lies Like Pine Resine
Pinacatontli	Little Beetle
Quetzalxochitl	Precious Flower
Quitzatzatia	He Who Shouts
Techoponia	Strikes Once
Teonochtli	Devine prickly pear cactus
Tetl	Rock
Tlapalilhuitl	Red Horizon
Tochancalqui	He Who Lives in My House
Zatepanpahtli	Last Medicine
Zipactonal	Sign of the Crocodile

Author's Note

I'm keen to point out that although this novel was inspired by some worthy historical tomes, it is not intended to be a weighty, scholarly work. The historical context is there to create a sturdy, believable warp through which the fabric of the tale can be woven. The eagle-eyed among you will have spotted that at no point during the body of the story have I used 'Aztec', as this term was only coined long after the Mexica had ceased to exist as a cohesive group of people.

Moctezuma existed (full name Moctezuma Ilhuicamina) and should not be confused with Moctezuma II, who was the tlatoani some fifty years later at the time of Cortez's invasion. His half-brother, Tlacaelel, was also a real person and held the somewhat bizarre title of Woman Snake. I have found no record of the names of the priests of Tenochtitlan.

Xicotencatl (Angry Bumblebee) was the ruler of the Tlaxcalan confederation of states, but the governance of Chalco was more complex. It seems to have been a confederation of previously semi-nomadic tribes (much like the Mexica who came from Aztlan), who banded together under two kings or 'tlatoani', each with their own separate royal lineage and title. At this point in time, *Chimalpahin and the Kingdoms of Chalco* [Susan Schroeder] suggests that one was Amihuatzin and the other was called Huitzilpopocatzin. I plead guilty to simplifying the story a little by dealing only with the former.

The ball game (ullamalitzli) has caused me the most lost sleep. Although variants of it are still played today, I've struggled to comprehend how a supposedly heavy rubber ball that caused bruising and broken bones could be kept in play using only the thighs and buttocks, let alone struck high enough to pass through stone rings set above head height.

Although the chapter names come from the named days of the Mesoamerican calendar, it was not my intention for each chapter to cover one day.

Most of my historical information came from *The Aztecs* by Nigel Davies [University of Oklahoma Press, 1989], *Book of the Gods and Rites and the Ancient Calendar* by Frey Diego Duran [University of Oklahoma Press, 1971] and *The Mesoamerican Ball Game* [University of Arizona Press, 1991]. These books present a fascinating picture of an extraordinarily complex people, who were both barbarous and yet had many civilised aspects such as building, irrigation and laws such as those designed to protect slaves against abuse.

Lightning Source UK Ltd.
Milton Keynes UK
UKOW041825311012

201475UK00001B/29/P